# The Passions of
# Mary Wollstonecraft

**By the same author**

**ADULT POETRY**
Amphitheatre
Steel Wings
Solving Atlantis
Selected Poems

**CHILDREN'S POETRY**
The Imaginator

**ANTHOLOGIES**
An Enduring Flame: The Bronte Story in Poetry and Photographs
Poetry in The Parks: The National Parks of England and
Wales in Poetry and Photographs
Journeys: Poetry and Literacy for The National Curriculum

**NOVELS**
The Other Concerto
Branwell Bronte's Creation
Wordsworth in Chains

**NOVELLAS**
Jupiter & Passage to Osiris

**NON-FICTION**
Introducing Information Technology

# The Passions of Mary Wollstonecraft

Wendy Louise Bardsley

METHUEN

First published by Methuen in 2017

1

Methuen
Orchard House
Railway Street
Slingsby
York YO62 4AN

A CIP catalogue record for this book is available from
the British Library

ISBN: 978 0 413 77786 7

Typeset by SX Composing DTP, Rayleigh, Essex
Printed and bound in Great Britain by CPI Group (UK) Ltd,
Croydon, CR0 4YY

www.methuen.co.uk

To John, Stella and Hazel, my beloved children

"Strengthen the female mind by enlarging it, and there will be an end to blind obedience; but, as blind obedience is ever sought for by power, tyrants and sensualists are in the right when they endeavour to keep women in the dark, because the former only want slaves, and the latter a play-thing. The sensualist, indeed, has been the most dangerous of tyrants, and women have been duped by their lovers, as princes by their ministers, whilst dreaming that they reigned over them."

*(Mary Wollstonecraft, A Vindication of the Rights of Woman, 1792)*

# 1

## *Beverley, East Yorkshire*

'There can be no worse travail than this,' said young Mary Wollstonecraft as she stood at the bedside of her friend. 'It is shameful that a woman must suffer like that to give birth to a child.' She spoke with tears in her throat. 'We were close. Now there is only the great space of death between us.'

The midwife swaddled the shrieking infant then handed it over to the father who stood in traumatised silence, pale and bewildered.

Fifteen year old Mary stared at the baby, its wet hair matted to its head, its features harsh and tight as if its voyage into the world had been a wearing endeavour.

'You are young to attend such a birth,' said the midwife. She looked at Mary and smiled admiringly. 'What you have witnessed may stay in your mind and torment you.'

'I have seen many things,' said Mary, slowly shaking her head. 'I feared the birth would be difficult, Agnes was never strong.'

There was a lot of blood on the sheets around the now stilled body of what had once been a vibrant young woman. Mary turned to the midwife. 'You were a long time coming,' she murmured. Anger and pity writhed inside her as she spoke. Why were there so few midwives, and why weren't they educated better in the workings of a woman's body? Did the wearing of stays disfigure a woman's organs? It was perfectly possible. But women were reluctant to discuss it. The man standing before them had provided

1

Agnes with elegant, stylish clothes, and stays she had insisted on wearing until almost the end of her pregnancy. Getting a doctor at short notice in Beverley could be difficult too. They must sometimes travel across the Yorkshire Dales to see a patient. And Agnes's pregnancy had been something of a secret; she wasn't married, whilst her lover was. But at least he'd had the decency to come to her now when she'd needed him most; the rest was his own story.

Mary gazed abstractedly at the white ceiling, then back to the woman on the bed. She knew so much, had observed so much and had experienced so much in her home, she felt much older than her mere fifteen years. Her critical and piercing observations were enemies as well as friends and she rarely felt happy. But she had felt some happiness with Agnes and had warned her about sleeping with strangers: "He comes from another town. He is wealthy and bound to be known. And he leaves his horse by the inn where he stays," she told her. "It means nothing," Agnes had said, straightening her slender frame and throwing back her shoulders. And it didn't. Her friend was *in love*.

The man who held the unfortunate child was wealthy. But no amount of money could have taken away the terrified look in his eyes. He gazed at Agnes's still cold body and shivered. 'I detest myself,' he whispered. 'I am wicked for this.'

He spoke as if seeking solace, but the midwife looked at him knowingly. 'She rejected the male midwife,' she told him. 'They often do. I was called very late. Forceps were needed for the birth, but I have none.' She sighed. 'Your child is well, but best baptise her quickly.' She gazed at the baby. 'She is unable to benefit from her mother's milk . . . Is there anyone you know who might feed her, a nursing mother perhaps?'

'No-one,' the man said confusedly. 'How would I know of such a person? And I dare not reveal I am the father of this child to anyone.' He stood tall before them, an elegant, cultured gentleman, apprehensive and shaky. With a look of dismay, he glanced at the shoulder of his frockcoat where the baby's head had left a large residue of blood. 'I need to think quickly,' he faltered. 'I am not sure how I . . .' His voice trailed off.

Mary glanced about, the midwife had brought but a small case of things. It lay wide open on the floor. There were a few pitiful instruments, a large pad of cotton wool and a pair of scissors. Nothing more.

The father stared at the infant in his arms. 'A girl,' he murmured. 'What am I to do with a girl?'

'You will think of something,' said Mary with a sigh. 'You must. She is yours.' The new born child looked strangely repugnant, she thought, like a water creature from the beck down the hill, wet and slippery, its eyes half closed.

'Yes,' he said, hesitantly. 'I have four grown sons but no daughter . . .' He smiled thinly. 'It would be good to have a daughter, under different circumstances, of course. – Oh, please don't upbraid me. I shall see she is taken care of ... But my wife must know nothing of this. You do understand?'

'Agnes's sister is to arrive from London this evening,' said Mary. 'She has been anxious.' She would be very distressed, thought Mary, to learn of the new situation.

The man returned the swaddled infant to the midwife.

'I am thankful we saved the baby,' said the midwife, her voice low and serious. The flames of the fire in the hearth raced up the chimney, eager and strong. The midwife put the child in a cot by the bed and Mary helped her bathe Agnes's lifeless body for her sister's arrival.

'Agnes?' the man whispered. 'Agnes, my precious?'

'She has gone,' said Mary in a measured and calm tone of voice. 'You must accept it. But you still have your daughter.' In spite of herself, she felt pity for this man who Agnes had loved. He had talked about leaving his wife. But it had only been talk; it would never have become reality. Now he faced the brutality of truth. She would like to have tried to probe him and discover what he *really* thought about Agnes. He had hardly considered her his equal. She had been his sexual servant. There were those in the town who had whispered the word, "prostitute".

'We had intended to eat at eight,' he said shakily. 'I brought some food.'

3

'She has done with eating,' said Mary. She looked at him for a long moment, then turned away her face in disgust. Agnes had been eighteen years old, a laughing elemental girl, who threw herself at the world with careless abandon, a fearless force for whom convention and gossip meant nothing. The midwife turned the cold ashen body with a gracious and tender ease as if familiar with the task before her, then she threw the blood stained lingerie and bedding on the floor. Mary brought new linen for the bed, angry and tense as her strong arms helped fix the sheets.

'She needs fresh nightwear,' said the midwife, in a formal and practised manner. 'There is something in the drawer over there. We must make her look peaceful . . . This sister?' she began, looking at Mary curiously.

'She will arrive any time now,' said Mary. 'It is arranged.'

'I have money,' the man interjected quickly. 'Please let me help.'

'Of course,' said Mary.

He braced himself. 'We must see she has everything she needs. I loved her.' He fumbled in his frockcoat pocket and brought out a purse-full of coins which he handed to Mary.

'I will ensure that her sister receives it,' she said. 'The midwife will stay until she comes. You must wait for the doctor too; he has things to write down. I cannot linger myself, I am needed at home.'

He went to sit on a chair in the corner and bit at his knuckles. His eyes drifted to Mary for comfort, but she had none to give. All her emotions were taken up with the woman who had once been her friend, now lying deceased on the bed. Mary had been called that morning since the labour had been sudden and early. It had been a demanding day, but now she must leave. 'She is a pretty, healthy little girl,' said Mary, forcing a half smile. It seemed to soothe him a little. Then she went to the cot and touched the tiny fingers. They were firm and warm and gripped her own with a fierceness for life that surprised her.

But the man's eyes rested on the bed. Then came the darkening room as the afternoon light left them, a light that would never be the same, thought Mary, it would never again shine for Agnes as she laughed and went through the town, the dark horror of injustice had found her. What would happen to the baby? Would the father fulfil his obligations or would the sister take her away so they would never see her again? Mary lifted her cloak from the back of a chair and drew it about her. She could not say goodbye, the word seemed frivolous in the face of what had just taken place. But she kissed her friend's cold hand. With that, she quietly closed the door and stepped out on to the street.

The bells of Beverley Minister chimed for the quarter hour. It was late afternoon, but the town still throbbed with traders. Wool, meat, butter, poultry, eggs, fish and more were for sale on the market. There was plenty to buy. She passed the large grand houses with their well-kept gardens, their throbbing heavy headed flowers and tall dignified trees. Tanners, shoemakers, all manner of traders lived in Beverley; it was a thriving, wealthy community. People were coming from the library where you might borrow publications on payment of a small subscription. Books, periodicals and pamphlets were increasingly available to the public. It was a treasured place to Mary and she could often be found there, but the seconds, the minutes, the hours, flew by too quickly. Someone was opening up the doors of the Beverley hall as she passed; there was probably a concert on that evening, or possibly a dance. She liked dancing. But she did not feel like dancing today. No, not today. She was moving fast from idea to idea. It frustrated her mother that she could not concentrate on one line of thought at a time, but she liked to capture ideas as they came and would not let a single one of them break free. There were days she suffered terrible headaches. She carried on walking through Beverley, trying not to think too much on the dreadful events of the day, they hurt her mind, they hurt her body, and she felt they hurt her future. She feared for all women.

The town of Beverley was the administrative centre of the East Riding of Yorkshire. It also supplied entertainment for the local land-owning families. The quarter sessions were held there, a time when lawyers would strut through the streets in their smart coats and hats alongside country militia who came to lieutenancy meetings. She glanced at the door of the Blue Bell inn where her father had gone to a meeting that day about land tax. He would be late and probably stay drinking, then he would abuse her mother. But her mother did not assert herself. It was a mystery. It was just as if she felt it her duty to allow him his ranting and raving. Little did she know how it tore her children apart.

She turned the corner to her home. Agnes's lover was gentry, and had probably come to Beverley on business at first, at the same time enjoying the other pleasures on offer, like horse-racing and lovely young women. Mary sighed. Had Agnes had something to do other than just be a woman, something that mattered to fill her mind, she might never have become so romantic. She was intelligent and could learn things, she might have learned French; they had practised together a lot. Mary thought of her own schooling, which hadn't amounted to much. The Day School she went to was dull and slow and she would rather study from books. But she passed on her learning to her younger siblings as best she could. Her school taught needlework, music and dancing and perhaps some painting, occasionally they might teach French, though not very often. Ned, her older brother, was lucky. There was good education for boys. Boys could learn languages, science and philosophy. Oh, to be a boy and be real, she thought at she made her way through the streets. So many stages of degradation lay waiting for girls and more awaited their womanhood. How she envied her brother. Did the world think girls had inferior brains, it was absurd!

A stray dog barked into the lonely air as she walked down the path to her house. She knew her mother would look at her confusedly with her curious penetrating eyes. The streets could be dangerous for young women out on their own, she would say, and it was almost dusk. Elizabeth Wollstonecraft was a caring woman, but far too tolerant Mary thought, of her abusive husband. When he drank he was worse than ever, and her mother always took the blame. He was far angrier with himself, her mother would argue, than he was with anyone else. He was ashamed because he did not prosper and could not correct his faults. "Don't you dare call me a failure?" he would shout, pointing his finger at her menacingly. "Just give me time!" Then he would disparage her further. "Had you been more supportive, understood my misfortunes and helped me, I might have done amazing things . . ." Mary had feared for her mother, the world of her parents was a sad, tangled mess that only they understood. There were always the same protestations, the same wild torrent of tears. Her siblings would cringe in their beds until it was over. But it was never over for long.

She was grieving deeply, but she knew as she arrived at the door, she must show restraint. Her mother had never liked Agnes, but if she criticised her now, it would be more than Mary could take. Agnes was trouble, she said, she did not live as she should. Well, now, Agnes was dead.

But it was necessary for Mary to return to the world of the living and she straightened as she entered her home. So many thoughts ran riot in her head; she might have lived a thousand lives and never understood them, try as she would. She knew she needed better education, and had an odd feeling she somehow belonged to history, to the army of ghosts who found things out and delivered knowledge to the world. She felt she was on a quest. But how would she do what she felt her destiny demanded? She rejoiced in her own singularity, she was strong, proud, and even pretty. There was something of the sage in her too, she thought, something ancient and eternal that would never be stilled. But in its oldness it was strangely new, and when she sat alone thoughtful, she loved to discover the fruits of her mind and enjoy them with delicious relish. Oh, her mind was a treasure trove of thoughts! But she could not stand her mother's heaviness of heart and had a dread of what lay in store for women; the awful none-life they must suffer.

'Where were you?' asked her mother, as Mary arrived in the parlour. 'You've been gone a long time.' Charles and James, her younger brothers, were playing at her mother's feet. Her mother bent forward to reach for a set of wooden blocks. 'You brought these pieces of wood to teach them the alphabet with, but they seem to like piling them up and knocking them over instead. You'll not teach them anything with these.' She shooed the boys to the stairs. 'Go and find Everina. – And Charles, don't you fall down!' They scuttled away like little stones in the wind. Elizabeth picked up her sewing and sighed. 'Ah dear me, anyone would think it was your father rather than me who was the offspring of an Irish Wine merchant. He'll be partaking of alcohol this minute. I saw he went off with money, though he has only gone to talk about land tax. Why would he need to take money? No, he's drinking, that's what he's doing, drinking and gambling.'

'He should buy us some books,' murmured Mary. 'We could learn and develop if he did. Ned is learning very well, but it won't be long before Father takes him to the races and ruins him. And he makes you suffer too. But what harm did you do, and we children are innocent. Those people out there create stories about us; say how they think we will be in the future. Why, Ned is already a good-for-nothing dolt, yet he says he wants to be a lawyer. – But there is something wild and careless about Ned, you know, that will always come to his aid. It's that fire in his eyes that never goes out. I doubt it is there in mine.' She shrugged; her mother's look said she wasn't listening. 'But you wouldn't notice, would you. I am only a daughter.' She removed her cloak and sat down with a sigh.

'You talk in riddles, Mary. You always do. Things have been difficult for your father in Beverley. There's a lot you don't know.'

'And there's a lot you don't *see*, Mother. You seem to think a woman's duty is to be blind to a man's foibles. But that way he will never mend them. You think I should find a husband and provide the next generation, and serve them along with their father. – Well, I won't, I tell you, I won't! Oh, woman, the eternal servant!'

'Is there really any need for you to work yourself up like this?' asked her mother, looking unhappy. 'Do calm down, you take life far too seriously. I can see that something has upset you.'

'Agnes is dead,' Mary said flatly. 'Just today. She died giving birth.'

Her mother looked up from her sewing. Her voice was quiet and pained. 'I'm sorry, my dear. I know how you cared for her . . . And the baby?'

'It was a girl. She is well. I left the child with the father and the midwife.'

Her mother sat silent, waiting.

'Oh, you need not worry about the child, Mother. The father is wealthy. He has given me money. I shall hand it to Agnes's sister as soon as I see her. I have it here in my pocket.'

Her mother watched as she pulled out the purse of coins. Mary glanced about the room. 'I must ensure it is hidden from father, for I cannot take it till tomorrow.'

'Are you calling your father a thief?' her mother retorted. She put down her sewing annoyed. 'Go then and put it away. Hide it beneath your bed.'

Mary did not move, and for a moment or two they were silent.

'And who is to take care of the funeral?' her mother said finally.

'I'm not sure. Jeremy Baxter is taking a clergyman to the house this evening.'

*'Jeremy Baxter?'* said Elizabeth raising her eyebrows. 'The carpenter? People will be pointing fingers. Poor Agnes, but she often had fits and flew into frenzies, you know; the birth was bound to be demanding.'

Mary took a deep breath. 'She did not fly into frenzies, Mother. She was deeply unhappy when neglected. He would leave her for weeks without contact. He wanted her just as it suited. I tried to say things, but I did not have the experience to argue, Agnes was a woman of the world.'

Elizabeth smiled wryly. '"*A woman of the world*?" She was only eighteen, and I do not believe she ever set foot out of Beverley. She was very well known, of course. From the age of twelve, her father sent her out on the streets to make money. It was disgraceful. I have often feared you might be influenced, my dear. You are comely, Mary, the eyes of men pass over you. But do not be deceived.'

'I am not deceived in the least. And I know that someone would have found an excuse to put her in an asylum once she was orphaned. But Jeremy found work for her sister who took good care of them both.'

Again they were silent.

'But you know how Agnes would rage about town,' Elizabeth Wollstonecraft murmured, 'telling people her father had murdered her mother by "smothering her life force". Now, that is your sort of talk, my dear. Be careful what you say.'

'I should think Agnes's lover is expecting her sister to take the baby back to London. That is where she works,' said Mary. 'His wife won't know anything about it. I saw the fear in his eyes. The sister will take care of the baby, I know. I have seen her letters; she has always been loyal to Agnes.'

'You are not to get involved,' her mother chided sternly. 'It is none of your business, and anyway, I need you here. There is a lot to do in this house, and money is often scarce. Your father squanders it whichever way he turns.'

'But you ought to be firm with him, Mother,' Mary said heatedly. 'He does not respect you, and we all suffer from his drinking. He cannot control his impulses – his need to gamble one way or another. But his gambles never pay off. And my father is no farmer either; he will never fathom how farming works for all his pomposity. Jeremy Baxter has offered to talk to him.'

'*Talk to him*? Jeremy Baxter? He's a ship's carpenter, what does he know about farming?'

'He is good at his work and intelligent.'

'Oh, I see.' Elizabeth sighed exasperated. 'So your father isn't intelligent? What will you tell me next? And you shouldn't discuss him behind his back.'

Mary continued, regardless. 'Jeremy was kind to Agnes. It was he who went for the midwife. He brought her in his chaise, but she arrived too late, the birth was well underway. He has promised to help with the funeral.'

Her mother straightened and frowned. 'Oh, Mary, there will be so much talk in the town about this. You must keep it from your father, you know, I warn you. He doesn't like trouble.'

Mary murmured some bitter though inaudible words. She returned the purse to her pocket. The children were making a lot of noise upstairs. The house was always a great disruptive force, like a land where you must watch your step or the earth might swallow you up or else burst into flames.

'I must give this money to Agnes's sister,' she said, tapping her pocket. 'After that it is out of my hands.' She gazed at space abstractedly as if lost in some difficult thought. Nothing could deliver her from the horror of Agnes's death, but she must try to find somewhere in her mind where it did not haunt her. She would continue as before, she would learn things and teach her siblings. She enjoyed teaching her siblings.

The front door opened and closed, then came the sound of her brother's stride in the hall. Her mother's features alerted. Ned was here, it was as if the house absorbed him. He smiled as he entered. 'Ah, Mary,' he said, slowly unbuttoning his coat and eyeing her curiously. 'You are here. I saw Jane Arden by the library, she asked where you were. I had no idea, so of course I had nothing to tell her.'

'Well,' said her mother quietly. 'She is here in this house at last, thank goodness. Do sit down and talk to her will you. She is in need of sensible counsel.'

'What else did Jane have to say?' said Mary.

'Not much, she was carrying books, but I couldn't see the titles. She said you should go to see her. I told her you'd be happy to visit them as soon as you could.' He raised his eyebrows. 'You will, of course, won't you, be happy to visit her, I mean?'

'My dear brother, how could you doubt it?'

Suddenly there was a clatter of heels on the stairs. Everina rushed in. 'Ned, Ned!' she cried. 'Did you see a cockfight?'

He coughed embarrassed and folded his arms, assuming the manner of the gentry. 'Of course not, I have been to look at books in the library.'

Everina's eyes dulled. 'I would love to see a cockfight,' she moaned.

'That's enough!' chided her mother. 'Why would you want to see innocent creatures fighting to their death? It's a horrible game, that is.'

Everina returned to her siblings upstairs, grumbling all the way as she went.

'I leafed through a pamphlet about the riots in America,' said Ned. He took a seat beside them. 'Do you remember when the colonists were protesting against British taxation and dumped all the tea in Boston harbour? There's a very good pamphlet about it. What a to-do. "No taxation without representation,"' he chanted.

'But we can't keep telling them what to do,' Mary said wearily. 'They are bound to revolt.' Mary had read the pamphlet herself, and had talked about it with Jane and Doctor Arden. Jane was a friend she shared books with, a friend she adored, but she hadn't seen much of her recently because Agnes hadn't been well and had needed company. But she thought about the riots. People's needs and anger could turn into action. And did.

Ned looked at her, then talked on intensely. 'The tax on tea is the only tax left, but they fully intend to get rid of it. John Adams believes the patriots were brave and sees what they did as a great historical moment. It has certainly changed things. And what with all that bother about stamp duty before, it won't end there; I suspect there will be more defiance. There is talk of a revolutionary government. Powerful stuff. General Gage, the British Governor, has been instructed from England to seize any weapons and gunpowder the insurgents might try to get hold of. It sounds like the colonists have the bit between their teeth.' He shook his head and frowned. 'It could turn into all out war.'

'Oh, I hope not,' murmured his mother, frail and fearful.

'Is there any more news about slavery?' asked Mary.

Ned took a deep breath, it was important for him to know things, and he liked to expound his views. 'Well, despite new rulings, people still return runaway slaves to the colonies. But matters are very confusing. I don't know the answers. Who does? But I am keeping an eye on developments.'

'Peasants are just like slaves,' murmured Mary. 'They don't get an education and are subject to some tyrannical family patriarch, who is often no more than a beast.' As she spoke she was aware of a fear entering her blood, the very same dread that overcame her when her father stormed about the house. She talked on quickly with passion. 'Slave, peasant, serf, woman, they are all the same! It is just subservience and fear.'

'New attitudes are emerging, dear sister,' said Ned, with a profoundness that made her look up. 'The intellectual capacity of black people is now being taken seriously. These people are human beings, not animals.'

12

Mary shrugged. 'But of course. And the intellectual capacity of women should be considered too. But it doesn't help men if women are educated, does it, any more than if they educate slaves. For what would they do if they at last faced the truth of their position?'

'Ned, did you meet with your father?' their mother asked, sighing. 'He went to the Blue Bell inn.'

Ned pursed his lips thoughtfully. 'Can't say I saw him. There are a lot of people out today.' He sniffed towards the kitchen. 'Something smells good. I'm hungry.'

'We must wait for your father,' said Elizabeth. 'You know what he's like if we don't.' Her tone was irritable. She was always at the end of her tether.

'Well you'll not wait long!' came a loud voice from the hall. 'Now then, Elizabeth, what are we eating? Is it ready?' Edward Wollstonecraft strode into the room rubbing his hands together briskly. 'And let me get near that fire. It's bitter out there.' He gave his wife a long and steady look and she held his gaze, her eyes narrowing with annoyance. Ned sighed loudly. He turned and went towards the stairs then climbed them slowly as if thoughtful.

'It will probably be a good half hour before the food can come to the table,' said Elizabeth. Her husband groaned.

Mary hated her father when he made her mother nervous. His brows knitted. He spoke through his teeth. 'But I told you the hour I would return. And am I not here as promised?'

'But you might have been an hour either way . . .' Elizabeth faltered.

'Are you saying I keep irregular hours?' he stormed. 'Stupid, uncaring woman. I suppose you thought I was drinking, didn't you? Oh yes, you did!' His tone was mean and aggressive. 'That's what you think of me, you see. You think I am a drunkard, yet I have not had a drop of alcohol today.'

Mary and her mother were stunned. It was a fact that if he went to the Blue Bell inn, he would return to the house inebriated.

'Well, have you nothing to say?' he growled. He cast out his large hands and opened his eyes in mock astonishment. Then he pulled out the pockets of his frock coat. 'See, they are empty. I haven't a penny. But I did not partake of any alcohol.' His skin tightened with anger. 'Don't start,' he warned. 'Don't start, I say.'

'It isn't fair,' Elizabeth whimpered. 'You left this house with lots of money. What did you do with it?'

He scratched his head. 'I think it might have been stolen. Sometimes I'm careless. Somebody picked my pocket, I think.'

'A fine excuse,' said Elizabeth covering her face with her hands. 'You have probably gambled it away.'

He glanced about shamefacedly, then continued his rant. 'Don't you dare!' he shouted, raising his hand. He collapsed down in a chair. 'You are not so clever yourself when it comes to money, my dear,' he said, sarcastically. 'I wonder what happens to it sometimes.'

Mary stayed silent, trying to shut away her fears. She hated her father's violence, her still dark eyes loathing the brutal belligerence he brought to their lives. Her mother watched the fire, sullenly stabbing at the logs. Mary thought she looked pale. 'Do you feel ill?' she asked her.

'Course she's not ill!' Edward Wollstonecraft bawled. 'Not unless you make her. Now let the woman alone!'

Mary felt stung and insulted. As she went towards the kitchen his voice rose louder. He sounded like a threatened animal, a bull ready to charge, and it disturbed her deeply that her mother should fall so limply into his hands.

## 2

# *Jane Arden*

During the last few months Mary had given a lot of her time to Agnes and had seen very little of Jane. Now it was a time of mourning, but also a time for reflection, and she had taken walks in the country to commune with the open air and listen to the sounds of nature. But nothing was the same as before. She had crossed some bridge and felt changed. People and things about her seemed unfamiliar. At night, in the silence of her room she could feel the force of her mind striving towards some goal she knew she must reach. It would make itself plain in time, of that she felt certain, but she longed for something to help her feel solid and alive, not lost as she was with the spirits of her thoughts and feelings.

Jane Arden, a dear friend, was daughter of John, a noted scholar and lecturer who liked to keep step with the progress in science and technology and was a member of the Royal Society. John lectured for pay and enjoyed teaching others. He would often stop on his walks about town to talk with any who had queries, and had even been known to make one or two drawings which they gratefully tucked away in their frockcoat pockets. He was generous in both thought and manner and very much liked. Popular scientific and technological books abounded and when it came to spreading the word Doctor John Arden was fanatical.

Mary thought the Ardens were kind and moral people and their passionate sympathies with the ways of the world had charmed her.

John would proclaim that even within the horrors of war, the calm beauty of hope would always shine forth, men would not desert each other, he said, love and goodwill would triumph. Mary found his enthusiasm infectious and she listened to all he said, but she did not always agree with him, she lived in a welter of uncertainty, always questioning, always concerned to minister to her own thinking. Jane was a devout Christian and liked to recite passages from the bible. That afternoon, as they sat at the table in her parlour, she decided on some lines from Proverbs, words, she said, that they both earnestly believed.

'Proverbs 4, Chapters 6-7,' she began, holding her bible before her. Her tone as she spoke was reverential. '"*Do not forsake wisdom, and she will protect you; love her, and she will watch over you. Wisdom is supreme; therefore get wisdom. Though it cost all you have, get understanding.*"' She lifted her head, her large blue eyes shining. 'There now, we have to get wisdom then we can know things.' She frowned and sighed. 'I've thought about it all morning. How can we get it?'

'I wish I knew', Mary said wistfully. 'I am most unwise myself. I think it is a gift, like perception.'

'But how do we get perception?' said Jane, resting her chin on her hand and gazing at Mary perplexed. 'I have talked with Father about it. It is often discussed at his meetings but people are always bewildered.'

'We must first have a good education,' Mary said straightening. 'Of that I am certain. Then our thoughts will have something to work with and provide us with answers.' But her eyes were filled with uncertainty. 'It's all so difficult,' she murmured.

'It's very interesting though,' Jane said, curious and tense.

'What matters most are the answers, don't you think?' said Mary. 'Never mind how we get them.' She spoke forcefully, but her tone was dubious.

Jane sighed loudly. 'Oh, you should hear the scientists. Father says they must know how everything works, the whys and wherefores of all things under the sun. They cling to facts like limpets on rocks and like to take matters to pieces.'

'But we can never understand "everything",' said Mary. 'Not the sun, the moon, the stars, or matters of the spirit.'

For a moment or two they were thoughtful. Jane went on. 'The philosophy of perception is immensely interesting to Father just now. All knowledge derives from it, he says.'

'So many mysteries . . .' said Mary, gazing about abstractedly. 'We perceive things, but how do we do it?'

Jane shook her head. 'Will these questions ever be answered?' She sighed, as if knowledge were a great heavy door to be opened on a new resolving world.

'I think they will in time,' said Mary. 'I like to question why we do things though, how we should balance our own desires and needs against those of others and attempt to be fair. I believe philosophy can help us with that, your father's work is important.' She grew excited as she talked. 'I heard that William Blake, the painter, is a philosopher as well as an artist. And they say he has immense wisdom. I wonder if it can be seen in his strange drawings.'

'I suspect it can,' Jane said thoughtfully. 'According to Father, Blake believes he is in contact with angelic realms.' She laughed, though she spoke in earnest. 'Father went to see him in London. He has a very interesting mind, though he is not yet twenty. His drawings are strangely singular, and display such mystical power, I believe they are quite forbidding.' She lowered her voice to a whisper. *'There are some who say he is mad . . .'*

Mary pondered on her words. People were quick to point fingers if you didn't behave as expected. She believed there were higher things than the world was aware of, perhaps Blake knew what they were.

Jane closed her bible. 'There is so much to learn,' she sighed. She gazed at her long slender fingers, which Mary thought much like Doctor Arden's. She spoke like her father too, and had the same kind of graceful manner. Mary had first met Jane at one of her father's lectures in Beverley. John Arden was the intelligent and learned father she yearned for and their conversations always thrilled her. At home she felt she could never say anything of value, but at Jane's she could talk and discuss and have an opinion. Here, at

Jane's, powerful ideas formed in her mind and there were days she felt radiant with power. She was little more than a servant at home with her family. But she would not be governed. She was temperamental and difficult and spoke as her heart commanded. The friendship she shared with Jane was devoted and intense, though she knew she longed for more than her friend could give, and feared she might drive her away with her often romantic ways. She would sit very close and stroke her ash blonde hair while they were reading which would cause Jane to draw back, looking uneasy. What could be wrong with one girl loving another she would muse as she returned to her home? Why was it frowned on? But her heart was bold and honest, some hearts were not.

'Father met a group of dissenters in town,' Jane said suddenly. 'They are brimming with fervour. They want to change things immediately, but Father says it is dangerous to change things too quickly. They are saying that state religion impinges on the freedom of conscience and are very much averse to monetary ties between government and church.' She smiled softly. 'Oh, Father tells me all he has seen and heard the minute he comes through the door. He gets so intense. They believe the doctrine of the Trinity and the theory of Original Sin can be dismembered and better constructed.' She rubbed her eyes tiredly. 'There is so much unrest in England.'

'And in France too, according to Ned,' said Mary, recalling a conversation earlier that week. But it was hard to voice her opinion when she talked with her brother. In Ned's world men did the talking and women listened. But she would rather hear him out than not. Crumbs, crumbs from his table! When would women have a proper slice of the cake and not just eat crumbs that men chose to allow them. 'Ned thinks the peasants in France are going to rise up against the government and try to overthrow it,' she said. 'They are poorer than ever now and wander the streets without shoes, starving and begging for bread. Their anger is dangerous, they have suffered terrible harvests, and they think their king and queen are too young and inexperienced and don't know how to rule.'

'It's true,' said Jane. 'The rich are too rich and the poor are too poor. The inequality there is outrageous; it is greed that does it.'

She frowned thoughtfully. 'Something is bound to happen. People are bringing terrible news across the channel.'

At that moment, from the top of the stairs there came the voice of her father, 'Jane! – Jane! – Go and bring your mother from the grocer's. I need her to find me some stockings. I can't find a single pair. – Did she wash them?' He arrived barefoot in the room. 'Good afternoon, Mary,' he said, looking surprised. 'I had forgotten you were with us today. I intended to talk with you didn't I? Do forgive me. I've been writing all morning.'

He was a tall, pale skinned man with long energetic limbs. Mary hadn't seen his feet before. He had long bony toes that almost looked like fingers.

'I think I might know where they are,' said Jane, rising from her chair and running upstairs.

Meanwhile Mary chanced to talk with John who had ensconced himself on the chaise longue in the corner. He looked pre-occupied. 'Have you been writing a lecture?' she asked, eager to hear what he was doing.

'Yes, I have,' he said, smiling. He was quick to talk and had strong sensitivities, pouring his emotions into every subject he dealt with. 'There are many vast empty spaces in our thinking, you see,' he said, gazing at the white ceiling. 'But they all somehow connect. We must find the pathways, for that is the way to true knowledge.' He straightened and gathered himself together as Jane arrived with his stockings and handed them over. He eased them on to his feet.

Mary watched him as he laced up his boots. John Arden was quite an enigma but she enjoyed his curious ways. He had an easy indifference to his clothes. The wrists of his frock coat were frayed and he never properly tied his cravat so that it sometimes fell loose as he talked.

'Did Father tell you I am intending to move to Norfolk?' Jane said casually, returning to her seat at the table.

Mary looked at them both by turns. 'No,' she said meekly. 'It is quite a surprise.'

'I am to work as a governess to the daughters of Lady Martin,' said Jane. She looked downwards and straightened her dress to avoid the obvious distress in Mary's eyes. 'You are welcome to visit me, of course,' she added warmly and reassuringly. 'And you can still see Father here at home.'

Mary flushed with feeling. She picked up her books and held them close. Would her books be all she had left of her precious friendship with Jane?

'It is a very good thing,' John Arden interjected. 'Jane can pass on her learning. She will teach, you see. And what can be more rewarding? She is older than you, my dear, I know, but I trust you will do the same when the time is right.'

Mary looked at them bewildered.

John continued, speaking in a kindly tone of voice. 'It is good that Jane is moving. My daughter has had enough of Beverley for now. – Not enough of you, my dear, never enough of you, but enough of the area. You, dear Mary, are quite a remarkable girl; your mind is quick and fertile. – Oh, please don't look sad. You have other friends in the town, I believe. You won't be alone.'

Mary discerned that her reaction had embarrassed them both. 'Of course not,' she murmured.

'I had intended to tell you earlier,' Jane ventured, 'but you haven't been around. – I heard about Agnes.' She frowned. 'How awful. The child, I believe, has been taken to London by her sister.'

'Yes,' said Mary quietly. She winced as she recalled the sad little funeral and the poor innocent baby in the arms of Agnes's sister. 'When will you go?' she asked miserably. She had no desire to talk about Agnes now. It had all been too cruel. But she had finally pulled herself together, and now there was this. It would be hard to lose Jane. She had been a precious friend, more than that she was an essential part of herself.

'Very soon,' said Jane. 'Ah, come, come,' she said, taking a hanky from her pocket and dabbing Mary's cheeks. 'You can visit me whenever you wish, and I shall return to see my parents in Beverley. It isn't goodbye.'

Mary bent her head. She wanted Jane to be happy and take on the world. But as a governess? No, never as a governess, she was far too exuberant for that, it would not suit her.

'Oh, you really shouldn't mind, my dear,' John Arden said frowning as he donned his hat and found his cane. 'You have a powerful independent spirit and should value it. We are alone in this world, dear Mary, and must learn to stride with our shadow.' For a moment he gazed at space. 'I will be giving a few more lectures before Jane takes off. I hope you'll be there.' He fastened up his coat and within seconds had gone down the street.

'I'm afraid I must go,' Mary said quietly. She couldn't bear to stay a minute longer. She rose and put on her cloak, then she embraced her friend and left.

Moody and irrational, she walked on steadily down a still country lane, the uncaring rain falling through the trees about her. She would let herself get soaked, yes, that's what she'd do! She would make herself ill so that Jane would feel sorry for leaving Beverley. She grieved so much to have lost her dearest heart. The sound of the rain and the rush of water in the ditches made her feel lonelier than ever. Thunder cracked through the sky, lightning lit the space about her, so that the wet dark trunks of the trees shone like silk. She stood beneath a tree listening to the bells of the Minster in the distance. It was late; she would be missing dinner. It occurred to her suddenly that the rest of the household would worry. But she had no desire to go home. She swayed slightly, her wet hair sticking to her face, her boots clogged heavily with mud. She felt dizzy, as if she might fall.

'And a sure test of patience it is!' came the voice of her brother through the rain. 'Mary, where are you? – Call to me will you! – I know you are somewhere down here. I found your glove on the path. Call to me now, this minute!'

Next came the voice of Eliza, her sister. 'Ned!' she cried, pointing. 'She is there by the tree. I saw her in a flash of lightning.'

'We were about to send out a posse!' said Ned, finding her at last and angry. 'Here, draw this shawl about your shoulders. The rain is abating, but we must hurry, you are shivering with cold.'

'Where were you going?' asked Eliza in a curious and frightened tone.

'I don't know,' Mary said shakily, pulling on the shawl. She saw it was one of her mother's. She fell to apologising over and over as if delirious.

'Oh, what silly creatures you girls are,' Ned said flatly, leading the way through the woodland.

'I think you have a fever,' said Eliza.

'I don't care if I die,' Mary said miserably. 'Then at last my soul will find peace.'

All the way back she shivered, till suddenly her mother was there in the doorway.

'She was wandering,' said Ned, sighing and looking baffled.

Her mother gazed at her with sad weary eyes. 'Ned went to Jane's and they said you had left some time ago. Oh, come and dry your hair by the fire, my dear, then Eliza will bring you some soup.' Elizabeth drew her daughter to the hearth and rubbed her hair with a towel. 'My strange, dear Mary,' she whispered. 'How oddly different you are. I never know what you are thinking.'

'She's thinking about Jane having gone,' said Eliza bringing the soup.

'Yes,' said Ned. 'She is to make another life in Norfolk, her mother told me at their house.'

'But Mary doesn't like it, does she,' said Eliza shrugging. 'I am not good enough, you see. I am not clever like Jane. And I believe I am far too quiet.'

'And heaven knows where that silence will lead you,' murmured Mary.

'Not down the lane in a storm wanting to die,' said Ned. He flung off his wet coat.

Mary's cheeks had started to shine as she partook of the hot soup. 'Now you are looking much better,' said her mother.

'I'm sorry,' she said, still shivering. She turned to Eliza. 'Please don't feel bad,' she pleaded touching her hand, still cold and damp from the rain. 'Jane has been my friend, and it hurts that she is leaving Beverley.' How her impulsiveness hurt people, she thought, she could be quite unkind and selfish. She would have to consider it. 'I needed to walk in the woodland.'

'Oh aye,' said Ned. 'In the pouring rain and all. And what a storm it was too. You might well have gone to heaven in that lot. But I doubt you'd have liked it very much. You'd be trying to sort out the angels. Ah, always fussing.'

'Ned, don't scold me,' she said shivering. 'Sometimes I feel so alone.'

'And sometimes you scare me,' Eliza murmured.

'Melodrama, melodrama,' said Ned, pacing the room.

'Where's Father?' asked Mary, glancing about.

Her mother shuffled in her chair. 'I have no idea,' she sighed. She bent her head, her soft blonde curls half covering her thin features. Then she spoke with sudden daring. 'Perhaps we should eat without him. He will grumble, I know, but it is getting quite late and you are all so hungry. And the little ones are wreaking havoc upstairs with Everina. The girl tries her best.'

'Yes, let's eat without him,' said Ned, clapping his hands. 'Good idea.' He stood before them and drew himself up, acting like head of the household. He went to his mother and slid his arm around her shoulder. 'If it upsets him, then leave him to me. I'll manage him, Mother, don't worry.'

Elizabeth Wollstonecraft gazed at her son and smiled. She believed he could manage anything.


A whole two weeks went by. Mary had developed a very bad cough and had taken to her bed. The doctor said it was pneumonia. Knowing that Jane no longer walked the streets of Beverley and had gone to live with a family where she'd be all but a servant had left Mary distraught. She did not care if she died, she said again to Eliza, and Eliza took the message downstairs. Her mother came and reproached her. 'For all your learning with that girl, what good has it done you?' she said. 'Learning should make you more sensible, not more foolish.' Elizabeth Wollstonecraft stood in the doorway annoyed. Mary did not reply, her mother had all the time in the world for her husband's cruelty but it took every scrap of her nervous energy and there was none for anyone else. 'You are quite lost!' she called to Mary, turning back to the stairs.

If anyone was lost it was her mother, Mary thought indignantly. Hiding her face beneath the counterpane she drew up her limbs. She felt like a captive waiting for rescue. But who was to make the rescue? She clasped her hands tightly together, crying and fretting, till at last exhausted she slept. And she dreamt of a forest where the wild creatures were bathed in glorious light and were never impaired by illness. She ran through trees of silver, and the trees knew her as their own, magical and mysterious, and she lifted herself up like a bird taking flight, over the hills, over the mountains, away to new places . . . Then all of a sudden she woke, sweating profusely. – But where was Jane? Where, oh where, was Jane? How was she faring in Norfolk? Did she think of her? Was she well? She would write her a letter straight away. She pushed back the bedclothes and took deep breaths. She felt better, so much better! After she'd put on her shoes, she pulled on her smock, then went to the stairs.

'And the dead will be raised!' Eliza exclaimed with a laugh, as Mary joined them in the parlour.

'Yes,' said Mary, 'though I never heard a trumpet.'

'That's a shame,' said Eliza with a shrug. 'You will simply have to imagine.'

'I am well again,' said Mary, smiling. 'Must your lives come to a halt because I am ill? Why all the fuss?' She spoke with mock amusement.

'People happen to care, that's why,' said her mother, sitting sewing. 'You have gone through the worst of your fever today. I'm glad you've recovered.'

'Is it time for dinner?' asked Mary. She felt strangely abstracted, her voice like the voice of a child's not quite clear of an illness but stepping back into life, fragile and tender.

'Not yet,' said Eliza. 'Father and Ned are still out. Shall I set you a place?'

'Please do,' said Mary. 'It seems like ages since I sat at the table. What are we having?'

'Mother made rabbit stew with onions and potatoes,' said Eliza.

'It sounds delicious,' said Mary. She took a seat by the fire.

'Ned's been quite worried,' Eliza continued. 'He'll be relieved to see you are well. You acted as if your whole life was shattered. It wasn't you know. Soon you'll be back to yourself again, battling with Father.'

Mary sighed. 'There isn't a lot of point in battling with Father, Eliza. He's not going to change.'

Her mother looked up from her sewing. 'Everina is teaching the little ones upstairs,' she said, frowning. 'We told them they had to be silent. I hope they were?' She bent again to her work, carefully moving her needle in and out of the calico and pulling gently on the thread.

'I didn't hear a thing,' said Mary. 'Thank you.' She must always steel herself when it came to talking with her mother, there was such disquiet between them. 'And my appetite is back, which is good. I feel I can do things.'

'And you've forgotten Jane Arden, I hope,' said her mother, folding away her sewing.

'Jane? Oh no, not at all. I do not intend to forget her. In fact, I shall write to her tonight and ask how she is.'

Her mother shook her head. 'You will have to toughen those emotions, my dear, or life will take hold of you and ruin you.'

'I must finish the ironing,' said Eliza. She went off into the kitchen.

Another three weeks passed by, then a letter arrived from Jane. The Martins treated her as one of their own, she said, and she often went out with them. She was meeting interesting people and had made new friends. "And the Martins live so splendidly," she said. "Their furniture is so elegant, and they have silk cushions on the chairs . . ." Silk cushions indeed! Mary thought irritably. What had happened to her mind? Were cushions important, whatever fabric they came in? And she didn't care a fig about furniture. She wandered into the parlour.

'What's the matter?' Everina asked her, with a poise she had developed lately. 'You are looking concerned.'

'It's nothing,' Mary murmured. But inside she was seething and her thoughts were chaotic.

'Nothing eh?' said Ned, closing his book. 'I know that tone in your voice. – So what does she say in that letter? You are dying to tell us.'

Mary did not reply.

'You're always abstracted,' said Ned. 'You walked in front of a horse and carriage yesterday. I'm glad I was there to pull you back.'

'You don't know what it's like,' she said quietly. 'You wouldn't understand, you could never grasp what I mean.'

'You are most insulting,' Ned said, screwing up his eyes and staring at her irritably. 'I understand things just as well as you do. Perhaps more if we're truthful. You are all emotion, it gets you nowhere.'

Mary smiled at him thinly. 'I do get lost in my thoughts, I know. It bothers me a lot, but I can't seem to help it.'

Her brother sighed loudly. 'You really are impossible.'

'Well, I didn't like Jane's letter,' Mary said finally. 'There is no point saying any different. I didn't like what she said. She says the Martins have silk cushions. Whoever cares about cushions? And she is making new friends.' She breathed in deeply and braced herself. 'One in particular, apparently, whose name begins with C . . .'

Ned got up and paced the room, his hands clasped behind his back. 'Oh, oh, it begins with C, does it? – Caroline, Charlotte, Camilla . . .'

'Stop it!' cried Mary, clapping her hands to her ears.

'Only an initial?' said Everina. 'How strange. That could be anyone.'

'It might be a *Charles*?' Ned offered, cocking his eyebrows. 'What if it's a gent? Jane is a good looking woman.'

'Don't be ridiculous,' snapped Mary. 'It won't be a gent. No, it sounds like a girl. But why does she need a girlfriend when she has me, here in Beverley.'

'Norfolk is a long way off,' said Everina. 'She will want a friend as a companion, someone to talk with. She will need . . .'

'Oh, be quiet, Everina,' moaned Mary. 'Both of you be quiet. If you can't make me feel better, then please don't make me feel worse.'

'You're jealous,' said Ned. 'It's childish. You really ought to let go. There are all sorts of people in Beverley. Chaps will look at you too. You're a beauty, dear sister, with that lovely sway of yours and those big shining eyes. You need to walk out more and not just lose yourself in reading.'

'I shall do as I wish,' she replied dismissively.

Ned gave her the steady stare she resented, as if she deserved it. But she did not falter. 'I like to learn things,' she protested. 'Learning for you is natural and expected. For me it is different. It is as if a girl must be cautious about taking in knowledge in case she lights up her mind too much and sees what she should not see.'

'Like what? said Ned. He smiled at her wryly.

She shrugged. She felt as if she were slipping away, slipping away from them all, moving into a solitary world of her own filled with surging ideas and new sensations, but lonely. She saw her brother growing older, bristle on his chin he must keep on shaving away; she saw how fast his limbs were when he went up the stairs, how agile he had been when he had pulled her away from the cart. And he did not suffer the difficult temperament of their father. What was more, their mother adored him. And what mother wouldn't? Everina, still very young, was trying hard to grow up, while people called Eliza "feminine". Mary knew she had striking looks herself. She had soft fair hair and Ned had said she had eyes that seethed with passion whenever she spoke from her heart. She knew it was true and could feel it. Ned missed nothing and would undoubtedly make a good lawyer.

Just then there came the rattle of a cart by the door. Elizabeth Wollstonecraft went to the window to look. 'Oh, my goodness,' she exclaimed. 'It's your father. Some fellow's helping him lift down a piece of furniture.'

Suddenly, their father rushed in. 'Ned, help me in with this desk!' he cried. The desk stood on the pavement in the dusk.

'And you brought it on that cart?' said Ned, watching the cart going off and shaking his head in disbelief. 'It looks like it cost a pretty penny. It's a fine piece of workmanship, that is. – Look at that inlay.' Ned ran his fingers over the wood.

'Aye, you hold that end and I'll hold this,' said his father, 'then we can get it through the door. It's to go in the room at the back.'

'What have you got?' said Elizabeth, dabbing her nose with her handkerchief and looking bewildered.

'It's a desk, woman. Can't you see? It's a writing desk. A man of means must always have a writing desk!' He pulled and shoved it with Ned until it stood halfway down the hall. 'Look at that!' he said proudly, smoothing his hand across the wood. 'Wonderful English oak, and look at that moulded-edge top and those mitred ends. And what do you think of these brass ring pulls on the drawers, eh?' He carried on talking, excited as a child with a gift. 'There are plenty of drawers for my papers in this. I can keep things tidy.'

'You will never use it,' murmured his wife. 'You buy these expensive things and they just gather dust. Those so-called Chinese ceramics, there on the dresser, I always fear they will break. We are often moving, Edward. We won't be in Beverley much longer, I'll wager.'

Edward Wollstonecraft stood before her and drew himself up, scowling. 'I don't care for your attitude, Elizabeth,' he said angrily. 'I am the master of this house, remember.' He took out his snuff box and opened it. The scent of powdered tobacco filled the long thin hall as he sniffed it into his nostrils. He turned his attention to the vases on the nearby dresser. 'I bought those vases for you, my dear,' he said haughtily. 'Fine thanks I got for it, too.'

'I did not ask you to empty your purse for vases,' she said with a sigh. 'I do not favour such things. And in any case, you did not buy them for me; you bought them for yourself, to impress those dull people you invite to dinner.'

Her husband braced himself. 'It is important to get to know such people. It is good for business.' He waved her off with his hand. 'You know nothing, woman, nothing.'

'Chinese ceramics are they? Well, however much you have paid for them, they are not in the least nice to look at,' she said. 'But you'll pretend to be a country gent, whatever it costs us.'

'And so I am,' he said, taking another pinch of snuff. 'My girls and you, my dear, are well turned out. Perhaps some of the gentry

28

dress better, but Eliza and Mary have silk handkerchiefs in their pockets. And Ned has a grand silk hat.'

She sighed and shook her head. 'Not a thing do you know about livestock or crops, but your arrogance will carry you along, I suppose.' She lowered her voice to a whisper. 'Though we are well near bankrupt.'

The desk was pushed into the room at the back where the evening light fell on it and made it look beautiful. Edward Wollstonecraft stood before it thrilled, gazing at it as if it were something holy. 'That's lovely,' he said with a quivering voice.

His wife turned away. She could not look at it. Mary gazed sadly at her mother. The desk would be sold when the family left Beverley, along with the ceramic vases. There was very little money left to live on. His need for things beyond his purse was intolerable. But her father listened to his own point of view and no other, and he could not learn from his mistakes.

During the summer Jane came home on a visit, bringing along her new found friend whose name began with a C. It grieved Mary to see them strolling about Beverley together, and she hated the thought of them both in the Arden household, perhaps sleeping in the very same bed. 'She has brought that friend,' she said to Everina miserably. 'I hate her.'

'But you don't even know her,' said Everina, in the condescending manner of their mother.

Mary pulled on her cape and went out, determined to go to the Arden household and knock on the door. Impulse ruled her again, but she could not fight it. She was in fear of Jane returning to Norfolk, leaving without as much as a word!

She rapped on the door and waited. A reserved Mrs Arden answered. 'Ah, I believe it is Mary?' she said coolly, as if she were talking to a stranger. She glanced back into the house.

Mary shook her head despairingly. 'Have I changed so much that I am scarcely recognisable?' she said curtly.

'Jane, do come!' called her mother, sounding nervous.

Jane came down the hall, looking surprised. 'Mary, how good to see you!' she cried, putting out her arms. 'Are you well?' Over Jane's shoulder, Mary saw that at the end of the hall the newcomer watched them.

'I am very well, thank you,' said Mary, self consciously. 'I heard you were back in Beverley. But I did not know you were coming.' She straightened. 'I am sad about that.' She fumed with jealousy as the guest came forward smiling, long golden ringlets swinging loose about her shoulders.

'This is Cecilia,' said Jane, turning and introducing them. Her mother had returned inside. 'Do come through,' said Jane. 'We were just taking tea. Father is away in London.'

Mary felt cold and looked down the long dreary hall. There was a thin light coming from the parlour through the partially open doorway.

'Shall I take your cape?' asked Jane.

Mary removed her cape and went through. The Arden house felt somehow ordinary now whereas before it had been sublime.

'Let me tell you about Norfolk,' said Jane excitedly as they all took seats by the fire. The new found friend stayed silent and cautious as if aware of an enemy in her midst.

Jane talked on about a play they were planning to see at the Beverley theatre. She glanced at Cecilia then they both looked downwards. Mary could see they were in some sort of silent agreement. So she wouldn't be invited. Well, let it be. But it cut through Mary like a knife. Jane's mother poured out the tea, though she said not a word. Mary longed for the presence of Doctor Arden; his warmth would have made things better.

'Well, then Mary,' Jane said awkwardly, stirring her tea. 'We are all rather tired. We were at an event in Beverley last night. We . . .'

Mary hated the *"we"*, and said she had things to do back home and would need to depart. She stood and pulled on her cape, thinking she'd been a fool to have come and put herself through such anguish. All the way home she felt furious. Jane's mother had treated her horribly. And Jane had been neglectful and awkward. She went along the lane to her home, pondering and studying the sky, watching the clouds as they slowly moved over Beverley, oh the great indifferent clouds! Everywhere was still. She bent for a shining stone on the path and gazed at the glistening specks in its surface. Who could understand the intensity of human feelings, she wondered. Was there anyone anywhere, who might know how she felt that minute? What if a simple stone were a solid body of intensity, she pondered, tumbled from the heavens, how it would suffer in silence. She cast it aside and walked on.

As she entered the parlour of her home, Everina looked up from her reading. 'What's happened?' she asked. 'You look sad?'

Mary's shoulders lifted and fell. 'That's because I am,' she said.

And the bad feelings remained and would not go. She did not visit the Arden house again and avoided places where she might encounter Jane with the dreadful Cecilia. She felt helpless with anger and wrote her another letter to say how excluded she'd felt at her home, complaining she'd been deeply offended and requesting Jane return every letter she had sent her.

Mary waited in agony, but Jane remained silent. Everyone in the Wollstonecraft household knew there was something wrong, but only Ned spoke up. 'Jane is allowed but a single friend,' he said flatly, 'and we all know who it is. Sometimes Mary, you are quite ridiculous. But it wouldn't be you if you weren't. It is quite tiring though at times, dear sister. I do wish you'd change.'

'I am true to my feelings,' Mary said quietly. 'I will always answer to my heart.' She was trembling, nervous and ashamed that she could not manage her thoughts.

'Oh, you will, you will,' shrugged her brother. 'Your heart demands a lot, and to hell with others who must suffer!'

'And how do I make people suffer?' she asked shakily.

Ned drew himself up and gave her an angry look. 'I will say no more,' he concluded. At that he went out. The others were upstairs with her mother. Mary sat down in the empty parlour and wrote another letter to Jane:

*'If I did not love you I should not write so; – I have a heart that scorns disguise, and a countenance which will not dissemble. . . . I am a little singular in my thoughts of love and friendship; I must have the first place*

*or none. I own your behaviour is more according to the opinion of the*
*world, but I would break such narrow bounds. . . . Love and Jealousy are*
*twins. . . . I have not time to write fully on the subject, but this I am sure*
*of, if I did not love you, I should not be angry. – I cannot bear a slight*
*from those I love. . . . P.S. I keep your letters as a memorial that you*
*once loved me, but it will be of no consequence to keep mine as you have*
*no regard for the writer . . . your humble servant, Mary Wollstonecraft.'*

'And she must promise to keep whatever I have told her confidential,' Mary murmured. 'Oh, I am such a fool. I have revealed so much!' She could hear the anger in her voice as she whispered. Her heart beat heavily as her emotions took over, she might have had a fire within her.

After she had posted her letter, Mary walked about town passing the great houses and little cottages, lost in a trance of feeling as if in a dream. She raised her face to the sky and prayed that Jane would reply.

But Jane had returned to Norfolk with Cecilia, and Mary waited to be pulled from her rooted depression just as sunshine dried up the rain. She walked down a lonely country track, a thin wind playing on her skin. It was good, so good, to be caressed by the free open air. She watched the branches of the trees swaying and listened to their songs, remembering the days of her childhood when nature had been close and healing. She would like to have stayed in that moment, in its richly imaginative pleasure, daring to feel like a child. But she wasn't a child, not anymore; she was an adult and must join in the fight. And she trembled in bitter resentment that her love and tenderness had been cast aside and she wasn't as important as she'd thought. In fact, she wasn't important at all. She shook her head irritably. How self-pitying she could be! How weak!

Gradually as she walked, she began to feel better and made her way home. Everina ran to greet her on the path. She was laughing and waving a letter. It was a letter from Jane! Upstairs in her bedroom, Mary almost wept as she read it. Jane was good through and through, and she ought to have trusted her constancy. Instead of taking offence, she'd actually been touched by her jealousy. But of course, of course, was she not a true angel? Mary held the letter to her breast.

'Is it good?' Everina whispered, peering round the door.

'Oh, yes,' she told her smiling. 'It is better than ever!' She put out her hand and beckoned her. 'Come to me, dear sister,' she cried. 'Let me kiss you!' You had to feel loved to love, she decided. Love was a flower from the garden of the Hesperides and its fragrance united all souls.

# 3

## *To Hoxton*

'Oh, without doubt,' Edward Wollstonecraft nodded assertively, 'it would have been far more difficult to sell if I hadn't had you with me. You are very persuasive, Ned. You'll be an excellent lawyer, my son, and a good businessman too, should you be so inclined.' The father laughed. 'Why, we sold that desk for more than I gave for it. And your mother's ceramics as well!' He patted Ned on the back. They sat alone on the floor in the parlour talking by the light of a candle. The rest of the family were in bed. A round white moon shone through the window. The Minster struck midnight.

Ned yawned. 'You hadn't had that desk very long, Father. We might have lost a great deal of money. We were lucky.'

'I know,' his father said wearily. 'Your mother was right, of course, I should never have bought it. But if I set my eyes on something, I must have it. I do as my mind dictates, I can't help it.'

'Perhaps you need a touch more discipline,' Ned said, cautiously. 'Apart from what's in those trunks in the hall, we haven't a lot to take with us; most of what we had has been sold.'

'Oh, we'll not come unstuck,' said Edward, assuming an air of confidence. 'I've sent some furniture on a wagon, and I still have some cash. All is not lost.'

'Glad to hear it,' Ned said quietly. 'Or we'll arrive in Hoxton penniless.'

'I have one or two ideas,' his father went on, his voice rising with his thoughts. 'They might not work, but at least I can try.'

'You always try,' said Ned, staring around the cold bare room. 'Would you like a drink?'

His father looked at him surprised. 'The tea is all packed away. We have to turn in.'

'I wasn't thinking of tea,' said Ned, tapping on one of the floorboards. 'Something stronger perhaps?' His father glanced at him baffled. Ned pulled on a thin floorboard by the window, then drew out a bottle from beneath. 'Yes, I do have a drink now and then,' he said, guiltily. It was a half of a bottle of whiskey. 'I have to say there are times when I feel the need.'

'I'm sorry about that,' his father said flatly. 'You are young. I never wanted to turn you into a drinker, my boy.' Edward Wollstonecraft looked despondent.

Ned pulled out the cork. 'We can drink from the neck of the bottle,' he said. 'Might as well empty it now.'

His father went first. 'I've always enjoyed a drink, lad. It's despair, you see, and the fear that nothing ever alters. There's a spell on me, Ned. By God, there's a spell on me I tell you. I'm damned.' He wiped his mouth on his sleeve. 'Let's sing a song,' he said suddenly.

'A song?' laughed Ned. 'What shall we sing? And we'll have to sing softly, we don't want to wake them all up.' He glanced at the ceiling.

'*Fare Thee Well*,' said his father. 'That's one of my favourites.'

'Alright then,' said Ned. 'Let's have a go.'

They sat their backs against the wall and sang in unison:

> "'*Fare thee well my own true love*
> *And farewell for a while.*
> *I'm going away, but I'll come again*
> *If I go ten thousand miles.*
>
> *Ten thousand miles, my own true love,*
> *Ten thousand miles or more,*
> *And the rocks may melt and the seas may burn,*
> *If I should not return.*

> *Oh don't you see that lone some dove,*
> *Sitting on an ivy tree,*
> *She's weeping for her own true love*
> *Just as I shall weep for mine.*
>
> *Oh come back my own true love*
> *And stay a while with me*
> *For if I had a friend all on this earth,*
> *You've been a friend to me.*
>
> *And fare thee well my own true love*
> *And farewell for a while.*
> *I'm going away, but I'll be back*
> *If I go ten thousand miles.'"*

The song finished and they both fell silent. 'Come on then,' whispered Edward. 'Bedtime I think. We've a tiring journey tomorrow.' They made their way upstairs, passing the bedrooms of the sleeping family. Son and father might have had other things to say, but there was no more time. It had been a long day.

The last of their belongings were loaded on to the coach. The house sounded hollow as Mary wandered the rooms looking for anything forgotten. But she wouldn't forget what mattered; she wouldn't forget what she'd learned from Doctor Arden and her talks with Jane. Her mother sat quietly in the coach, unhappy about moving to the East End of London and wondering what lay ahead. The children stared broodingly into the distance, they too would leave friends. Ned and his father talked with the coach driver. There had been a lot of concern that year about criminals holding up coaches, always a danger on the roads. And the weather was bad. The journey to Hoxton was going to take at least two days.

'France has a new young king,' said Ned.

'Aye, a mere sixteen year old lad,' the coach driver frowned. 'The queen's even younger.'

'Marie Antoinette,' said Ned with emphasis, enjoying the expression as he said it. 'Daughter of the Holy Roman Emperor, Francis I, and the Empress Maria Theresa. Sounds very grand doesn't it.'

'Grand or not,' the coach driver shrugged. 'It seems they've got no more idea, than two birds sitting on the top branch of a tree. The little girl bride got married in a gown as was dripping with gold and sapphires, and all while the peasants are starving.'

'France will change very quickly, I think,' said Ned, in his new-fangled serious way. 'The aristocrats and clergy have too much money and the peasants are like beasts of burden. Something has to be done.'

'A beast of burden, that's me!' laughed his father, with the careless manner he often adopted on the move. The driver secured a trunk beside him, while Edward gave it a push to make sure it was safe. It was a heavy cargo for the four waiting horses that must pull it mile after mile along muddy uneven roads.

'Talk about beasts of burden,' said Ned. 'Horses take the prize.'

The driver checked all the harnesses and hooves of his steeds, then climbed into the driving seat and waited for his travellers to take their places.

'The British parliament has declared Massachusetts in rebellion,' said Ned, standing by the coach, his arms folded as he glanced at his father who was wrapping a strap around a trunk. 'Did you know? – The American Revolution can't be stopped. There is going to be such a bloodbath.'

'Well, look here,' said his father, gazing at the darkening sky. 'There'll be another bath soon if we don't get a move on. I think we're in for a storm.'

The worldly-wise coach driver nodded and pulled down his hat. 'All ready then, sir?'

'I think so,' said Edward boarding the coach with Ned. They talked on about what was happening in America. It seemed as if the whole world were about to explode into chaos.

Men and war, thought Mary, and the coach wheels chanted, *"Men and war, men and war,"* as it went. As she sat in the coach she did not know where they were going or what to look forward to.

She felt she was losing sight of herself, whisked along by her parents into a remote, unknown, world where she must meet new people and find new friends. Her heart beat fast at the thought of it. Now and again in her mind she caught a glimpse of her future waiting in a fading sunset, or she might catch it in the tones of a song, but it was always gone within seconds. And so they were heading south. What would it be like? What new world would she encounter?

The house their father had rented was in Queen's Row, Hoxton, in the East End of London. Mary had thought the travelling would never end, and they had stopped two times overnight. Her father was grumpier than ever because the inns had been far too costly. "Worse than highwaymen!" he'd cried. "Nothing but daylight robbery!" The weather was poor and they were all exhausted.

The house, they found, on arrival, was only partially furnished, though a wagon load of furniture was due to arrive very soon Elizabeth told the children as she wandered the bleak cold rooms. She went to sit in a chair in the parlour while Ned got to making a fire. Edward Wollstonecraft was checking the windows around the house, while Mary, Everina and Eliza went to investigate the kitchen. Just then they heard a knock on the door.

'How do you do, sir,' said a small distinguished looking gentleman. He put out his hand to Edward, who looked him up and down curiously. 'I am Reverend Clare from next door. I believe you have come from Yorkshire?'

At that moment Ned came forward and introduced himself. 'You expected us, then?' He smiled, across his father's shoulder. 'I can't shake your hand sir, for my own, as you see, are filled with soot from the fire.' Ned ran his hands down the sides of his frockcoat, still crumpled and shabby from the journey. Mary peered around the door of the kitchen, excited by the sight of the friendly new neighbour.

'Yes, oh yes. It is very good to see you,' said the reverend. 'My wife is next door. She has asked me to invite you to tea – only when you are ready of course. Any time you like.'

'And my own wife is suffering from a cold,' said Edward. 'I fear it was the rain, we had very bad weather.'

'It was a long way too,' said Ned. 'A most unpleasant journey.'

'My daughters will be getting our dinner very shortly,' said Edward, glancing back. There were sounds of activity in the kitchen. 'But that's a very kind gesture, Reverend. And we'll certainly take you up on it when my wife gets better.'

'We will look forward,' said the reverend. 'Always best to look forward, never much point looking back.'

'Indeed,' said Edward. 'There is much comfort in the thought.'

'I do my best,' said the reverend. With that he smiled at them warmly and returned to his house.


Settling in was made easier with the amiable Clares next door, thought Mary, who were kind and thoughtful people. Elizabeth Wollstonecraft was glad of it, she said, for she never knew what to expect from her restless fiery husband who was often like someone possessed.

'Reverend Clare often looks pale and overwrought,' Elizabeth said to Ned one morning at breakfast. 'I wonder if his holiness wears him out, for the man is indeed holy.' She shook her head at the thought.

'Holiness and badness can be equally tiring,' said Ned. 'I believe we should keep them on the sidelines for their own due season.' Mary, Ned suggested, might tire Reverend Clare further by constantly plying him with questions. Seated at the table, she curtly replied that the Clares enjoyed her company, and asserted she borrowed books from the reverend's library. He was much like Doctor Arden, she said, and enjoyed conversation.

'Books, books, books,' her mother chanted censoriously. Eliza wasn't too bothered about learning, she said, and neither was Everina. 'The boys like making discoveries,' she added. 'But boys always do, even if it means they must break things to see how they work.'

Mary smiled wryly, then went upstairs to find Charles and James who were due for their lesson.

'I heard Reverend Clare might be suffering from tuberculosis,' said Elizabeth to Ned. Ned sat reading at the table.

'Yes, I heard the same,' said Ned, sighing at the thought.

'It could mean he is dying,' his mother said, looking serious. 'Most people die if they suffer from tuberculosis,' For a moment she was thoughtful. 'His wife takes care of him well enough though from what I gather. But he doesn't go out much.'

'He might have something mild,' said Ned abstractedly. 'That's probably why he stays in. The weather in England is often so damp.'

After another half hour Mary came down and picked up a set of books from the chaise longue.

'More reading?' murmured her mother. 'Those Clares get no peace from you, Mary.'

'We're involved in an important discussion,' Mary replied ponderously.

Her mother gazed at her confounded.

'Would you prefer I stayed in?' asked Mary, sitting down beside her.

'You need to mend your stays,' her mother said crossly.

'I am quite disinterested in stays,' Mary murmured.

'Oh, women and stays,' said Ned, turning the pages of his book and biting his lip. 'They do make a woman's form look good though, I admit. But they can't be healthy. You, dear sister, have no need of them. You possess the shape of a goddess. And your eyes sparkle like great shining dewdrops.' He laughed loudly.

'Don't talk nonsense,' said Mary. '"Great shining dewdrops" indeed! Such matters are merely superficial.'

Their mother sat twisting thread about her finger abstractedly. 'Would you like me to mend them while you're out?' she asked. 'It's only a small tear, but it'll get bigger if it isn't attended to.'

'I can do it myself, Mother,' said Mary loftily, contemptuous of her mother's lack of respect for her desire to improve her mind. Ned needn't concern himself as to how to acquire knowledge, he'd received a good education and was now intent on working with a law firm in London.

'So what will you read with them today?' asked Ned, rather tiredly.

Mary glanced at him, cheered by his enquiry. But she frowned at the thought of discussing her beloved reading with Ned, who might try to make her feel stupid. 'It's a poem by Thomas Day, the abolitionist. He wrote it with his friend John Bicknall quite recently.

Mr Clare got hold of a copy. We're reading it together. I could let you look at it sometime if you like.'

'I daresay you could,' said Ned, stretching his arms above his head and yawning. 'Though I doubt I would care for it much. They do go on, those poets. And they all drink laudanum you know. A lot of their ideas are quite muddled.'

Mary looked at her mother, her eyes intent on her sewing. Ned gazed at the white ceiling above him. 'The poem is written as an attack on the slave trade,' said Mary. 'I'm sure you'd appreciate the words. Perhaps the end of slavery can only be accomplished when poets, artists, politicians and the rest of us can combine our unique sensitivities. That's when our souls are most generous.'

Ned replied with a sniff. Her mother's head stayed bent. Mary continued. 'It speaks of the wretchedness of slaves on plantations and their complete loss of hope. It's a sort of suicide note I suppose, depicting the slave's feelings, his anger at the system that has led him to think of shooting himself.'

'"*Shooting himself?*"' said Ned, closing his book and looking at her straight.

'Yes, the poor man shot himself.'

'Oh dear, that's pretty serious,' he frowned. 'Go on then, read it. I'll listen.' He sat waiting attentively.

After a brief silence, she reached for the poem. 'It's the true story of a negro who was abducted from Africa. It tells of the happiness he found with a family in England and the love he shared with a lovely white servant girl. They had hoped to be married. There was a ruling that said no slave could be made to leave England against his or her own will and be returned to their so-called owners. This slave was to suffer that injustice.'

'Damned awful,' murmured Ned, his cheeks reddening with feeling.

Finding a section, she kept the place with her finger. 'It's quite sentimental,' she warned. In a strange way she was afraid of it. She was trying not to be too sentimental or romantic, but she did love poetry and poetry was full of romance. She glanced at her mother, who was now poking the fire. 'Do *you* want to hear it, Mother?' she asked.

Elizabeth looked at her straight. 'What, that poem?'

'Well, not all of it,' laughed Ned. 'It's bound to be long.'

'And so it should,' Mary contended defensively. 'There is much to be said. Poets are serious thinkers, and a lot of them are active in politics as well. I think they write poems to discover their deepest thoughts and give the rest of us a chance to share them. Poetry can be like the wings of song, I think.'

'Aye and every bit as fanciful,' said her mother.

'The negro was detected and forced on his master's vessel,' said Mary, dismissing the slight. 'Finding he couldn't escape and unable to face the terrible voyage back and the horrors awaiting him, he shot himself with a gun.'

Apart from the crackle of the fire, the room was silent as Mary read out the poem:

> *"When some sweet maid receives her lover's vow,*
> *And binds the offered chaplet to her brow.*
> *While on thy languid eyes I fondly gaze,*
> *And trembling meet the lustre of their rays,*
> *Thou, gentle virgin, thou didst not despise*
> *The humble homage of a captive's sighs.*
> *By heaven abandoned, and by man betrayed,*
> *Each hope resigned of comfort or of aid,*
> *Thy generous love could every sorrow end,*
> *In thee I found a mistress and a friend;*
> *Still as I told the story of my woes,*
> *With heaving sighs thy lovely bosom rose;*
> *The trickling drops of liquid crystal stole*
> *Down thy fair cheek, and marked thy pitying soul:*
> *Dear drops! upon my bleeding heart, like balm*
> *They fell, and soon my tortured mind grew calm;*
> *Then my loved country, parents, friends forgot;*
> *Heav'n I absolved, nor murmured at my lot;*
> *Thy sacred smiles could every pang remove,*
> *And liberty became less dear than love."'*

'A moving piece,' said Ned, his eyes dark with sincerity. 'I wonder what the girl thought though, if she ever got wind of it. Sentimental and romantic, without doubt, but I doubt the slave would have wanted to leave an epistle like that for his beloved to read later on. These poets don't half take liberties.'

'Oh, Ned,' sighed Mary. 'Must you always think so judiciously? Sometimes you just have to *feel*.'

'And what trouble it causes when we do,' Ned murmured.

Mary tucked her books beneath her arm and walked out into the hall. 'I shall probably be something like an hour,' she called back.

'A half of an hour, more like,' her mother corrected. 'I shall need you in the kitchen soon.'

Later that week while walking round town Ned encountered a cohort of students in heated conversation by the library. They were men from the Hoxton Academy. 'They are young and need to use their energy!' somebody shouted.

'Dissenters? – Send them to war!' cried another. 'They stand about talking nonsense.'

The Hoxton Dissenting Academy was thought to be the best in the country and some fine questioning young minds attended it. Dissenters had been excluded from national universities because they would not conform to the articles of the Anglican Church; they'd been therefore compelled to set up their own institutions. Their schools of learning however were often excellent and might offer a variety of subjects from politics, rhetoric and logic, to classics, mathematics and natural philosophy, though some complained that the diversity of subjects was sometimes at the cost of depth.

'I was first schooled by Caligula!' a voice cried from the middle of the group. The strong looking fellow waved his fist in the air. 'A spiteful instructor if ever there was one, who I was always expected to agree with. Ah yes, I tell you, I was! But we must fight the good fight and attempt to discover the truth! You see, my friends, there *is* a truth beneath the rubble if we can but find it. – I say to you now, we must speak for what we believe in. Human beings are all susceptible to the same joys and sufferings, and whatever a person's place in society everyone deserves fair treatment and a chance to improve their mind.' He threw out his arms. 'Is it not so?'

Someone asked him to clarify his comment about Caligula and he claimed that the teacher he spoke of had been a Samuel Newton of Norwich. 'I loved him and hated him,' he cried. 'And with equal vigour too. – Do we not despise the shackles of gratitude we feel towards those who would control us, and from whom we seek constant approval? Such shackles cripple our thinking.'

'Is it not the same in marriage?' cried one of the group laughing. The others shared a smile.

'I abhor marriage, my friend,' continued the speaker, 'where a man might suffer from attempting to mould a woman to his own whims, and where a woman might be subject to her husband's beliefs and disposition. – Oh no, I shall never be married!'

Ned thought the speaker looked a similar age to himself, and someone he thought he might talk with. The group dispersed and he strolled forward towards him. 'Sir,' said Ned, thrusting out his hand. 'How do you do! My name is Ned Wollstonecraft. I have recently come to live here with my family. My father is a gentleman farmer.'

The man looked him up and down. 'Do you intend to be a cleric?'

Ned straightened. 'Sir, I intend to be a lawyer. In point of fact, I shouldn't care to be a man of the church.'

'Ah, we are all such fiends!' laughed the other. He shook Ned's hand. 'I am William Godwin. I attend the Hoxton Academy. You are a man who knows his own mind that much is plain.'

'I would like to think so,' said Ned. 'I have a sister who insists on knowing hers.' He shook his head despairingly and smiled. 'I fear for her though. She is very strong in her assertions.' He laughed briefly. 'She is a fighter, is Mary. – She is so full of anger about slavery and the plight of women. Slaves and women are very much the same to my sister. Fairness and justice is all she thinks of. She is quite a gorgon.'

William Godwin stood his hands in his pockets, looking deeply interested and thoughtful. 'So she has living snakes for her hair, and her look would turn me to stone?' He opened his eyes widely in a playful gesture.

'Well, it might,' said Ned, frowning and serious.

'Perhaps you can arrange for us to meet,' smiled Godwin. 'I would very much like to talk with this gorgon.'

'You would not thank me for it!' laughed Ned. 'She is all but a girl, though her mind is much advanced through reading.' But the conversation was getting too personal. Ned turned to look down the street. 'I am in a bit of a rush,' he said. 'But I hope I will see you again.'

'You no doubt will,' Godwin said abstractedly.

Ned looked back and saw that Godwin stood for a while trans-fixed before walking the opposite way.

At that moment, Mary was seated in a chaise with Mrs Clare, who was on her way to a friend's in Newington Butts. Frances Blood, better known as Fanny, was two years older than Mary, 'and a very accomplished young woman,' Mrs Clare asserted as they travelled. 'I know you will like her. She sings and plays the piano, and you will find she is widely read.'

'Does she expect me?' asked Mary, inspired but nervous.

'Of course, my dear, she looks forward. We have exchanged a couple of letters. She has only the children today, her parents are out.'

It seemed to Mary that Fanny's family was very much like her own. The mother had borne seven children and Fanny often took charge if her mother was ill or resting. The Bloods were also of Irish descent like her mother and originally came from County Clare. The father had once been a landowner, but he had somehow squandered his money. Mary knew all about fathers squandering money and the similarities were striking. Mrs Clare shook her head as she delivered the story to Mary. The money had largely belonged to Fanny's mother, she said, but Mr Blood had wasted it, and had constantly fled his creditors, first to Limerick, then Dublin, now London.

'But how do they live?' asked Mary, knowing the struggles a family experienced when money was scarce.

'You might well ask,' said Mrs Clare, shaking her head despairingly. 'I believe Mrs Blood does some sewing, but she doesn't make very much money. Fanny supports them mainly through her artwork.'

Mary looked at her astonished. 'She sounds very talented.'

'Indeed, she is,' said Mrs Clare, proud of her young friend. 'She makes beautiful drawings of wild flowers which are published in the *Flora Londinensis*, a wonderful book. William Curtis, the publisher, has a number of artists work for him. They say he makes generous payments.'

It was music to Mary's ears, and she braced herself to meet this friend who she knew would be different from all others. How she needed a friend to be close to and admire, another woman she could talk to without the strains and constrictions of family. Even though she felt tense, she was aware of a bud in her soul opening up to the sun. Two years older than herself, just like Jane Arden, and with a family similar to her own, perhaps Frances would bring some zest to her jaded soul.

Mrs Clare continued to talk. William Curtis had a garden, she said, where he cultivated wild flowers to observe their development. 'It's a sort of scientific exercise, I think. The drawing styles of his artists are expected to be consistent, that is in thin black lines, each part of the flower carefully shown and named.'

For the rest of the way they were silent. Mary felt she was about to enter a new and exciting world, and she put aside her despair.

Frances Blood had a cordial and happy manner as she opened the door to greet them. Mrs Clare introduced them and they stood shaking hands, looking at each other searchingly. Mary felt she might be seeing her reflection in a pond they were so much alike; her spirit and Fanny's were the same and the two young women felt an instant affinity. 'Well,' laughed Mary, seeing so many children in the room, and trying to talk above their voices, 'This is like home!'

'It's a bit of a strain,' smiled Frances, 'but they are all good humoured. And to tell you the truth, I much prefer children to adults.' She smiled. 'Excepting present company, of course. I believe you are often at the Clares.'

Mrs Clare bent to the children and they welcomed her familiar chatter.

'It is fate,' smiled Mary. 'I am drawn there.'

'Likewise,' said Frances. She glanced at Mrs Clare with fondness. 'I don't believe it is fate though, I believe it is effort that moves us towards what is best. If we follow our true feelings there will always be something valuable to find on the way.'

'I have heard a lot about you,' said Mary, taking off her cloak and sitting down by the table. Frances poured them each a cup of tea. How slender and lovely she was, thought Mary, watching as she bent to her siblings. She cast her eyes about the tidy and charming room with its noisy children's voices and pleasant pictures of the countryside. 'Is this your own work?' she asked, rising to look.

'Indeed,' said Mrs Clare answering for her friend.

'You appear to do it all quite naturally, the work looks effortless,' said Mary. Her thoughts and feelings just now were filled with unbounded pleasure. It was something of a fashion to hang water-colours, but to paint them yourself was a triumph. 'They are beautiful,' she murmured, fascinated by Fanny's expertise. 'You have a passion for the countryside, then?'

'Oh yes,' smiled Fanny, delighted to have Mary's attention, 'especially wild flowers. It is as if they are my very own, you see. I draw them in their natural places – foxgloves in fields, violets in ditches, broom on the hillside . . . I draw them in all their stages too; that is how I capture them best.'

'And do you always paint your drawings?'

'Not always. When I do I use only the slightest brush of colour. They must seem to grow from the page. But the energy and skill has to come from the heart not the hand.' She placed the flat of her hand on her breast. 'I must *know* them here.'

Mary had lost herself to Fanny, as if she herself were rooted. All the way back her mind revisited those last few hours. Could anything really be so perfect? They would write to each other often. A new and flourishing spirit was ready to come into being.

# 4

## Imagination and Wild Flowers

Mary was now in a haze of happiness. How good it was to have inspiring friends to share time with, she thought, the Clares were a godsend, and Fanny Blood was adorable. Mary helped her mother with the house and continued to teach her siblings, though with much more verve than before. They were reading well and making drawings which they showed to their mother with pride. The problems between her parents did not change, but now she could set them aside as theirs and not hers. There was a new radiance in her soul and she lived for her times with the Clares, visiting their home like a busy bird building a nest, for in it lay the seeds of her most important ideas. Fanny would often come to join them, her books and drawings tucked beneath her arm. Heaven itself could hold nothing more joyous for Mary than the times she shared with Fanny Blood, her drawings of wild flowers could have softened the hardest of hearts. Sometimes they sat for hours together in the woodland, Fanny's pencil tracing the shape of a flower on her pad, the image emerging like a gentle delicate ghost. She would whisper its shape and structure as she moved her pencil on the page. – The flat surface of a leaf was known as the *lamia*, the leaf was joined to the stem by a stalk called the *petiole*, while the angle the petiole made with the stem was the *axil*. The petals, known as the *corolla*, were the most beautiful features of all, she said, for they were often brilliantly coloured with a delicious sweetness at their centre for bees, butterflies and moths. Interest in the countryside was flourishing in England

and scientific particulars and medicinal uses for plants were important to the publisher of *Flora Londinensis*. Fanny's knowledge was vast and she had much to offer. They would scour the hedgerows together, stride over streams to sit by a chosen flower, and if she must reach across a ridge, Mary would clasp her feet so she didn't fall over. They laughed at such activities and enjoyed a unique and fulfilling harmony. Fanny asserted that flowers were drawn best in the very spot where they grew, fresh and thriving, and they must always be rooted for finest coruscation. She occasionally slipped into the stream and dirtied her smock, but she was never disagreeable or sullen if she must walk back home grimy and dishevelled.

The propaganda of revolution and anarchy however was everywhere, and Mary felt it worse than ever as she walked about Hoxton that day. At the other side of the Atlantic, the colonists were arguing that taxes imposed by the parliament in Britain drained them of economic independence and were unconstitutional. – "Who can deny it?" people reasoned on the streets, and they shook their fingers in warning. "The colonists are about to tear the government limb from limb!" Every day the voices of liberty pierced the air and refused to be silenced. And the king's spies crept through the land like spiders, hiding away in spider holes and coming out to scout, for surely the troubles in France were contagious, liberty could be a wild and livid creature that might well run amok.

And it did. Thirteen colonies formed a Continental Congress and had set up committees and conventions in a bid to seize power. A petition had been drafted and sent to King George in an attempt to resolve the situation, but it seemed the king had ignored it, and the Congress had issued a declaration claiming they would rather die free than live the life of a slave! British forces were harassed and shot at. Colonists' weapons and supplies were destroyed, and British muskets and bayonets were seized. The blood of the colonists was up. War was underway. General George Washington was appointed to take charge of the troubles in Boston and took command of the Continental Army. The surge for freedom and liberty was disseminating like a plague, and who could know its inclination.

Hoxton brooded, then shifted into livid talk. Histories awakened. Forgotten ghosts stood up and walked from their graves. Times past reminded of a little known MP called Oliver Cromwell who had led a civil war against the king and sent him for execution. "The colonists have worked themselves up into mania!" people cried in the streets. "The echoes of history are upon us!"

Now the Continental Congress issued a Declaration of Independence, and the British assembled forces. The threatened monarchy in France was eager to maintain its hold, and the colonies hoped France might aid them in the war against Britain. King George was angry and indignant that anyone dared question his authority and proclaimed the colonies would be closed to all trade that year.

Mr Clare and Mary went to the library to try to lay a hand on 'Common Sense', a fifty page pamphlet written by Thomas Paine, an English-American philosopher and political activist who had gone to live in America. The pamphlet had been widely distributed and was heatedly discussed. It indicated Paine's support for American Independence and the wrath of the government was stirred. Thomas Paine was dangerous. But America, Paine insisted, didn't just argue for herself, she argued for the whole world:

> *"These are the times that try men's souls: The summer soldier and the sunshine patriot will, in this crisis, shrink from the service of his country; but he that stands it now, deserves the love and thanks of man and woman."*

And –

> *"As to government matters, it is not in the power of Britain to do this continent justice: The business of it will soon be too weighty, and intricate, to be managed with any tolerable degree of convenience, by a power, so distant from us, and so very ignorant of us; for if they cannot conquer us, they cannot govern us. To be always running three or four thousand miles with a tale or a petition, waiting four or five months for an answer, which when obtained requires five or six more to explain it in, will in a few years be looked upon as folly and*

*childishness. There was a time when it was proper, and there is a proper time for it to cease . . ."*

A leviathan had set itself free and there was no way of knowing what fruits its loins might deliver. Britain watched and waited, people read what they could. No-one knew what to fear or what to hope for. The wind whispered in the trees. The rain battered on windows as if in warning. People stopped thoughtful in the street. Could all that commotion thunder through the cities of Britain? It could, it could, there was injustice everywhere.

It was a fresh sunny morning as Mary sat with her mother in the parlour. But there was nothing sunny about the look in her mother's eyes. Elizabeth Wollstonecraft was annoyed and jealous over Mary's attachment to Fanny and the Clares and struggled to comprehend it. Along with Everina and Eliza, she felt rejected. 'I sometimes wonder,' she said cruelly, 'why you don't go to live with them. You are far more often with them than you are with us.'

Mary looked at her straight. 'Do you not see how I am treated in this house?' she said quietly. 'Everything I do is criticised. No matter what I say, not one of you listens or hears me out. I am *real* at the Clares. I can live and learn things.' She peered thoughtfully at her hands, observing a scratch where she'd protected Fanny from a hawthorn branch by a stream. Her mother looked confused.

'But you follow that girl everywhere,' she murmured grudgingly. 'I don't see what you can learn from drawing flowers.'

'All knowledge is linked,' said Mary, struck by the thought and pondering on something John Arden had said to her once. 'Fanny's drawings are spectacular. And she writes down everything she knows – their names and parts and the way they connect, like people who study medicine do when naming the parts of the body.'

'She'll be getting a young man soon. What are you going to do then?'

Mary recalled an Irishman by the name of Hugh Skeys who'd been trying to court Fanny for a while. Skeys was young and good looking. He wasn't without means to support her either, though nothing had developed. 'She isn't too enamoured of men, and I have to say I am glad of it,' Mary said quietly.

Elizabeth gazed at her daughter, perplexed as ever. 'But a woman always wants to marry, or what is her life to be about? Will she waste it in drawing flowers?'

'There has to be more to life than being married, Mother,' Mary said curtly. 'Marriage makes you lost and wretched.' She looked at her darkly. 'See what has happened to *you*.'

'So what's the matter with *me*, then,' said Elizabeth Wollstonecraft, taken aback and straightening. 'I have a good enough life. I have seven children and a husband.'

Mary sighed exasperated. 'Father is unreliable; one way or another he'll disgrace himself. I suspect we'll be off again soon.'

Her mother sat wringing her hands. 'Well, from all I hear, those Bloods aren't anything special. I wonder why you want to befriend them. She is quite beneath you, that girl is. Her father is a heavier drinker than yours, and I believe he wastes all their money. What's more he can become quite violent. Oh yes, I have heard things.'

For a moment or two they were silent. Elizabeth gazed at space.

'Fanny does well considering what she puts up with,' said Mary assertively. 'She is strong and determined.'

'I too, have strong-willed children. I am very proud of my children.' Elizabeth Wollstonecraft's forehead tightened as she spoke.

'Well yes,' Mary said hesitantly. 'But we had better not talk about Henry, had we?' She looked downwards and dropped her voice. 'We must never talk about Henry.' She spoke in the tone of a secret.

Her mother glanced at her sharply, her cheeks flushing. 'Everything has its place in life, and some places are silent.'

'We do not speak of my brother at home, but I have heard him spoken of elsewhere. The world is not silent, you know.'

'Are you saying that people in Hoxton speak of my missing son?' She looked annoyed then fearful, her voice strained thinly. 'They know nothing about us here, unless your father lets his tongue run loose when he's been drinking. Henry was known in Beverley but not in Hoxton.'

'Word travels, Mother. If only it didn't.'

'What *word*?'

'Word that would break your heart. It is strange how my brother disappeared. You will never allow us to speak of it, yet I loved him dearly. I always worried when I heard him crying in the night and have often thought it strange that he left us so silently. I wondered why we didn't keep searching.' Her eyes glazed over with tears. 'Why didn't we search for him, Mother?'

'What sort of things have you heard?' her mother asked quietly.

'Well, if you want me to tell you, then I shall, though you will not like what I say.'

Her mother waited, straight and strong.

Mary continued. 'I heard some talk about youths being stolen for students studying anatomy. A boy half-dead in the hedgerow is as easily stolen as a boy lying in a grave.'

Her mother shivered. 'That's enough,' she said, sternly. 'Sometimes, Mary, you are quite insensitive.' For a moment the room went silent. 'There are things to be done,' she murmured. 'Everina's hair is livid with lice. She needs help with combing them out.'

'Just a normal everyday event,' said Mary. 'Head lice are innocent and will survive however they can.'

'Those lice will have the lot of us soon,' sighed her mother.

'Yes, they have the time of their lives.' In the soft morning light, her hair so tidy and her clothes so neat, for all her worries and woes, her mother was a wonder to Mary. That she suffered and did not run away was curious. But in truth she had no alternative. Her husband held all the power in the household and knew it. She must endure his barbaric behaviour and the children must suffer it also, never mind Henry's disappearance and Eliza's near mad behaviour when she screamed and hit out at the walls and wished she were dead. Mary knew she was much more selfish than Eliza, and would fight against any such condition. But to talk about these things with her mother was a futile activity; she might have been talking to stone.

Elizabeth Wollstonecraft shrugged. '"*The time of their lives?*" You do say the strangest things. Everina scratches day and night while those lice are having their parties! She had blood on her fingernails yesterday. She has gone to her bed exhausted.' For a minute she bent her ear to the stairs then turned back to Mary. 'You say that Fanny is helping you with your writing?'

Mary nodded. 'Yes, I have improved immensely. Not only does she draw, she also plays the piano and sings. I only wish I were so accomplished. I do rather love her, you know.'

Her mother stiffened. 'Well,' she said flatly. 'I too might have learned how to draw and sing in the past, but the world has attempted to crush me.' She sighed. 'But I have always got up again, you see. That's how it is for some of us.'

'It is what you have chosen,' said Mary. 'What I should like most would be for women to try to be *themselves*, become the best they can be and stop being guided by others who would form them to their purpose.'

Her mother shook her head. 'Where do you get these notions?' she said shrugging. 'You will drown in the depths of your thoughts.'

'I won't drown, Mother. Sometimes the most precious gems of our thinking are found in those depths. I like to swim deep.'

'Too dark down there,' Elizabeth murmured. 'You will lose your way.' She rose from her chair and went to the kitchen.

There was a certain majestic air about her mother, thought Mary, a sort of strength that allowed her somehow to be savaged, get up, lick her wounds, and carry on. But it would not do for herself and she would fight to the death for her rights rather than be wounded like that. But her mother had allowed her life to be consumed by others. It had happened a long time ago.

5

# To Laugharne

Just as Mary had expected, again they were on the move, over the rocky stones, beneath the cold glaring moon, the coach making its usual hollow sound of going nowhere. It was more than likely her father was fleeing his debts, thought Mary seated with the others, for there had scarce been time to pack their things. They were indeed making a getaway and had left in the night light.

Each time they moved they lost money. And Mary lost friends. She hadn't had chance to tell Fanny she was leaving Hoxton, or why. But why might have been awkward. Wherever their father led the family must always travel with him, just as the horses of the coaches did that delivered them to their next refuge.

They were now on their way to Laugharne, a town in Carmarthenshire on the estuary of the River Taf, a river in West Wales. Laugharne was noted particularly, her father had told them, for its abundance of sea trout, and he intended to fish. *Fishing?* He had enjoyed fishing in the past, but she had never known him fish in her lifetime. She travelled in silence, her emotions spent, her thoughts in turmoil.

The River Taf ran for 35 miles and entered Carmarthen Bay at Laughharne. Oh yes, it was a place of refuge, thought Mary, with so many hills about it and so much quietude. It was certainly peaceful, if peace was what you were after. Crushed against her mother and ignoring the talk in the oppressive coach interior, she stared from the window. They had travelled much of the night and had stopped at an inn, rising early next morning to travel again, then another stop for rest, before continuing to Laughharne. The young ones were half asleep rubbing their eyes and Everina was fidgety, complaining she felt achy and scratchy. The countryside was quite spectacular, Mary thought as the coach went along, and she knew she'd enjoy the wild-life. How good it would be to walk out and smell the fresh air. There was little fresh air in London with its nasty odours and dirty unlit passageways, dangerous after dark when criminals lurked in the shadows. But the city thronged with people. Who could she talk to here? She could hear her father telling her brother James about the Laugharne birdlife, as if the sounds and sights of birds might compensate for lack of people. Not a soul could she see anywhere. 'Keep your eyes open, son,' said her father, 'there are dippers, warblers and ducks around here, and if you watch carefully, you might even see a bird of prey!' James sat drawing in a sketch pad.

'I didn't know you cared about birds, Father,' said James attending to his picture of a blackbird.

'Your father's been doing some reading,' murmured Elizabeth.

'But who shall I have to talk with?' said Mary, distressed at having left Fanny.

Her father ignored her.

'You wouldn't understand, Father, would you,' she moaned, 'that I need to have someone to talk to.'

'And what's wrong with Eliza and Everina?' her father said, frowning. 'Why can't you talk to your sisters?' He glanced at his wife. 'Or even your mother?'

'Oh, Mary talks to me,' said Elizabeth, straightening her clothes, 'but only to complain. She thinks it is good to complain.'

'But it *is*, Mother,' Mary said emphatically. 'Boys complain, men complain, why can't we? It's wrong to stay silent if you feel something strongly. You need to voice your opinion and not let life roll over you and *crush* you, as you say.'

'What's all this then?' said Edward, swelling out his chest. 'Life rolling over you and crushing you, Elizabeth? You never told me that.'

'It's Mary,' murmured her mother. 'She gets me to say things.'

'Oh, what a muddled mind you have, Mary,' said her father. 'But you'll not be arguing with *me,* girl. I'll not accept it. And I'll thank you not to argue with your mother. It gives her a headache.' His eyes wandered through the window. Then he sniffed and leant back in the coach staring at his hands and muttering. 'You women are impossible.'

'Heaven knows why I wed you,' Elizabeth murmured. 'Or maybe hell knows better.'

'Listen here, Elizabeth!' Edward Wollstonecraft shouted, leaning forward and making a fist. 'I'll not let you speak to me like that. I'm your husband and I'll have you know it!'

'And neither would you shout at your wife like that,' she retorted, 'if Ned was here in this coach.'

'Bah, you and your Ned!' snapped her husband. 'You've wanted him all for yourself. That's what you do, you women, you destroy us men from the start.'

'If women were more themselves, and didn't rely on men for their thinking then they might not cleave to their sons so much,' murmured Mary. 'Perhaps we would all feel better.'

'Oh, yes, and us men could live without worrying how to put food on the table, could we? Talk about slaves. I am a slave to this family, that's what I am, a slave!'

'And I am a lady of leisure, I suppose,' said Elizabeth. 'I wonder sometimes what happened to all those silk handkerchiefs your family used to make. We had boxes and boxes of them once. Where did they go?'

'Well, let's not argue over handkerchiefs,' Edward replied, dismissively. 'Ned will do well at Tower Hill, I'm sure, then we'll see. He'll do something useful with his life, I know it. And he's a good inheritance awaiting him too.' He stroked his chin thoughtfully. 'He has quite a bit of money to come to him, Ned has. He was considered.' He slumped and frowned. 'Good for him.'

'Yes, Ned was considered, that's right,' said Elizabeth. Her voice trembled as they travelled the stony road. 'But you weren't left without. You never do anything properly though, do you.' She shook her head and sighed. – 'Oh, I'll not find fault with your trying. I know how you try. And I shall always stand by you, Edward, the same as ever.' He stared at the roof of the carriage.

'See!' cried her husband, nudging James. 'There, can you see it? That's the castle I mentioned. It's twelfth century, that is. We can go and have a look if you like.'

'It's just a romantic ruin,' said Mary, following the line of his gaze. 'Wars, sieges, cannon fire, men have destroyed it.'

'Men must always go to war,' said her father, bracing himself. 'We must protect the women and children.'

'From men,' murmured Mary. She changed her position, confined as she was in the coach and close to her father, she felt more oppressed than ever.

'Do they have cock fights in Laugharne?' Everina asked suddenly. She had been silent most of the way. 'Ned likes cockfights.'

'I shouldn't think he does,' sighed her mother.

'I wouldn't be surprised,' said Mary. 'But I doubt we'll see much of Ned. He'll be staying in London. Why would he come out here?'

'Blackbirds don't fight,' said James, who was gentle and sensitive. 'I do like blackbirds and robins.'

'I would have thought men fought for principles, Father,' said Mary, returning to their previous conversation. 'Not just for women and children. Given the chance, women can fight for themselves.'

'A fighting woman is most unattractive,' said Edward. He looked at his wife, half smiling. 'Women should be calm and silent. Best leave the fighting to men. Ned would agree with me, I know.'

'You presume he's like you,' Mary said irritably. 'Perhaps he is different.'

'Now then, Mary,' said her mother, touching her daughter's hand. 'We are almost there. What is the cottage like, Edward?'

'I know no more than you do, Elizabeth.' He reached into the pocket of his frock coat. 'I have an address. The driver knows where to take us. We ought to get something comfortable though. Rents are quite cheap around here and it really is the loveliest of places.'

'That's if you love grey skies and dampness,' murmured Elizabeth.

Edward turned to Charles, who sat with his eyes tightly closed. Charles got sick in coaches and the coachman must keep on stopping. 'You know how you like those fossils?' Charles raised his eyebrows, though his eyes remained closed. He was fascinated by the fossils Eliza had found in Hoxton when they'd been out walking. 'Well, you'll find plenty of fossils in Laugharne,' said his father. 'I'm told some of them are ice-age.'

Eliza sat, her arms folded, displeased at being moved from Hoxton so fast. She showed not the least emotion about the idea of looking for fossils and Mary thought she must have grown out of it.

'I heard they have a very good cockle industry too,' their father continued. 'Not that I am fond of cockles.'

'Is that what you'll do?' said Elizabeth, gazing outside. 'Will you sell cockles?'

'Or maybe get involved in a bit of piracy, Father,' Mary said wryly.

'Oh, piracy's been done away with,' laughed her father. 'Time moves on.'

'Much like we do,' murmured Mary.

'You'd be good as a pirate,' laughed Elizabeth. 'It would suit you down to the ground.'

Mary knew that a part of her mother delighted in her husband's free spirit, though much to the annoyance of her children. The horses clattered round a corner and went down a hill. Soon they arrived in Laugharne. From here they could see the ruined castle properly, rugged and broken against the sky. It stood on a cliff by the estuary.

'How dark and sad it looks,' James said dismally.

'In Arthurian legend, back in the sixth century,' said their father dramatically, 'the wizard Merlin said, "Kidwelly was, Carmarthen is, and Laugharne shall be the greatest of all three!"'

'Will it really be *great* in Laugharne, Father?' asked James, gazing through the window.

'Wizards aren't real,' Everina said shrugging. 'They are just made up.'

'I don't believe there are ice-age fossils here either,' said Eliza peevishly.

'What happened to the soldiers who fought in that castle, Father?' asked James. 'Will there be skeletons in the ruins, or were the soldiers just thrown into the sea when they died?'

'When can we go to the beach?' asked Charles, opening his eyes and stretching his neck to see above his brother's shoulder. 'We might find a few old skeletons. Skeletons last for ever, you know.'

'Not long now,' said his father. 'We'll be getting out in a minute.'

'How long will we stay?' Mary asked gloomily.

'Be quiet, girl,' grunted her father. 'Or I shall get bad tempered.'

'And we don't want that, do we,' said his wife, fussing with the bags of luggage at their feet. There were sounds of shuffling and elbows poking into sides as they all climbed out.

They stood together on the earth of Laugharne, unmoving as the hills about them, lost in what felt like a dream. It was a fine clear day and the sky was a soft pale blue. The air was indeed fresh, thought Mary; she could even taste the sea. Her eyes searched earnestly for something happening, just a figure moving on the pathway, an animal making its way perhaps, anything, but there was only the sound of peace, a peace she shrank from.

Edward paid the driver who helped him down with the trunks, then the coach rattled off.

'Well then, this is the place,' said Edward, looking the house up and down.

It was a rather diminutive dwelling, thought Mary, with a small piece of land to the side. A man was walking towards them from over the road.

'Owen Laugharne at your service!' he shouted. 'I live nearby. You said you were arriving today, and it is good to see you. I hope you will like the cottage.' He glanced around the small assembly. 'It isn't very big though.' He was tall and broad shouldered with a ruddy complexion and long flowing golden hair. Mary thought he looked about thirty. James whispered he was Merlin. 'No connection with Laugharne,' laughed Owen. 'I just have the same name. One of my ancestors liked it, so now it is mine.' He felt in his pocket and drew out a large heavy key. 'You should find the cottage quite warm, I've been lighting the fire two days. And there are steak pies waiting in the kitchen. My wife baked them yesterday and she swept all the floors.' He handed the key to Edward. 'You have quite a sizeable brood.'

'I used to have a brother called Henry as well,' James burst out, as his father opened the door. 'But he just disappeared.'

Eliza pulled on his arm. 'You haven't to speak of Henry!' she whispered. 'Not to anyone!'

'But Merlin is magical; perhaps he can bring him back,' James protested.

'Hush,' said Eliza, pulling his arm even harder.

'Go in and have a look upstairs,' said their father, 'and take those bags with you. I need to inspect the land.' He turned to Owen Laugharne. 'Is it possible I might buy a cow or two and maybe a dozen hens?'

The man nodded and threw back his hair, which gleamed and dazzled in the sunlight. 'I have a couple of cows you might like,' he pondered. 'They are good for milk. And I can get you half a dozen hens for now if that's alright.'

'That's good,' said Edward, with enthusiasm. 'Let me have the cows as soon as you can. We are quite familiar with cows. I thought I saw a cowshed out there.'

'It hasn't been used for a while, but we can soon sort it out,' said Owen.

'And to whom do I pay the rent?' asked Edward.

'That will be me,' said Owen, smiling and showing a perfect set of glistening teeth. 'The cottage is mine. It has been in my family for years.'

Edward took some coins from a bag and passed them across. 'Here you are,' he said, smiling. 'I think that's what we'd agreed. You are to be paid once a month. Is that correct?'

'That's right,' said Owen. 'And you must pay for the cows and the hens now, sir. I shall bring them without delay.'

'Ah, of course. I'm presuming they are strong and healthy,' said Edward Wollstonecraft imperiously.

'All my animals are healthy, sir,' said Laugharne, looking insulted. 'They cannot be any other.'

Mary heard Owen Laugharne curse beneath his breath. 'We are all but a short walk away from my farm,' said Laugharne pointing. 'I've boxes to carry the hens in and the cows will follow me anywhere. I can let you have feed as well, and after that you can buy it as needed. The winter is coming and the feed is better stored with me.'

Mary and her sisters went inside. Just as the man had promised, there were pies on the table. The cottage was comfortable and clean, with a busy fire in the hearth. It wouldn't take long to settle in, she thought. For the time being.

Six long weeks dragged by. Mary, her sisters and their mother, washed and cooked and tried to make the place homely. There was always something to do. Some days Mary went down to the beach with Eliza, listening to the sounds of the sea and watching the waves. On the small plot of land by the cottage, Eliza would stare with fascination when the hens came running towards her. And she would stand in a kind of bewilderment watching them peck at their feed. "How eagerly they live," she would whisper. "But they don't know the first thing about us. We steal their eggs for breakfast and they don't seem to notice." Mary's eyes grew duller each day and the pain in her soul would not budge. She needed to see Fanny desperately. Eliza went off on her own searching for fossils, returning to the cottage with one or two slivers of rock and staring at them curiously. "All I can see are shadows," Everina would tell her dismally. "Those creatures have died long ago. Fossils tell lies.'

There was a strange quietness in Eliza now, thought Mary. She wanted to do things alone. Everina too was often silent, whilst they all three washed and hung clothes and got on with the sewing and cooking. Charles often sat weeping and would break his toys on purpose. James continued with his drawings. But it was useless trying to draw birds, he said, for they didn't stay still very long, and after a while he grew bored.

One day down on the beach out walking, Mary and Eliza talked of their heartfelt concerns. Mary said she felt she would die if she didn't see Fanny soon. 'I must go to London for a while,' she moaned. 'But I'm worried about what will happen to mother. What if our father bursts into one of his rages?' Slowly they climbed up the hill back to the cottage. 'He is always raging,' Mary continued, breathing in deeply. 'He enjoys it.'

'Oh, Mary, don't hate him like that,' Eliza said frowning.

'Why shouldn't I? I think he's brutal. I shall hate him if I wish.'

'You could go to see Fanny while Father is away,' said Eliza with a sudden idea. 'He's in London next week. There isn't time for a letter to Fanny, I know . . .'

'No, I can't send a letter, it's too late,' Mary said flatly. 'I shall simply arrive at her house. I know she won't mind. She will miss me like I miss her.' She spoke wistfully. 'I did not think I could ever find a friend like Jane, but I have found one I love even better.'

'Yes, it's true,' sighed Eliza, used to her sister's flights of fancy when it came to her female friends.

'Owen is going to a market in London very shortly,' said Mary, thinking quickly. 'We could travel together when Father has gone, and we'd be away for the same length of time. Owen knows what he's like, and is sure to understand. I have a little money from the sale of my silk handkerchiefs.' The seagulls above them screeched out Mary's frustrations. She felt she was close to madness. Where did her father go when he went to London, she wondered. Her mother said it was business and never asked questions. But she brooded. "He must collect the rents from the houses on Primrose Street," she would say. "They don't amount to much, but those rents are often hard come by." They rarely referred to the Primrose Street rents which were often a source of trouble.

'Why do we never speak of Henry,' Mary murmured to Eliza as they climbed the hill to the cottage. Her voice quivered with feeling. 'Something terrible happened, I'm sure, but Mother insists on silence. I know she suffers.'

'And ought we to break it, the silence, I mean?' said Eliza, her voice almost a whisper. 'Why can't we speak of it? I do think we should.'

'What good would it do?' Mary said painfully. 'I have thought about it a lot. Henry had a strange condition; he was often running away, or else sitting in corners screaming. It was very upsetting.'

'But Father didn't help much, did he,' Eliza said unhappily.

'I don't think he could. Father doesn't understand us. But he did go searching; sometimes he was out till day break.'

All around them felt thick with the mood of evening. The smell of the sea was strong. They were silent a while, pondering.

Eliza spoke shakily. 'Please don't mind me saying it, Mary, but do you think Henry is in the *madhouse*?'

Again they were silent.

'I have thought about that myself,' sighed Mary. In the darkness she felt her sister's cold hand on her own.

'It might be true,' whispered Eliza. 'What if Father put him away and never told us?'

There was another long silence. Mary said finally. 'I shall speak to Mother tomorrow, and tell her I want to visit Fanny. Owen can get me a chaise.' She was anxious but determined. She knew what she had to do. She would stay for a couple of days, and she would speak about Henry. Fanny could be trusted. She would visit Bethlem hospital at Moorfields where she knew there were lunatics. If her brother was a lunatic, then she must know. Her skin went cold at the thought and her heartbeat quickened. For a moment or two she despised her parents if they had driven Henry to lunacy. But perhaps it was something else. Perhaps he had run away to sea. Or he might have committed a felony which had to stay secret, though it hardly seemed likely, her brother was a kind individual, who would never do anything criminal. What could have happened? They were all being forced to forget him. She shuddered. It seemed so cruel to pretend he had never existed.

Owen Laugharne was a very busy farmer, endlessly working in the fields or else herding his cattle. Harvest was in the air and his wife and daughter were out with him gathering apples and forking the hay. It was a time when the community came to life with competitions and there was much to-ing and fro-ing around Laugharne that season.

'I would very much like to see Fanny,' Mary said to her mother in the kitchen as they kneaded dough for the bread.

'But when?' asked her mother, though she didn't look surprised. 'I've been watching you; I knew you would have to see her sooner or later. More's the pity.'

'Not at all,' said Mary, sighing. 'I miss her.'

'And how long do you intend to be away for? There's a lot to be done in this cottage, you know. I don't know if I can manage.'

'A couple of days, that's all . . . You have Eliza and Everina to help you,' Mary said grudgingly. 'A visit to London would be good for me, Mother. I long for stimulating company.'

'Ah, how you insult us,' her mother said shrugging her shoulders. 'It's a wonder we talk to you at all the way you slight us. Were you thinking of going soon? – If you were, that could be difficult; your father's in London from Wednesday. He has gone this minute to get a chaise from Owen Laugharne. Why don't you travel with him?'

Mary sighed. 'I believe Owen Laugharne is taking a pig to market this week. I doubt he would charge me for the journey if he is going to London regardless.' She lowered her voice. 'I don't want to travel with Father, and he is bound to take umbrage when he learns I want to see Fanny. And I'd rather you didn't tell him. We'll travel a few hours behind him and return before he gets back.'

'Oh I don't know,' said her mother, banging her fists into the dough. 'But your plan will hardly go smoothly.' Mary went to haul a bucket of water from the well. 'I suppose you must do it,' said her mother, when Mary returned with the water, 'or I'll not hear the last of it, will I?'

Already Mary felt drained, yet she must carry out her plan. She sliced some apples and laid them in neat little pieces on a plate. She was making an apple strudel for dinner.

'Your father will stick some buns in his pockets and be off,' said her mother. 'He rarely sits at table with us nowadays. You must go and sort out your journey with Laugharne, but don't stay in London too long. There are days when I ache from head to foot, and I can't move my bones.'

Mary always felt sorry for her mother. But she determined to visit Fanny, and discover what she could about Henry.

'I think I told you,' said Owen, when she went to see him at the farm. 'I must take a prize sow to London this week and would be glad of your company, but I shall have to make stops on the way. I will not charge for the journey, but you will have to stand the cost of one night's stay at an inn.'

Mary nodded gratefully. 'And how shall I return to Laugharne?'

'Leave that to me. When did you want to come back?'

'I intend to stay for a day or so with a friend in Hoxton. But I want to get home before Father.'

Owen Laugharne smiled. 'That won't be difficult. As soon as I know where you're going, after I've sold the sow I can arrange to collect you.' He scratched his cheek thoughtfully. 'I'll not let her go for a song.'

'I am hoping to stay at my friend's two nights, and if you would be so kind, you could collect me on the third day.'

He thrust his pitch fork deep into the earth and leant on it. 'Is it a man you will stay with?' he asked, talking to the soil at his feet.

'No,' she said awkwardly. 'It's a girl friend. I don't have friendships with men.'

He looked up and his eyes ran over her. 'Did you have a bad experience?'

'Perhaps,' she said quietly. 'Men can make women unhappy.'

'Not always?' He spoke assertively. There was a slight chill in the air, as he rolled down each of his sleeves. He looked at her again, his eyes narrowed with thought.

'Mostly,' she murmured.

'I'm sorry you feel like that,' he said, stretching up. He threw back his shoulders. 'I doubt my wife would agree with you. She is happy enough with me. Or at least I hope so.'

'Perhaps she is lucky.'

'We are both in luck together,' he said smiling.

For a moment or two they were silent.

'So I'll come for you Thursday late morning, then, when Edward has left,' said Laugharne. 'You'll not want to meet him on the way.' He turned. 'Now I must go to my sow. She'll not be too happy about moving out from the others, but that's how it goes.'

'Thank you,' she called as she watched him stride off. She had made up her mind. In some small way she felt triumphant.

6

# London and Bethlem

It was nearing the end of autumn. The bruised skies of November were hovering when Mary climbed into the chaise beside Owen Laugharne. The sounds of his protesting sow in the crate behind them were loud in the bright white sunshine. She was a heavy weight market-pig, and Owen had needed the assistance of a local farmer to help lift her in. He covered the crate with a blanket. 'That'll keep her warm, and she doesn't like too much light,' he said. 'Don't let her worry you. She'll soon settle down.' He glanced at Mary's clothing. 'It's as well you're in decent clothes. It might get cold.' They had a sort of understanding between them. Owen didn't like her father any more than she did and had made a considerable effort to comply with her plans. They would be gone five days.

Arriving at Fanny's house in Hoxton, it didn't take long to explain the situation and Owen behaved like the gentleman he was, courteous and patient, promising to return for Mary as planned. After that he drove off, the sow squealing and grunting in the crate behind him.

Fanny took Mary's arm and pulled her through to the parlour excitedly; calling to the others that Mary had been brought by an angel with long golden hair. The children came laughing and dancing. She was always welcome, Mrs Blood told her; the chaise longue could be easily vacated and was perfectly comfortable to sleep on. Mary felt like a returning relative and was treated as such.

But she knew the high spirits couldn't last; she would need to tell Fanny of her errand.

Next morning they went out walking.

'You look pale and tired,' said Fanny. 'I don't suppose you have many acquaintances in Laugharne, the place is so quiet.'

Mary looked at her and smiled. 'You know my moods very well,' she said sighing. 'You are right. How dismal and dark my mind is when my thoughts have nowhere to go.' It was a calm sunny day but it did not reflect her feelings.

Fanny walked slowly beside her, her face serious. 'But it isn't just that,' she said tentatively. 'There's something else isn't there?'

Mary gazed at the sky. 'I would like to tell you,' she said anxiously. 'It weighs down heavy on my mind.' She spoke with a strained voice. Did she really want to tell Fanny her terrible fears?

'Is someone seriously ill,' Fanny asked searchingly.

Mary hesitated a moment. 'I'm not really sure, but it's possible. The not knowing makes it worse.'

For a while they were silent. 'I am your friend. Tell me whatever you like, however hard it is to say,' said Fanny, linking her arm. 'You are often in my thoughts. Please don't worry that you left for Laugharne in a hurry. I know how it is with your father, mine is the same, of course. It's a sad state of affairs but we make the best of it, don't we?'

They walked down a narrow country lane and stopped by a little pond. Mary struggled. The words were so difficult to voice. 'I never told you about Henry, did I?' she said quietly. Speaking his name in the still clear air made the loss more real. It was as if she were summoning his spirit out of the woodland.

'"Henry"?' Fanny frowned curious. She gazed at Mary and waited.

They didn't normally keep secrets from each other and Mary could see that it bothered Fanny that she spoke without her usual confidence and was acting withdrawn.

But this was something her family did not speak of, something locked away in the past. She wanted now to unlock it once and for all. 'He is one of my brothers,' she said, filled with a sudden tender feeling. Tears fell down her face.

Fanny stared at the ground. 'You have never spoken of Henry,' she said softly.

'I have never been allowed to. No-one speaks of Henry. He hasn't been seen in ages.'

Fanny looked at her earnestly and waited. 'What happened?'

'I don't know. That's what I have to find out.' She spoke shakily. The reflected sun glared up from the water, cold and dazzling with light. Fanny listened intently, but Mary's words came in their own good time, slowly and painfully. 'We sort of lost him. But worse than that, we daren't speak his name. Henry wasn't well, he had fits of screaming and there were times he ran away, but he always came back, or else Father would go out searching and find him.'

'I have heard of such things,' said Fanny, quiet and serious. 'And I understand what you fear.' She lowered her voice. 'You fear he is in the asylum.'

Mary made no answer. For a couple of minutes they both stood silent and thoughtful, gazing into the pond, their faces staring back nervous and worried. Mary said finally, 'I might as well be in the madhouse myself when Father launches a tirade. I know that Mother is afraid. Ned doesn't live with us now and Father is worse than ever.'

'It's disturbing about Henry,' sighed Fanny. 'I wonder what we can do?'

Mary spoke firmly and precisely. 'I shall try to find him,' she said straightening. 'If he's in Bethlem I intend to unearth him. Perhaps I can take him home. I believe they let you inside.'

'I'm not sure they do anymore . . .' Fanny said pondering. 'They might want a fee, not a lot, just a small contribution, but things have changed, I think. And you might need the official on the door to sign you a ticket before you are allowed entry. Visitors have been bad for the patients apparently, and the governor has become quite cautious. Do you have money?'

'I have enough,' said Mary abstractedly.

'But Henry might have gone somewhere else,' Fanny said biting her lip. 'He might be in a private home with sick young people like himself.' She lowered her voice to a murmur. 'If they don't get better then they send them to Bethlem later. Oh, Mary, how awful. But that is often the way. I have talked about it with mother. There are many such homes around London. Just small institutions, not horrible places like Bethlem. He might be in one of those. But it is hard to discover where they are, impossible even. People keep quiet.'

Mary put her hands to her face. 'Bethlem is hell. I have heard such talk in Hoxton. People can die there. What if he died and they never informed us?'

Fanny took hold of her arms and tried to stop her trembling. 'He might not be there anyway, my dear, so reserve your strength. If, as you say, he was prone to take flight, he might have gone to sea. Lots of boys go to sea. – Oh, Mary, I feel for you so much.'

They walked on further.

'Well, if I can't find him, it will ease my thinking a little,' Mary whispered. 'If he died in Bethlem at least I will know, and God rest his soul. But I despise my father all the more if he made my brother insane.'

'People become insane for all sorts of reasons,' said Fanny sympathetically. 'Sometimes it's the way they are born. It's unfair to just blame your father. Our fathers often have too many duties and concerns. Mine looks to drink for solace as yours does. But it rarely helps, and I believe they hate themselves for that and plague their families.'

'But people should try to be rational,' Mary asserted, bracing herself. 'Or life becomes nothing but chaos. I so want to find Henry, Fanny. I must. Can you get me a chaise to Moorfields?'

'Of course,' said Fanny calmly. 'Do you really want to go on your own? I'll join you if you like.'

Mary shook her head. 'Thank you,' she said, sighing with gratitude. 'But just to have told you is enough. I need to go on my own.'

'I know of someone we can trust,' said Fanny, again taking her arm. 'We can go and find him right now. He will take you and bring you back to me. You must let me pay for the journey, I insist. It's the least I can do.'

Mary left later that day. She was now on her way to Bethlem hospital. Her heart beat hard with anxiety. She was firm in her purpose. She would discover her brother's whereabouts, but what would she do if she found him?

The hospital had been the priory of *the New Order of St Mary of Bethlem*, started in 1247. The monks watched over their sad inhabitants those days, people who were deemed insane and committed to their care. By the seventeenth century, the old building was decrepit and there was need for a better establishment. The new hospital at Moorfields, north of the city, was a beautiful palatial looking building thought Mary as she walked along the hospital footway. But she feared the imposing appearance belied what was happening inside. Against the tall grand structure, she felt fragile and unfitted for her task, and could almost feel the physical and mental anguish of the patients who lived there. What sort of *living* was it? What might her brother have suffered and *still* be suffering? When she came to the official at the door, she kept her head bent low for she feared he might see the tears running down her cheeks.

'Do you wish to enter?' he asked, looking her up and down.

'If I may,' she said meekly.

'You will have to pay, I'm afraid,' he said frowning. 'We are cutting down on visitors now.' He put out his hand. 'A couple of pennies should do it.' He shook his head as Mary handed him the coins. 'You are only a girl, and on your own. I saw you coming down the walkway, it is better to have someone with you, you know. It can be very upsetting in there.' He gave her a curious look, the coins shining in his palm. 'Have you no-one?'

She steeled herself as she spoke. 'I am a great deal stronger than you think,' she said forcefully. She glanced all around her; she would scour each nook and cranny of the building, however long it took. If Henry wasn't there, then she might find some peace in her soul, but her heart feared her eyes might alight on him. Henry, her long lost brother, confined in this horrible place, screaming as he had at home, his head shaven of its brown curled hair and his limbs fettered.

'Let me get you an attendant,' said the official. He entered a room then came out with an elderly gentleman who indicated Mary should follow him.

'Do you want to walk along the gallery?' he asked as they went. 'I warn you though, the lunatics are often fearsome.'

The atmosphere was stale and airless; the smell of excrement was strong. She stopped and gagged. There were screams and shouts all around her that sounded to Mary like the very voices of hell. 'I do not fear them,' she said quietly, though beneath her cape she trembled.

'Is that so?' the attendant said, turning to look at her. 'The sight of madness causes most young women to faint. Do you have any smelling salts?'

She looked at him boldly. 'I will not faint. Please proceed. I would like to see everyone here.'

The attendant looked at her straight. 'Have you ever seen madness, Madam?'

'Madness is everywhere,' Mary said quietly. 'The wretched souls in here were probably like everyone else at first, but the great dark beast followed them too closely and devoured them.'

'Oh yes,' he laughed facetiously. 'And a great dark beast it is!' They continued down the corridor. 'Some of our patients are possessed. Their humours are unbalanced, you see. You will hear blasphemies and curses. Some of the men howl like dogs, others roar like lions, or else sing at the tops of their voices. And others indulge in practices you will find abhorrent.'

The air about her was shadowy with the mist of madness. She could feel it entering her blood. Her heartbeat sounded in her ears like the regular beat of a drum.

They were now in a long thin gallery with cells either side. It was possible to view the sad suffering souls through a window in the door of the cells. Each time she looked she shuddered. It was painful to see women clamped and screaming, young mothers possibly, or just women who could take no more in their lives and had flung themselves into insanity. She thought of her mother back in Laugharne. Might she too find herself here if matters were to worsen at home?

'We have had every level of society visit this hospital,' the attendant said as if proud. 'Even Lords and Ladies. They attempt to talk to the lunatics, but it is futile. The patients have lost their minds. But the rich leave generous contributions.'

'It is justice not charity that is wanting in the world,' murmured Mary.

'Well, you'll not find much justice in here,' he said, kicking a discarded shoe that lay in his way. 'I wonder if you find it anywhere.'

'Have you had training to work here?' Mary continued.

'"*Training?*" How can you train for this? Some sit weeping, some sit laughing, others are raving mad and have to be restrained. We have doctors come in to see them . . .'

'What kind of doctors?'

He scratched his head through his thin grey hair. 'A visiting surgeon and an apothecary come, though it's usually anatomists. But what do anatomists know about lunatics, I ask you?'

'And what do these people do to help the patients?'

'Well, they try to restore the balance of biles mainly. It is most important. Black bile makes for badness, you see. It makes itself plain around their eyes. The doctors bleed them and force them to vomit it out.'

Mary shivered with disgust. 'Some of these people are naked – and look, they are heavily bruised?' She spoke suspiciously.

'It is all their own doing,' he answered in a tone of authority. 'They rip off their clothing and pinch themselves or else bang their heads against the walls. – Oh, what can you do? They are tortured souls. We sometimes immerse them in cold water to help control their wayward spirits, but it is only of marginal effect. Some of the treatments are harsh and if a patient is frail they can die.'

She looked at him astonished. 'And yet you continue to do it?'

'Of course, it is the treatment.'

Mary put her hands to her cheeks; her face felt hot with anger. 'And if they should die?'

He threw out his arms in a cold unfeeling gesture. 'We always inform the relatives if a patient appears to deteriorate or might be dying. But lunatics are often forgotten, they are an embarrassment to their families, you see.'

'If that is true, it is wicked,' she whispered. She talked on quickly. 'I have heard that the bodies of people who die in Bethlem might be used for anatomical studies.' She glanced all around her with a sudden sharp thought. 'Could the dead be used like that, without their family's permission?'

His shoulders rose and fell. 'The anatomists are eager to discover why madness befalls these people, so sometimes dissect their brains, though it is all for the furtherance of science.'

She shook her head in disbelief. 'Families should think very carefully, before committing their relatives to this torture. – That woman over there, what is she reading? She is talking to herself and weeping.'

'They are pictures she looks at all the time, but she does not cause us any trouble.'

'But what sort of pictures are they?'

The attendant smiled amusedly. 'They are scenes from *The Rake's Progress*. They . . .'

'I know the story,' said Mary, raising her palms. 'I know it only too well.'

'She thinks the rake is her father,' he laughed. 'And for that reason she is mad. But it gives her something to do. All she ever says is, "Look! Look! This is my father; do you not see the resemblance? For his sins, he is in the madhouse, now I am here too."' The attendant laughed loudly as the woman waved them goodbye.

'And you answer?'

'We tell her she is right. What does it matter, the woman is deranged. She is probably here for life. The one next door thinks he is a famous politician. He likes to give speeches. He has a good grasp of politics though, and I suspect he has studied them, before he became insane, of course.'

Mary noted with relief as she left that not a single one of the patients had the least resemblance to Henry. Neither was Henry Wollstonecraft listed in the deaths. She felt tired and weary and could search no more.

Returning to Hoxton that evening, she sat at the table with Fanny, low and dispirited. The rest of the family were upstairs and Mr Blood was away on business.

'You needn't tell me about it,' Fanny said with compassion. 'I can see how you are. But you didn't find Henry, and in a way I think it's a blessing.'

'I'm not going to search anymore,' Mary said softly, watching the darkness through the window and wondering where her brother might be. He was either with the living or the dead. But wherever he was, she somehow felt better for her search. Fanny lit a candle. Enough words had been said. Perhaps they would find more words tomorrow before Owen Laugharne came to return her to Wales.

# 7

# *Robberies*

'You're telling me you let her go to London to visit that Fanny Blood without letting me know?' Edward Wollstonecraft shouted. 'I heard it from Eliza just now.' He threw down his hat and gloves, then pulled out a chair and sat down heavily.

Elizabeth worked faster at her sewing and made no reply. Having him come home earlier than expected was something of a shock, he was much more likely to be late. Eliza had gone up the hill for water; the others were feeding the hens. Her husband's eyes flashed with anger in the midday light. 'They've swindled me again,' he moaned, slurring his words. 'They always defraud me.' He was inebriated.

Elizabeth looked up. 'So who has defrauded you, Edward?' she asked, in the peculiar quiet tone she used when he came home drunk. This mood of his was a torture.

'All of them?' he said. 'The whole damn lot of 'em.' He drew his hands down his cheeks and his blood-shot eyes bulged as if trying to escape. 'Oh, you wouldn't understand. How could you? Damned robbers! That's what they are. – Ah, what do you care?'

'Of whom do you speak?' she asked, afraid of his rising anger and what he might do. Must they move house yet again, they'd scarce had time to settle in. She spoke calmly. 'Whatever it is, it won't do the least bit of good to raise the roof with your shouting.'

He glowered at the fire, then turned on her suddenly. 'You don't know anything about the way I struggle for this family, do you? Not even half of it.'

She worked fast with her needle. 'I know that you need to calm down,' she murmured. 'Then perhaps we can talk. Do relax, my dear.' He was silent for a moment, his face pale and his eyes mad with frustration. 'If we've been robbed then we must work to get straight again,' she said. She thought she had soothed him a little. But he wouldn't be soothed over Mary's visit to London. She waited.

'We're done for, Elizabeth,' he said wretchedly. He stood and paced the floor. 'I fear I am at last cleaned out.' The children's voices could be heard outside. Everina was calling to Charles. Eliza came in with the water and went to the kitchen. Elizabeth looked at him anxiously. 'It's a long journey to London, and she'd have to pay for it, too,' he said, his eyes narrowing with annoyance. 'Did Laugharne get her a chaise?'

Elizabeth kept perfectly still, then spoke in a monotone voice. 'He was intending to travel to London himself, he had to take a sow to market, so he invited her to share his carriage. She didn't have to pay him any money.' She continued explaining how it was, how Mary had felt morose and had wanted to visit Frances Blood.

'She's always morose about something,' he grunted.

Elizabeth sighed. It was true. Mary roused a fury in him nowadays; she was so headstrong and defiant.

'And he's bringing her back, is he?'

'Yes, today I think. Or that was the plan.' She bent her head to the window. 'There, I think I can hear them.'

A clattering sound came from the road along with the barks and yelps of Laugharne's collie.

'There's a good dog!' laughed Laugharne. 'There's a good dog!' He got down and ran his hands along its sleek black and white markings. The dog licked his fingers and shook its tail wildly. 'He's a worthy stud is this one,' laughed Owen. 'Must have fathered a hundred.' He pointed. 'Talking of fathers, Mary, I see that yours is with us. He is there at the door to greet you.' He spoke scornfully, as he always did when he spoke of Edward Wollstonecraft. 'It looks like we didn't make it.'

'I can see he's been drinking,' said Mary, as her father came across. His face looked grey and tired and he staggered slightly as he joined them.

'Your mother tells me you've been to see that girl in London,' he shouted. 'Gettin' about a bit aren't you, going off to London without telling your father?' He turned his eyes to Owen Laugharne. 'She has a friend there, you see, a girl who likes drawing flowers.' He glanced again at his daughter and laughed. 'All the way to London to watch a girl drawing flowers.' He wiped his nose with the back of his hand. 'And did you like them then, those flowers?' He laughed again at the muddy ground at his feet.

'It's her work,' said Mary coolly, but her blood convulsed with anger that he should speak to her so crudely in the presence of Owen Laugharne. 'She draws for a publication and is highly accomplished. But you would not know of the book if I told you its name.' She spoke self-consciously. Owen Laugharne knew all about her stay with Fanny but they hadn't discussed it, and she'd been silent about the asylum. 'Fanny Blood has opened my mind.'

Her father laughed. 'Opened your mind? Well, I doubt she'd find anything of use in it. – Get inside that cottage. There are things we need to discuss.' He gave her a slight push.

'Don't be so rough!' cried Laugharne, standing tall by his dog.

'Keep out of it, you,' grunted Wollstonecraft. 'Give her that bag off the chaise and get on your way.'

'Thank you for your assistance, Owen,' said Mary, taking the bag and disgusted with her father's manner. 'You need not worry. I am quite familiar with my father's drunken behaviour.'

'That's enough!' shouted her father. 'Watch your lip!'

'She isn't a child!' said Owen, in a loud and commanding voice. 'She deserves some respect.'

'Well!' her father exclaimed with a laugh. 'She'd get some if she deserved it. Her prattle causes endless bother.'

Owen went back up the hill in his chaise, the collie running beside him, while Mary followed her father into the cottage. Her mother glanced at her, then away. She was bound to have heard all the fuss, but Mary knew she wouldn't defend her; she would shrink from her husband, as always. Mary hated it all. Her tour around the asylum had bruised and battered her. She felt tired and ill and despised her home just then, and the fact that her mother endured it as if it were just bad weather. But the anxiety she'd felt about Henry had somehow lessened. She had decided he'd run away to sea and imagined him having escaped. There was work at sea and Henry had been strong. Whatever the answer, some weight had lifted in her soul.

The details of her visit were soon passed on to Eliza with an assurance that it was kept between themselves. She could not speak of it to her parents or the rest of the family; what she had done was all too bold and Eliza gazed at her in awe. Not another word must be spoken about Henry, Mary insisted; the episode would be consigned to history.

Life continued much as before in Laugharne. Though in the noisy world outside there were many interesting developments. Fanny wrote that the brilliant dissenting clergyman, Joseph Priestley, writer and speaker, who was also an excellent scientist, had discovered a new kind of gas called oxygen. Amongst other experiments, he had kept a mouse in a jar of air until the poor creature collapsed, but had discovered in doing so that if the mouse was kept in the jar with a plant, it survived. Fanny thrilled at the breakthrough. It seemed that plants could restore to the air what breathing animals removed, such was their magic! This chemical substance had been given the name "oxygen". She had decorated her script with drawings of her most beloved flowers. And there were lots of other things happening. On the military front the Commander in Chief of the Continental Congress, George Washington, had become the first President of America and they were building a new naval fleet. There was much talk of it in Hoxton.

Fanny's letters alleviated Mary's loneliness a while, but she was all too often depressed. Such days she went out walking. But it did not satisfy her need to exchange ideas. For she felt ideas were almost like living things and it pained her if she could not discuss them, her limbs ached and a great tiredness came over her. She read Fanny's letters as soon as they were brought to the door and replied as fast as she could, but pens and paper were wanting in the cottage and as much as Owen provided them, she felt sick in her soul at the thought of some vital idea escaping her mind. Fanny wrote that the last execution for witchcraft had now taken place in Germany. Witches, vampires and ghosts were most unhealthy preoccupations, thought Mary, though she had recently encountered a peculiar vision of some frail ethereal looking creature standing at her bedside, a girl who looked very like Agnes.

One evening the family was summoned to a meeting in the parlour. There had been a lot of commotion the previous day and her father had been pacing like a tiger on the path by the cottage, frowning and mumbling. She could not bear to watch him, for she knew that something terrible was coming for her mother. He would not take the burden of his problems alone. He must see their mother weeping and wretched, then the bother was hers and not his, and he could bid her calm down and be sensible. As they all took their seats that evening, Mary saw that her father's eyes were desperate. His voice seemed to echo about the cottage as he explained they would have to move house yet again, for the state of their finances was dire. His hands were clasped so tightly that his knuckles were white and he bent his head with shame as he spoke. In spite of his constant assertions that he could always sail close to the wind and win, he was now stony broke.

'So you want to rob the children's inheritances, do you?' her mother said gravely, casting her eyes about the company. It was rare she had anger in her eyes, but she did that evening, and Mary was glad to see it. 'I can see what you're after,' she said to him sharply. 'I wondered when it would happen.' The tense, unhappy tableau stared at the fire.

'Have I got some money?' Charles asked his mother, looking surprised.

'Listen, cock sparrow, you've more money than your father,' said Edward Wollstonecraft, stroking his son's hair and speaking in a soft kind voice.

'You've all got some money,' snapped Elizabeth. 'But not if your father gets hold of it. – Oh, Edward. How did it come to this?'

'Ah, matters get difficult you see, and I sort of get tied in knots.' The young ones half asleep, lifted their heads anxiously. Their father knitted his brows. 'I only mean to *borrow* it, my dears. Otherwise it's away to the workhouse for all of us!'

'Don't frighten the children like that,' said his wife. Charles shuffled closer to his mother.

'I am sorry to have to say it,' said their father, 'for it very much disturbs me. But I intend to take us back to London. Perhaps I can find some work.'

'"*London?*"' cried Mary, clapping her hands with delight. She felt suddenly luminous, as if something was happening at last in the depths of her being. She could *live* if she went to London. She could see her friends and talk, and through talking she could learn and grow.

'Matters are always changing,' said her father, drawing a deep heavy breath. 'Money, money, money. Everyone wants money, you see, and you have to sort of make it somehow. I'm not much good at doing that, try as I will.'

For a moment or two they sat silent, wondering where they would live. They waited for what he said next. Their father's voice came soft and serious through the air. 'I am your father, my dears and I must do what is best for us all. Arrangements will be made for whatever inheritances you have to be loaned to me.' He pressed his hand to his chest. 'I say loaned, of course, just *loaned*. You can imagine how hard it is for a father to say it, but there now it is said.'

'You'll get nothing off Ned,' said Elizabeth irritably. 'He's much too sensible for that, whatever his sympathies.'

'I've already seen him,' her husband said flatly. 'He will lend me a little. And he's working something out for the others. I shall borrow from my children for a while.' He wiped a tear from his eye. 'You have no idea how hard it is to say these things.'

'So you went to see Ned, did you, to take money from the children's legacies? What depths must we fall to? – And you, Mary. What do you say?'

'If it means we can return to London, then yes, he can borrow from me if I have money.'

'I shall find a nice house to rent and we can start a new life,' said her father, smiling at her strangely and showing his uneven teeth.

'But you can only take money from me if I can live near Fanny,' Mary said flatly. 'I must live near Fanny or you won't have a penny.'

'Ah, my soul!' cried Edward jumping up. 'Must that flower girl rule our lives? Why, she is here in this very room, standing in the shadows. She is everywhere we go.'

'She is always with me,' murmured Mary. 'And always will be.'

Her father threw logs on the fire and sparks shot into the air. But he said no more. The boys fell asleep by the hearth. Everina and Eliza sauntered off to their bedrooms with Mary. Mary had now made her mark. She had forcefully pulled away from her parents and family. She had demanded her father find a house for rent near Fanny, and she believed he would try to do it.

# 8

## New Vistas

And so they were off once again. Owen Laugharne's wife had given them a parcel of food, for it was obvious, she'd said to her husband that for Elizabeth Wollstonecraft the move was deeply distressing and she couldn't think straight. She'd been constantly dabbing her eyes with a hanky and could scarcely stand up.

Everina, Eliza and the boys got in the coach. 'Don't you think you might lend a hand here?' the father shouted to Mary as he loaded the luggage. Mary stood with her mother, trying to console her; it was a cold wet windy day. 'Stop snivelling now,' the husband shouted, 'and don't get the children in a state!'

Mary looked at him angrily, furious that her father should treat his family like Owen treated his cattle which were constantly shifted around the fields. She was pleased though to be returning to London. Her father looked unkempt as he worked, like a poor farmhand, and he'd scarcely allowed her mother time to get dressed, her hair was as dishevelled as her mind and her dress was heavily crumpled. In the worst of tempers, she stood ignoring his cries.

'The hound is howling,' said Eliza. 'Do you not hear it?'

Mary gave her an exasperated sigh. 'The hound doesn't frighten *me*,' she said flatly. Her mother looked pale and distant. People had little deaths, thought Mary, as a way of getting through the horrors of the living moments. How many little deaths did a person have to suffer, she wondered, before the final darkness?

'You will get it for demanding he finds us a house near Fanny,' said Eliza. 'And you have dared to ask for a room of your own.' She sighed as if with despair. 'Oh Mary, he has argued with mother so long and cruelly about that.'

'I'm sorry,' said Mary, still standing by her mother and defensive. 'I intend to write and need privacy. I will not fear him, Eliza. He is a coward. If he knows you fear him he will come for you all the more. I have had my fill of him!'

'Get over here!' her father shouted again. 'Mary, have you gone deaf? I need you to help with these trunks!'

At that moment Owen Laughharne came striding down the hill towards them, his face beaming like the sun, his hair flowing about him. 'Allow me to assist you!' he called. He advanced quickly and managed the trunks with ease.

'That's good,' said Wollstonecraft, disgruntled but relieved. 'You are a younger man than I am, and stronger I suspect.' He waved a finger. 'Though not when I was your age. Oh no, not then. At your age I had the strength of an ox!'

'And the mind of one too,' murmured Mary. She smiled wryly at Laugharne. She was fond of this simple farmer, who had little education but an abundance of easy-going warmth.

'So where are you off to now?' asked Owen, addressing Edward.

'It seems we are going to Walworth,' said Wollstonecraft, straightening. 'It isn't what I wanted, but that's how it is.' His eyes narrowed menacingly as he looked at Mary. 'Mary wants to live near her friend. And see how I accommodate her wishes. I am not all bad, you see.'

'I trust you will find the house in order,' said Eliza, glancing back at the cottage. 'We have cleaned it thoroughly. It has been good to live there and thank you for the package of food.'

Mary stood with her arm around her mother's waist. 'Yes,' she murmured. 'Thank you.'

'Well, we can't stand about saying thank you,' Edward Wollstonecraft grunted, heaving his chest. 'We have to get going.'

'Our lives are nothing but journeys,' sighed Mary. 'Journeys to nowhere.'

'Let your mother alone now,' Edward said brusquely, 'or you'll give her a headache.'

Seagulls screamed overhead. The morning sky was dull and grey and Mary's heart beat fast with agitation. Her mother coughed and shivered. 'Do get into the coach, Mother,' she said. 'I think it is starting to rain.' Soon the family were all in the coach and the doors banged shut.

Famous for its fruit and vegetables Walworth was a London suburb, very busy and thriving. Many of the residents made their income from selling poultry, wool and honey, and the locals were allowed to let their animals roam the common. The weather had taken a turn for the better and Mary gazed from the window of the coach, hearing the sounds of squawking hens and laughing children as they passed through the neighbourhood. The last part of the journey had been smooth and pleasant, and the coach driver had told them the roads to the town had been much improved, which had brought prosperity to the area; it was now much easier for wealthy Londoners to come to and fro. The Old Kent Road, he said, was constantly active with an abundance of horse drawn carriages and stagecoaches. Mary decided that coming to Walworth had been an excellent idea.

The family was to lodge with a young married bank clerk by the name of Thomas Taylor. He had a passion for Greek philosophy and liked to attempt translations. Translating was something that interested Mary greatly, and she was eager to talk with him about it. To keep with the voice of the author and capture the music of the language and thought while holding on to the culture of the work, seemed like a fascinating challenge.

They all disembarked from the coach and went in the house. Well, at last they could settle and relax, thought Mary, even if only temporarily. And she was right where she wanted to be. But her father failed and failed again, and she puzzled over his decisions, if he ever made decisions at all. Where would they move to next?

Taylor though, Mary discovered, was alive with ideas and her own yearnings for knowledge suited his energies. They talked together a lot until the candles burned low in the parlour. Which Greek philosophers did he read; she asked him, which translations had he done? And he told her, revealing some of the pitfalls of translating and also the joys. He occasionally got into scrapes, he laughed, when he'd translated something wrongly and had caused offence, things could sound ridiculous sometimes, though such matters were soon corrected on a second printing. Her father had gone to London and would be away three days, so she relaxed in Thomas's company, enjoying their conversations and learning new things. That week she went to see Fanny. 'I now have a room of my own,' she told her excitedly. 'Only a small one, but it's somewhere to write, and we can see much more of each other now I'm in Walworth.'

'And we can visit the Clares like before,' Fanny said happily. 'They know you are back. I sent them a letter. "That's wonderful," they said. "Mary will wake us all up!"'

'It will be good to see them,' Mary replied warmly. Now she had energy for growth, and though the air in Walworth could never be compared to the purity of the air in Wales, she felt she breathed better and the pains in her limbs had lessened. 'How their spirits move me,' she sighed. 'I have missed them. Laugharne is beautiful, but I was very lonely, and with the aches and pains I was getting I felt older than Mother. I fear it was depression.'

'I knew you were depressed,' said Fanny in her calm, gentle way. 'I felt it in your letters. You need to have interesting people to talk to. Family is all well and good, but sometimes it seems as if they don't know us. It makes you frustrated.' Fanny looked downwards and sighed, Mary knew that much like herself, she felt captured.

Mary moved on in her thoughts. New knowledge burned within her and fired her with ideas. When all her woman's concerns brought their worst heartaches, she thrust herself forward addressing them bravely, fearless of any opposition. Learning was the answer to progress; this was an essential truth.

One day out walking with Thomas they chanced on the subject of Plato. 'Plato perceived the nature of Absolute Goodness,' Thomas told her intensely. 'Can you imagine that?' He smiled at people as they went and was obviously quite well known. She decided she would no doubt be talked about by people who passed. 'An amazing idea,' he continued. 'I think it is inconceivable. I wish I could understand these things, I keep on trying, but a lot is beyond us.'

'Yes,' she replied. 'Poor creatures that we are, much is beyond our understanding, like love, for instance, or God.' She recalled her talks with Jane. 'How can we know what is good – I mean *truly*?' she said. She turned to him. He was a tall smart looking fellow, who held himself proud and was much like Doctor Arden, she thought. 'Perhaps there is no such thing as absolute goodness,' she said abstractedly. 'Circumstances confuse us. There are times when something seems bad whilst at other times it seems good and we cannot think why.' She recalled one of the last times she'd talked with Jane, and how they had talked about the nature of wisdom, another great mystery.

'True knowledge, according to Plato, is composed of perfect models from which all things take their pattern.' He made strange shapes in the air with his hands. 'He calls them *"Forms" or "Ideas."'*

Mary gazed ahead. She had read some Plato just recently, trying to fathom his notions. 'But do these Forms actually exist?' she said curiously. 'If we simply take them on faith, can we ever really believe in them? Imagination isn't enough.'

'I think they exist,' said Thomas, his brow furrowed with thought. 'We have to perceive them. We must allow them to enter our minds then accept them, though we may not always comprehend them.'

Mary remembered Jane's question. *"How do we get perception?"*

Thomas went on. 'Plato considered those elevated states of being, like truth, beauty and justice are derived from the Form of the Good. Aristotle argues however, that if they are not of the world of physical reality how can they help our understanding of human ethics?' He stroked his chin as he walked. 'Hmm. I need to think about that.'

'It is as if we walk in darkness,' said Mary. Could it be that there were questions without answers, she wondered, questions that simply belonged to themselves and remained as such for ever?

Thomas spoke again. 'Plato claimed that knowledge gained through the senses is no more than opinion and that in order to have real knowledge, we must gain it through philosophical reasoning.' He gazed at space abstractedly. 'Not so easily come by ...'

'But true knowledge, can be *felt,* surely?' Mary said searchingly.

'No,' said Thomas with a sigh. 'I do not think so. We must simply be open to the light, in the way that the countryside is open to sunshine, then we can see what gifts unfold from its promise.'

For several moments they were silent, lost in their thoughts.

'Vices and other base things prevent us from achieving the higher states that are possible,' Thomas said finally. 'Of that I feel certain. Justice, for instance, involves the fair and moral treatment of all persons . . .'

'And that includes women,' Mary added quickly, casting him a serious glance.

'Well, yes,' he said, looking surprised. He gazed at her curiously. 'And animals too. Brutes have rights, you know. Would you not agree? The man you see passing this house early morning, beat his dog to death yesterday, all because it wouldn't stop barking. What a wicked thing to do. How could the creature protest, other than to keep on barking? Now it is silenced for good.'

'Are you saying women are like that? Not hearing, not listening to their husbands who always expect to be served, and who in the end would beat them to death for lack of obeisance?' She knew that she sounded angry.

He tipped his head sideways and spoke in a kindly tone of voice. 'I have no such thoughts, Mary. I did not wish to offend you.'

She made no answer. He spoke again. 'I suspect under certain circumstances, women might become wicked as easily as men do.'

'Oh, yes,' she said, sharply. He had come to her most vital concern. 'They can turn into terrible mothers, spiteful wives, frustrated and unhappy beings if they do not have rights and education. – They can even become insane. – It is wicked to bring up girls as empty headed playthings for men and society. The man is devoted to the acquisition of wealth and property and the woman is devoted to the man's ardent eyes, and should those eyes darken she is lost, for she has no real being of her own.' She covered her face with her hands. 'It is all so wrong. Let women have rights, allow them to become more rational and society will improve. A man's education is designed for independence. It is not so for women.'

Again they were silent.

'I long for wisdom,' she said painfully. 'The wisdom to understand and know.'

'Ah yes,' said Thomas. 'We all want wisdom. It is a rare and beautiful thing. Oh, that we might find it! As Plato tells us, man is a being always in search of meaning. But where is meaning?'

They walked on further, deep in thought, then turned and went back to the house. Mary went to her room and got out her paper and pen. There was much she needed to write.

Time moved on. She learned a lot from Thomas Taylor, and it was always good to be with Fanny. When they were together, she watched the clock, scarcely able to bear it when she had to return to her family. And despite the pleasure of Thomas's company, she hated the family squabbles and the outrageous behaviour of her father, who came and went like a madman. Fanny had suggested she leave and come to live with them, or failing that move away and take work. But what work would she do? Would she have to take work as a governess, cut off from the world, tutoring children in their home in amusing though unprofitable subjects? The thought made her panic. Why couldn't women work in business like men did, or train to be lawyers like Ned? Or at best become writers and spread their ideas. How she would love to be a writer! Could women not be loved and cherished for their minds and not just their usefulness to family?

'Mother is tearful,' said Everina that morning, as they all sat together in the parlour.

'She is always tearful,' sighed Mary. 'That is the reason marriage must change. I believe it can kill you.'

'How awful,' said Eliza, surprised and afraid. She stared at Mary perplexed. 'You say the most terrible things.'

'It doesn't kill everybody,' said Everina, thoughtfully. 'If you marry the wrong person, you are bound to be unhappy, that's obvious. Then you might die of misery. It happens mostly to women though, doesn't it, Mary.' She looked at her for confirmation.

'I believe that's right,' said Mary.

'I thought it was childbirth that killed you, not marriage,' said Eliza.

'Knowledge of childbirth is neglected,' said Mary pondering. 'Much can be done to stop women losing their lives and their babies.' A quick painful thought went though her mind. She closed her eyes and took deep breaths. Oh Agnes, poor Agnes!

'I'll not be a fool,' said Everina flatly. 'You won't see me getting married. And I don't intend to have babies.'

'Oh, you will,' laughed Eliza. 'You'll be wed before you know it. – Ned is getting married, did you know?'

Their mother looked up and dabbed her eyes with her hanky.

'No I didn't,' Everina said crossly. 'Who told you that?'

'Mother did,' said Eliza, casting her a glance.

Elizabeth Wollstonecraft shook her head. She was not happy about her son getting married. 'Yes, he told me last night,' she sighed. She looked at Mary. 'You were writing in your room. It was a hurried visit.'

'He wrote me a letter,' Mary said quietly. 'I suppose he expected me to prepare you, Mother. But I felt he should tell you himself and not just leave it to me.'

'And I suppose you will know that Eliza and I will soon be going to school,' said Everina.

'Yes,' said Eliza, shrugging. 'We're being packed off.'

'You're lucky,' said Mary. 'A boarding school in Chelsea will be better than being in this house with Father.'

'But who is to pay for it?' said Eliza. 'Father has nothing.'

'Ned is to pay for it,' Mary said quietly. 'Don't ask me how.'

There was a silence.

'Do you know what it's like?' Everina asked Mary, suddenly worried. 'That school, I mean.'

Mary gazed out of the window. 'A bit mediocre I believe. I expect you'll learn drawing and singing, maybe some sewing, and a little bit of French. Training for a governess, I suppose.' She lifted her shoulders and dropped them despairingly. Mary felt sick at the thought of being left in the house with just her parents and younger brothers. 'I long to get away, myself,' she murmured. Her mother, silent by the fire, frowned. 'And *you* would too, Mother, if you were me. Where is my life? I want to have a life!'

'What life do you want?' asked her mother in a low and exhausted voice.

Mary shook her head frustrated. 'Oh, something different from this, for certain.' She spoke quickly, knowing that what she said would be hurtful, especially now Ned was getting married, but she had to say it. 'I could move in with Fanny and her family,' she faltered. 'They have invited me to do so.'

Her mother looked up surprised. 'You want to live with the Bloods?'

'You and my father are constantly fighting and my nerves are in shreds. Something bad is in my blood, Mother. I fear it will destroy me.'

Her mother shook her head in despair. Her voice trembled as she spoke. 'But that father of hers will cause you even more suffering than your own does. And isn't Fanny unwell? She is always coughing. And didn't you say there was a man who wanted to marry her?'

Mary recalled Hugh Skeys, who still visited the Bloods, though nothing had come of it yet. 'Yes, there is, and he often goes to the house, but he does not ask her to marry him. And to tell the truth, I am glad of it. The worst thing a woman can do is get married. The very idea makes me weak.'

Eliza went to her mother who had resumed her weeping. 'See what you've done,' Eliza said, crossly. 'Ned has gone, and we are about to depart, and you say you want to leave home. You are most insensitive, Mary. Mother can't bear it when you say you want to leave. You know how it hurts her.'

'You talk as if I am about to do something wicked,' Mary pleaded. 'I just want to save my life, that's all.'

'You are very cruel and selfish,' sobbed her mother. 'And you did not learn it from me.'

'Do you not love us?' asked Eliza. Her voice quivered as she spoke.

'I think a woman can want to develop her mind, yet still love her family,' Mary said flatly. 'But she should not be a sacrifice to it.' She raised her voice. 'I won't be a sacrifice! I won't!'

'Do stop pacing, Mary,' her mother said shakily. 'You always want to fight like your father. It never does the least bit of good. You should try to be calmer.'

'And silent, no doubt,' said Mary, taking a seat and sighing. 'That silence can drive us insane.' She thought of the asylum she had visited, though her mother knew nothing of that, and she hoped Eliza hadn't told her. 'There is too much happening in my mind, Mother, for my thoughts to be confined to silence. It isn't in my nature. Please understand.'

'I know, my dear,' said her mother, struggling to gain her composure. 'But the girls are leaving. If you leave too, who will be here to take care of me and the boys?'

'I can get you some help. I'll see Ned. – Ned has a life, he takes it as his due, why not me? – Because I am a woman that's why! And you expect me to live in this hell!'

'Oh, Mary,' cried her mother. 'Is it really that bad?'

'It isn't hell!' said Everina. 'You are quite right Mary, you like to speak your mind, but you ought to consider other people.'

'I'm sorry if my words upset you, Mother,' Mary said quietly. 'But I am subject to powerful feelings and such a fast rush of thoughts sometimes. If I can't express them I feel as if I shall scream.'

'Well yes,' said her mother. 'I know how you are. But think how ashamed I should feel if you decided to live with the Bloods.'

'Oh, I won't do that, said Mary, desperately. 'Not really. It was just an idea; you know how I like to be with Fanny. I shall have to go away, though I don't know where to go.' She stood biting her lip.

Eliza and Everina stayed silent. The boys came running down-stairs.

'Mary might leave us,' said her mother to James.

'Why – is she getting married?' he asked, looking at Mary with wide-eyed boyish surprise.

'No, James, I am not,' Mary said quietly. 'Ned is getting married, not me. I shall never be married. How many times must I tell you? I need to find work.'

'But what will you do?' said James. He went to sit by his mother and stared at Mary worriedly.

'I shall become a lady's companion,' she said. 'I can send money to Mother from my earnings. I have seen an advertisement for an appointment in Bath; I think I might like it.'

'You wouldn't like it at all,' murmured Eliza. 'And you know it. What has happened to your truth?'

'What would you do as a companion to some silly old lady?' said Everina curtly. 'She won't talk to you, you know. And you'll soon grow weary of giving her all that company.'

'But I shall meet new people, you see. That could be interesting.'

'I doubt it,' sniffed Eliza. 'Though it can't be worse than our school. You *will* write to us, Mary, won't you?'

'But of course,' sighed Mary. 'I shall write to everyone.' She went across to her Mother and kissed the top of her hair which was warm from the fire. 'I'm sorry, Mother. But I have to do it.'

'And you must be the one to tell your father,' murmured her mother.

'I will,' said Mary. 'Just as soon as he's back.'

'And what a to-do it will cause,' said her mother, gazing about worriedly.

'It will have to be endured,' Mary said resignedly. She sat for some time in silence, surprised at what she had accomplished in the last fifteen minutes. A strange feeling of euphoria came over her. And at the same time a great sense of sadness. Something had come to an end. She needed to talk with Fanny again and speak of her intentions, and she must talk with Thomas Taylor. Thomas Taylor, in particular, perhaps Plato might have a few words of wisdom to help ease her mind.

# 9

# *To Bath and Windsor*

'Fool's courage, that's what it is,' argued her mother, when Mary had finalised her plans. 'This is all Fanny Blood. She's encouraged you. It is she who has advised you to leave us. No wonder your father is furious. You are going to become a companion to some wealthy conceited woman, oh, and never mind me. – Ah, I see you have bought another hat.' She lifted a hat box from the floor and looked inside. 'And a very nice hat it is, you intend to go up in the world do you?' She laughed. 'Companion indeed, she will treat you like an inferior and you'll hate it.'

'I have to leave sometime, Mother,' Mary said dismally. 'We have talked about this so often. Please let me go in peace – the coach is waiting.' Mary was fully aware of the dark path she must take and the obstacles she might encounter. It made it no easier when her mother harassed her like this. But as she spoke to her now, she felt a certain glow in her soul she had never felt before, though the guilt lingered.

'But who will companion *me*?' her mother continued mournfully. 'It won't be your father, for certain. The girls will have gone, you will have gone, I shall be all alone with the boys. For all my efforts and sufferings I am at last abandoned. You'll be a servant to that woman I tell you, and she'll want you to know it.'

'You won't be neglected, Mother. The Taylors came in to talk to you last night, remember. They are your friends.'

'Oh, are they now?' answered her mother, with a sudden Irish accent which she sometimes assumed when emotional. 'Well, I'm glad they're my friends, to be sure! But your father will have us move again shortly. Oh, he will, he will. He'll not stay lodging in this house. You are leaving me, Mary, and that will be the end of it.'

Mary went over their previous conversations and tried to console her. The girls would visit her. Ned was now living closer and would bring round his wife. 'You say I am about to abandon you, why do you think so?'

'Instinct,' said her mother in a resigned and quieter tone of voice. 'A woman's instinct. We know things. And I know I have lost you.'

The city of Bath was in the valley of the River Avon in the countryside of south-west England. This was where Sarah Dawson resided, who Mary had gone to assist. Mrs Dawson was the daughter of a Windsor Canon and the widow of a wealthy merchant, a wealthy woman, who it was rumoured, had a difficult temperament and rarely kept companions for long.

Well, never mind, thought Mary as she walked through the town that morning, life at home had prepared her for the worst and she would shoulder whatever lay ahead with her usual fortitude. She hadn't seen much of Mrs Dawson since her arrival, but from their brief encounters she had appeared quite pleasant and kind, suggesting places Mary might like to see and trying to put her at ease. She liked her room, which was luxurious and light, complete with a writing desk, a pen and a bottle of ink and a good supply of paper too. It was pleasing to think that the woman acknowledged she would want to write letters, rather than sit about sewing.

She gazed in the shop windows, seeing expensive furs and jewellery, bought by women haughtily passing by. She felt she had entered a rich and hollow world and wondered how she'd fit in. Not so satisfactorily, she decided. Bath was a spa, and baths had been built there by the Romans in the seventh century. Might the waters help ease the aches and pains she had started to suffer from lately? Perhaps she would give them a try. She saw that the city also had a theatre and heard it had secured a royal patent just recently, which made it highly prestigious. In time she might get to see a play.

She stopped and leant on a wall. It was there again, the horrible pain in her side. She did not think it was sickness, well, not of the physical kind, but more a result of her acute sensitivities for it came on worse when she worried. Just now she was thinking of her mother, hoping her father would show her some affection, for Everina had said he was always less difficult when Mary was absent. And she was thinking, too, about Eliza and Everina and wondering how it would be at the Boarding School, and how wrong it was that their education must be paid for by Ned, and a meagre education at that.

She braced herself and walked on. Bath was a beautiful city, the lovely honey coloured stone of the buildings glittered and flashed in the sunlight. She felt hopeful for the future as she went about exploring. There was plenty to see, and she hoped to meet new people. The newly built Royal Crescent was a set of thirty terraced houses, all very grand, and designed in a sweeping half moon, a very clever design, she thought and pleasing to the eye. She would write to Fanny about that and try to draw it. She had lots to tell her. She noted the city housed many people of leisure, people who went to balls and horse racing and generally had fun. Though, just as in London, there were always the forgotten poor. Squalor abounded in the alleyways and people sat begging on the pavements. She was glad of the oil lamps on the streets for it might be dangerous after dark.

It was now afternoon. Mrs Dawson wasn't at home. She had gone to see a friend, and Mary had learned that she normally stayed in Windsor during the summer. Being a companion wasn't so bad after all, she thought. And how good it would be if Mrs Dawson took her to Windsor. She pondered on that as she walked. She would like to see the castle, built by William the Conqueror in the eleventh century. Her brother Charles would certainly be interested in that. Already she was thinking she had made a wise decision in coming to join Mrs Dawson and hoped they'd get on. She was though a distant kind of person and looked right past her when she spoke. Mary didn't think they'd have many useful conversations.

Having reached the age of nineteen, Mary was reviewing her past. She'd been shaken and bruised, but not hurt, and she was still in one piece! She hadn't worked away from home before and the experience was strange, neither had she worked for money, she must learn about that on the hop. But learning on the hop could be fun, and she thrilled at the thought of having money of her own. To be hired and paid however was thought of as a kind of servility in the eyes of many. Oh, the terrible judgemental ignorant eyes of others! She contemplated the possible truth of her future. Would this be her life, to suffer the condescension of some dull wealthy woman, or to try to teach witless children? What if her mind stagnated and she must just become a servant with no ideas to grow from. She trembled at the thought, listening to the frivolous voices around her, feeling like an outcast. Carriages trundled by, market traders selling their wares called out to pedestrians. – Then all of a sudden, out of the blue came a face she knew.

'Dear Mary! – Good Day!' John Arden cried. 'What are you doing in Bath?'

'Doctor Arden,' she said laughing. 'Am I in a dream? I am working as a lady's companion. It seems so long since I saw you.'

'Indeed it is,' he said, gazing at her in his usual pensive way. 'Some four and a half years I should think. Now tell me what you are up to.' He glanced all around and they found a place to take tea.

The tea room was filled with fashionable people, and Mary saw that some of them scowled at her dowdy attire. John Arden smiled wryly. People sometimes complained, he said, if *ordinary* people went to take tea there, but such looks were best ignored. 'They give themselves airs and graces,' he whispered. 'Many of these women are ladies of rank but they mainly talk nonsense. They have very fine feathers and twitter away like birds saying little of value.' Mary looked down at her old well-worn boots. The constant peering annoyed her and she returned the looks with a cold unflinching stare, then straightened and smiled at John Arden. Did such women think of nothing but wealth, she wondered. And what if their money were suddenly taken away? It happened constantly, the times were unpredictable and the poor were increasingly hostile.

John Arden glanced about for a waitress. 'Well then, what would you like?' he asked, smiling broadly. 'There are scones, tartlets, éclairs . . .' A waitress came over and they ordered tartlets and tea. 'I am giving some courses at my home at present in experimental philosophy. Do come along if you wish, you are always welcome.'

It surprised her to learn Jane's sisters were also in the city, and that Jane still worked as a governess in Norfolk. Mary asked if she were happy, and her father answered she was. 'That's Jane,' Mary said smiling. 'I only wish I were so easily contented. She is quite remarkable.' She cut into a delicious strawberry tartlet.

Just as they were finishing their tea, Jane's younger sister Ann walked in with a man. 'Ah there you are, Father!' she cried, hurrying across. 'I thought I might find you here.' John Arden stood and invited them both to take a seat, then explained how he had stumbled on Mary and had been catching up with her news. Ann's companion bowed briefly then pulled out a chair for Ann, then he sat himself down, all the time smiling at Mary.

'Ah, Mrs Dawson, an awkward lady, I am told,' said Ann. 'But it is all hearsay, of course.' She laughed. 'We should always be careful of hearsay.' She turned to her companion. 'This is Joshua Waterhouse; his father is a yeoman farmer in Derbyshire. Joshua was at Cambridge and ordained as a priest a few years ago.'

He smiled at Mary artfully and clasped his hands before him as if in prayer. He was strikingly handsome, she thought.

'People say terrible things about me, as well,' said Waterhouse quietly, 'but I care not a jot.'

'Joshua is a fellow of his college,' said John. 'Though he doesn't appear to do very much teaching or researching.' He glanced at Waterhouse, who bent his head and frowned. John went on, leaning back in his chair and keeping his eyes on Waterhouse, who Mary thought looked embarrassed. But this was the way of John Arden, he spoke spontaneously just as he felt and was a fearless crusader for truth. He continued. 'Joshua would rather frequent the tea rooms with pretty young ladies, I think, and the watering places attended by wealthy women.'

'Now that you mention it John,' said Waterhouse, stretching out his legs and smiling. 'Are you not sitting in a tea-room yourself this very afternoon, and with a rather lovely young lady?'

'Indeed, I am,' said Arden. 'But I have to be on my way very soon. I am about to give a lecture.'

'Ah, philosophy?' said Waterhouse. 'A dizzying subject, I can't make head or tail of it myself.'

'But you are Cambridge educated?' said Ann, giving him a curious look. 'You are being disingenuous, I think.'

'I am a man of common sense,' said Waterhouse, swelling out his chest. 'Most matters can be solved by common sense.'

Mary gazed at Waterhouse, watching his strong hands as they pushed back his loose dark hair. He met her eyes and smiled. She looked at him flirtatiously, hating herself as she did so, but nevertheless enjoying the exciting encounter.

'Joshua says one thing while believing another,' Ann said tiredly. She shook her head. 'That is the way of men.' Then she turned again to Mary. 'Do you not think so, Mary?'

'It is the way of people in general, I think,' said Mary. 'Even the way of ourselves, if we are honest.'

'Ah, so you believe matters can be *honest,* do you?' John Arden said, seizing on her words. 'I am not so sure about that.' He waved a long finger. 'Philosophical enquiry cannot always solve things, of course, but is "common sense" an answer?' He put his hand to his forehead, as he often did when thinking. 'I do not think so.'

'So what is the answer?' said Mary, eager to learn something new, and wishing she had Thomas Taylor seated beside her.

'Prayer, perhaps,' said Joshua. 'The last resort of despair.' He brought his hands together again and closed his eyes. For a moment or two they were silent. Then he turned to Mary and leant to her, smiling. 'Might I take tea with you sometime, Miss Wollstonecraft, when you are free?' His tone was low and seductive. 'Just the two of us, I mean?'

'I doubt she will be free very often,' said Ann, annoyed that he had turned his back, and determined he should know he'd been heard.

For several moments they were silent. John Arden folded his napkin slowly, vexed and uneasy. 'You're not going to trifle with Mary now, are you,' he said quietly. That he did not like Waterhouse was obvious.

'He trifles with us all,' said Ann, indignantly. She turned away from the table and glanced all about her. Already a number of elegant ladies had set their eyes on Waterhouse. He cut a dashing figure in the tea-room and his proud deportment and easy dignified bearing made him exactly the type they looked for.

'Who me?' said Waterhouse with a sudden hurt look. 'What makes you say that, my dear?'

'I say it because it is true,' said Ann with a sigh. 'You tell me you can never marry because of your fellowship, yet you flirt with every woman in sight – and worse still, you make them fall in love with you.'

Waterhouse laughed and widened his eyes mischievously. John Arden stared at him coldly.

'Oh, Father, do not worry,' said Ann, with a little embarrassed laugh. 'I shall never fall in love with Joshua. I am far too sensible for that. It is all about common sense, you see.'

Mary was silent. She wasn't sure she could say the same herself. Already she could feel the blood surging in her veins. And though she resented it she could not cool her feelings. 'I'm sure I might steal an hour one sunny afternoon,' she murmured. She did not dare call it love, for it was quite a different feeling and had come on her fast. This was *desire*. She sat confused.

'But what would you tell Mrs Dawson?' Ann interjected frowning.

'I would tell her what she needed to know.' Mary smiled sideways at Waterhouse, even coquettishly.

'And what if she wants to join you?' said Jane. 'She might, you know. People like her do.'

'Then I shall change my mind and arrange another time,' said Mary, all the time looking at Waterhouse.

Again there was silence. John Arden paid the bill then reached for his hat and cane.

'I met Joshua by accident earlier,' said Ann, as they all went out. 'I was looking for you, Father, and he offered to assist me.'

'And we found you,' said Waterhouse nodding at John as if in a gesture of success. 'Au revoir,' he said, finally, giving them a little bow, and he strode away down the street.

*Au revoir*, thought Mary. Waterhouse would probably send a note to Mrs Dawson's, or at least she hoped so. Would he not act like the learned and dignified gentleman he was and ask Mrs Dawson's permission? They wandered the shops for a while and John Arden bought Mary a little engraving of wild flowers, it was extremely delicately worked and beautiful, something Fanny might have made. She would keep it on her desk and try to describe it when she wrote to her that evening.

Two weeks later, Mary had sunk in spirit. Joshua Waterhouse hadn't made the least contact. But it wouldn't have made any difference had he bothered, for Mrs Dawson held her like a prisoner and constantly watched her. She wrote to Jane, saying how thrilled she had been to meet her father and Ann in Bath, and she told her of the moves and troubles with her family and how they had worn her to distraction. She explained how she and her siblings had been forced to yield their inheritances to keep their father out of prison – or so it had seemed – and how they had fled to Walworth. But she related with immense pleasure that she had spent some time with a clergyman in Hoxton, an excellent man who had helped her cultivate her mind, just as she and her father had in Beverley. And even more importantly, she wrote about Fanny, *"I enjoyed the society of a friend, whom I love better than all the world beside, a friend to whom I am bound to every tie of gratitude and inclination: To live with this friend is the height of my ambition . . ."* But Fanny was quite unwell and would benefit from a warmer climate, she said, and she now had a suitor, an Irish Merchant by the name of Hugh Skeys. Writing his name caused her hand to tremble and her words were unclear on the page. She feared for the future, she said. Mary had received but little instruction on Christian doctrine, and her parents had never been devout, but she, herself, had always gone to church, and had no doubt been influenced by the piety of Reverend Clare. Just now though she could not call upon the Lord for any comfort, for she still felt guilty at having left her mother. She told of her sisters at a Boarding School in Chelsea, saying Eliza had become particularly pretty, and that Ned, her eldest brother, was happily married and had now become a father. She was delighted, she added, to hear of Jane's brother's being married, and wondered if she, herself, had met *"an agreeable Norfolk Swain"*, and to please send details if she had. She did not speak of her self betrayal with Joshua Waterhouse, how she had fallen for his charms and demeaned herself in the presence of Jane's sister and father. She felt resentful and aggrieved, a shadow of her former self. There was something unbearably shameful about it; she had allowed the man to take hold of her feelings so quickly.

One dark day in late summer, Mrs Dawson moved to her family home in Windsor, and Mary went with her. The sense of feeling lost in a void was now becoming familiar. Her dreams offered more vivacity than her daily activities and she was losing touch with reality. She feared for her sanity. It wasn't as if Mrs Dawson treated her badly, nothing was as bad as she'd imagined, and she wasn't treated like a servant. Mrs Dawson wanted her company and conversation. But it was only conversation of a sort. And it all robbed her of time. How could she converse with someone who thought in such a different way to herself? She was forced to play a role and make her employer feel important. Just as her mother had warned, she did, indeed, hate it. "You may sit with us, of course," Mrs Dawson might say when they attended some patrician function. "But only after dinner." Rules, orders, and commands were the order of Mary's day. It hurt her to the marrow of her bones. She had a very nice room with a window, and the light in the mornings was excellent if she felt like reading or writing, and all her meals were provided, but she saved all she could, for she always intended to flee. But where she would flee she did not know though she desperately needed to escape.

Then came a letter from Jane. Ann, her sister, had started a school in Bath and Jane intended to join her. Mary's heart leapt as she thought of it. How she would love to start a school! In her abstraction, she forgot to join Mrs Dawson for breakfast and sometimes even for dinner when she had guests. It was not good, and the relationship became uneasy. But whoever would want to be a lady's companion if they could start a school of their own, she thought. Such a venture, however, needed money and time. Was there not a way to do it? She wrote to Jane:

"*. . . I have ever approved of your plan, and it would give me great pleasure to find that you and your sister could contrive to live together; – let not some small difficulties intimidate you, I beseech you; – struggle with any obstacles rather than go into a state of dependence; – I speak feelingly, – I have felt the weight, and would have you by all means avoid it. – Your employm' tho a troublesome one, is very necessary, and you have the opportunity of doing much good, by instructing good principles into the young and the ignorant, and at the close of life you'll have the pleasure to think that you have not lived in vain, and, believe me, this reflection is worth a lot of care . . .*"

Oh, to start a school with Fanny! thought Mary. She had things to do, ideas to pass on to the world that as yet were still taking form, but she knew they were strong and true. Windsor was closer to Fanny than Bath and while she was there she arranged a full week's holiday with her. There was much to consider.

'All good things must move in stages,' said Mary. It would have to be a sort of process. They would plan it out together – where they would have their school, the costs and number of pupils. It was as if she were giving the whole of her soul to this one wonderful idea; this school with Fanny. She hoped they might live together, she'd said, it was her earnest wish. Hugh Skeys wasn't spoken of and hadn't been anywhere near throughout the week of her visit. Mary had thrown the whole of her scorching heart at Fanny's feet but Fanny's tepid response had hurt her and made her nerves feel raw. She'd been interested, but nothing more.

# 10

# *Summoned to Duty*

It was now 1780. The *British Gazette* and the *Sunday Monitor,* the first British Sunday newspapers, were issued to an eager public. The world was abuzz with activity and there was much to read and discuss. Along with the constant wars a lot of peculiar things had been happening that some said were "acts of God," warnings that meant mankind must stop and take measure before it was all too late. At the beginning of summer a mysterious darkness fell on New England and part of Canada. Animals scuttled into hiding, people fell on their knees and prayed. The cause was never discovered, but mercifully light returned. Captain James Cook, however, did not. When HMS *Resolution,* in which he had made his second and third voyages to explore the Pacific, came back, he was lost from his crew. Landing on Hawaii Island at first, Cook and his men had been feted by the natives, fascinated by the novelty of the European ships. After a while though, familiarity caused a change in their mood and Cook and his crew had thought it best to depart. Their ship suffered terrible seas and violent weather and was so severely damaged he was forced to return. Fierce quarrels ensued between Cook and the natives, and Captain Cook was murdered. A horrible ending for a man who had worked so hard and courageously, said his supporters. Others claimed Cook had been foolish, for who was to know the minds of people who lived on remote islands. But there was other, happier news to be had. Louis XVI of France had put an end to torture as a means of gaining confessions and men breathed better for that.

Mary's parents had moved yet again, this time to Enfield with her younger siblings, a rural area straddling north east London. James had left for sea. At twelve years of age, he had boarded the *Carysfoot* and gone, whether from his own choice or some naval request, Mary didn't know, but she comforted herself that it was often the way of boys to choose a life on the waves. The romance, though, would soon wear off, she mused, when her sensitive and melancholy brother experienced the terrible food and dampness and the ways of sailors at sea. Eliza wrote that she and Everina had now been brought out of school, for help was needed at home and money was in short supply. Charles, she said, would follow Ned and take Articles. Eleven year old Charles, Mary reflected, had always been cheerful and did not dwell too long on the despair of the household. But as she walked down the long country lane in Windsor, Mary could feel her life ebbing away. There were days she felt physically sick, always at Mrs Dawson's beck and call.

It pained her too when she learned Jane's school had failed, though in truth it could hardly have succeeded given such heavy competition from the prosperous and more established schools in Bath. But Mary understood how important it had been to Jane, and she had no doubt lost much of her investment. Speculation meant taking chances and taking chances was risky. Her father had taken too many. It was almost as if the essential art of life was to know when to take chances and to discern when to withhold. She'd been determined to try to start a school with Fanny. Jane's loss though had damaged her will. Might she still try? Or would she simply go forward into nothingness.

Deep in thought, she wandered. The closest she could get to Fanny now were the wildflowers she saw in the hedgerows, it was as if she dwelt within every quivering head. She stopped and leant against a tree, then covered her face with her hands and took deep breaths. She was falling into a well of emotional turmoil and knew she must force herself out of it. She focused her mind on matters more rewarding; she was practising her French and enjoying her writing. Yes, she had started to write, really properly write, she would tell Fanny about that, she would go to her room and get out her pen and paper and write until the candle burned low. "Une femme est pas un jouet!" she would say into the silence of her room. Her soul was always in conflict with her father over his demeaning and cruel ways, and she had seen the pattern repeated in Fanny's family. A lot of men revelled in acting superior to women, she thought, and she believed it happened right across the social spectrum, the pitch changing according to wealth and position, but no matter what class they came from women were treated as mindless creatures who could not think for themselves, and worst of all they let it happen.

She probably seemed like a very sad creature indeed to the fashionable women of Bath and Windsor, she thought, and sometimes she fell into depression at the task before her, but she determined her concerns would finally be written as literature for both women and men to read; it was her mission. Women needed help to become rational and genuine for many of them lived a false and empty existence. Education had to be the answer! They must open their minds and think, or were they not slaves? In a second hand bookshop in Windsor she had picked up a book called *Harris's List of Covent Garden Ladies*. It gave details of prostitution in Covent Garden. There were names of streets where prostitutes might be found and the exact location of brothels. Intimate details of the prostitutes' physical appearances were given, even to genitals. Her skin went cold as she read it. So many women and not the least hint in over a hundred and fifty pages of the cold matter-of-fact nature with which they were listed, they might have been animals for sale. Addresses and costs of sessions were listed also, along with a woman's social standing and whether they could sing and dance, or were good conversationalists. The Introduction to the book argued that prostitution was of benefit to the public and helped curb violence in men. Was it not a tragedy that such behaviour existed, such lack of respect for women? How could anyone condone it? She wondered how many children were born to such women and what happened to them after their birth; it was hardly likely that the men who had fathered them would stay around to find out. She fought against the desire to be dispassionate and detached. She was a woman. All she wanted was freedom to think and be herself. She longed for liberty and equality. Turning the pages the energy drained from her body. The list of women varied from "low born errant drabs", to "genteel mannered courtesans, worthy of praise". Even names of their clientele were disclosed, and many were men of high status. She stepped across the puddles in the rain. 'Such is the reward of youthful innocence,' she murmured. Many of the women were probably just girls who had run away from home as boys ran away to sea, in the hope of finding something better. A sharp pain of sadness went through her as she thought of Agnes. Then she turned again to thoughts of starting her school. Yes, she would try! She would harness her energies and formulate a plan. She must write to Fanny without delay.

But the following day a letter arrived from Enfield. It took her time to focus. Her hands trembled as she read it. The words went through her like a knife. Eliza wrote that their mother was seriously ill. How seriously ill was she, Mary wondered frantically? Guilt raced through her veins. She'd left all the caring to Everina and Eliza, how selfish she'd been, how obsessed with her own concerns, and how coldly she'd left them, how cruelly. But she had grown so weary of self sacrifice. Might she not have a life of her own, ever? She had strained on the leash of family and had finally broken free. Her father had been forced to find help, and Mary had closed her eyes to it all. She was filled with wild confusion, lost between past and future, wandering alone. For all their problems she felt a tender respect for her mother and was surprised that she'd asked for her now, for she believed she had cast her aside. Not once had she written, and it seemed she did not speak of her either. But now she needed her, and Mary felt that need in the deepest part of her being. She would leave Mrs Dawson and return to her family forthwith. Bad as her home life had been, she loved her mother and carried her sadness everywhere she went as if it were the Ark of the Covenant, and she hoped that unhappiness might one day spring into a host of fighting women. This was her solemn prayer.

# 11

# *The Death of*
# *Elizabeth Wollstonecraft*

Arriving in Enfield, Mary wondered what help she could give to her family now at this difficult time. She felt so estranged from them all, and especially her mother. She watched the flow of life on the street, chaises passing, people walking to and fro, traders going about their day, and she thought of her childhood, remembering her mother, young and beautiful, her hopes for the future, their talk as they'd walked in the woodlands or trailed around markets searching for bargains. Eliza's letter had sounded so terribly final and Mary's imagination had plagued her all the way there. The horror of not knowing, not seeing, and having been away so long made her feel lost for words. She, the eldest daughter, how could she have been so cruel? Here in the open air, her distorted life seemed to order itself with the sunlight but she knew that once inside the house her senses would twist and cringe and she would feel again the pains of her youth and the pains of her mother's suffering.

'Thank goodness you're here!' cried Eliza, opening the door to greet her and kissing her. 'Mother is delirious; I fear she might die any minute! Oh, Mary, you have no idea. She talks to invisible people; she argues with them and sings to them too. Songs I have never heard before. Do come to see her!'

'Oh yes!' called Everina, following on her sister's footsteps.

'We have watched the clock, longing for your arrival.' The sisters gathered her things. Eliza said their father was away and would be gone several days. Mary, as ever, was glad of it. She followed them both upstairs and they entered their mother's bedroom. And as if in a strange leap of time, Mary changed from the studious young woman of the world she had become to the eldest daughter of the household, the fears and responsibilities of her past seizing her once again. Her sisters stood by their mother's bed like dutiful soldiers, but they looked to Mary for solace, hoping she would take on the burden of what came next. As she gazed at her mother's pale features, her dark sunken eyes and bony outstretched hands, Mary's plans for the future fled. All she could think of was now. Her mother had grown so old, she thought, strangely taken aback by her shrunken features; the dark veins in her hands looked prominent and stubborn, fighting for life. Amazing strength came in all shapes and sizes, Mary decided, even in the small frail body of her mother, who had suffered so much for them all.

'Mary, dear Mary,' her mother said weakly. 'We could never understand each other, could we, and now it is all too late.'

Her words were lost in the still dank air of the room, but the words *"too late"* resounded in Mary's ears. What had happened while she hadn't been there that was now too late to address? What duties had she neglected, thinking on other matters? Wasn't home and family the most important matter of all? The jigsaw pieces of life were constantly scattered, she thought, so you could never quite see the picture of how things were. Her mother clasped her hand tightly, and her touch felt warm and right. And Mary felt suddenly that she *was* her mother, taking on her obscure and complicated power, feeling her emotions and the strength of her sacrifice. Her mother, she thought, had endured such robbery of her being, suffered such self abnegation, that she had made herself subservient to everything before her, forgetting herself as if she no longer existed. 'It isn't too late,' whispered Mary. 'By the grace of God we are united at last.'

The days and nights were long. Ned made visits and sat in the chair in the corner of the bedroom reading. But he could not read for long and kept on pacing the floor. Eliza and Everina grew increasingly tense as their mother's strength left her body. There were times Mary felt dazed as if in a nightmare. Nothing had changed with her father. He could not cope with the separation from the woman who had absorbed his every weakness and allowed him to see them as hers. He was cowardly in the face of her illness and went about the house making guttural murmurings that were thankfully out of hearing. From time to time her mother got up from her bed, though only for brief periods, her limbs were so swollen and painful. Seeing her cold grey eyes, the lack of life in their depths, Mary knew she was dying. It was just a matter of time, the doctor had told them, her heart was failing. But even against her will she lingered, clasping her hands in prayer and saying how she'd always loved them. Then at last she expired and gave herself up to the end.

'Let *me* sort it out,' said Ned who made visits back and forth and sat long and late with Mary deciding what must happen for the funeral. Her sisters showed great fortitude and the boys behaved with dignity. But their father was lost to it all. He broke into relentless weeping. He could not deal with his grief, and went about looking through the rooms as if searching. But his wife had gone. And Mary had seen a look in her eyes in those final moments of life that suggested she were summoned to a far better place. "Have a little patience and all will be over," she had murmured peacefully. And Mary had gathered those words into her memory, holding them close. They were the very core of her mother's lonely strength.

Spring 1782 came upon them fast.

'I suppose,' said Everina, 'that Father might become more pleasant now he has married Lydia.' She sat sewing by the fire. 'He soon moved on, didn't he?'

'He is good at moving on,' said Eliza. 'But yes, he must moderate his behaviour now, Lydia won't tolerate his nonsense. But then she doesn't have to, does she, there are no children to restrict her from thinking of herself. Mother kept quiet for our sakes I think. And silly as it seems,' she added abstractedly. 'I do think she loved him. He won't find that sort of love with Lydia.'

'That love was sick and sad,' sighed Mary, sewing the pocket on her smock. 'It shouldn't be allowed. It's too sacrificial.' She shuddered. She was suddenly the young Mary Wollstonecraft again, her dreams had fled.

Lydia had been a housekeeper in the Wollstonecraft household and while she was there her father had toned down his temper. But his attentions to Lydia, Eliza reported, had been quite inappropriate and it had caused their mother much anguish. Mary poured out her woes to Fanny in letters withholding nothing. The tremendous passions of her soul were leaving her, she said. She felt as if she were apart from herself, looking on. She even wondered if she'd died with her mother and was now in the land of the dead. Oh, the agony of being half dead! How could it be? Was this how a person grew mad? she said. Then she feared she'd been weak and had put too much pressure on the dearest love of her life.

But Fanny invited her to live with them again. And for a day or so she forgot the darkness and imagined how it might be. How the thoughts exalted her! What solace imagination provided. But reality was always waiting. Something would have to give. She would not return to Mrs Dawson. She would go to live with Fanny instead, and discover her lost vitality. How well the ardour of the human heart could communicate, she thought, when all was imparted without fear. She would go to live with her dearest love. She must.

And Everina, Eliza and Charles, went to live with Ned, though much to his chagrin. – "Why don't I take the lot of you?" he'd shouted irritably when Mary had implored him, "Father and that woman as well? My wife and child are of little consequence in the grand scheme of things, of course." And he had stood before her scowling. "You, dear Mary, can only think of the grand scheme of things, you see. You have permanent employment there, but your ideals will never bear fruit. The ways of the world are far more complex than you think." "Can you not remember how it was for us?" she'd groaned. At that he had laughed. "I must remember how it *is* each passing moment, dear sister, or how am I to work?'" She had seen he was disturbed and desperate, but reminded him that *she* would be living with the Bloods and that Eliza now had a suitor and would soon be off his hands. "I shall be happy living with the Bloods," she had said, "even though my work will be humble. I can take in sewing. The pay will be meagre, but for now it must do. Everina has no such happiness. Eliza will probably be married soon, and you have an excellent wife, all will be well for you Ned." He had stood his arms folded and she had seen the lines of worry deepen in his brow. "And will Father take that woman to Laugharne?" he'd said, still irritable. "For that is where he said he might go." Mary had sighed despondently. "Yes, that is his plan. But our sisters refuse to live with them. They are asking to live with you." "And so it is all arranged?" he'd sighed. "My sisters will arrive just as the dawn does, as if it were the way things go." He had gulped down a glass of whiskey and stared at space. "Everina is a good looking woman; she too should be married soon," he'd murmured abstractedly. "I suppose that's something." Mary had laughed wryly. "Dear brother, Everina is poor. Few men will marry an inferior. And as regards Meredith Bishop, Eliza would seem to have done very well, but let's see, women can often be deceived and their hearts irreparably broken." She had not hidden the anger in her voice, and had stood strong before him, turning then to the window to gaze at the darkening sky, as if the world were a place she did not belong in, a place that wearied her soul. Then she'd seen that Ned had taken a seat and was resting his head in his hands. Well, she had done her best. She had not dared go forward to kiss him for fear of annoying him further. All was silence now, the hopeless silence of surrender.

Living in Newington Butts with the Bloods, Mary could see quite plainly that Fanny was in love with Hugh Skeys. As they sat sewing, she talked of his beautiful hands, as if she longed for their touch, she talked of how he walked down the street so vigorously to see her while she waited at the door for his warm and heartfelt embrace. 'I do believe he cares for me,' she said one morning at breakfast. 'I have no dowry at all. I have nothing to give him but love. And I am none too well, either. I tire so easily. But I do think he loves me.' And she went on helpless, carried along by her feelings. 'You say that men are fickle and can often put on an act. Why would he want to do that? What has he to gain?'

Such words were a torment to Mary. Skeys would often turn up at the house to sit by Fanny as she played the piano and sang, and she would smile at him sweetly as if he were her entire world. But Mary felt he only enjoyed the flattery of knowing she loved him, he would not marry her. And what of her health if he did and then she fell pregnant, might she not die giving birth? She trembled at the thought. The very idea of pregnancy horrified Mary. If a woman did not die, she went on having children who took every scrap of her time and patience and left her ever more vulnerable to the vagaries of her husband's nature. A great rush of terror came over her. 'Please don't get married,' she said urgently. 'A woman is weakened by marriage. You have seen how it is. He will tear you up by your roots and you will be all but a pressed flower. – Oh, Fanny, forget him, I beg you!' So often Mary felt alone, dangerously close to the edge of some precipice she was doomed to fall over. It was as if her destiny told her she would plunge eventually into a great dark void of confusion, and each day she feared for her sanity.

Fanny sat motionless and thoughtful. 'I believe I love him,' she whispered, her eyes shining with bliss. 'I would like to have a husband. I think it makes a difference.' The two young women sat on their own in the parlour.

Mary shook her head and sighed. Fanny gazed at her wistfully. 'You shouldn't be so scared. There are lots of good men in the world.' She smiled and spoke calmly, though flushed with emotion. Just then Mrs Blood came in with the others. They had been out walking.

'What is it?' asked her mother, seeing their serious faces. She took off her bonnet and sat down.

'He hit me!' one of the boys cried suddenly. 'Please, Mother, stop him!' And he clung to his mother, who frowned with frustration.

'You're not to get violent,' Mrs Blood said sharply. The older boy stood before her looking angry. Then he advanced on the younger and hit him again. 'Stop it, I say!' cried the mother. And she gripped his arm, trying to pull him away. But his eyes grew even more determined. 'Go upstairs and join the others this minute!' she shouted trembling. 'I tell you, I will not have it. It is giving me palpitations. Why, one of these days I shall fall down dead!' The boys went off and within minutes were at their play, noisy and laughing. Mrs Blood drew a breath and closed her eyes, then sat for some minutes in silence, robbed of her dignity and robbed of her energy. This was the life of Mrs Blood, for better or worse.

That summer Eliza married Meredith Bishop, her suitor. He was a Bermondsey shipwright and a close friend of Fanny's beloved Hugh Skeys, through him he had found Eliza. Ned had said he was quite well off, which had pleased him a lot, and it had pleased their father no end. Eliza though wasn't yet twenty and Mary thought she was far too young to have made such a crucial decision. Getting married was a serious business. On visiting her at Ned's behind the Tower, she had voiced her opinions unreservedly. There would be all manner of household tasks to consider, she'd told her, and if children came she must forget any needs of her own and always put children and husband first. Was it really what she wanted? Without doubt it would tire her out, said Mary, or she would just get used to it, grow old and know no different. Eliza had argued it was right and proper for a woman to put husband and children first, and if she forgot herself, so be it, for wasn't that nature's way? And she had talked on fast and mechanically, already trailing after Meredith in thought like a little pet dog without a mind. She would soon be his creature, thought Mary, and submit to it all in silence.

And so it was done. Eliza, blank faced, walked down the aisle and their father gave her away. Meredith Bishop looked happy with his new acquisition, thought Mary, or that was the way it seemed. But her sister's proud and indomitable bearing had gone in the twinkling of an eye.

Visiting her in her very grand house in Bermondsey, south of the Thames, Mary thought she looked stranded as if living on an island. She was observing all the wifely niceties, and had taken on a new adult voice, though it always seemed to disappear when Meredith entered. Her husband was the dominant force in the household, cutting her short if she dared to voice an opinion and forcing her to enter that terrible wifely silence Mary despised. She removed her cape and sat down by the fire. Only Eliza was in.

'So how do you like being married?' Mary asked her, smiling. Her eyes wandered the room. Meredith had bought two Chippendale mahogany chairs since last she'd visited, like some she'd seen at Mrs Dawson's. Chippendale's carpentry was highly prized and expensive. The house was comfortably furnished with a fine upholstered chaise longue and comfortable velvet chairs. The oak sideboard had ivory inlay. The place was looking quite splendid, if that was what you wanted, to look at things and admire them. She hoped it was what Eliza wanted; for furniture did not keep you company or love you. A beautiful oak Longcase clock ticked away the time close by.

Eliza rang for the maid. 'Ned's wife came to see me with the children,' she said smiling. 'It was all very pleasant.' She bent to a toy on the floor. 'See, they have left this little doll.' She placed the doll on her lap. 'I love to see them, but how noisy they are.' She laughed. 'That is the way of children.'

'Yes, children are noisy,' sighed Mary. 'A mother learns to be obedient. Men are invariably out. The mother is left with the children, and oh, how subtle their demands are; she must suffer them in silence, that is unless she is wealthy and can pay to have them taken care of so she can sit and do embroidery, or play the piano . . .'

Eliza scowled at the fire.

'Would *you* like to play the piano?' Mary asked her.

Eliza shrugged. 'Perhaps, but I haven't thought about it much. I like to draw, as you know.'

'Indeed,' said Mary. 'You draw very well.' The maid came in with tea. 'Are you happy?' asked Mary as the maid went out.

'But of course,' said Eliza, with an all embracing smile. 'Domestically it is all quite easy. The maid comes a few days a week . . .' She broke off and looked downwards. 'I am learning to dance . . . Properly, I mean.' Her eyes lit up as she spoke. 'Dancing is so enjoyable.'

'That's good. Fanny likes dancing,' murmured Mary. 'I wish I could dance better. I do love music, especially Handel, though Handel is not to be danced to. You must listen and hear what it says.'

'And what does it say?' Eliza asked curiously, daintily picking up a teacup.

'I suppose he speaks of feelings,' said Mary reflecting, 'and the feelings are gathered in our hearts.' Eliza, she'd noted generally yawned at concerts and played with her gloves.

'How lovely,' said Eliza with a little gasp of wonder. – 'Do drink your tea, dear Mary. You must not let it go cold. We are so lucky to have tea, you know. Meredith gets it from a man who lives near the Tower.'

'Thank you, 'said Mary. 'It is very good tea.'

Eliza rested her hand on Mary's arm. 'Do not be concerned for my welfare. I am perfectly happy.'

For a minute or two they were silent. They talked a little more, but it was soon time to depart. Already her sister was trying to learn the art of artificial conversation, what to say, what not to say, and when to stay silent. 'I must go,' Mary said finally. 'Fanny will be waiting. She does not play her piano just now, she has rhapsody enough with Hugh Skeys.' She laughed briefly. 'I fear she is lost to him, poor darling.'

'I'm glad,' said Eliza. 'We must take our pleasure as we can; it is often in short supply.'

But Mary felt fearful for the lives of the women she loved, as if men were out to destroy them. Ned's wife was strong and might offer Eliza good counsel. Ned had learned from his father the way not to be and he and his wife were content. But Ned had travelled a very different path from his sisters. And what's more, their mother had adored him. Mary reached for her cape. 'You will let me know if you need me, won't you?' she said. Dear Eliza would see her marriage through rose tinted glasses, thought Mary. But at least she was letting some happiness into her heart, if only for now.

'Goodbye then,' said Eliza, embracing her. 'I look forward to seeing you again.' The words sounded formal, as if she were talking to a stranger. Mary looked into the eyes of her sister and wondered if Eliza might be a stranger for good.

## 12

# *The Collapse of Eliza's Marriage*

That year, Mary felt she was losing Eliza, her letters became short and factual, and she felt as if their relationship was fading away. She had given birth to a daughter and had called her Mary. Mary thrilled that the child had been given her name. But she saw when she went to visit, that her tiny namesake wriggled in her sister's arms as if she did not belong, and Eliza's heavy coiled hair had started to look grubby and untidy. She was growing increasingly wretched as the demands of the child took over. Seeing the sad situation Mary stayed silent, but a cold fear dwelt in her bones. Meredith observed the state of affairs bewildered and anxious. 'Is it not wrong for a child to turn from its mother?' he said to Eliza confounded. 'What did you do to cause her to behave like this?'

'Do not berate her,' Mary said softly, though the tears on Eliza's cheeks made her angry. 'I own that the child is difficult, but temperaments can be helped or hindered by parents. It is problematic, however, if the child has a stubborn nature.' Her sister had never been fearful of anyone and seeing her weep was hurtful. 'These things are rarely straightforward,' she murmured.

'But the child refuses the breast – surely it needs to feed or will it not perish?' He fell to pacing the room.

'I have tried and tried,' wailed Eliza, 'but she just wants to bite.'

'"*Bite*?"' Meredith shouted mockingly. 'She has no teeth! How can she bite? Oh, Eliza, why is everything so difficult for you, it tires me. Feed her, I say! Or I shall have to find someone else to do it.'

'That can be done quite easily,' murmured Mary. 'If you can pay.'

The young husband glanced at her and frowned. 'Of course I can pay. But I do not want your opinion, Mary. If I did I should request it.' Just as his voice grew louder, so did the baby's shrieks.

'It can sometimes take a while for a mother and child to get used to each other,' Mary said composedly, ignoring him.

Meredith continued harshly. 'You have far too much influence on Eliza. She will never do her own thinking if you constantly advise her.'

'Oh, not so, Meredith,' wept Eliza. 'Mary is a good sister. I value her counsel.'

'She has no experience,' Meredith murmured, pacing again. 'She thinks she knows everything, but let me tell you, she doesn't. She . . .'

'Stop it!' cried Eliza. 'Mary can see how things are. I will not have her abused, do you hear?'

Then she wept profusely. Mary reached across and took the child from her arms, though it wrestled like a wild creature. It had been a difficult birth and it was possible the baby had suffered. But she saw that Eliza was now at the end of her patience, and it was hard to see how the child might be comforted when its mother recoiled from it in horror.

'Well, the cruel little thing need not care about me!' sobbed Eliza. 'For I cannot care about her if she hates me like this!'

'Eliza, Eliza,' urged Mary. 'She does not hate you; she is all but a baby.'

'She keeps being sick!' screeched Eliza. 'How can I ever feed her, if she constantly vomits? – Oh, why did I ever have her?' She pointed a finger at her husband and narrowed her eyes as if she were delivering a curse. 'It is all because of you that I suffer. I was almost torn asunder bringing her to birth, but she does not appreciate that.'

'A baby cannot *appreciate*,' Mary murmured, clinging to the child. She gazed at the little red faced infant in her arms, who appeared to have entered the world with a terrible vengeance. A child had come into existence but her sister was almost insane.

Meredith's thick dark brows came together. 'It's unnatural,' he said coldly. 'Why can't you feed her?'

'How dare you!' Eliza screeched through her tears. 'But you do not know what it is like, do you? You are a man! You don't know how she almost kicked me to death in the womb, she hated me even then. – And don't look so shocked, it's the truth. She never liked me in there, and she likes me no better out here. She hates me I tell you, don't you see?' Her voice fell to a shudder. 'And I think I hate her too.'

Meredith glanced at her angrily.

'Don't look like that,' cried Mary. 'It isn't long since the child was delivered. My sister is unwell. Please treat her gently.' Again she felt the chaos of her life with her family. But the child fell asleep in her arms. Oh, the bliss of falling asleep. But it was only the sleep of exhaustion.

Later, as she travelled back, she felt overcome with anxiety. She couldn't accept what she'd experienced. Eliza had made a terrible mistake. What could be done?

Then came the letter, and it was just what Mary had expected. She read it with trembling hands. Her sister was in a predicament, earnestly begging for help. "He will kill me!" she wrote. "He has neither time nor patience to consider my needs. I am bruised both heart and soul. But I will not die or be put in a madhouse! Please don't be angry with me, Mary; do not be bitter towards me because I have failed. I was mistaken in thinking him good, for he is not. And I do not have the necessary strength for the baby. I bleed and am often in pain. Ned's wife is good and often comes calling. She has so much kindness in her soul. But I have nothing to give. I am lost . . ." Mary read on shakily, then came the appeal. Eliza had given her the name of a street near Ned's where they might meet up. She needed to talk. She could not come to Fanny's, she said, and Mary dared not visit her home, for Meredith had come to abhor her.

'You are pale,' said Fanny, entering the parlour that day. She was aware of Mary's tension over Eliza and saw she was holding a letter. 'Is it bad?'

'It's worse than bad, it's a tragedy,' sighed Mary. It was also, she thought, inevitable. 'It's happened,' she whispered. 'Meredith will never forgive me for interfering. But I had to, you see. I couldn't stay silent. I needed to give her my support.'

'Of course you did.' Fanny put her arm around her shoulder, and Mary loosened into tears.

'But it has come *so* soon,' Mary continued. 'I never expected it so quickly.'

'So what will you do?' asked Fanny.

'I must get her away from him somehow,' Mary answered shakily.

'But will she let you?' said Fanny, concerned and looking afraid.

Mary felt the pain of indecision. But the need to protect her sister was overwhelming. She braced herself. 'Help me not to be impulsive, Fanny,' she said. 'You know how I am. Let me be rational and sensible.' But the plaintive note in her voice spoke the truth. She would steal her sister away. She could not suffer as their mother had done. It dare not happen! 'I know I shall be the shameful incendiary in this shocking affair of a woman leaving her bedfellow,' she murmured, 'but I must try to get Eliza to a secret location. I have to find her somewhere to hide.'

'What, with the child?' said Fanny, looking troubled. 'She legally belongs to the father, you know. The law is bound to favour Meredith, however Eliza pleads. If a woman leaves her husband she is forced to relinquish her child.'

'She is not fit to take care of her,' said Mary wretchedly. 'And she doesn't want to. I have exchanged letters with Everina. We fear Eliza will deteriorate further and Bishop will then take serious action against her.' She bent her head and breathed in deeply. 'I think we know what that means don't we. But she cannot be ruled by her husband and child. For they *will* rule her, Fanny, oh yes, they will quite absorb her and think she is their slave. Her eyes will dull and her vitality will leave her for dead.'

For a few moments they were silent, thinking things through. 'You hold this man in very low esteem, that much is obvious,' Fanny said sighing.

Mary's eyes flashed with feeling; her mind was split in so many ways. 'I cannot forgive his contemptuous treatment of my sister.

He believes Eliza is his property and he can treat her however he likes. Is it not the law of the land? Her husband is her master. If matters do not proceed as he wishes then he roars like a lion and wants everyone to tremble before him. And he'll pretend at innocence if it suits him. He is very convincing there; I have tried to talk with him. He is certain the troubles are the fault of Eliza and you cannot rationalize with him, he has his own opinion and will not budge an inch. He thinks from an accustomed perspective.'

Mary sat for some time by the fire, the wounds she had suffered from her father aflame in her heart, and she could not suppress the burning sense of injustice.

She chose a lodging house in Hackney for Eliza's escape. As they travelled in the chaise, she saw that her sister's bloodshot eyes stared into space and she constantly bit at her wedding ring as if her very teeth might tear it away from her hand. The child, she moaned, was barely five months old, it was all too much, and she burst into tears saying she despised herself for leaving. But she did not want to turn back. Hackney would be safe, thought Mary, steeling herself against Eliza's sobs. Bishop would never find her there, but she felt as if she were embroiled in a fight, as if wrangling with the Fates for her sister's sanity.

And so they would take refuge in the home of a Mrs Dodd. It had taken some time to find a suitable place and someone they felt they could trust. "Well," Mrs Dodd had replied, when Mary had first approached her. "I don't want her bringing me trouble. This kind of thing could be awkward." "Each situation is different," Mary had pleaded softly, "and my sister needs care and tolerance."

The woman's features as she came to the door to greet them now, were aloof and detached and she scowled at them at first as they stood outside in the cold. Eliza shivered and gathered her cape more tightly about her shoulders. But the house was warm inside and the woman showed them to a room where there were two single beds, a wardrobe and a dresser. No more. But it was clean and cosy and would do for now, thought Mary, for she could think no further than that. There was a little window above one of the beds, and she gazed out on to the street, advising Eliza to keep herself hidden, so she wasn't noticed. She did not look like herself and she did not act like herself, she was a woman ready to scream. Should they need provisions, Mary said she would go out for them; Eliza must stay inside. It was a horrible bleak situation like imprisonment and Mary hated it.

After a couple of weeks, she wrote to Everina. "I fear that knock on the door," she said. "Eliza is often sleeping, she is so exhausted, but I am constantly ready for Meredith, even the creak of a floorboard stirs me." Eliza though, she noted, was less concerned about Bishop now, and one evening they dared to visit Ned.

'Hugh Skeys's brother has been to see Meredith,' Ned told them, pouring out a large glass of whiskey. 'I can't get involved though,' he said, and in a slightly pleading tone. 'Meredith seeks reconciliation and says he intends to try harder . . .'

'I know about that,' snapped Eliza, 'Everina brought me his letter. And I have replied with an emphatic no. I want to be rid of him.'

'You are bitter,' Ned said quietly. 'I am sad to see it. My pretty, celebrated sister has wilted like an un-watered rose.' He glanced at Mary with disapproval.

But wasn't this what she'd expected? Now she would be charged with procuring her sister's escape and destroying her marriage.

'And don't blame Mary,' said Eliza straightening, and with a newly found strength. 'I am able to think for myself, even if Meredith thinks I can't. I am grateful to Mary for helping me.' She ran her fingers through her curls, which shone as if lighted with life.

'Yes,' murmured Mary. 'She can.'

Ned's wife came backwards and forwards bringing refreshments.

'You must help me,' Eliza said to Ned, her eyes gleaming with hope. 'You must secure me a legal separation. I know you can do it.' She leant forward and grasped his hand.

It was just like the days of old, thought Mary, when Ned had been close and they were young, except the family had changed profoundly. Ned and his wife were happy. Their mother had suffered. And Ned was no longer a child, now he had power and could at least prevent further suffering for Eliza.

'Please, please Ned, I beg you,' said Eliza in earnest as Ned bent his head and sighed.

How passionately Eliza craved freedom, thought Mary, the need was there in her eyes, fixed determinedly on their brother. And just for that moment in time, he did not judge, but fell instead on his profession, the profession, which he believed was of fairness and justice. He did not speak of his personal feelings for Bishop and considered what could be done. 'Unless one has committed some serious crime, like bigamy or incest, then divorce is out of the question, of course,' he said thoughtfully. 'And I do not know if we can get him to release any money. He . . .'

'I can earn money myself,' Eliza interjected forcefully.

'But what will you do?' asked Ned, raising his eyebrows with confusion.

'I can sew and draw,' she said, her eyes lighting up at the thought. 'Mary and I have talked about it with Fanny. We intend to work hard and make money.'

Ned pursed his lips, baffled. They were all silent a moment. Ned's wife came to sit by.

'See how hard it is Ned,' sighed Mary, 'for a woman to have any independence. Eliza has so little choice. She could become a companion, as I did. God help her. Or she might take in sewing. It is easier for Fanny; she is quite established as an artist. Eliza can draw, but the standard required for publication is exceptionally high.'

'I shall work and learn,' Eliza insisted irritably. 'I have always had a talent for drawing. Meredith will see that the child is well taken care of.' She shrugged. 'He will say he is entitled to everything and that I deserve nothing. I do not think he ever loved me. Love is not in his nature, the lack of it disturbed me. I reached for it, but could not find it; there was no tree in his soul which bore such issue.' She laughed scornfully. 'I presume he does have a soul, for I believe God blesses us all with a soul.' She spoke quietly, a sudden pallor in her cheeks. Her eyes were busy with thought.

Mary sat tense and abstracted; Ned and his wife's faces were lit by the light from the fire. And Eliza's face was lit with profound change. She was springing back into life.

# 13

## Towards a Business

Baby Mary, however, Everina had written, was behaving like a child possessed, constantly kicking her legs and screaming, though the doctor could find no cause. Her shrieking terrified Bishop with its persistence and he accused Eliza of eluding her responsibilities, hiding away from her child and refusing to acknowledge her existence. Mary sent Fanny's brother to try to reason with Meredith, George was a good talker and could usually win in an argument, though he too thought Eliza in the wrong for having fled her child. And in any case Bishop had his own sad story, which man to man, George would probably believe. Bishop though sent ten guineas, which was certainly helpful, since Eliza was suffering financially. But had he sent her a fortune, she would never return, she said. She knew she had not a single right to anything and was by law her husband's property, but she would never return to Meredith. She saw herself now though as more of an individual, a grown woman with her own purpose, for in the midst of her tears she would raise her voice and proclaim she was Eliza Wollstonecraft and not Eliza Bishop. And as night-time fell each day Eliza grew stronger.

Everina came to the house surreptitiously on a wet Friday afternoon. 'You can't keep living like this,' she told them frustrated. 'It's very peculiar, you know. People are talking.' Mrs Dodd stood listening and looking, her arms folded as if she herself were weary of the odd situation.

'Might we have a little privacy please,' Mary said to her, smiling. Mrs Dodd sighed and walked away. Mary saw that Eliza looked contemptuously at Meredith's ten guineas in her hand, then dropped them in the pocket of her smock.

'It must seem like a rather grand gesture,' said Eliza laughing. 'He hopes for my return, all for a handful of guineas? Well, it isn't Eliza he wants; it is his own dignity, for people are probably wondering why his wife ran away. And just like you say, the baby has proved to be a problem.' At that she fell into a chair forlorn, and Mary saw that a look of delirium had returned to her eyes. 'But it has to be remembered, Mary,' she said, shaking her finger. 'I could not console her however I tried. You know how it was – *you* know!'

It hurt to see Eliza so frantic, constantly turning to the window like a captured animal. Mary knew that whilst she disavowed it, Eliza was afraid of her husband and what he might do if she did not comply with his demands.

She turned to Mary and spoke to her pleadingly. 'I was forced to leave her, or what would have happened to me?' she moaned. 'Well, we know the answer, don't we? You have helped me, dear Mary, and for that I am grateful.'

'He is obviously desperate,' Mary said with a sigh. But Bishop's slightly softer approach did not weaken her resolve and only reinforced her convictions. Though now she felt drained of energy.

Everina left before dark and Eliza went to crouch by the fire, resting her head in her hands. She always professed to have strength, but it rose and fell like the tide. Let women have rights! Mary maintained determinedly, and they would grow more rational and sensible and not succumb to the emotional bondages that tied them to misery. She felt this truth with every beat of her heart and her own tumultuous life had endorsed it. She thought on speedily – yes, that's what they'd do. They would form a business! They'd sell drawings and take in sewing. They were all proficient in sewing. Eliza could draw and Fanny's drawings were superb. She wrote to her straight away suggesting all three of them meet and decide what to do. Perhaps Ned would help them financially? She wrote to him also, outlining her ideas and begging his assistance. Several weeks passed by. Not a single word came from Ned. Fanny's reply however was favourable. She would come to talk with them; the prospect of a business excited her.

'But she vacillates,' said Eliza, reading through Fanny's letter. 'I fear she is unreliable.'

'She can be a little weak at times,' said Mary pondering. 'She forgives her father too readily and somehow thinks suffering is the way things must be. It is as well to remember that Bishop is friends with Hugh Skeys as well, and Skeys of course, is Fanny's chosen. She might be persuaded to take the side of Bishop.'

'Surely she wouldn't do that?' Eliza said earnestly.

Mary sighed and dropped her voice. 'She does not have my vision of the way things can be and steers her ship through the waters according to the weather. I care nothing for the weather, you see, and will fight for what I think is right.'

'Oh, but Mary,' murmured Eliza. 'Such a ship could crash on the rocks.' She went to sit by the window, a rigid figure just then in her own dark fear.

'Not if we remain strong,' said Mary. 'Ships at sea suffer changes in weather? The weather is its own master, and a good commander must battle it. We must be good commanders of life, Eliza, and look for comfort from that Being who will never desert us, and Divine Grace will be our guide.'

But there was no Divine Grace to be had. And Ned had told Everina he would not be drawn into the problems created by his sisters, he had a family of his own to consider and could not spread himself too thinly. But Fanny was enthusiastic and came to see them within the week, silently and obediently removing her cape and delivering herself to Mary's wishes. 'Well then,' she said, her eyes wide with wonder, and smiling as she spoke. 'But what do we know about business? – Not a lot.'

'But you and I can sell drawings,' said Eliza to Fanny. 'And Mary is excellent at sewing.'

'Do you really think it will work?' said Fanny, taking a seat. She frowned dubiously. 'Who will bring us their sewing? And who will buy our pictures. I sell mine to *Flora Londinensis*, of course. But I doubt I could sell them otherwise.'

'We can do it,' said Mary firmly. 'I shall write once more to Ned and ask again for his support.' But she hated this bowing and scraping to her brother, though there was nothing else for it. The eldest son in the family, he'd been taken good care of from the first. At a distance she loved him dearly, though she was angry at his entitlements. Why should men be so privileged, she thought irritably. And whenever she'd complained her father had called her a shrew. But she would not betray her plan. 'Think of how it would feel to earn our own money,' she laughed, clasping her hands with joy. 'We must think rationally and calmly and not depend on men for our identity.' She felt like a smouldering fire, a fire that would burst into flames when its moment was ready.

Fanny sat frowning and worried. 'But can we really succeed?' she said anxiously. Her parents, she said, did not approve of the enterprise and feared they would lose their investment.

'Of course we can,' said Mary. 'Have courage, my dear. Be strong. I shall continue to plead. If Ned will help us, I believe we can achieve great things.' She sat down and stared at the fire. Money was vital for independence, and how might money be acquired by a woman who was poor, except through surrendering the very quintessence of her self? There had to be a better way!

'And baby Mary?' Fanny whispered. 'Can we not get her? You say she is unwell.'

Eliza recoiled and put her hands to her face. 'It is far too awful to think of,' she groaned. 'I am in agony over it, but I dare not visit her and no-one can bring her here. My heart aches for my child, but what can I do?'

Mary looked at them both, searching her mind for an answer. They could not steal the baby. Eliza had abandoned her and the law was on Meredith's side. And just as Fanny sat yearning for her lover, Eliza sat yearning for her baby.

And Fanny did vacillate, just as Eliza had warned; she grew disloyal, writing to Ned of her concerns, saying she had seen Eliza's efforts with drawing and feared it would never be sold. She apologised for having encouraged her and owned that dear as she was, her work was too amateur for business. But she admitted she had a passion for the relentless flame that was Mary. It was almost as if she could not survive without it. Mary's flame warmed her, gladdened her, enchanted her. And when it entered her they burned as if with the same torch. But she did not think Mary would be happy drawing and sewing. They needed another idea.

Mary got very little sleep that fortnight as she thought up scheme after scheme and talked endlessly with Eliza and Fanny about the way girls needed to open up their minds to knowledge. Then came the thought of a school in Newington Green. It would be such a daring venture and there was much competition in the area, but the plan excited her. 'According to Plato, "Knowledge is the food of the soul"', she said, smiling at Fanny. 'And it is also the food of progress. We will educate young women and teach them to think about fairness and equality. They will learn how to see themselves differently. We will be in the business of teaching and learning, what could be more important?' In her craving for parity with men she did not care that Ned doubted her and saw her as troublesome, would he not rejoice when he saw her at last succeed? She would hide her anxieties from Eliza and Fanny and lead. Life needed leaders. All would be well, she told them.

And the idea of the school rose high in her mind and buoyed her along. She thought hard about how they would do it – costs, profits and possible losses. Would they take lodgers? If so they would need a house that was big enough, and money must be borrowed from somewhere. Who might they ask?

They ate frugally and saved. And Ned gave financial assistance. They didn't mind going without for they all had a vision. Through thinking, reading and planning, they were getting to think like business women, paying attention to detail, carefully considering finances and writing things down.

In the meantime however, baby Mary grew increasingly weak. It was chiefly the difference in the tone of Everina's letters that suggested something serious, and on several occasions Eliza had suggested she go to see Meredith, but she'd changed her mind, deciding it would probably just weaken her resolve and she would find herself back in the trap from which she'd escaped. But from the gaps in the windows the wind brought sounds of a crying child and she was constantly anxious. To her horror her baby passed away, just before her first birthday. Phantoms descended on her then. She wailed and paced the house, said she was damned, threatened to kill herself and said she was worthless. The others gazed downwards confused. The conflict was gone, but so was the child. They were all overcome.

'We've been quite neglectful,' said Mary. 'I'm so sorry, Eliza. We ought to have fought him. The child should have been here. He kept her from you, and it isn't your fault. Did you not send him letters? Did we not plead? Were we to smuggle her away?' Mary wept as she spoke.

'It isn't *your* fault either,' said Eliza, also weeping. 'The sad little creature had always been sick. But I might have done more. I ought to have cared for her better.'

'Well,' said Fanny quietly. 'We can always do more. But we do what we do.'

Mary glanced at her. She knew Fanny was thinking about Hugh Skeys in Lisbon who had asked her to marry him. At that moment, her sister and her friend were hardly in mind to start a school. Mary pressed her lips tightly together, she had determined to confront all obstacles with strength but it was hard to find it today. She looked at herself in the mirror. Her face was blanched and her eyes had lost hope. Beginning a school was far from her mind now baby Mary was dead. She must help Eliza write to Ned, but what would they say? Eliza sat in a chair by the fire sobbing and moaning but all words had gone. Fanny stood silent by the window. Mary knew that her thoughts looked towards Lisbon. She would not stay with them long. She wanted Hugh Skeys.

At the end of the week, Mrs Clare came to visit. She brought them food and wine and an offer of financial assistance to help start the school, if they still had it in mind. She promised to always support them.

In spite of all difficulties Mary's hope held strong. "In general terms there is no such thing as happiness on Earth," she wrote to Everina, that day. "It requires severe disappointment to make us forbear to see it and be contented with that endeavour to prepare ourselves for something better." She could feel the blood rising to her cheeks as she wrote. Did not affliction educate? Everina must join them, she said, for what they intended to do was vital to the lives of women. Eliza was recovering and had not fallen into the depression that so often claimed her. She was morose but coping. It was good.

The idea for the school burgeoned in Mary's mind. Truths and virtues might be found in the natural world, she thought, and nature offered the best understanding of life. In this she followed Rousseau. She also had an aversion to rote learning. Children might repeat facts so they did not forget them, and facts might add to a bigger idea, which was important, for ideas were related, but facts alone were like disorientated stars in a lonely universe. Other things came to her mind which she scribbled down quickly. Much had to change.

And help was at hand. Along with Mrs Clare, a very good woman by the name of Mrs Burgh, "a strong minded widow of excellent character", Mary wrote to Everina, had generously provided a loan to help with their project, and she was also helping them search for a house big enough to use for a school. They were not forsaken. The Reverend James Burgh, her deceased husband, had been a radical thinker and author and a highly respected schoolmaster in nearby Newington Green, a place where affluent merchants resided in grand Georgian houses surrounded by leafy elms. On the northern side dissenters got together in a chapel, and though she was of Anglican persuasion, Mary enjoyed the vitality of dissenting ideas and the excitement of new developments. 'I would like to hear their arguments. They have strong opinions and are eager to give them life,' she told Eliza as they sat in the parlour that morning. 'And they do not have the least support from the state. They spread their convictions purely from the strength of their feelings.'

'And what do they say?' Eliza asked curiously.

'That's what I want to find out,' said Mary pondering. 'Their thoughts are complex. They talk together a lot, to sort out ideas I imagine. I suspect they argue atrociously. Mrs Burgh's husband wrote *The Dignity of Human Nature and Thoughts on Education*, I believe it is an excellent book. The dissenters are interested in change and growth. There's a great deal to learn from them I think.'

'Then I shall learn, too,' said Eliza, intently. She turned to Fanny who had arrived yesterday on a visit. 'And what about you?' she asked her. 'Will you come with us?'

'Where to?' said Fanny abstractedly.

'To hear the dissenters at Newington Green,' said Eliza.

'I'm not sure,' said Fanny, dabbing her nose with a hanky and looking downwards. 'I know of the Meeting House, but I fear their talk might tire me.'

Mary could see that Fanny's thoughts as well as her heart were with Skeys. 'I have invited Everina to join us,' she said undaunted. 'She is more than eager. We shall soon have larger accommodation, then she will come on board.' But Mary felt she was speaking into a void. Fanny had no intentions of staying in England; she would join Hugh Skeys in Lisbon.

# 14

## *More Thoughts on the Future*

A good sized house suitable for the school was found in Newington Green and Everina arrived in due course. They employed a maid and a cook and fashioned a prospectus, advertising for pupils and lodgers. At last, thought Mary, their lives were in their own hands. It was a thrilling time and they all peered over the prospectus reverentially as if it were a bible. They took on the manner of teachers, turning the pages of their books in a scholarly fashion and making profuse notes. They were on a different footing and believed they were on their way to something important.

'I used to be young,' Mary said quietly, her eyes moving by turns between Fanny and her sisters. 'Once, you know, I was young.'

'And now you are not?' said Eliza, frowning curiously. 'You are hardly old, Mary.'

'No, but I feel I've matured.' She looked at Fanny, who gazed at the roof abstracted. 'You are still with us, my dear, aren't you,' she asked, a little uncertain.

'Of course,' Fanny replied vaguely. 'It is the best work anyone can do.'

But Everina knew the truth. Fanny had never for a single moment been with them. Not for a second. Her mind had always been in Lisbon.

The school, however, was set in motion and they each put their shoulder to the wheel. But Eliza mourned the death of her baby. No matter how she tried, she could not remove the guilt from her soul and it worsened by the day. She went pale when she spoke of the passing of her child, her voice trembled and she whispered the baby's name over and over as if it were a kind of incantation that might bring her back into being. But the dead never returned, and Mary told her she must forgive herself for any imaginary sins for life itself demanded it and the dark side would always torment her.

But Eliza's vitality had left her. It was as if she belonged elsewhere in a realm between life and death. There were days when Mary thought her sister might try to kill herself, but Eliza had hidden strengths and she would try to help her rediscover them. There were days she taught well, other days she said she could scarcely think. She taught in fits and starts sometimes smiling and kind, then suddenly depressed, even weeping, having to take a seat before her class who stared at her in confused silence. It would not do, Mary pondered, the situation was precarious. People would remove their girls if something didn't change, word got round very quickly in Newington Green.

Fanny still pined for Hugh Skeys who wanted to marry her. And Eliza struggled with her mind. Alone in her room, Mary felt instinctively that her enterprise was doomed to failure. Were her aspirations just dreams, fading like the summer sun?

There was a stillness in the parlour that morning where Mary sat alone with Eliza. Fanny and Everina were out walking in the woodland. A few of the girls had been removed from the school by their parents, those who were left were a thin murmur of sound elsewhere in the house. Today was one of her sister's better days, thought Mary, she was coming to see there was life outside her despair and was gradually getting better. 'I wish I had Fanny's enthusiasm for art,' she said, lifting her head from her book and trying to smile. 'She teaches drawing so well, and I know it comes from her heart. How good it must be when it comes from the heart, like that. Teaching doesn't come naturally to me; I must always plan out my lessons so carefully before I deliver them.' She bent again to her book then looked up curiously. 'Carl Linnaeus, you know, couldn't draw people and landscapes very well. Don't you think it's strange?' She turned to a page of his sketches. Eliza was criticised for want of a confident hand and sometimes spoke grudgingly of others. 'His sketches of plants and insects are almost as good as Fanny's, but only almost, and the rest of his work is wanting.'

'I doubt Fanny will stay much longer,' Mary said pondering. 'She will go to Skeys in Lisbon.'

'To be married?' Eliza threw back her head indignantly. 'She's a fool if she marries Skeys.'

'My exact sentiments,' Mary said flatly. 'But she says she loves him.'

'How delightful,' said Eliza, passing her a wry smile. 'And you, my dear?' She gazed at Mary and waited. 'Do you want a lover too?'

'Ah, love is a beautiful thing,' Mary said wistfully. 'But it's so destructive sometimes. I'm not sure it's meant for this earth. It's as if it belongs elsewhere, in heaven perhaps with the angels, who are better than we are of course.'

'You want too much,' said Eliza quietly. 'Perhaps your idea of love is too spiritual. We must not expect perfection, we cannot give it ourselves, so why expect it.'

'But we can *feel* it,' said Mary earnestly. 'And is not feeling real?' Eliza sighed loudly.

Mary put out her hand as if to stop the flow of talk. 'Hush, do not speak of it now,' she whispered. 'It disturbs me.'

'Fanny is going to leave us and it upsets you. But what sort of life will she have if she stays?' Eliza became subdued and thoughtful. 'I do not believe our school can succeed anyway. We have good times, I know, but we tumble over each other's words. Three sisters are bound to be in conflict and the teaching suffers. The lodgers have heard us arguing, you know, one of them told me. Everina and I will be back on Ned's doorstep 'ere long. Ah, poor Ned.'

'Poor Ned, indeed,' said Mary straightening. 'You must always remember Eliza, he had a far better start than we did. We are as hatchlings pushed out of the nest and made to fend for ourselves, unless we go squawking to some man for shelter and protection.'

'Perhaps it is what we teach that causes us to fail,' said Eliza pondering. 'The girls will take our values back home, and their parents might frown. Our vision of education is different from that of the other schools around here.'

'Well, yes, and I hope it is,' said Mary. 'That is my exact intention. Our school has the home at its heart and learning is imbibed with morals and self discipline. It is always difficult to change things, I know, people find change exhausting. We teach our pupils values, but we do not teach them artificial manners, and that must be a blessing. Honesty is vital. Also, their reading must be part of their thinking as a whole, rather than practised passages learned for effect, which is far too often the case.' She knew that her sisters believed in her ideas, but there were awkward times with the girls, who heard of different ways of learning and must contend with their parents' insecurities. Mary taught within a framework of love, her sisters asserted, and an essential truth that had grown from the roots of her life, a life they had shared. She took comfort in the thought. 'We shall succeed, Eliza,' she added firmly. 'I will not allow misguided dolts to triumph. Some of the mothers appal me. "Oh, how I love the sublimity of Milton, the elegance and harmony of Pope!" they coo. But they say what is fashionable, all that matters is the contemporary way of thinking and should you inquire any further they gaze at you with mindless eyes and defer to their husbands. – I deplore the way girls are made to become demure, fainting creatures just to please men. Those who are lucky enough to have schooling should be taught how to *think*, which means knowing first they have a mind to think with, a mind with its own observations and opinions so that they need not take the first offer of marriage that comes their way. – And they should not see themselves as weak and artificial, they must speak from their minds, rationally and with vigour.' She talked quickly, this was everything to her.

'But what of their role as mothers?' said Eliza. 'They can't just forget they are mothers – and weaknesses come with motherhood, there is always a need for self-sacrifice, mothers can feel so helpless, which is when we need men to be kind.'

'Ah yes, men must be kind.' Mary laughed briefly. 'We always need men to be kind, don't we? We are reliant on them for money, you see, oh, for our very lives! I do not suggest that a woman forget her role in the home; the love she provides, the guidance and care, oh, no. The role of mother is sacrosanct, as is the role of a wife, but those roles can also be intelligent. What use is a mother or a wife without informed opinions? She will simply fall back on gossip and nonsense and care nothing for important issues or the world at large.'

Eliza braced herself and breathed in deeply. 'I am not educated like Meredith, did that make me dull and stupid?' She stared at Mary, waiting.

'That's not what I mean, and you know it. You are intelligent, Eliza, and you have used your intellect as far as you can, but you have never been allowed to blossom.'

'Men like women to be silent,' Eliza said quietly.

'They do. And in such a situation a woman is brutalized if she dares speak up for herself. – I wonder if Meredith was faithful. You have never thought of it, have you?'

Eliza looked at her resentfully. 'I never considered infidelity. But I . . .'

'And you? – Did you ever look at others after you were married?' Mary held her gaze. 'Did you ever desire other men?'

'I was married. What do you mean?'

'Men look at other women, and women look at other men,' she said half smiling, 'regardless of marriage. We too are sexual beings, but self-restraint comes first with women, and men too should put duty over sexual pleasure if a marriage is to work. Rationality comes before feeling. Feelings are vital, of course, but feelings within duty and loyalty, that's what I mean. There ought to be harmony between action and feeling just as there is harmony in nature. There are divine laws in nature we must try to understand, but they exist within the law of reason; a *natural* reason. For the sake of a higher cause we must be disciplined, for that which is unreasonable brings along its curses.'

'You think too much,' murmured Eliza. 'Ned always says it and he's right.'

But Mary went on intensely. 'I do not suggest we eliminate

feeling, not at all, but that we practice within it the principle of reason, for when human beings give complete free rein to feeling and forget their responsibilities a price will be paid, for nature retaliates if its natural order is disturbed. So with nature, so with us.' Her voice fell to a murmur. 'But Fanny could be fortunate. She and Hugh Skeys are *friends*. I believe he respects her.' Her shoulders rose and fell. 'I pray it is so.'

'Is she to leave us soon?' asked Eliza. She sighed.

Mary could hear a hint of envy in her tone. 'Yes, I believe she is. But as you have seen, she is none too well at present; she has a harsh persistent cough. I hope that the air in Portugal will be of benefit.'

'You are sad that she is leaving though, aren't you.' Eliza looked at her straight. – 'You can hardly bear it.'

There was a silence.

'Yes,' Mary said finally. 'It will break my heart to lose her. But she loves him.'

'And *you* love her,' Eliza said quietly, focusing her mind on a flower she was trying to draw.

'Please don't say it like that,' Mary said softly.

'But it isn't fair,' murmured Eliza.

'What isn't fair?'

'That you love her best.'

'Do I?' Mary said, awkward and hurt.

Eliza looked up then away. 'Of course you do. You always have. But I cannot think as she does. I cannot draw as she does. I am nothing compared with Fanny.'

Mary touched her arm gently. Eliza continued with her drawing. 'It is different, that's all,' she said tenderly. 'I can never be anything to you except Mary Wollstonecraft at home, Mary your sister, Mary being abused, Mary being angry. I have to be more than that.' She breathed a sigh of despair. 'Family will never let you grow; they always want to keep you as you were, with all your pains and weaknesses. Fanny has made me feel strong.'

'And now she leaves you for a man.' There was a slight mocking tone in Eliza's voice.

'Yes, but I always expected it. That is how it must be.'

'And I am no comfort, of course,' said Eliza brooding. 'All because like Ned, I know only too well that you are sometimes sulky and overbearing.'

'Well, there we are,' sighed Mary. 'I think too much and I talk too much.' She looked in on Eliza's drawing. 'You have improved with your sketches of flowers, Eliza. And you have brought out the talent in a few of our girls too, that is all to be applauded.'

'Would you have preferred to be a man?' Eliza asked boldly, looking up.

Mary laughed briefly. 'I am envious of their privileges, oh yes. But I am proud to be a woman. What life does to women though disgusts me.'

'You are right, dear sister. And how I wish others could hear you. But women shut off their ears to what they don't like. That way it is far more comfortable.' She gazed again at her drawing. 'Though I cannot know what life would be like had Meredith and I been better suited. Is Skeys suited to Fanny?'

'I don't know. But Fanny would think so and I value her opinion. But I do not think she should hand herself over to marriage so soon.'

'You advised me the same, but I did not listen. The urge to be married is strong for women. Marriage makes you feel respectable. You are at last made whole.' She laughed and shook her head. 'It is what we are made to believe.' For a few moments they were silent. 'I think Meredith might have put me in the madhouse you know, I felt so wretched.'

'But you escaped, you see. You are free.'

'But my baby is dead,' murmured Eliza, collapsing in on herself as she always did when she talked about the death of the baby. 'Perhaps it was I who killed her.'

'You can say it as often as you like, but it doesn't make it true. What do you want me to do, Eliza? Do you want me to call you a murderer, a devil?' Just then there was only dark frustration and tension between them, for who could say why the baby had died, babies died all the time. 'Perhaps we should go to the dissenting chapel tomorrow and hear what they're saying. It might distract us a little and give us other things to think of. I believe Reverend

Price is an excellent speaker, he is deeply interested in moral philosophy and corresponds with notable people like Thomas Jefferson.'

Eliza looked at her intently. 'I have heard about Thomas Jefferson from Ned, something to do with America becoming independent I think, though I don't know very much about it.'

Mary smiled with pleasure. It was good to have Eliza interested in politics. And it seemed she had talked with Ned about the ways of the world. The woman in her was developing quickly; she was less of a stranger now. 'Jefferson was the primary author of the Declaration of Independence,' she said. 'I believe he is a man of many talents and can read five languages.' She was happy to talk about Jefferson, a man she admired. 'He also likes to gaze at the stars and the planets and try to discover their secrets. And he keeps a book with facts and drawings of the plants and animals in Virginia where he lives.'

'He is interested in both heaven and earth,' smiled Eliza thoughtfully. 'I want to know more about this man.'

A thrill went through Mary's veins as she listened to her sister's words. The two of them had formed a beautiful tender bond in childhood and it remained. Mary looked at her in silence. Did she not realise that what Jefferson had done must also be done for the rights of women? Words must be shouted from the hills, written in books, passed by word of mouth! Her thoughts had the force of a hurricane, but how to release that energy into a conditioned world of women was hard to imagine.

'I do want to learn things,' said Eliza, 'the same as you do. And I would much rather listen to Ned than tidy the parlour. I remember you told me that the famous Rousseau thought that a woman's education was only to help serve men. That made me very angry and I started arguing with Meredith, or trying to argue that was. He refused to listen. I thought about it, you see. But Ned said I wasn't to talk with you, Mary, because you would make me unhappy.'

'Ah, I am dangerous, am I?' laughed Mary. 'He likes to think I am dangerous.'

'But if what you say is true, then should it not be said?' asked Eliza, frowning.

'Not by a woman, Eliza. You are better to put your head in the sand than listen to me.' She sat down frustrated.

'It doesn't matter,' cried Eliza. 'Don't be upset. Meredith was cruel anyway. If Ned thinks I made Meredith cruel – and he might you know, I've seen how he looks at me – but he's wrong. Meredith likes to boss and I won't be dominated. I won't be docile. If a man wants a woman to be compliant and subservient, like Rousseau professes, then a man must be kind. They will not get gentleness from a woman if their behaviour becomes tyrannical.'

'I have made you into a man-hater, my dear,' Mary said sadly.

'Not so,' said Eliza. 'I think for myself. You have simply shown me the way, and for that I'm thankful. I was locked in darkness before. Now I can see more clearly.'

Mary's cheeks burned with emotion. 'I have changed you, my dear,' she said shakily. 'I have given you a new song, it is unfamiliar, it is a song you must sing in a lonely place and I fear it. Nevermore will you be the laughing Eliza.'

'I did not laugh very much,' Eliza said, suddenly serious. 'Sometimes I pretended I was happy for the sake of mother. I am happier now in my soul, I know it. It is a real happiness and I'll grow from it in time. I do not abuse your words, Mary. I value them. I too am impatient of the way things are with women and much has to change. But oh, what a burden it is.'

At that she broke off to gather her books. She had a lesson to teach and her pupils were waiting in her room.

# 15

# *Newington Green Unitarian Church*

Newington Green was an open space of land in north London. Here stood the chapel where the Reverend Richard Price gave his sermons. It didn't take long to get there from where Mary and Eliza were lodging and they'd decided to make an appearance that morning. A mild autumn breeze blew across their faces as they went, migrating birds flew across the sky close by, neat and in line as if an other-worldly hand were tracing their flight in the streaks of pink and gold. 'See how they all fly together!' cried Eliza, pointing. 'And so much noisy excitement.' They stopped and watched. 'Soon they'll be gone,' she said sadly. 'And the land will grow silent.'

They passed up the hill, then gazed ahead at the little Unitarian chapel, a small intriguing place, thought Mary, scarcely bigger than a large London mansion. It had been opened in 1750 by Mrs Burgh's husband, the Reverend James Burgh, who was a British Whig politician and an important promoter of radical reforms. His book *Political Disquisitions* argued for universal suffrage, religious liberty and freedom of expression, and Mary reflected as they walked that his widow had come to her aid when she'd wanted to start her school, James Burgh would have applauded that.

The little chapel was afire with explosive opinion and speculation. Anti-Trinitarian notions had abounded for ages, Mary pondered, and in many places Unitarianism was making good ground. She was, however, Anglican at heart. But she challenged the authoritarianism of the Anglican Church and concluded its slavery to forms sometimes made religion seem farcical. She would only submit to the moral laws which her reason discerned as true! She took issue, as well, with the doctrine of original sin. People were not by nature evil, no, no, they were not! There had to be room for the expansion of the human soul in all matters. God was in nature all about her and she had felt the force of the creator most strongly while walking with Fanny. True grace arrived with an independent mind, of that she was certain, people were victims of society, it brutally defined their roles and how they should live, and often according to falsities.

She gazed on the group who stood at the entrance to the chapel. Doctor Price indeed had a wealth of interesting acquaintances, though there were only men there today. She must somehow find a place for herself amongst them, a place amongst men. Her mind moved quickly. She knew her worth, yet in the private part of her being when she lay thoughtful in her bed, she felt a great sense of aloneness, almost akin to fear. After the days of Cromwell and the restoration of Charles II, many people in England and Wales who did not belong to the Church of England felt spiritually lost. Was she spiritually lost she asked herself, perhaps Price might teach her how to find herself again. She was impatient of the Anglican Church. The sermons no longer reached her, and the angels she'd seen in childhood had all departed. She thought she might find an affinity with the dissenters. Public Office had been restricted to Anglicans and the Act of Uniformity had made hostilities worse. A lot of clergymen had left the established church and various struggles had ensued causing much dissent. To add to the fray, non-conformist clerics were prohibited from living within five miles of a parish from which they'd been banned, so wherever a minister went, his supporters followed. And this had continued until the Act of Toleration in 1689, whereby various oaths of allegiance and registration of a chapel's location and leader allowed for freedom of worship to certain gatherings. But existing social restrictions, such as exclusion from political office and the universities brought constant outrage.

'Let us stand here and listen,' said Mary, touching Eliza's arm. 'We are early.'

'Do you think the sermon will be long?' asked Eliza.

'I don't know,' said Mary, her eyes scanning the group. 'But once it is started we must wait until it is finished, just as in the Anglican Church. And I want to speak with Doctor Price if I can.'

'Will you speak to him of women's rights?' asked Eliza, nervously. 'You know how people look at you, Mary, if you do. You are ever so hard on men.'

'I probably shall, but Price is popular, as you see.' She straightened. 'Though I am just as important as any of those men, and I shall have my say.' She spoke firmly with purpose.

Eliza's face looked pained. She worked her fingers together in her thin leather gloves. 'Don't embarrass us, will you.' She sighed, worriedly. 'It's just that you talk so earnestly sometimes and I wonder you don't get tangled up. And whatever you say, nothing will ever change.'

'Not if we don't fight,' Mary said earnestly. 'Make no mistake Eliza; Doctor Price is deeply concerned about the rights of women, as much as he is about anything. He is a passionate social reformer and his chapel is visited by the likes of John Adams and Benjamin Franklyn, writers and campaigners too, like Thomas Paine. Philosophers, scientists, writers, poets, all manner of people come to hear him.' She breathed in deeply at the thought, and her senses tuned in, she would find her place amongst them all, only at their peril dare they ignore her!

Price's voice rose up from the group as he talked, he was strong and certain of his notions, warm to others and encouraging. Mary tidied her soft fair curls which had blown about in the breeze. She was a good looking woman, naturally so, without all the daubing of the face most women seemed to like. And Ned had said she walked with a sway. Did she really walk with a sway? She felt vaguely uncomfortable needing to even consider it. But what could be wrong with beauty? Wasn't beauty admired for itself – beautiful flowers, beautiful birds and beautiful scents were all admired and cherished. Fanny would sometimes play the coquette and make

145

men laugh, though Mary would never have done so herself. Or perhaps she would . . . She thought of Joshua Waterhouse in Bath . . . Yes, perhaps she would.

'I doubt you'd get elbowed out,' said Eliza, smiling. 'No-one talks better than you do.'

'Well, this chapel will change our lives, Eliza,' she said as they both stood musing. The sight of the building roused her. She knew that her soul was big and could fly to heights from which she could view humanity with clarity and try to make sense of it all. She would speak. She would write. But when and how would she do what had to be done? She had so little money and when would she find the time? There was life and death and the space in between where you consumed yourself. But if the mind seized a truth, should it not set it free, unlock the door to what mattered, the door to progress and liberty? Doctor Price had argued in support of the revolt of the colonies and believed in the American Revolution. He had rejected the notion of original sin and trusted human nature was perfectible. But how could a woman's nature become perfectible if she did not get an education? Would it not struggle in the dark reaches of ignorance?

Mary leant towards Eliza. 'Listen,' she whispered. 'They are talking about population, can you hear them? Come, let us move in further.' She enjoyed how the men argued; the way the tension rose and fell with their emotions. Thoughts surged through her mind. Her face screwed into a frown. Population? If there was better care for women in childbirth, proper instruction, then babies and their mothers wouldn't die. She wondered if anyone would say so . . . For now she'd stay silent and stand by the corner until everyone had gone into church.

'Your essay about the population of England was most valuable, Reverend,' a tall, thin fellow was saying. 'There is a lot of enquiry into sicknesses at present. Your work was of great interest, to young Thomas Malthus, I'm told, who I happen to know very well.'

'I believe it was,' said Price, in a joyfully alive manner. 'He sent me a letter.'

The man went on. 'Priestley's contribution was excellent too.

Undoubtedly the spread of smallpox is very disturbing; it is quite ubiquitous. Thousands die every year and survivors often go blind.' He glanced around at the others for confirmation.

'Young Malthus does not agree that human nature is perfectible,' said Price, suddenly thoughtful. 'And he believes population is consistently checked by famine and disease – and rightly so, it is a sort of mathematical equation for him. But young Thomas has a great deal of work ahead of him, and he will do it. He is a very discerning young man.'

'But I believe he sees famine and disease as divinely imposed, a sort of check,' said the tall thin man.

Price scratched his head and frowned. 'We must continue to investigate the causes of sickness. Too many people are dying.'

'The Poor Laws are an important factor,' said another member of the gathering. 'The Society published something just recently.'

'Ah yes,' said Price pondering. He turned to a sturdy figure beside him. 'Johnson my friend, you are very quiet this morning. Does our talk lack lustre? Please recite us a poem. I believe you have published something of late by Cowper, and at your own expense I'm told.'

'Ah Cowper, yes. And I was well rewarded too, it had very good sales.' Johnson chanted softly as they all listened:

> *"God moves in a mysterious way*
> *His wonders to perform;*
> *He plants His footsteps in the sea,*
> *And rides upon the storm.*
>
> *Deep in unfathomable mines*
> *Of never-failing skill*
> *He treasures up His bright designs,*
> *And works His sovereign will."*

'Excellent!' cried Johnson, clapping his hands. 'I learned them by heart.'

'Well done, well done!' laughed Price.

So this was Joseph Johnson! – Mary's heart beat fast as she listened. Johnson was a man who took risks for freedom and liberty, an established and respected publisher, who writers sought out for his bravery, oh yes, he was brave, very brave, brave enough to publish all manner of opinions. His home, Mrs Burgh had told her, was a centre for all kinds of discourse. But he was often unpopular when disputes arose over notions he'd brought to attention. In 1777 he had brought out the book, *Laws Respecting Women, as they Regard Their Natural Rights.* It was a work to help vulnerable women and Johnson had published it anonymously, but Mrs Burgh had told her she knew the name of the author though would never disclose it. Mary had thought the author might be the dear Mrs Burgh herself, for she was active and immensely capable.

'Come Eliza, let us go in,' said Mary. 'People are entering the chapel.' As they moved to pass by the group, Reverend Price turned and addressed them.

'Forgive my rudeness,' he called, bowing briefly. 'I believe you have come from the school? Mrs Burgh said we might have your company.'

'Ah, did she,' said Mary, suddenly embarrassed. 'Yes, I am Mary Wollstonecraft and this is my sister Eliza.' She spoke quickly and nervously. 'I am glad to meet you Reverend Price. I am loaded with so many questions; you had best avoid me for I shall fire them at you like bullets! – My sister too wants to speak with you when you are free.' She laughed and saw others were watching. Eliza flushed and bent her head; she always found it hard to speak when being introduced.

'I'm afraid I have spent too long out here,' Price laughed. 'We are such an excitable bunch. Now I am running late.'

'Mary Wollstonecraft?' said one of the men, pushing forward. 'Ah, the gorgon herself – well, according to your brother, that is!' He stared at her and smiled.

'I see' said Mary a little abashed. 'Is that what he says?' She looked at the man straight, annoyed by his bold manner.

'Have no fear,' laughed the stranger. 'He spoke of you proudly.'

'Did he, indeed, yet he calls me a gorgon. I shall ask him about it. Where did you meet him?' She spoke in the way of a rebuke.

'He was walking on the street in Hoxton a while ago, near the Academy. I was talking with friends . . .'

'It is wrong to refer to a sister like that,' she said, looking annoyed. Ned hadn't mentioned it. What liberties he took sometimes! She felt Eliza touch her sleeve.

'Is there a problem?' Reverend Price asked, concerned. The others had entered the chapel.

'Not at all,' said Mary. She gave the stranger a look of disdain. 'A sensitive disposition like mine is hard to endure. I apologise.'

'Godwin is a very fine fellow, my dear. He is always kind and friendly. What has he said to upset you?' He gazed at Godwin and frowned.

'William Godwin,' said the stranger, putting out his hand and bowing lightly. 'A spontaneous disposition like mine is also hard to endure. I am sorry. I did come forward rather quickly.'

But Mary's spirits had sunk. She turned to Eliza who had read the situation correctly.

'Shall we go back?' said Eliza with a sigh.

'Not because of me, I hope,' said Godwin, looking sad.

'No, because of me,' said Mary in a low and vanquished voice.

'My sister is a little tired,' faltered Eliza.

Price stood watching them confused. 'Well, I hope to see you again,' he said hopefully, a little bewildered.

'Of course,' said Mary. She did not know what to do with herself when her spirits sank low. They hurried away from the chapel fleet footed as mountain hares. She wondered if she would ever visit it again.

# 16

## *The Lure of Lisbon*

Mary did not visit the chapel the following Sunday, nor indeed the Sunday after. February proved viciously cold and matters moved quickly. Fanny left London and went to Hugh Skeys in Portugal and they were married. Then March was soon on its way. Wild daffodils swayed in the hedgerows, buds burst from the trees and the blinding rays of the sun enticed them to flower. Streams rumbled furiously past as she walked the woodland paths she had walked with Fanny. All about her was busy, yet she could not feel her life moving within her. She might have melted into shadow for such was her substance. She was full of bitterness towards Skeys for stealing her beloved Fanny Blood, who now had the name of Fanny *Skeys; it* sounded passionless and cold.

Everina and Eliza were as ghosts wandering the house. They were all three teaching competently, yet Mary felt somehow defeated and constantly thought of Fanny. – Was she happy with Skeys? Was she *really* happy? How was her health? Did he care for her as much as he ought? She built the fire in the parlour higher, it brought more warmth to the household and the house warmed to satisfaction, though her heart did not. Always, she awaited a letter. When the church bells rang, her thoughts turned to Fanny and she imagined them calling her, though not to prayer but to her friend who needed her. Did she not whisper from the shadows? Was she not there in the darkness? She tried not to think of the blood on her lips when they'd parted at the harbour, the cough that was slowly getting worse. Would Skeys allow a little brandy in her tea; it always eased the pain in her chest. Every hour was like forever. But she must not get carried away; her imagination was powerful and could weaken her. She had to be rational. Always rational! But try as she would her emotions always took charge. George, Fanny's brother, had written that her health had grown worse, and what's more she had become pregnant.

'She ought to have told me in her letter,' Mary said moodily to Eliza that evening. 'Why must I hear it from George?' She gazed at Eliza puzzled.

'Perhaps a letter got lost.' Eliza spoke gently, trying to ease Mary's irritation. 'You know how the post is.' She was making a drawing, but the lead in her pencil kept breaking. The lead was weak, she said, she needed another pencil, for however often she sharpened it, it was certain to break again. She carried on talking. 'Or maybe she didn't want to worry you. She knows how you burden yourself. You are easily overwhelmed, my dear.'

Mary shrugged, annoyed that her love seemed obsessive. 'Well, I know what she *needs* and I'm not sure Skeys can provide it. Fanny has a great core of strength, but I fear the pregnancy could break it, and if her cough has grown worse, heaven knows what might happen.' She shook her head worriedly. 'I am so far away . . .'

'You mustn't interfere,' said Eliza, in a tone of admonition. 'You know how Ned says you meddle.'

'Does he?' Mary looked thoughtful for a moment. 'Well, if we want appreciation, the last place we'll find it is in our family. But I really don't care what Ned says.' She shrugged with annoyance. 'I'm concerned about people, you see, whereas Ned thinks only of himself.'

'You like taking over,' Eliza said straightening. 'Oh, you do, you do. You relish the power.'

'"*Power*"' gasped Mary, taken aback and offended. 'I fear for people, that's all. I just want to help. But power and fear are part of each other anyway; we must decide what each of them is made of and act accordingly. They are cunning spirits.'

'You put such strains on yourself,' Eliza said tensely. She went to sit by the fire and gazed at the flames. 'It disturbs me to have you constantly concerned. It affects my health. And yours too I should think. The world will go on without us, whether we are in it or not, if you lose your mind because you can't control your thoughts, what then?'

Mary felt suddenly cold and shook her head confusedly. She was getting the pain in her side.

As the months went by she thought even more about Fanny, who wrote of her exhausting pregnancy and what had now become advancing consumption. There were beautiful woodlands in Lisbon, she said, and the flowers had wonderful scents, but they wouldn't be Fanny's woodlands, thought Mary, not the flowers she loved and knew.

Letters continued to arrive from Fanny, written in a shaky hand, and letters arrived from Skeys also, who was quite distraught. 'We can manage,' said Everina, who sat by the fire sewing. 'I know you must go.' It was a dull wet evening, rain lashed against the windows, chaises on the roads sounded louder than ever their wheels pounding the rain. Everina looked at her sadly. She said very little, but her feelings were strong and loyal, also her drawings had improved and she'd become an excellent teacher, she and Eliza would keep the school on course, she said. Fanny's help and instruction had been invaluable, she asserted, and she too had felt her loss. Mary's foremost thought was to reach her quickly. She was drawn as with an astral force. Mrs Burgh would pay for the journey, she said, believing that pregnancy must always be taken seriously, let alone consumption, and that Mary should go without delay.

The gales were strong and there were times when the vessel was in danger of being done for, battling an army of waves. It was impossible to take refuge in her books and Mary turned her attention to assisting a sick fellow passenger who was determined to keep on vomiting. She hoped they would make it to Lisbon, for there were occasions when even the sailors grew nervous, arguing and getting aggressive.

She had been on the sea a fortnight when the ship finally dropped anchor. She made haste to Fanny's address, sighing with weariness as she stood in the hall of her home. Nothing had ever been dreamy and lovely for Fanny; she had somehow been landed in the hostile reality of life right from the first. And she had met that hostility with goodness, wanting no more than to trace the petals of a wild flower or listen to the song of a bird. She asked for so little. You could not buy the light of happiness with money, it was a singular peculiar thing, which came and went with the sun. Much more available was the dark reality that rushed at you with deathly open arms. 'Dear God,' she whispered, 'please let Fanny be well. Do not take her yet!' She remembered their days in the woodland when they had searched for wild flowers together, Fanny's delight in finding the precise specimen. Always, even then, she had noted her breathlessness, the way she had needed help climbing the bank, the occasional drop of blood on her lip . . .

The maid came downstairs, Skeys hurrying behind. He looked both glad and afraid. 'Thank you for coming,' he said. 'Fanny will be most appreciative, she suffers so badly.' He shook his head miserably. 'I do not know how to help her.'

'Where is she?' asked Mary. Her voice sounded thin and nervous. She would do what she could for both of them now; she would venture within their sacred space, for she feared the worst. Quickly, she followed Skeys and the maid to the bedroom.

Fanny was writhing and moaning as she entered. 'Mary!' she cried through her pain. 'I knew you would come!'

Throwing off her cape, Mary shut out her fears and gave what assistance she could. The midwife, a tiny, delicate woman, who might have seemed unfitted for the task, smiled with gratitude and went with the rhythm and vibrations of the struggle proficiently, while Skeys wandered the house murmuring and sighing.

A few more anguished hours brought the weak cry of a child, and the tiny red shape of a bloody little boy entered the world. Fanny fell back exhausted. 'I have a son?' she said thrilled and relieved.

'Yes,' said the midwife, wrapping the child and placing him in Fanny's arms. 'And he is quite perfect.'

Fanny gazed at her baby with tired wonder, then closed her eyes and rested.

He looked disturbingly small thought Mary as the midwife lifted him from Fanny. 'He is very tiny,' she murmured.

'He is,' said the midwife quietly. 'But with care and attention all will be well. I doubt the mother will make milk however, the labour was so intensive and she is ill.'

'My dear Mary,' Fanny murmured, reaching and clutching her hand. 'I have prayed so much to have you near.'

Skeys came running upstairs. 'You have a son,' said the midwife, handing him the swaddled child. Skeys took the baby, looking bewildered.

'Baby William is quite beautiful,' Fanny said softly, 'but how hard it was bringing him to birth.'

'You came through it, my dear,' said Skeys, with an air of gratitude. 'It was such a terrible business. I have never known anything like it.'

'I am so glad Mary was here,' said Fanny, coughing slightly and wincing with pain.

'Well, yes,' said Skeys, gazing at the baby with wonder. 'Though I'm sure we'd have managed. I was very concerned because you'd been unwell throughout the pregnancy and you kept on asking for Mary.' He turned to her. 'Fanny has been quite ill, like I said. But she's had all the attention I could give her.' He looked at the midwife confusedly. 'I don't know what to do if she cannot feed him.'

'We must find a wet-nurse,' Mary interjected boldly. 'Do you have any addresses?'

Fanny pointed to a drawer in her bedside cabinet. 'I believe I have some in there. Mary, can you get them? I cannot lean over.'

Mary saw that Skeys watched her, cold and aloof, as she handed the small piece of paper to the midwife. His dislike of her was almost palpable.

'My dear Mary,' Fanny murmured feebly. 'I cannot be a mother to little William. I am so sorry.' She sobbed quietly as she spoke, then her voice trembled with fear. 'I think I am dying.'

For a moment or two, apart from Fanny's gasping, the room was silent. The little scrap of a child lay in a cot beside her, silent now and coming to terms with his existence. But Mary was reminded of death, the deaths of young women, the deaths of babies, the inadequate training midwives received for such serious work.

'You will soon be well again,' said Skeys, hesitantly. 'I'm convinced, and our baby will thrive.'

'My husband is right,' said Fanny, pressing Mary's fingers. 'If you can get us one of those women on that piece of paper, the baby can grow strong, can it not?' Her eyes searched Mary's frantically.

'I knew that Mary's arrival would upset you,' said Skeys with a sigh. 'I warned you.'

Mary held her nerve, Skeys would rather be nasty than thankful. Mary felt she had failed in letting Fanny come to Lisbon. Had Skeys ever loved her, she wondered, had Fanny ever loved him? The doctor arrived in the room. Skeys looked at him with the eyes of a doleful dog. 'Will she get better?' he asked formally, as if he were a farmer enquiring about the state of an animal.

The doctor's face creased with unease as he opened his bag and found the things he would need. He listened to Fanny's chest, then carefully looked into her eyes. 'Her pupils are very small,' he murmured. 'And her breathing is poor.'

Fanny pressed her hands on her chest. 'It hurts so,' she whimpered. 'Will you be here when I'm buried, Mary?' she asked anxiously. 'Please say you will.'

Skeys tipped on his toes and gave an irritable sigh. 'She is here for some time,' he said. 'And you will not die, my dear. I promise. I have sent for one of those nurses to feed our son. The maid will bring you some soup very shortly. You need to eat, my dear.'

The doctor stood a bottle of medicine on the bedside cabinet. 'I shall return tomorrow,' he said. He turned to Skeys. 'Should I be needed in the night, you know where I am.'

'Thank you,' said Skeys. The doctor turned and went downstairs with the midwife.

'Now then Mary,' said Skeys, stretching to his full height. 'Fanny must have time to recover. This has been most distressing. I am glad the birth of the child is over and done with.' He spoke calmly, with authority. 'You are welcome to stay but you cannot be always beside her. You do understand?'

'Please?' begged Fanny faintly. 'Don't be unkind.'

'I am only thinking of the best all round,' said Skeys, in a warmer tone of voice.

Mary turned away and looked at the small, almost lifeless creature lying in his cot. What could she do to help Fanny now? Her dear, beloved Fanny whose spirit had almost gone, she could not feel it in the room, all that was left was a worn moaning misery. She bent to her and kissed her forehead. 'Can you find me a ribbon for her hair?' she asked Skeys. 'I know how she likes it. It is matted with sweat and I dare not wash it. I see there is blood in it too.'

Skeys went for a yellow ribbon and handed it over bewildered. Mary arranged Fanny's hair, much to the man's confusion.

The intensity in the house lessened with nightfall. The child scarcely made a sound. Skeys walked about softly and bid Mary good night. But she rose repeatedly to listen by Fanny's door. Though it did no good, for no matter if Fanny moaned or was silent; it was all Mary could do to stop herself lifting the latch, and she had promised Skeys she would not visit her at night-time. Skeys would be there for her himself, he said, and he slept downstairs by candlelight. It comforted Mary to think that Skeys had some warmth in him, though she couldn't understand its nature. If only men and women could talk with each other more easily, she thought. What was wrong with expressing the truth of emotion, did it not belong to rational thought as it were its perfect partner?

She went to see Fanny after breakfast next morning. Skeys stood by her bed, silent and tired. But the nurse had come early and the eager sounds of suckling governed the room.

'Mary, dear Mary,' whispered Fanny, putting out her hand. 'Come here.' Her voice rose as she spoke. 'I am so much stronger today. And I do not fret for the baby like I did. See how he feeds! The woman is good for him.'

'Can you not eat some bread, my dear?' said Skeys, looking at the tray of food she hadn't yet touched.

'I would rather rest,' she answered lifting the bedclothes to her chin. 'Will you give me a spoonful of medicine? I would like to sleep if I can. Oh, how I need sleep!'

Skeys poured a drop of medicine into a spoon. His hand was steady as he lifted her head and took the relief to her lips.

'I have to write a letter,' said Mary. She touched Fanny's hand. 'Sleep now, my darling. I shall come again later this morning.'

'There is all you will need in the writing desk,' called Skeys as she left. His tone was kind, but he had not looked at her yet.

Back in her room, Mary sat with her pen and paper, wondering how to start her letter. What should she tell her sisters and what might be best kept back? Sunlight shone through the window. It would seem the world was calm and at peace just then. But there was little peace in her soul. She could scarcely think and the pen shook as she took it to the ink. She could hear the sound of the stream back home in the woodland where she'd wandered with Fanny. She could hear the songbirds. She was in that place again where reality merged with dreams. It was a dizzy disturbing place where she wanted to pinch herself into life, a place filled with guilt and uneasiness. She had spent the whole night pondering, half asleep. It had been impossible to rest for fear the angel of death stood in the shadows and would seize on Fanny while she slept. She was face to face, up close with the future, the past cared nothing for her now. The little child lay upstairs by Fanny in its cot. Its life lay before it, a mystery of movement, joy, wonder and undoubtedly pain. But what would happen to Fanny? Might she stop dead like a fallen tree in a wood, never to blossom again, or feel the wind in her hair? She gripped her pen tightly then dipped it into the ink, braced herself and began:

'*My dear Girls,*

*I am now beginning to awake out of a terrifying dream . . . Before I say any more, let me tell you that when I arrived here Fanny was in labour and that four hours after she was delivered of a boy — The child is alive and well and considering the very very low state Fanny was reduced to she is better than could be expected . . . My mind is quite unsettled — Fanny is so worn out her recovery would be almost a resurrection — and my reason will scarce allow me to think 'tis possible — I labour to be resigned . . .'*

But she stopped and could write no more. Finally giving in to her desire for sleep she fell fully clothed on her bed.

The next few days were filled with anxiety and fear. She had been to gather some small blue flowers from the side of the house and had taken them to Fanny, placing them by her cheek while she slept so that she might see them and smell them on waking. But Fanny was leaving them fast. The church bells pealed loudly with a melancholy air. Mary sat for a while by Fanny's bedside, then returned to her letter:

'*. . . Fanny has been exceedingly ill since I wrote the above I entirely gave her up — and yet I could write and tell you so, it seemed like signing her death warrant — yesterday afternoon some of the most alarming symptoms a little abated and she had a comfortable night — yet I rejoice with trembling lips — and am afraid to indulge hope, she is very low — Her stomach is so weak it will scarce beat to receive the lightest nourishment — in short if I was to tell you all her complaints you would not wonder at my fears — the child tho' a puny one is well . . . I am tolerably well — and calmer than I could expect to be — Could I not have turned for comfort where only 'tis to be found, I should have been mad before this — but I feel that I am supported by that Being — who alone can heal a wounded spirit — May He Bless you both — Yours Mary*"

The weather had turned cold and damp, heralding November. Last night there had been a storm. The wind had rattled the windows and the thunder had boomed through the house. Mary had felt as if everything around her was angry and had repeatedly crept to listen by Fanny's door, occasionally hearing her talking, as if she were somewhere else, at home perhaps with her siblings, for the talk had been happy and joyful. Apart from her own footsteps she heard nothing, the entire house had been silent, and the night had seemed endless. By the parlour window downstairs, a dog had kept on barking, and had howled three times through the rain. But when she'd gone to look, no dog could be seen. She wondered what Everina would have said, who believed that dogs had senses denied to humans. If a dog howled twice, then Death was coming for a man, if it howled three times it was a woman. Mary shivered at the thought of Fanny dying, but she knew it was inevitable and would happen very soon. But she knew that if God took Fanny it would hurt her so much she would never recover from her sorrow. Her heart stirred as if breaking. Her blood hardened against it. It could not happen. What would she do with her anger? She would rage and rant at her creator. She would refuse to pray. Her muscles would alert and she would take the sword of injustice in her hand and with all the power of her being she would smite, smite, smite!

But the very next day her dreadful fear was realised. The child had been taken to the home of the nurse and Mary braved the terrible emptiness of Fanny's death, telling a stupefied Skeys that she had lost her "best earthly comfort". But Skeys wasn't listening. He had retired into a world of his own. They both sat mute looking downwards awaiting the sound of the doctor's footsteps on the stairs. Fanny's dead body lay on the bed silent and still. She was no longer with them.

'I'll see she has a good funeral,' said Skeys, with more feeling than she'd known he possessed. He shook his head and bit his lip, tears glinting in his eyes. Then he paced the room, all the time murmuring a prayer. Mary had thought him an imperious and cold individual afraid to acknowledge his emotions, but now he seemed mad with grief.

'I would rather not return to England until after she's buried,' Mary said quietly, a strong new tone to her voice.

'Of course not,' said Skeys lost in his own misery. 'I understand perfectly, and would like you to stay for a while.'

'Well, nothing can save her now – she has passed,' Mary said quietly, repressing her sobs. 'She will honour God with her presence.' Fanny however, was a Protestant being buried in a Catholic country and proceedings would need to be discreet.

Once the funeral was over, Fanny's brother George suddenly arrived in Lisbon. Skeys had promised him work with the British consulate and he had come to investigate the offer. But Mary knew he wouldn't settle; George abandoned post after post, relying on family for money and always counting on others.

'Mr Palmer's servant girl?' Mary said tentatively, as they sat having tea in her room. 'Are you the father of her child? Come now, George, tell the truth. She has charged you with it enough.'

George sat by the fire, hiding beneath his thick black eyebrows. 'She can say all she likes. I'll take it on the chin, but I'll not have her get me by the throat.'

'And so you are not?' Mary passed him the tea and looked at him dubiously.

George leant back in his chair and frowned. 'She would like to think so, though it isn't as if I could support her anyway. I didn't even touch her actually, bonny as she is.'

'Are you going the way of your father?' said Mary with a sigh. 'You know he can never be trusted.'

'Ah, my father's a scoundrel, but he never got a woman in the family way, apart from Mother, of course. Fanny would have told you that.'

'You have damaged my friendship with the Clares, George, you do realise, don't you?' Mary sat down and frowned.

'Old Clare thinks people should be perfect, but they are not. I'm sorry he's disappointed. I know he recommended me. But I ask you, Mary, how could I stay in a haberdashery sorting out buttons and ribbons? No, it wasn't for me.'

'And all those other jobs you've left, what about them? Skeys has found you a decent position, but you know you won't keep it.'

'Well, more fool him if he couldn't see my aptitude,' laughed George.

'And what news do you bring from home?' asked Mary, sighing again.

There was a long frustrated pause. 'Not good I'm afraid.' He straightened and folded his arms. 'I am sorry to report that your school is going down the drain.'

It was a dull grey morning. The house was silent. Skeys had gone out, the maid was busy in the kitchen downstairs and the baby was at the home of the nurse.

'Oh, I'll see the job through, don't worry,' said George, suddenly guilty because Mary's stupendous efforts with her school were failing. 'I won't disappoint him.'

'You mustn't waste your chance,' urged Mary. 'The school I started was doomed from the start. I shall return home soon and surrender the venture to history. Everina and Eliza can go to live with Ned.'

'I suppose they'll find work somehow,' George said pondering.

George was always irritated by having to work. He wanted an easy life like the rich. He reminded Mary of her father, though their fathers were much the same.

'And what about you?' he asked. 'What will you do back home? You won't go to Ned, for certain.'

'I've been thinking of going away – to another country, I mean. But everywhere seems so uncivilised. You are lucky that Skeys has found you something worthwhile. I hired a horse and went to look around here. Fanny wouldn't have liked living here, I'm certain, women are treated so badly.'

For a moment or two they were silent. Mary said finally, 'There are a couple of posts in Ireland that interest me.'

'What sort of posts?' He bit into a slice of cake the maid had brought with the tea.

'I shall work as a governess somewhere,' she told him, unhappily. 'I have debts.' She rested her head in her hands, recalling how hideous it was to be socially isolated between employer and servants. There had to be another way.

'You could live with my family if you wanted,' said George, 'doing like you did before, taking in sewing and stuff. Mother would be glad of your help I'm sure. – Or why not forget your debts and just run away. I have done so myself quite often.' He laughed and slapped his thighs.

Mary's heart sank. She was annoyed and weary of George's way of doing things. 'It's the wrong way to live, George,' she said as if speaking to a child. 'We must always pay off our debts.'

'I doubt anything can change with me,' he said quietly. 'I've made a living out of debt.'

Mary got up from her chair and reached for her cape. 'The sun is shining,' she smiled, peering through the window. 'Let's take a walk.'

# 17

# A New Direction

Baby William was now in the care of Skeys' sister, and Mary hoped the new arrangement might help the child flourish. She was sick at heart over the terrible events in Portugal. The sea was moody as she sailed back to London as if in accord with her feelings, and the wind sang songs of death that chilled her to the bone. She had made some notes for her novel, *Maria*, and tried to read them through, but the pages trembled before her and she put them aside. She pulled on her shawl, then turned to practising her French, speaking her favourite phrases over and over.

'Are you alright?' The frail voice of an elderly gentleman could be heard through the door. He tapped softly. She opened it on a tall white haired fellow. 'I knew you were alone,' he said meekly, 'I was concerned and thought you were delirious. The waters are quite unfriendly today, highly conducive to sea-sickness I think, which I suffer from myself. A most unpleasant business.'

'Ah thank you. How kind of you to care,' she smiled. 'The sea was unfriendly when I was coming, and it is most unfriendly going back. I deduce from that that no matter which way I go, the sea doesn't like me very much.'

The man looked her up and down concernedly. 'I hope you don't think we'll sink. Ships often do, you know. I have lost a couple of relatives in wreckages.'

She shrugged. 'Let's not think about that,' she sighed. 'We have almost reached the shores England.' She endeavoured to cheer him up. 'I fancy you have had many relatives who have often made the journey successfully?' He looked like a man with considerable wealth, his clothes were well cut and he spoke with a cultured accent. 'Well, there you are,' she smiled, as he nodded. 'Don't worry.'

He ran his hands through his soft white hair and smiled. 'You are absolutely right. My father travelled the world over and over. He was never frightened of the sea, but I own to feeling nervous myself.' Again he enquired of her welfare.

'I am well enough, thank you,' she said, smiling. 'I am trying to improve my French. I'm far from proficient, as you probably heard. I have opened a school in England and would like to teach French to my pupils.' She shivered with cold.

'Would you like me to bring you a blanket?' he asked. 'The cabins are rather chilly.' And he asked her why she wasn't wearing something warmer than a thin cotton smock.

'I have other clothes over there,' she replied, glancing at her bags. She had only allowed herself an hour that morning for packing and hadn't thought it through; her body had moved so slowly through space she had almost come to a halt, such was her grief over Fanny. 'My clothes are all packed away.' She pointed to her luggage. 'The vessel is much too unsteady for me to find them.'

'Then do let me bring you a blanket,' he said, turning to leave. 'Warm things are vital on journeys like this, otherwise you might catch a chill.'

'Thank you' she said, shuddering lightly. His smile was warming. She liked his long white hair which fell about the shoulders of his frockcoat. He looked like an artist or an actor.

After a couple of minutes he returned with a thick woollen blanket which she drew across her shawl. She felt warmer now and lay on her bed feeling eased. There was a vital energy in kindness, she thought. It was essential. She closed her eyes and lapsed into a dreamy sleep, until the vessel gave a series of jerks and lodged its anchor. At last, she was home!

She gathered together her things; rejoicing she was back in England, though knowing full well there were further struggles ahead. But at least she could be there by her sisters who were bound to have found things difficult during her absence. She must set her mind back to business now and drag it away from her suffering, though she wondered if that were possible and was forced to admit that just now she cared nothing for the school. Let it all fall apart, she thought languidly. What does it matter? If it came to that, nothing mattered anymore. She set her feet on the English soil and hailed someone to help get her things in a chaise. Within minutes she was travelling to London.

As she opened the door of the house, she was met by the gloomy faces of her sisters. It didn't bode well. She stood in the hall motionless, concerned to know what had happened in her absence to cause such unwelcoming looks. 'So what are you going to tell me?' she asked, making her way to the parlour. The house was silent and cold.

'You stayed too long,' said Everina. 'We thought you'd never come back.'

'Don't be ridiculous,' said Mary. 'You know what happened. It was disastrous. You see how I am?'

'It has hardly been easy for us,' said Eliza, unhappily. 'We didn't want to tell you the worst in our letters, matters as they were.'

'Well, you had better tell me now,' sighed Mary. She did not remove her cape, and instead sat down in her outdoor clothing by the still empty grate. It was a miserable wretched scene, the house silent and chilled, her sisters hiding in their shawls on the edge of despair. She learned that her school was much as George had reported, "Going down the drain." Her sisters talked on frantically of how it had been, their faces flushed and their voices high pitched. 'There was nothing at all we could do,' said Eliza, on the verge of weeping. 'Thank goodness it's weekend. We can at least save money on heating when the girls have gone home.'

'Nothing at all we could do,' Everina echoed, in a thin wavering voice. 'It was as if some carrion-like creatures had come to devour us.' She made gestures with her fingers; sounds came from her throat like the sounds of marauding seagulls at Laugharne. It was as if she were almost insane. 'There are other institutions around here, you know,' she continued, 'who think they can do better, and I'll tell you, they can. It isn't our fault. We have done our best. People have talked and tried to destroy us.' Some of the boarders had left and others were thinking of departing, she said. And some had gone without even paying off their debts.

Mary sat trying to console them, but it was only what she'd expected. Hope was one thing, reality was another.

'They really have a nerve,' cried Everina. 'That girl with the rather large nose left without a word and hasn't paid her bill.'

'It was all very underhand,' said Eliza quietly. 'What can you do but trust people?'

'Whether you trust them or not, they will still deceive you,' said Everina, livid with anger. She sniffed and wiped her nose on her handkerchief.

But Mary knew she would have to pay off the debts, and with boarders gone and some having left without settling their accounts, they could not rent the large house on the Green any longer, they would have to find something smaller. She felt heavy hearted at having failed, and thought she'd failed her sisters too. 'Well,' she said lightly, feigning nonchalance. 'So much achieved and so much lost. We have worked very hard but our hopes have met with disaster.' She frowned, determined not to weep. 'And now we must try again. At least we have health and strength. And there are several boarders and pupils left. If we find somewhere smaller and manage our money more carefully, I think we'll get by.' For several moments all three of them were silent. 'We must review our budget,' Mary said earnestly. 'We shall have to lose the maid for a start.'

'But our living conditions will deteriorate,' moaned Everina. 'We can't do everything ourselves.'

'We must,' replied Mary, bracing herself. 'We can do no other.' She went upstairs with her bags, then returned again to the parlour, deep in thought.

'We have been very upset about Fanny,' said Eliza. 'You might have held something back. You throw everything into your letters, Mary, perhaps sometimes it is good to withhold a little, for what could we do to help, and there was so much commotion back here. We loved her too, you know, and I felt so bad about the baby.' Eliza covered her face with her hands and spoke through her fingers, 'How dear Fanny must have suffered. I dare not think of it.'

'I'm sorry' said Mary with a sigh. 'You are right. My heart is so fierce when I write that it is all I can do to keep my pen from screaming. You know how I break the nibs. I try so hard to withhold things, but I can't, I must tell you it all. I do not believe Hugh Skeys ever trusted me at all. It was as if I dared not love her, as if she were his alone. He is selfish, just like the rest.'

Everina spoke quietly. 'Ned gets so angry with you, Mary. You always make him feel bad. It is almost as if you think all men are devils.'

'No, no, Everina, not that.' Mary protested. 'It is the way they are made to be, it is the tools they are given for power which they sometimes use to sculpt the lives of those creatures they call their "wives". Oh, that's what it is. Anything clever they do will offend them. Women are at their mercy, they have no tools of their own to fight with and have to fall back on coquetry and that sort of nonsense.'

So there it was, Mary's belief, painfully transmitted to her sisters with a voice on the verge of breaking. The strangeness of the new situation was deeply oppressive. Everything had changed and they went about the house quietly expecting all manner of disasters. A pack of hounds at the door couldn't have frightened them more and Everina jumped at any unusual movement.

White winter sunshine shone through the window but they could not feel its warmth, they were lost in dismay and frustration. 'Did you ever visit the chapel?' Mary asked Eliza one morning.

'I'm not likely to have gone without you, am I?' said Eliza, annoyed at Mary's presumption. 'I do not wish to come face to face with Mr Godwin,'

Mary glanced up. 'Ah, William Godwin, a very talented fellow I believe, though he is rather impertinent I think.'

'And in any case there were too many troubles here to think about the chapel. I did see Doctor Price though on the street. He asked how you were. I told him you'd gone to see a friend in Lisbon.'

'And did you talk long?'

'No, not at all, he was walking with that publisher, Joseph Johnson.'

Mary continued to look at her. 'And did you speak to Johnson?'

Eliza gasped. 'Oh, Mary, I am not like you. I would not stand around in the street talking with two strange men.'

'But they are not "*strange men*", Eliza. They are both well-known and learned. How curious it is that you fear them. Have I not said to speak out? You must have had questions, surely? Politeness is one thing, but what do you learn from politeness?' She sighed. She must visit the chapel soon, but she doubted Eliza would join her.

Despite her despair, Mary moved with alacrity, selling the furniture from the school and dismissing the cook and the maid. Then she found somewhere to live with Eliza and they continued to teach the last of their pupils. Everina went to live with Ned. Mary and Eliza scraped along, but Mary knew that the school couldn't last; her dream was over.

On a cold sunny lane in January she met Mrs Burgh who was about to pay them a visit. She had found Eliza a teaching post, she said, breathless from rushing, in a town called Market Harborough in Leicestershire, the job wasn't anything grand, but was it not a chance to earn money and become independent? Eliza left without delay.

## 18

## *Eliza in Market Harborough*

With little hope for the future and dreading the thought of throwing herself back on Ned, Eliza was now in Leicestershire. But taking the job had been a bit of a reckless decision, she wrote to Mary. "I certainly shan't stay with these dreary self-righteous people, who I know don't like me," she said. Her spirits were lower than ever; her colleagues were far too pious, and she was bored.

Mary's relationship with Eliza had been tetchy for quite some time. She had interfered about the baby, and she had interfered once again, encouraging her to take an appointment she did not like. But it seemed to Mary that Eliza was buckling before she had even started. "You must give it a little longer," she said, writing back. She was irritated by Eliza, who must always ask her for guidance, then blame her when things went wrong; she had not liked her marriage, she did not like the school in Market Harborough, what next? There was something seriously wrong thought Mary, Eliza had lost all confidence, and worse than that she had lost her grip on reality. She would have to pay her a visit.

Market Harborough certainly looked a pious place thought Mary, as she made her way through the town. At the centre stood the St. Dionysius Church, a lovely building, rising directly from the street. Dating back to the thirteenth century, it was a very old church, and Mary thought the lives of the parishioners were no doubt grounded in its values. There were many notices on the doors and a lot of people came in and out absorbed in conversation. Eliza wasn't especially disposed to piety and complained that her colleagues were obsessed with fears of hell. She was sure to go to hell, she'd said, and could tell from the way she was treated that she wasn't welcome. For wasn't she bad? Oh, yes, she was sinful! She had left her husband and child. It was not done. They were sure to have uncovered her past, she said, there was so much whispering around her. The spiritual life was important to Eliza, but she did not want to devote her life to worship, neither did she regret leaving Bishop, even when her colleagues looked at her strangely and murmured to each other. Mary saw that many of the people in the town were weavers of cloth, though there were bakers, brewers, butchers, carpenters and many other traders at work there. It was also a stage coaching town and a lot of coaches passed through. Eliza had moaned that she could not count the number of times she had wanted to climb on board and escape.

Mary felt frustrated. She imagined a more fulfilling life for Eliza, oh, the freedom of imagination! There was always something better to imagine. But you could not live in dreams, she told her one evening at her lodgings, and disappointment could torment you to death.

'I can't bear it,' wept Eliza, biting her nails. 'These people despise me.'

'I wish I could help,' said Mary straightening. 'But if you want an independent existence, you might have to work in places you don't like.' She knew that from experience. 'I doubt it's as bad as you think though. Like Shakespeare says, "There is nothing either good or bad that thinking makes it so."'

'But Mary,' Eliza pleaded, 'I *know* it's bad. Never mind poetry. I am miserable.'

Mary looked at her straight. 'Feelings cannot rule us Eliza. It is for us to rule them. This is one of the reasons women get married, security, of course, and the chance to retreat from the world. But they are only captured again. Society must change. It will take some time.'

'By then I shall probably be dead,' moaned Eliza.

'You might be right,' Mary said sighing. 'You can't come back with me though. What will you do?'

Eliza trembled, then turned aside as if ashamed. This was something else that infuriated Mary; women were always ashamed, ashamed of struggling and suffering. Fanny though, would have argued that life was just the same for men, and that the whole of humanity suffered. But for Mary that wasn't enough. Men took all the power from the world; they drained it to the bottom of the cup while women were parched. She could not dampen the flame that raged inside her and her heart went out to Eliza now. She was lonely, she was afraid, and she was sad. But Mary knew that her sister had hidden strengths. They would come to her aid in time.

Several months later when the spring brought blessings of renewal and blossoms hung heavy on the trees, Eliza miraculously settled and accepted her fate. Her fears had melted with the snow on the hills and she was starting anew. Reading her letters Mary smiled with relief, the tensions she felt decreased and the pains in her limbs lessened. She wrote to her forthwith:

*". . . Indeed my dear girl I felt a glow of tenderness which I cannot describe − I could have clasped you to my breast as I did in days of yore, when I was your nurse . . . I was pleased to find you make the best of your situation, and try to improve yourself − You have not many comforts it is true − yet you might have been in a much more disagreeable predicament than at present . . ."*

Fanny was no longer alive, but Mr Blood certainly was. And he was always in debt. Nothing in the way of financial help came from Skeys. Fanny's father wrote to Mary of a caretaker's job he wanted in the Church of Ireland. He would very much like to apply for it, he said, but he didn't have the wherewithal to get there. He asked her for money. She sat for a good half hour wondering how she might help him. She needed money herself, yet she would like to assist him if she could, if only for the sake of Fanny. And she did not know the whereabouts of George to get in touch. Had he reneged on his work? She could not turn to Ned, and went for advice to the Reverend John Hewlett, a friend and well-known teacher at Shacklewell Academy in Hackney. All the time they talked she felt desperate. He stood before her his hands clasped behind his back, his features serious, while she sat on the chaise longue pouring out her woes.

'He is always destitute,' she complained. 'He can't come to grips with the fact that his drinking wastes money. We've had all that with my father. It really wears you down. My mother was often beside herself with worry, but she just let it happen. She was weary to the marrow of her bones. Mr Blood is the same, you see.'

'A lot of men are like this,' said Hewlett, frowning and thoughtful. 'They like to speculate, and when it doesn't work out they drown their sorrows in drink. It's hard to know how to stop it; it is cause and effect, a way of life in the end, taking chances is all that is left.'

'Indeed,' said Mary, catching her breath. But such words didn't make her feel better.

It was however, a very productive conversation. Hewlett told her he had written a book, soon to be published by Johnson. The blood came up in her cheeks as she listened. *Writing!* How wonderful it was to write, it was better than a string of pearls!

'Why not write something yourself?' he said, as if reading her mind. 'I'm sure you could, and if Johnson likes it, who knows?'

'Why not!' she exclaimed. 'And I think I could do it. You have given me a surge of energy!' The idea filled her with elation; it was just like manna from heaven and she thanked him profusely. 'I would like to write a pamphlet on education for girls,' she told him. 'I have so much to say.'

A strange new passion danced inside her as she returned to her lodgings, as if something important lying dormant had finally sprung into life. She had a wealth of experience to bring to the project and the emotion and authority to deliver it. She trembled with eagerness as she sat in her lonely room. Her thoughts were so wild she must tame them! She found her pen and paper and set to work on a proposal. Her heart beat furiously at the thought of this new direction. She had other books growing in her mind, great books, useful books she thought Johnson might like. Her pen flew across the page.

Two whole weeks went by. How many times must she pace up and down her room? Why was Johnson taking so long to respond? He did not care for her work, that's what it was! Her writing did not suit him. Her temper grew difficult. She went out walking and returned again and again to the place where she collected her post. But there was nothing. She waited longer.

Then came the letter. She opened it with bated breath. – Yes! Yes! He had accepted her submission and had made her an offer of ten guineas! She gasped. 'Ten guineas,' she murmured, slowly sitting down, the letter trembling in her hands. 'I am about to become an author!' She had not dared imagine it, and prayed she didn't disappoint him. Johnson was giving her money before she'd even put pen to paper, how generous he was. Now she could pay the fare of the Bloods to Dublin and Fanny's father could take up the post he wanted. She wrote to him explaining what had happened, thrilled she could help them. It was as if she were helping Fanny, she said, and she felt as if her spirit watched over them. She also wrote to Eliza. Mr Blood would probably be extremely glad that Fanny's spirit watched over them, Eliza said in reply. Though she doubted he believed in spirits, she said, well, not the ethereal kind.

Mary set to writing there and then. She knew that her pamphlet would be special. It was important to write simply and clearly, she thought, so that people understood exactly her point of view. She had so much to say and mustn't get carried away, which she knew she was wont to do. She must keep to the point and not allow emotion to distract her. She dipped her pen in the ink and began:

*"Mary Wollstonecraft – Thoughts on the Education of Daughters"*, she wrote at the top of her page. She had started! The book would be addressed to mothers, young women and teachers. In silence she listened to the disparate noises on the street, the cry of a trader, the screech of the wheels of a chaise, the laughter of a woman. Her

soul spread wide its wings, she could fly wherever she wanted, say whatever she would, and Joseph Johnson would read it, the illustrious Joseph Johnson who published such profound writing. She felt like a child of God, standing in a field of wild flowers and filled with existential wonder. Her pamphlet would explain how girls should be educated from infancy through to marriage and motherhood, chapters would include *"The Nursery"* and *"Moral Discipline"* contending that the shaping of a rational mind had to start early. She would make a point of explaining the importance of realistic education, rejecting the bloodlessness of artificial manners and the emphasis on dress and makeup, and arguing that monies saved might be used to help the poor and sick. A good education was always key to the progression of healthy thought, she would add, for base appetites could often take over if minds were left vacant.

She sat back for a while and read through what she had written. She had learned so much with Fanny. Nature itself was a profound teacher, she was wholly convinced of that, and it was far too often ignored when pupils were shut in their homes when they might better be learning in the countryside. – And she had never seen the point of rote learning; ideas kept separate decayed and could not grow! – Long and florid words also had to go; they were often used for effect and nothing more. She aimed for simplicity and clarity, where speech and thought were natural, not affected or artificial, and always, always, rational. – And she would endorse breast feeding too, she firmly believed in that, though it was very much argued over in families, but ought not a mother to suckle her child if she could? Was it not the natural way? She wrote on quickly:

*"Her milk is their proper nutriment, and for some time is quite sufficient. Were a regular mode of suckling adopted, it would be far from being a laborious task . . . The suckling of a child also excites the warmest glow of tenderness – Its dependant, helpless state produces an affection, which may properly be termed maternal. I have even felt it, when I have seen a mother perform that office; and am of opinion, that*

*maternal tenderness arises quite as much from habit as instinct. It is possible, I am convinced, to acquire the affection of a parent for an adopted child, it is necessary, therefore, for a mother to perform the office of one, in order to produce in herself a rational affection for her offspring . . ."*

Another hour went by while she fervently scribbled words on the page, constantly dipping her pen in the ink until she had emptied the bottle. In her intensity she had worn out two quill pens.

# 19

# *Highs and Lows*

This was how Mary felt when elated. She flew! But oh, the curse of hubris, her wings failed and she crashed like Icarus to earth.

Next day, as expected, she fell into deep depression. This was the way of her mind. She fretted. Johnson was publishing her pamphlet, but would he be able to sell it? And what would the readers think of it if he did? She stiffened herself against censure. Her writing would either be applauded or rejected, was it not the same for all writers? At best she wanted it considered and believed in her words. She recovered herself and decided to go out walking. A walk always helped. She went out on to the street where she talked of trivial things to people she did not know. Then she wandered into the nearby woodland to commune with nature.

Arriving by the pond she knelt down in the grass and gazed at her reflection in the water. How lovely the water was, she thought, with its thin melancholy smiles and its gentle flute-like music meandering through the waving reeds. Thoughts of Ophelia entered her mind. Dipping in her hand she filled her palm with the pure crystal substance, then watched the heart shaped droplets fall like little buds of light. 'Ophelia, Ophelia, where is Ophelia?' she murmured, chanting:

> "*When down her weedy trophies and herself*
> *Fell in the weeping brook.*
> *Her clothes spread wide;*

*And, mermaid-like, awhile they bore her up:*
*Which time she chanted snatches of old tunes;*
*As one incapable of her own distress,*
*Or like a creature native and indued*
*Unto that element: but long it could not be*
*Till that her garments, heavy with their drink,*
*Pull'd the poor wretch from her melodious lay*
*To muddy death."*

She sat for a while and pondered on how it might be to be in the place beyond life, the place where Fanny was now? Was it just eternal blackness or might it be a place of everlasting peace, far better than anything on earth? She thought of Paradise. Did it really exist? Might it be a place where everything people sought to put right was at last resolved, not a demon tormentor in sight, only the people you had known and loved finally redeemed and perfect. She gazed at the vast sky. But what was perfection, a flat plane of light perhaps offering sinners a reflection of themselves cleansed of what the world called transgressions? She murmured the Lord's Prayer: *"'Our Father who art in heaven, hallowed by thy name. Thy kingdom come, thy will be done on earth as it is in heaven . . . but deliver us from evil . . .'"*

*Evil, evil, evil . . .* the word echoed in her mind. Had she committed evil? She probably had without knowing. She laboured so hard to be good, but it was almost as if doing good in one place meant doing bad in another, tearing the human spirit asunder. How much of her life had had its being without her knowledge, she wondered She thought of those moments of discovery when something terrible had happened in a sort of darkness she hadn't been aware of, but a darkness that was all her own doing. She bent again to the water, dipping in her hands, then she wetted her face. How good it was to feel the water on her face! Water was indeed holy. She wanted it to embrace her, to embrace the whole of her body. She wanted it to surround her, to swallow her into its depths. 'Oh, the peace, the peace of it!' she cried. And she remembered a passage from Voltaire:

*"I have wanted to kill myself a hundred times, but somehow I am still in love with life. This ridiculous weakness is perhaps one of our more stupid melancholy propensities, for is there anything more stupid than to be eager to go on carrying a burden which one would gladly throw away, to loathe one's very being and yet to hold it fast, to fondle the snake that devours us until it has eaten our hearts away?"*

At that moment there came the song of a robin nearby. The bird came close, almost touching her smock, all feathers and cleanness as it thrust out its bright red breast. 'What a brave little creature,' she laughed. 'And you are all alone, careless of the trials of humans. What do you know of better or worse, dear thing? You fly from tree to tree neither loving nor hating anything.' The robin hopped about on the bank. She remained still for a while, imbibing the elixirs of nature. She would like to have stayed the night there, but the weather was bound to grow damp and cold, and she wasn't a robin; she was human and must suffer for that. She rose slowly and the bird flew off. But in those precious moments her soul had returned to her body.

But she could not support herself writing pamphlets, she pondered as she walked back home to her lodgings. And in any case one pamphlet did not make a writer. She needed some work!

She visited Mrs Burgh and learned of a post for a governess in Ireland to the daughters of Lord and Lady Kingsborough. She would no doubt be given a beautiful room and lots of good food, but would the appointment suit her. The Anglo Irish Lord and Lady Kingsborough were exceedingly rich, but the girls were probably spoiled and might prove difficult to teach. She didn't know anything about them, but felt confident she could get good references from Joseph Johnson and Reverend Price; she had been to a number of Price's excellent sermons and knew Johnson because of her pamphlet. Working as a governess, however, wasn't something she wanted to do, but she still had outstanding debts and needed to pay them. She had lots of ideas to offer about teaching and learning that might benefit the Kingsborough daughters if the girls liked her. But talking to a man at the library she began to think again.

The previous governess had been quickly dismissed with a comfortable sum of money. Was that generous or merely expedient? Did his lordship have a roving eye? Had there been problems? Nevertheless, they had brought into being seven sons and five daughters. Bad marriages constantly delivered large families which tied women down all the more and weakened their health; she had seen that with her own. Society marriages were often based upon wealth, but if there were love, she wondered how it might stay strong within such a restricted lifestyle. She had not seen the love she believed was possible between her parents. But was the sort of love she could imagine ever possible? At least a wealthy woman could pay for assistance and it did not fall on the lot of the eldest daughter to act as a second mother, a daughter who was committed to drudgery and would always be stuck in the mire.

She returned home tired, though it was only mid afternoon. London felt quiet that day as if in slumber, it was a very unusual silence like something waiting. The thought of becoming a governess made her despondent, especially if she must teach the daughters of people like the Kingsboroughs who would be haughty and condescending. She thought and thought. She didn't have a great deal of choice things as they were; there was nothing else for it. Ned always said she thought about things too deeply and wouldn't leave a single stone unturned, that way, he asserted, she was bound to find something disagreeable. She knew he grew weary of her boundless energy which often led to depression. But she had never felt as alone as she did right now.

She sat by herself in the parlour, her head in her hands, then the church clock chimed in the distance. It was time to take action.

She completed her application and was immediately sent for. Now she had accepted the post and was travelling to Michelstown Castle. This was the largest neo-Gothic house in Ireland, the former home of the Irish Earls of Kingston and located in County Cork. It had been built in the fifteenth century by the White Knights of Michelstown, but had since been refurbished and modernised, finally passing to Caroline Fitzgerald, granddaughter of James, 4th Baron Kingston. Reading about Caroline, Mary had felt sympathetic, filled with a conflict of pity and esteem for her ladyship. She'd been married at the age of 15 to her cousin Robert King, Viscount Kingsborough, Earl of Kingston, scarcely much older than herself. In those tender years, she could scarcely have known what was happening. The Kingsboroughs were only in their thirties and seemed like contemporaries. But she would have to obey their orders and the salary of forty guineas would certainly help pay her debts. If only she weren't so proud, she brooded, if only she didn't have so many ideas bounding around her mind. But she could not stop herself thinking and must always make notes.

It was a dark damp day as she passed through the high steel gates of her workplace. What would be expected of her here, she wondered, as she gazed on the grandeur of the castle, it was as if she were about to enter the dark Bastille in Paris, the prison fortress she'd read about, used by the kings of France to secure their enemies. The girls she was about to teach were fourteen, twelve and six. Margaret, the eldest, spoke several foreign languages, and was obviously highly accomplished. Teaching her would be a challenge. The girls knew a lot of English history, but Lady Kingsborough had stressed emphatically in her letter that her daughters were not to read novels, novels being the new form of story-telling publishers like Joseph Johnson were eager to get out to the public, and which many mothers referred to as "a pack of lies". Margaret would no doubt want to read them, Mary thought smiling, but she would not broach the subject with Lady Kingsborough. Forewarned was forearmed.

She was introduced to the daughters as soon as she arrived, and was glad to get to know them. But Mary thought the atmosphere of riches they lived in ill-fitted to the sort of education she intended. What the girls missed out on most, she thought, was the moral example of adults they were close to and loved. Their mother seemed cold and authoritative and Mary saw she shrank from their questions, acting detached and withdrawn. Her own way of relating would be kind and affectionate. She would charm them with her large blue eyes and strong soft voice and manner. Her ladyship though had made it plain that Mary mustn't get too close to her charges; after all she was only a governess.

The very next day, Mary was summoned to the parlour. Standing by the window looking out, her ladyship asked if Mary's room was to her liking. 'The maid thought you rather reticent,' she said. 'It's a lovely room on the east side of the house. The views are very good, and . . .' Suddenly there was a noise of gunshots from the grounds. Lady Kingsborough peered across the quiet trees and lawns. Everywhere looked empty.

'What is it?' asked Mary, seeing her distressed.

'Nothing, my dear,' she replied, though she was trembling slightly. 'Lord Kingsborough behaves quite erratically at times. He likes to wander the grounds firing his gun, sometimes at nothing at all.'

The maid ran in and peered outside.

'It is a fox, I think,' she said. 'It comes for the hens.' After that she curtsied and left.

'The room you have given me is beautiful, my lady,' said Mary, returning to the previous conversation. 'Forgive me if I did not say so. I often internalise my feelings. And the desk will be useful; I am hoping to write.' In the afternoon sunlight from the window, Mary thought her ladyship's hair was far too heavily powdered and her cheeks too heavily rouged; the redness did not become her and made her look artificial. Why did she want to make herself into a doll, Mary mused curiously, she was a pretty woman and did not need such cosmetics.

'We hope you will enjoy being with us,' Lady Kingsborough said in a warmer tone of voice. The gunshots had stopped. 'And you needn't keep curtseying, Mary, I am sure it is tiresome. I am a sad little creature really and not at all how I should be.'

'But how should you be?' Mary asked, surprised by her ladyship's candour.

Lady Kingsborough's eyes flashed with confusion. 'I am supposed always to act superior, but it is such a bore. And when my dogs bound up to me, I embrace them wildly like a child.' She glanced at Mary nervously. 'There is nothing wrong with embracing your dogs, is there? My husband does not like it when we have guests.'

'There is nothing wrong with it at all,' said Mary perplexed. Indeed, it was true; a woman should never marry too early and Caroline Kingsborough had married at the age of fifteen. 'The children look much like that painting on the wall there,' said Mary. 'Margaret is the prettiest I think.' She frowned and looked downwards. 'I apologise. I am far too direct.' She smiled at her words, though Lady Kingsborough wasn't listening.

'It is good to act like a child, don't you think,' Lady Kingsborough continued, fingering the lace on her cuffs. 'I love to run through the gardens with my dogs.' She laughed. 'I believe Marie Antoinette is the same. She lost her childhood, you see. They forced her into that marriage with Louis. Childhood passes so quickly, and you can never get it back.'

'No, my lady, it is true.'

Lady Kingsborough was thoughtful and seemed unhappy. 'So much of what we wish for never comes to pass,' she murmured. Then she straightened proudly. 'But my husband is good and hardworking. He is commanding colonel of the Michelstown Independent Light Dragoons, you know.' She laughed again lightly and put her hand to her mouth. 'It sounds like a march doesn't it. They have only recently been formed in case we should need them.' She looked down worriedly. 'I hope there won't be an invasion. You never know what is happening with France, and we sometimes get dreadful news.'

'Lord Kingsborough is praised for establishing schools also,' Mary added quickly, eager to turn the conversation away from war. 'And, I believe he created a library . . . Oh, and did he not plant a few thousand mulberry trees too?' She smiled.

'Ah, the mulberry trees, yes. We must have silk, you see, and it is work for the peasants, of course.' She stood for a moment gazing at space as if lost in some private sadness.

Mary spoke softly. 'I did not mean to upset you. I have scarcely been here a day and I cause you distress.'

'Oh no, my dear, it isn't you,' said Caroline, twisting her hanky in her fingers. 'My children like you, and for that I am grateful. I feared they might not. I'm afraid I am often tearful.'

Mary realised suddenly that her place in the Kingsborough family was not only to educate the girls but also to befriend her ladyship, who despite being surrounded by exquisite objects and statues, focussed her most earnest feelings on the dogs she always kept beside her.

'I was nine when I lost Mama,' Caroline said tremulously. 'Her death was a terrible thing.' She rubbed her arms and frowned. 'I know people die all the time, but I thought Mama was eternal. But she had gone, quite gone, not a sign of her anywhere.' She talked on even more painfully. 'And I was mother of two when I was just seventeen. Imagine?' She looked at Mary sharply; it was almost a look of anger. 'How can it be that I was mother of two when I was all but a child myself?' She sat down heavily in a high backed chair and straightened her curls. 'But they expected it of me, you see. I had to keep bearing children.' She gave a strange little laugh. 'I have borne twelve of them in all, seven boys and five girls. Oh, I have been making babies for ever.' She sighed. 'It is *so* exhausting. And I must always be firm with them, you see, or I believe they would overrule me just like their father.'

In the last half hour in her desperate need to confide, Lady Kingsborough had delivered the secrets of her soul. It seemed like a sort of sacrifice, for she had also yielded her power, and Mary knew that a woman's power was often consumed in her distress. Caroline's significance in the real order of life had been robbed, she was abandoned in a make believe world.

'I'm afraid I got carried away,' Lady Kingsborough faltered. 'Perhaps I have said too much.' She glanced at Mary sharply. 'It is all confidential, of course. I have had a very good life to tell the truth. We have done much travelling.' She twirled momentarily on her shining silver shoes. 'I have been to so many balls. – And do you know I have attended the court of Louis XVI and Marie Antoinette. Oh, I have! I have! Her clothes are quite exquisite – silks covered in jewels so that she dazzles like a star!' For a moment she gazed into space, then sighed.

Mary stood silent, trying not to stare, fighting against the overwhelming fascination she felt for Caroline Kingsborough and eager to hear more of her thoughts, but she would not prompt her further, she had a lesson to prepare for the girls and must go to her room. Also, she needed to think and record her impressions. Nothing was ever as it seemed.

'Do you play the piano,' asked Caroline as Mary was about to withdraw.

'I am sorry, I don't,' murmured Mary. She did not think she could ever have found the time, and pianos were costly, she said. 'Nor do I sing. I believe there are more important things for girls to be learning.'

'Like what?' She spoke some words in French, but Mary couldn't grasp them.

Mary saw that Lady Kingsborough was waiting. 'Like matters to do with the opening of the mind.' She gazed ahead, thoughtful.

Caroline Kingsborough smiled and assumed a patronising air; she was a clever woman with busy intelligent eyes and a grasp of French well beyond Mary's present standard. 'Tell me, my dear, how will you open their minds?'

Mary drew a breath then spoke in a soft tone of voice, quite opposite to that of her ladyship whose forceful confident inflexions jarred on the nerves. 'I shall see what sparks their interest and work from that. The best education springs out of interest.'

'I do believe you are right,' said her ladyship abstractedly as Mary gave a brief curtsy. She looked Mary up and down then turned and went to her dogs waiting on the chaise longue.

# 20

# *Life with the Kingsboroughs*

The Kingsboroughs had many guests, and Mary was able to talk with them all freely, and she was given a lot more liberty it seemed, than the previous governess, or so said the cook. But she did not feel she belonged at Michelstown Castle, not even remotely. Their aristocratic pretentions annoyed her and she wondered how such intensity could be generated from what seemed to her like theatre and very dull theatre indeed.

'Take care,' said one of the female guests as they all sat down to talk after dinner one evening. 'Lady Kingsborough is a jealous woman. You have brought new light to this house, a light too bright for her ladyship I fear.' She smiled and continued. 'Do you ride?' she asked genially.

'I do,' said Mary. 'But I haven't been riding in Ireland.'

'Then we must take you out with us sometime,' said the woman. 'Lord Kingsborough likes to go shooting. Oh, he shoots all the time; it is a sport he relishes. My husband and I sometimes accompany him. Her ladyship does not care too much for riding.'

'What does he shoot?' Mary looked at her curiously.

'Oh, *things*, you know anything that runs or leaps.' The woman leant in closer. 'I do believe he might shoot Lady Kingsborough half a chance!' She laughed at her words. But Caroline was coming across. The female guest smiled sweetly and spoke with practised mendacity. 'I have been telling the governess here what wonderful food you serve at Michelstown Castle. I haven't eaten venison in

185

ages, it was quite delicious, and how fresh those vegetables were. – I believe they are grown on the estate?'

'Indeed, we grow them ourselves,' Lady Kingsborough said proudly, 'and the venison is from our deer park.' She fanned her rose red cheeks.

'Yes, delectable,' said the guest, nodding approval. 'How lovely to have a deer park.' She rose slowly from her chair. 'I am afraid we must leave however. I see my husband is beckoning. Do excuse us my lady.'

'He said goodbye to me earlier,' said Caroline, glancing over. 'It was good to have your company, and I hope you will come again soon.'

Lady Kingsborough went across to the piano and began to play a piece by Schubert. As she sat by the window, Mary saw that a man was coming her way, some lord whose name she had forgotten. He smiled as he approached then he bent and whispered in her ear, 'You are the best looking woman in the room, my dear. I am sure you know it.'

Mary cringed and felt the poverty of her position immediately; this was often the way that aristocrats behaved to their inferiors. She moved further away, but he moved in closer and pressed his body against her own. She desperately wanted to leave, but she knew she was captive to the Kingsboroughs. She could not do as her will commanded and was as good as bound and shackled. 'The way I look, sir, is of no importance,' she told him flatly. 'It is a woman's person that matters not her appearance.'

He started and laughed. 'Your modesty is a little false I think, for I have seen you twirling your curls. I wonder who for? You wear no rouge, but I suspect you pinch your cheeks when no-one is looking.' He glanced about the room then put his hand on her hair. 'Your hair is a lovely colour,' he said in a soft and intimate voice. 'I imagine it shines like fresh yellow grain in the sunlight.'

'Do not touch me, sir!' cried Mary, with a slight shudder. 'I will not be treated like a plaything!'

'Oh, come now,' he smiled, his eyes half closed with amusement. 'Does a woman not like the company of a rogue now and then?'

'I do not know such women,' Mary replied shakily. She looked across at the group around the piano. His wife stood close to Lady Kingsborough. 'I believe your wife is singing. Should you not join her?'

He looked at Mary and scowled. 'And shouldn't you mind your own business, dear governess? I find no pleasure in singing; my wife is used to me and knows it.'

Mary rose irritably. 'I must bid you goodnight, sir, for I am tired.'

Finding her room, she sat down in despair. She could still hear voices and the sound of the piano downstairs. But the darkness of the night emanated through her bones as if it would take her with it. She felt humiliated and demeaned. But most of all she felt angry.

It was a lonely life she found herself in at Michelstown Castle. The servants had their own society and the Kingsboroughs had friends of their own, but she had no-one to relate to and must live in a world where she ate alone in her room, her one delight teaching her pupils. Fourteen year old Margaret proved to be an excellent scholar and was invigorating company. But there was often a frown on Lady Kingsborough's face should the girl laugh too loudly or show her governess affection.

'We have never had a governess like you,' said Margaret that morning. 'My sisters read like they have never read before. It is as if we are learning for ourselves with our very own hearts.'

'That is the way it should be,' said Mary with a glow of satisfaction. It was curious how her relationship with Margaret was complementary. For as much as Margaret learned from her, Mary learned from Margaret who had a lively and questioning mind.

'I want to be just like you,' said Margaret one day in the parlour, 'to feel and think as I wish and act as I like.'

'Is that how you think I am?' smiled Mary. 'Oh, I dare not act as I like, my dear. If only I could.'

'But you seem so free,' said Margaret gazing at her with wonder. 'Nothing is real in this house, and I'm not sure Mama and Papa like each other now . . . They used to, but now Mama often cries and Papa is always out shooting.' She gazed at the grounds through the window. 'The peacock there isn't a peacock, you know, it is an eidolon. I believe an Indian maiden is trapped inside it.'

'My dear,' said Mary gently. 'How lovely it is to dream. But it is just a peacock. Let it be a peacock.'

'Alright,' said Margaret in a low and thoughtful voice. And she fixed her great dark eyes on Mary for a moment, then murmured quietly, 'It is just a peacock, a very lovely peacock, but only a peacock.'

That year the Kingsboroughs moved to Dublin and Mary went with them. To her surprise, she was treated like one of the family, visiting the theatre, meeting actors, and talking with all kinds of people. Much good reading was sent to her from Newington Green and she was never short of something to write. Life was better, and the months passed quickly.

Soon they were moving to Bristol, and Mary felt pleased with the way the girls were progressing; they came to their lessons promptly and went off to their rooms exuberant. It was all going well. But Lady Kingsborough scowled a lot and sat thoughtful, always watching, and Mary felt anxious as she went down the hall on that cold morning she was sent for. Caroline was out to find fault, and she sat a dog on each arm, looking at Mary haughtily. It was time for her daughters to have a change, she said, and learn from someone else. 'I shall ensure you have excellent references,' she said. 'The girls have enjoyed your instruction.' She bent her head all the time, fondling her dogs. 'But you said you were a little too direct, my dear, and I fear it is true. You have offended my guests.'

'Which guests have I offended?' Mary asked boldly. But Caroline made no answer. Mary felt she had failed, though she knew she'd succeeded with the girls. But Caroline Kingsborough was a jealous and lonely woman. Even the pretty faced dogs seemed to glare as if ready to pounce. She would be glad to leave those ridiculous canines anyway. She braced herself and tried to be strong. But her heart was torn when it came to leaving Margaret. She had listened so carefully and had learned so much. She felt as if her very heart's blood beat in the girl now. Would Caroline let her say goodbye, or was it all over? She went to pack her things, trusting the girls might come to see her tomorrow. But it was doubtful. It was indeed all over.

# 21

## *Back in England*

So the Kingsborough year was over. The time spent with the family had been invaluable though to Mary for she had heard and experienced many new things and was passionately longing to write. She prided herself on the fact that she'd kept her dignity and had refused to think herself beneath them. She had retained her self-respect, which was no easy task. But her pride had incurred her ladyship's wrath and now she'd been dismissed. Well, Lady Kingsborough had been an anxious woman, manifest often as an excess of emotion over trivia, like finding a tiny spider in the drawing room, having lost one of her combs or a beloved hat pin. Mary had listened to her grievances, offering what sympathy she could. A spider would do her far less harm than a human, she'd told her, and in the autumn they came in the house to get warm, and her comb and hat pin were bound to turn up, for they were surely somewhere in her room. After extensive searching the precious items had been discovered beneath a dresser, though why they were there was anyone's guess, the cook and maid however were known to play pranks on her ladyship. Caroline Kingsborough though was a learned woman and Mary had enjoyed their conversations. But Margaret had been special, she had been a loyal friend and they'd promised to keep in touch.

But the dreary weight of what to do next was with her again as she sat in her London lodgings. Joseph Johnson with his exceptional kindness and generosity had found her somewhere to live. He had come to her aid. She had felt like a child again back home, powerless, useless and having to fall on others to help with her vicissitudes. Johnson, it seemed, understood more than anyone about life's vicissitudes and always gave a helping hand. It wasn't too far from the chapel at Newington Green and his home where he often held dinners for his literary friends. Perhaps he would invite her sometime. How she would enjoy it if he did. She could listen to his friends and make a contribution herself perhaps, for she had learned so much over the year and was much more experienced. He had told her she seemed quite changed when he'd taken her to the house on the Green. And perhaps she was. Others saw changes more than you did yourself, she reflected. Would Ned and her sisters also think her different? Had they changed too?

Johnson was much admired for the encouragement and assistance he gave to aspiring writers, sometimes much to his cost, for he published material that often caused a stir and brought government officials sneaking around his premises. But his inexhaustible interest in all manner of new ideas spurred him on and he constantly reached out to as many readers as possible. But Mary's heart was full of disquiet just now and despondency, and she was feeling lonely. She intended to visit the chapel on the Green very soon, to listen to Price's sermons and talk with some of the dissenters. Johnson was a strong dissenter, he had no respect for the establishment, but the man was nobody's fool and his wits were always kept sharp. Halfway through printing a book he might decide in a flash to abandon it because the text was too dangerous and the authorities were on to him; there were always spies around dissenters, especially those with a press.

The work of Jean Jacques Rousseau, the Swiss born French philosopher, and William Paley, best known for his natural theology, had taken up a lot of Mary's thought just lately and her mind was teeming with ideas. There were also many national developments to catch up with. It was now 1787; an important year for anything concerning slavery. A new society had been formed that May by the well-known abolitionists Thomas Clarkson and Granville Sharp. Ned would want to talk about that. She had heard too, that eleven ships had left Portsmouth recently taking 700 convicts and at least 300 crew to start a penal colony in Australia. Doctor Price would no doubt be speaking about it in chapel.

She bent to her books and found one by Paley she'd been reading earlier. She turned to a page on "Happiness". Finding a comfortable chair, she settled by the fire to read:

*". . . Where there exists a known external cause of uneasiness, the cause may be removed, and the uneasiness will cease. But those imaginary distresses which men feel for want of real ones (and which are equally tormenting, and so far equally real), as they depend upon no single or assignable subject of uneasiness, admit oftentimes of no application of relief.*

*Hence a moderate pain, upon which the attention may fasten and spend itself, is to many a refreshment: as a fit of the gout will sometimes cure the spleen. And the same of any less violent agitation of the mind, as a literary controversy, a law-suit, a contested election, and, above all, gaming; the passion for which, in men of fortune and liberal minds, is only to be accounted for on this principle."*

Paley's words went round and round in her mind, attaching themselves to scenes from her past and filling her with a sense of turmoil. Her life, she felt, was a constant struggle of ascent and descent, and she could not tell where it was going, or indeed if it was going anywhere. But there was always the urge to somehow climb out of some sort of magical shell and grow into something splendid like a caterpillar did when it changed into a butterfly. Why couldn't people do that? Oh, those precious awakenings! And what of the ideas that shimmered like stars then died, the deaths of wonderful people who had lost their lives through war and disease or other misfortunes, babies who had expired because the world didn't want them. She had seen such babies, grey, shrivelled and lifeless, attempts at a life that could not be.

She read a little more of the book then put it aside. Tomorrow she would visit the chapel and listen to Reverend Price. She would talk with Johnson and assert herself as a writer, someone with something important to say, equal to his friends – yes, equal to the men! She would be Mary Wollstonecraft political writer! And let them smile if they dared, she would rage at any who did. Her great stubborn spirit was ready to seize its destiny and demand recognition, and others must take notice and learn!

She gazed outside through the window. How good it was to be back, she thought. The air wasn't fresh like the air in Ireland and everywhere was noisy with the to-ing and fro-ing of carriages, the endless chatter of people and the clatter of barrows from coster-mongers selling their wares, but oh, how she loved it! She had an endless fascination for London with its tall monumental buildings and the great river Thames. Even the taste of the air on less smoky days like today brought a feeling of home to her tongue. The lodg-ings Johnson had found her were in George Street, a familiar street where he'd said she might live rent free until she could find her feet. What a generous person he was, and he did not deem himself holy, his loving and caring came purely from the goodness of his heart.

Next day she rose early, determined to visit the chapel. She cut a slice of bread and covered it with butter then brewed a pot of tea, thinking as she did so of the time it had taken Lady Kingsborough to take breakfast and prepare for the day. First she partook of an excellent repast from a tray, then her maid would come to fix her hair, bringing a number of hair pieces and fanciful slides. Her ladyship's mirror was probably her most prized possession. Her own mirror, Mary reflected, was a gift from Ned in her teens. It had lost a lot of its silvering now and she could only see her features when she moved it to catch the light, but she saw them from broken perspectives, which was much as she saw herself in truth, so it didn't particularly matter. Ned had remarked she had the most beautiful hair in the world and had bought her a bunch of coloured feathers once to place in her curls. But it was all light-hearted and always accompanied by laughter. "How you women waste your time!" he had chortled. "And all to please men!" Then they'd argued, saying unforgiveable words that could never be taken back. She wondered what had happened to the feathers, then recalled she had given them to George, who had probably passed them to a girl. George had a lot of girlfriends.

She lifted her curls with a thin coloured scarf and tied it loosely around her head, allowing some of her thicker curls to fall on her face. She wasn't a beauty like Eliza, but she knew she had something striking about her that turned men's heads. That she liked to turn men's heads disturbed her for she was guilty then of the very same thing she despised in other women. But even animals liked to be attractive, didn't they? It was quite natural. Some of them performed the most elaborate rituals in order to attract a mate, and were animals not innocent of vanity?

She sighed deeply and sat down. She would like to have a mate. But a mate with a mind! Her own mind was a chaos. She was trying to regain control of her will and felt overcome with anxiety. The tensions inside her were so great they felt like buds trying to burst from a tree, but she did not know their fruit? Would it be good or would it be rotten at the centre. She drank her tea. Soon she would arrive at the chapel and Doctor Price would discover how she'd changed. Or that's what she hoped for. Was it not good she should change? Did she not dominate people? Was she not over intense? Eliza and Ned had said so.

As she made her way to the chapel, she heard the sound of animated voices through the trees. She could hear Doctor Price involved in a discussion with others.

'Passions are most peculiar,' Price said solemnly. 'They are outside the realms of ethics I think and have their own entities.'

As Mary approached she saw that Joseph Johnson stood beside him. So far no-one had seen her.

'It is perfectly possible,' Price continued, 'to still have a soul, even if you lust for power.'

'A dangerous soul I should think?' said the questioner, gazing at Price thoughtfully.

'Quite,' said another. 'We all have a soul, even the worst of us. Though I do not know what it is.'

'What are you talking about?' asked another.

'This thing called a soul. What is it?'

'Ah, we must discuss it at dinner,' said Price, turning to Johnson. 'Tell us your thoughts, my friend. They are always worth hearing.'

Joseph Johnson folded his arms tightly, the sun shining on his neatly cut wig, he pursed his lips and frowned. But he did not speak.

'My friend, what do you think?' asked Price with a laugh.

Johnson shrugged. 'I try not to think at all if I can help it. Thinking,' said Johnson, waving a finger, 'can cause the most violent headaches. We are often over-thinking.'

'My family accuse me of over-thinking all the time,' said Mary, coming forward. 'But how do you stop yourself doing it?'

'Ah, Miss Wollstonecraft,' said Price, with a look of pleasure. 'How kind of you to join us.' He bowed lightly then glanced around at the gathering. 'This is Mary Wollstonecraft,' he said. 'Joseph, you know her, of course. Is she not one of your writers?' Johnson bowed, but did not speak. Price continued, turning to another of the men. 'Paine – you haven't met Miss Wollstonecraft, have you? She has much to say that is of value. And I can guarantee she is sure to be familiar with your writing.'

'Thomas Paine?' said Mary, facing him with interest. 'Yes, I have read your work. How do you do?'

'Not very well sometimes,' said Paine, smiling. 'I take it you are well yourself, Miss Wollstonecraft.' He gave a light bow and looked kindly at Mary, who he appeared to have taken to immediately. 'Well, Miss Wollstonecraft. Has my work inspired you?' he asked, looking charmed.

'Your pamphlet *Common Sense* cannot help but inspire,' Mary said fervidly. 'It is right to challenge the authority of the British government and the monarchy. And the language you use to speak to the colonies is much to my taste. I am all for plain language. It was brave to encourage independence.'

'They were being devoured. The pamphlet had to be written. And you write also, Miss Wollstonecraft?'

'I have written all my life,' said Mary, smiling with confidence. 'Only small pieces at first, but they blazed with the fire of youth.'

'Ah, the fire of youth!' Paine looked at her pondering. 'Do you still have them?'

She shook her head sadly. 'Only in my mind. My father didn't like them. He is not a man of ideas, though he isn't very practical either.' She frowned in annoyance at the thought. 'You were a founding member of the anti-slavery society in Philadelphia I believe. My brother would love to talk to you.'

'I'm sure that can be arranged Miss Wollstonecraft, such allegiances are always valuable. Ah yes, slavery, a terrible business.'

'Revolutionary ideals have now spread over to France,' said Mary. 'There is much strong feeling. Your pamphlet caused a lot of discussion.' Paine straightened his hair which was blowing about in the wind, and she saw there was a scar on his hand. 'The scar?' she asked, frowning. 'It is a cruel one?'

'Oh this,' he said, dismissively, examining it as if he'd forgotten it. 'A lot of the time I have had to fight my way through. The buggers were always after me.' He stopped abruptly, emotional. 'I do apologise Miss Wollstonecraft. I should not swear in the presence of a lady.'

Mary smiled. 'Oh, do not regard me as "a lady", Mr Paine. I am a *person*. No, no, I am not a lady.'

The group lowered their voices, talking quietly together. Paine nodded slowly, and gazed at Mary through serious and thoughtful eyes. Price cut in. 'Well then, Mary, what have you been doing in Ireland?'

'Teaching, Doctor Price and writing – lots and lots of writing. I have one or two ideas I would like to discuss with you sometime.'

Joseph Johnson raised his eyebrows. 'Ah, writing,' he said quietly. 'I see. Would you care to join us for dinner at my house this evening? Tonight a fiddler will entertain us.'

'You are kind,' she said, delightedly, glancing about. She could only see men in the gathering.

'I wonder what you are writing?' said Johnson. 'You are an interesting person, and I suspect that interesting thoughts will come from your pen.' He had begun his career, he told her, publishing medical books and had moved into literature with a desire to reach the general public. 'I published William Cowper recently. His poetry has sold very well, my publications are most diverse, you see. – But come now, we must first hear what Price has to say in that den of iniquity.' He pointed to the door of the chapel.

'I'm sure it will be most rewarding,' said a voice from behind them. Mary turned to look. It was a small though strong looking fellow with a foreign accent. He stared at her and held her gaze, then he turned quickly, but not before she had noted his interesting features and busy dark eyes.

'Henry Fuseli, the writer and painter,' Price said with vigour. 'Meet Mary, Mary Wollstonecraft. I have told you about her before. She is a woman with a singular mind.'

Mary felt the blood rising in her cheeks. She had heard of Fuseli but he did not look how she'd thought, he was smaller than his reputation might have suggested. 'Thank you Doctor Price, I always hope for more learning,' she said quietly.

'"*Tell me and I forget. Teach me and I remember. Involve me and I learn,*"' said Price sonorously. 'Benjamin Franklin, of course.'

'Absolutely,' said Fuseli. 'Wise words.'

The group made their way up the path to the chapel. 'You are a painter, Mr Fuseli?' said Mary, her eyes shining with interest. 'What do you paint?'

'Yourself perhaps, Miss Wollstonecraft,' said Fuseli, smiling mischievously. 'If you so wish.'

Mary flushed again. 'Oh, I hardly think my face is worthy of a portrait Mr Fuseli.'

'Let me be the judge of that,' he said, looking at her sideways. 'I paint things that are marvellous, things that are supernatural, horrific things too.' He lowered his voice to a whisper. 'And things that are erotic.'

For a moment Mary went silent. But her spirits wouldn't be suppressed. 'I do not see where I come in your list, Mr Fuseli,' she said calmly, though deliciously taken aback. Fuseli told her as they walked that he'd been born in Zurich and had once been a priest, but he'd condemned corruption in positions of power and had therefore been made to flee the country. Now he was an artist, a far less harassing occupation. 'Do sit for me' he said. 'I promise to make an excellent likeness.'

They were about to enter the chapel when a voice called out from the crowd. 'My dear Price, I feared I might not make it!

Someone caught me on the street and the time passed by without notice.'

Mary saw it was William Godwin the man who had called her a "gorgon" on an earlier visit. She looked at him now as the sunshine fell on his face. He had a proud and arrogant bearing. She did not like such men, and made to quicken her pace.

'But you are here, dear Godwin. And I'm glad,' said Price warmly. 'And Mary Wollstonecraft is with us also.' Mary looked at Godwin coldly.

'Please don't look at me like that, Miss Wollstonecraft,' said Godwin, stopping and bowing to her briefly. 'I am sorry I caused you to run from me before, I did not mean to offend.' He glanced at Price. 'Please introduce me, sir. I would be most grateful. I fear Miss Wollstonecraft distrusts me.'

Mary turned her back.

Reverend Price leant towards Godwin and whispered. 'Do not trifle with her Godwin, for her heat may scorch you!'

William Godwin frowned. 'It was her brother who called her a "gorgon" not I, if I remember rightly. And it was all in good humour.' Mary strode ahead with Fuseli. Godwin's features tightened. 'Though I think he was probably right.'

'I think not,' said Price. 'But she is a woman with her own mind. And I mean her *own*. Nothing she says is from the mind of anyone else. She is quite an original thinker. I think you misjudge her. Have another try.'

'Oh, I am not as desperate as that,' Godwin replied, annoyed. 'I have never abused her in the least, yet she is quite determined to ignore me.'

'Never mind', said Price, 'it will all work out eventually.'

'Will it,' laughed Godwin, shaking his head in wonder.

'Certainly,' said Price. 'These things generally do.'

Later, at dinner, Mary found herself seated between Paine and Godwin. She was eager to talk with Paine, but she did not want to talk with Godwin. There was no denying he was a man with charisma however, and she'd seen how the others respected him. Was he a difficult customer? Well, what of herself, she could be difficult too! She gazed about at the company, still wondering why Godwin had held on to the word "gorgon" and thinking of Ned and her father who thought they had the right to cast names. But she did feel possessed by some sort of demon . . . yes, perhaps it was a gorgon-like creature. She recalled the Gorgons, the three female monsters in Greek mythology, daughters of Echidna and Typhon the mother and father of all monsters. The names of the daughters were Stheno, Euryale, and the most famous of all, Medusa, who was a winged human female with a hideous face and living venomous snakes in place of hair. Any who gazed on her face would turn to stone. Was *she* Medusa and were Eliza and Everina her gorgon sisters? She drew her shawl further about her shoulders. For a moment or two she recoiled in its folds and concentrated her attention on Thomas Paine. In his pamphlet *Common Sense*, he had brought moral and political arguments together in a way that ordinary people in the colonies could understand. He was a fine writer and had certainly been brave. The work had been published anonymously in January 1776 at the start of the American Revolution. A radical and provocative piece, it had sold worldwide and had been read out loud in taverns and wherever people gathered to talk. Mary recalled he had gone to the colonies in 1774 whilst the thirteen colonies and Great Britain were forever sniping at each other. The idea of independence hadn't been yet considered; even to think of it would have seemed traitorous. Then in 1775, Paine had hit the nation with *Common Sense*, and ideas of independence had exploded throughout the world.

'You must be proud of what was achieved,' Mary said to Paine. 'You opened everyone's eyes and gave them a different vision, for life is quite different when seen through the eyes of independence.'

William Godwin leant forward to try to speak to Paine across her. 'I believe you intended to use the profits for mittens for General Montgomery's troops! Quebec is bitterly cold, of course.'

'Oh, I didn't make any money,' said Paine with a sigh.

'There are dangers in anonymity,' said Mary.

'More dangers had I revealed the name of the author,' said Paine, smiling wryly. 'I might not have been here today to enjoy this wonderful food.' Johnson was slicing into a sirloin beef roast and passing it on plates round the table. Next came the vegetables; artichokes, carrots, French beans and potatoes. 'Yes, splendid,' Paine murmured.

'There is a lot of writing about potatoes,' smiled Mary. 'It is a wonder there is so much to say. King Louis XVI of France and his court are quite devoted to potatoes, you know. I am told that Marie Antoinette once wore a headdress of potato flowers to a party.'

Paine laughed. 'Ah, the queen wears her hair in ridiculous ways. I believe she must bend her head to get into a coach.'

'I suspect she suffers very bad neck ache,' laughed Mary.

For a moment or two they were silent, passing round the food.

'The potato has replaced the turnip as foodstuff for the poor,' Paine continued. 'We should be deeply thankful to Sir Walter Raleigh for bringing it to England, don't you think?'

Mary glanced sideways at Godwin, whose face was serious and stern.

'Tell me about Ireland, Miss Wollstonecraft. How was it?' asked Paine.

'Quite depressing actually,' said Mary, spooning several artichokes on to her plate. 'The poverty hurts me, and like everywhere else, the rich are far too rich. Oh, how I loathe the complacency and arrogance of the rich!'

'I can see you have no wish for discourse on Ireland just now,' smiled Paine.

'No, no. I'm sorry. Much of Ireland is beautiful. But I am left with the tension of inequality and the fact that I cannot address it. Not only inequality between rich and poor, but also of the sexes. Women are equal to men if they would only realise their abilities, but they won't you see, they can't, they need to think better of themselves.'

'I am in full agreement, Miss Wollstonecraft,' said Paine. 'Much needs addressing there.'

And they continued to talk until the end of the meal, Mary's voice rising and falling with her feelings, Paine earnest and frowning, then laughing at something light hearted.

Godwin though had little to say and half turned his shoulder. When they were taking coffee after dinner, Johnson came over and whispered in his ear. 'My dear Godwin, it seems you've had a rather bad day. Stay around for a while and we'll take a night cap together. I must walk Miss Wollstonecraft back to her lodgings first though, but it isn't so far.'

The faces of the company grew tired and they were ready to leave. Mary pulled on her cape and gathered her gloves. As she did so, she felt the flat of a hand on her own. It was the large warm hand of Henry Fuseli.

'Miss Wollstonecraft,' said Fuseli. 'May I walk you to your lodgings? It is rather dark out there and the weather has turned quite chilly. It would save Joseph the trouble. I can see he is putting on his coat.'

'Thank you Henry,' said Johnson. 'Are you happy with that?' he said to Mary. She did not need to reply, the answer was there on her face.

## 22

## *Fuseli and Desire*

Next morning when she opened her eyes the events of the previous evening came to her vividly – the talk by the chapel and the dinner at Johnson's house, her meeting with Paine and Fuseli. She had successfully become a member of Johnson's circle and had arrived where she felt she belonged.

Her conversation with Paine had been most agreeable. She had suffered no sense of inadequacy with Paine, however much she talked he listened, his busy discerning mind thinking on her words. She mattered. She recalled however, that she had not spoken at all with Godwin. Nor had she allowed him to spoil her conversation with Paine. Thomas Paine was popular and she wondered why Johnson had been so good as to place her next to him. Johnson, it seemed, knew everyone, and as a long established publisher he liked to bring people together to share their ideas. He probably thought the best ideas came into being through discussion, which was a theory close to her heart. Let people talk and learn!

What a lively party it had been, so much enjoyable conversation, appetizing food and a very good fiddler in the background. There was life to be had in the nooks and crannies of loneliness; all you had to do was find it. And for the whole of the evening Fuseli had glanced across at her smiling. That he found her attractive was obvious, for he had scarcely spoken to anyone else that evening. She thought him strangely stirring. Never before had she seen a man kiss another in the way he had kissed Johnson on arriving for dinner. But Fuseli was a law unto himself. Some had said he was cold, even pugnacious, but everyone believed he had great ability as a painter.

In spite of her thoughts, which she would like to have dwelt on that morning, she knew she had to get on, for she had two special guests to breakfast – none other than Johnson and Fuseli. Fuseli wanted to make a painting of her, and she could not help but feel flattered; he was famous and very particular. But what would become of it, she wondered. Would she hang on a wall like Lady Kingsborough? She smiled at the thought. She didn't think anyone would want her portrait on their wall. What did you do with such paintings?

It was going to be a busy morning, she thought, flinging aside the bedclothes. She wondered what she could give them to eat for breakfast, for all she had in the larder was a sponge cake Mrs Burgh had brought her yesterday. She felt ashamed of her poverty. But her friends had been more than generous. Johnson and Mrs Burgh had paid off her debts, and by courtesy of Johnson she was living rent free in her lodgings. Yes, she'd been most fortunate. People admired her and cared for her and she ought to be mindful of that. But she didn't feel loved by her family. Eliza and Everina sometimes said she was discourteous. And she knew Ned thought her opinionated and conceited. But her thoughts came fast and courtesy often cut you off from people when something important must be said. Courtesy it seemed was mainly administered to the rich, for few were courteous to the poor. Yet however wealthy he might be, was a man always courteous to his wife behind closed doors, or a wife her husband? Not so. Experience had told her differently. She knew she would never marry, but what would she do for a living? The thought of becoming a governess again made her weak. Might she gain independence through writing? Was it possible? Could she make sufficient money? She had much to write and Johnson was eager for the kind of work she could deliver. Might he rescue her from the dark fate she feared; the fate of *oblivion?*

Her thoughts moved on towards Fuseli. His bold erotic stare was etched in her mind. She had seen his painting *The Nightmare* in The Royal Academy, a picture of his wife that men gazed on with desire, and which women didn't dare look at, a painting showing a near naked woman on her back draped across a bed, her head hanging down, her long hair loose and her beautiful neck exposed. She shivered at the recollection of the incubus perched on her belly . . . As she wrapped her scarf about her hair she hoped Fuseli wouldn't want her posing like that. Fuseli's wife was beautiful and quiet apparently, a woman who moved about the house in the way of a ghost. She glanced about the parlour. There was nothing of interest to look at, no ornaments, no trinkets, nothing. But she hadn't been back in London very long, she would buy things in time and cheer the place up. She got the fire into action and swept up the grate, then she filled the kettle for tea and sliced Mrs Burgh's cake.

Everything done, she waited for the knock on the door, flattered that Fuseli and Johnson were coming to see her, though both men made her feel nervous for different reasons. One had hold of her erotic imagination, and the other had hold of her future. She imagined Fuseli dipping his brush in his paints then taking her image to the canvas, carefully, slowly, precisely . . . What would she look like, she wondered, in paint on canvas, every brush stroke applied with thought and feeling. Or perhaps he worked quickly with confidence, knowing her inner self already in the way of an artist. He had probably taken her in with his eyes and searched her every feature. Her skin tingled at the thought.

It was half past ten when they arrived. Opening the door, she spoke to Fuseli first, though nervously. 'Ah, Mr Fuseli, you have come to talk about the painting?' She spoke quickly. 'London has been very influenced by Paris I think when it comes to art, though Rococo portraits invaded Germany I know. – I do like the work of Hogarth, his conversations and moral fables are fascinating I think.' Joseph Johnson standing behind Fuseli, bid her good morning.

'I am hoping you will come to my studio, Miss Wollstonecraft,' said Fuseli. As they entered the parlour, the sun from the window shone on Johnson's immaculate grey wig and the silver buttons on his coat. Fuseli's hair was loose and powdered falling about his shoulders. They both wore coats and waistcoats and close fitting breeches.

'Thank you, Mr Fuseli. I would like very much to see your studio,' she said. She glanced at Johnson who sat clasping his hands in his lap. It was Johnson's practise to listen more than talk and he did not look the least resentful at seemingly being ignored. She went to bring the tea and cake from the kitchen and offered them each a small plate. 'It was baked by Mrs Burgh,' she said to Johnson. 'She is quite an angel.'

'The woman exudes virtue,' Johnson said with a sigh.

'And she bakes a very good cake,' smiled Fuseli, biting into a slice.

Johnson sipped his tea. Fuseli sat gazing downwards. Mary couldn't help thinking about *The Nightmare*. What were Fuseli's intentions, she wondered.

'Fuseli can't stay very long,' said Johnson. 'He has a meeting somewhere at one. But he wanted to see you.'

'I did,' said Fuseli quietly. 'I am determined to know you better, Miss Wollstonecraft, so I thought I would visit you this morning with Joseph. I am hoping you'll allow me to paint you.' He looked at her and waited. For a moment or two there was silence. 'So when will you come to my studio?' he asked, narrowing his eyes and holding her gaze.

'Next week,' she said quickly, 'Wednesday afternoon.' She did not know why she'd decided on Wednesday afternoon though, it was just a feeling.

Fuseli rose slowly. 'Wednesday afternoon, it is. Now I must bid you good day. I have to be off.'

'I'll talk to you later,' said Johnson nodding farewell to Fuseli.

Mary showed him to the door.

Alone with Johnson she felt emotional. 'He makes me have strange feelings,' she said awkwardly.

'*New* feelings?' Johnson lifted his eyebrows and smiled, he missed very little.

'I have never met anyone like him,' she murmured, staring at the fire. He . . .'

'He *excites* you?' said Johnson, glancing about the parlour. 'You are lonely, my dear. If you like you can have a room at my house, I mean as a sort of office. That way you needn't spend all your time in here. It would give you a change. I shall continue to pay for your lodgings, so you need not worry.'

For a moment or two, apart from the crackling of the fire, the room was silent.

'You are far too good to me, Joseph. You'll take care of the cost of my lodgings, and you offer me a private room in your home as well. How can I ever repay you?'

'That isn't the way to look at it. I am offering my friendship. I see myself as a father figure, if I may.'

'You, Joseph – my father?' She smiled with a flood of warm feeling.

'But why not?' he gasped. 'From all I can gather, it seems your father neglects you.'

She started. What did he know about her father? He talked a lot with Mrs Burgh but she did not gossip. She might have let something slip though accidentally. Mary rarely heard from her father, but he'd married again since the death of her mother and she would not think to interfere. Her relationships with Eliza and Everina were strained; love still survived though sharp at the edges, it was much the same with Ned.

'I am starting a new magazine called *The Analytical Review* with a Scotsman called Thomas Christie,' Johnson told her, standing. 'He will live in my home, so you will probably see him around.' For a moment his face was sad. He looked downwards and spoke quietly. 'Fuseli lived with me once, but we parted. We are still very fond of each other.' He lowered his hands into the pockets of his frock coat and braced himself. 'Yes, I am fond of Fuseli. He is easy to take to but his passions are wild. If you fall in love with him, my dear, you had better be careful.'

'Oh, I won't fall in love with him!' she gasped. 'How could you even think it?' She could feel her face reddening, and she wondered about Johnson and Fuseli. She waited for more, but Johnson stayed silent, his face turned towards the fire. 'What sort of writing will you want from me?' she asked, cheering.

Johnson burst into talk. 'I am keen to branch out into foreign ideas. A degree of translating would be needed. Would you like to do something like that? How is your French?'

'It ought to be better,' she said, excited but awkward. 'I do intend to improve.'

'You will need to, dear Mary, for I have work that will take some brain power. I'm sure you have plenty of that. – And might you write some reviews? It is always good to have reviews from a thinker like yourself, an 'analytical' thinker for the new magazine. What do you say?'

'I could certainly try,' she said, smiling and drawing a breath.

'"*Try?*" Oh, that isn't good enough, my dear. You will have to do more than try.' He was making to leave. 'Now I must get that room cleared over the kitchen. It is light and warm and the pigeons don't perch there so much.' He straightened his immaculate wig. 'I think you will like it.'

'I'm sure I will,' she smiled.

'Then that is all sorted,' said Johnson finding his cane. 'Now I have things to attend to. And so do you. Your life is about to take a turn for the better I think.'

# 23

# *Johnson's Mansion*

It was only a short walk to Johnson's house, but Mary was frustrated, deep in thought and gazing down at the pavement as she went. He was paying the rent for her lodgings in George Street and finding her a room in his home from where she might work, that was all good, but she was feeling far from independent. Alternatively though, if she tried to see Johnson as a father, as he'd suggested, and wrote for his new magazine – the thought of which made her tense – then might it not balance things a little and make her feel better? In truth, she had little choice. She wondered how much she should reveal to Everina and Eliza in her letters. They would wonder at Johnson's generosity. And Ned might even think the worst and roll his eyes as he sometimes did if he thought she'd made the wrong decision. She breathed the fresh morning air deep into her lungs. Well, she wouldn't reveal anything!

She arrived and rapped down the knocker, greeted immediately by Johnson in his dressing gown and without his rather grand wig. She saw that his soft brown hair was slightly thinning. He looked quite different, she thought, without his wig, more like the gentle fellow he actually was and not the sometimes austere publisher who strode through the streets.

'Come in, my dear,' he smiled. 'The maid will bring us some tea. And then I must make myself decent.'

She was now in his sitting room which was large and warm, furnished with long velvet curtains, a lovely slate blue colour with little flecks of white, bringing to mind the cliff faces of Wales. The heavy easy chairs and sofa were dark sea green, softened by blue satin cushions. It was all very colourful and cheering. A fire glowed in the hearth.

'Do let me take your cloak,' said Johnson, putting out his hand. 'There now, have that seat by the fire and make yourself comfortable.' He rang a bell and a thin elegant young woman appeared in the doorway.

'Louise, please bring my guest some breakfast. And thank you for sorting out the room. I take it everything is ready?'

'Oh Monsieur, je suis désolé, there were no flowers to be found at all this morning,' she looked at Mary and gave her a quick curtsy. 'I was to place some flowers on your desk Mademoiselle, but I could not get them.'

'Well, there we are,' said Johnson. 'We can get some later. Are you quite comfy?'

The fire flickered, and early morning light entered through the window sleepily. 'Your home is most pleasant,' said Mary. 'Thank you.'

Johnson gave her another welcoming smile and went off.

The maid left her but returned quickly with food and drink on a tray which she placed on a low table. Mary thought she had a worried look in her eyes; something that spoke of suffering. Johnson had probably rescued her from some fearsome fate; he was always out to make a rescue. 'Please ring the bell when you have eaten,' said the maid. 'Then I can take you to your study. The second floor staircase is only short. Mr Christie is over the landing. You will like him, no?'

'So he is here?'

'Ah yes,' said the maid delightedly. 'He arrived early this morning.'

'And do you live here also?' asked Mary, buttering a croissant.

'I am sharing a room with the cook; it is down by the kitchen. You will meet her later.' She gave another light curtsy and left.

After another fifteen minutes, Johnson accompanied Mary upstairs. Now in his wig and day clothes he wandered her room, looking around with a view to her comfort. 'There is a writing desk there for your use by the window,' he said. 'I am rather partial to it actually . . .' He ran his fingers around the edges of the shining wood.

'It is well crafted. I shall make good use of it. I know I shall love it,' she said, excited by the new arrangement.

'Well, I see you have brought your books,' he smiled. 'If there's anything you need, writing things and such, you can ring for the maid. As for me I must go to the shop.'

For a moment or two he talked on in his friendly, happy manner. Whatever he expected her to write for him, she would do it to the best of her ability; she wanted to please him.

'You do not mind if I leave you?' he said, awkwardly. 'You can come and go as you wish, of course. I thought if you were here in my house, you could meet other writers and converse with them. They are always coming and going. Such splendid people drop by, people who write for me, of course, in the main.'

'I don't mind at all being left on my own. I am used to it.'

'That's good then,' he said, clapping his hands and smiling.

There came the sound of footsteps on the stairs.

'Ah, Thomas, meet Miss Wollstonecraft,' said Johnson, opening the door and making a gesture towards Mary. 'Mary, this is Thomas Christie. I am sure you'll make very good colleagues.'

Christie, she saw, was tall with a tightly drawn forehead suggestive of business. 'I hope to get to know you,' he said, his eyes shining with pleasure.

She wondered, as he said it, who in fact *she* actually was. "I intend to be the first of a *new genus*", she had once said to Fanny, "a new genus!" She smiled to herself, Fanny was never far away. It was as if she had made her a promise.

'We are to undertake an exciting new venture, Miss Wollstone-craft,' said Christie excitedly.

'Yes, Mr Christie. I have talked about it with Joseph,' Mary said equally exuberant. 'Though I have no idea what I shall write for your review. I'm practising French and German very hard. I believe I am to do some translations.' Christie, Mr Price had told her, was a brilliant young man who had once been a bank clerk but had discovered an interest in literature and science. He had also studied medicine but had found himself writing articles for magazines instead and had wanted a life of letters. He had corresponded with many famous people, Johnson had said, the likes of Erasmus Darwin and the scientist Joseph Priestley. And he had latterly discovered Johnson who he now proposed to work with. *The Analytical Review* was to cover all kinds of subjects from matters philosophical, medical and moral to miscellaneous items of interest on theology, education and history. Christie's background, Johnson had said, was priceless.

'Your knowledge is admirable,' she said, a little diffidently. 'I cannot begin to match it.'

'Dinnae let it worry ye, lass,' Christie said playfully. 'You are a clever woman, and I am a clever man. Knowledge is a mystery until you understand it. Then it is yours. Welcome tae the world o' mysteries! We are about to take over the universe!'

'I am glad you are hopeful,' smiled Johnson waiting by the door. 'But come now Christie, we must get to the shop, we are late.' He turned to Mary. 'Do come and join us if you wish, when you are ready. Christie's energy seeks a focus, or it will lose itself in mischief.'

For the first time in years, as she settled into her room, Mary felt happy. And she was suddenly feeling elated again, for her *Thoughts on the Education of Daughters*, Johnson said, had been getting good sales. He was eager to raise the educational standard of society, he said, and the moral tone of the people. He did not like aristocracy any more than she did, or the buying of privilege, and he and Christie were hell bent on getting *The Analytical Review* up and going to help change the times.

'Mademoiselle Mary,' the maid said breathlessly one morning. 'It is Monsieur Fuseli. He requests to see you immediately. He is most insistent.'

'And where are Mr Johnson and Mr Christie?'

'They have both gone out to the shop. I do not know what to do. Will you come to see Mr Fuseli, he waits in the parlour downstairs?'

She set aside her work and went to find him. The door to the parlour was open and she could see him pacing intently. 'What is it?' she asked. She looked at him concerned.

'It is *you*,' he said quietly. 'You promised to pay me a visit, but it seems you forgot. I came to remind you.'

Mary held back, confused. Fuseli spoke again. This time his voice was harder. 'Tell me, my dear. Did you dare to forget about Fuseli? Do you not know of my genius? I asked you to sit for me. I requested it and have thought of it often.' He looked at her intensely. 'I wonder if you thought about it at all.'

She gazed at him worriedly. His eyes were angry. She hadn't forgotten. Fuseli was there in her mind every day, so much so that she had resisted going to his house for fear she would succumb to his power. The maid stood watching in the doorway. 'Thank you, Louise,' said Mary. At that she left and closed the door.

'This sort of thing has never happened before,' said Fuseli in his thick accent. 'If I wish someone to sit for me, they normally come to my studio quickly. What happened to you Miss Wollstonecraft, do tell me. I am offended.'

She began, hesitant and nervous. 'I am writing for Joseph . . . I am very busy learning. I must study my French and German. Joseph thinks they will be needed for . . .'

Fuseli stopped her with his hand. 'It is more than that.'

She looked at him straight.

'I unnerve you, Miss Wollstonecraft. I know it.'

'Not at all,' she said sharply, and straightening. 'The new magazine is taking up a lot of our time. And I am expected to do some important translations shortly.'

'Ah, translations can often be troublesome,' he said frowning. He made a gesture with his hand. 'It is the *feeling*, you see. It is sometimes lost in translation. What is the use of language if it loses its feeling? It is just like a body devoid of its blood. – I helped the poet Cowper translate some Homer once. Not easy.' He looked at her with his dark penetrating eyes. 'I am sure Johnson can part with you now and then. I'll ask him myself if you like. I doubt he expects you to constantly stay in your room, hiding away like a mole.'

Mary was roused and affronted. Johnson had not insisted on a strict schedule and she was free to come and go as she wished. She had not wished to visit Fuseli and had tried to forget her promise. 'I can come right now if it suits you,' she told him coolly. She rang for the maid to bring her cloak. 'I do not know how long I shall be gone,' she told her. 'But please inform Mr Johnson that I have gone to Mr Fuseli's house.'

Within minutes they had left.

Soon she was treading the tall dark hall of Fuseli's home. The soft sound of piano playing came from a distant room. 'My wife,' said Fuseli. 'She plays rather well considering she taught herself. I am very fond of her. Should you speak with her, though, do not bother her with questions for she is not learned. She was one of my models.'

'I believe she was your model for *The Nightmare*,' said Mary.

'Yes,' said Fuseli intensely. Several canvases and drawings rested on the sides of the hallway. He drew out something rolled up. 'This is the sketch I did for it.' He unrolled it and they looked at it together. Then he stood stroking his chin, his eyes narrowed. 'I was able to explore the deepest of my emotions on the canvas. I could enter the painting, you see. It is a wonderful piece.'

'"Enter it?"'

'Yes, an artist must enter his art, not just slide across its surface. That piece I entered quite forcibly.'

Mary gazed on the woman draped across the bed. Was she dead, or did she just sleep? Might death be a kind of long unending nightmare? Fuseli took out more of the sketches in the dim light of the hall and unrolled them. Though it was almost midday, there was too little light to see the pieces in detail. He went for a candle and it seemed the drawings sprang to life in the flickering light.

'You work is exaggerated,' she murmured with a slight shiver. 'What living man has thighs so primed for violence?' She gazed at one of the sketches with nervous curiosity. 'The arms are like those of a brute that would tear you to pieces. – Oh, those eyes are not human Mr Fuseli! They are the eyes of hell; they are the very same eyes as the eyes of the incubus that sits on the woman in

*The Nightmare.*' For a moment she covered her face as the blood rushed to her cheeks.

'You are very observant,' he whispered. 'And you would see much more on the canvas, but I do not have it at present.' She saw in that moment that his own eyes harboured almost the very same look. The incubus came from himself, it was his own creation. She stepped back. What was Fuseli's potential? The music played quietly on from afar, lending an eerie reality to the fearful drawings. She could feel her spirit draining from her body so that she was all but a shell of herself. She braced herself back into being.

'Enough of these sketches,' said Fuseli, rolling them up and putting them back into place. 'Let me take you to see the hangings. My ideas might not work for you – in the way of pleasure, that is. I do not know what I do exactly, but my models have enjoyed their sittings, in whatever postures I require. They do not always appear the same however, once I have their essence. For we are each many things – human, beast, yes, even plant life I think. The lives of plants are extraordinary. They take on such interesting forms, and belong to us in ways we are yet to explore.'

'Undoubtedly,' murmured Mary. She thought instantly of Fanny and a cruel pain passed through her. But she would not fail her; she, Mary Wollstonecraft, would be a new genus, of that she was certain. But what was she doing now in Fuseli's house like this, with his wife playing music downstairs. They went down another corridor then up a flight of stairs. The sound of the music sounded farther away. Soft warm fur brushed against her leg momentarily. She started.

'A mouse,' he said calmly. 'They insist on coming. But they do us no harm.'

The air had a musty smell as if the rooms were not often used, and having no windows where they walked, the lighting was dim. They entered another room. 'My best work stays in here, until I let it go, that is. I hate to let it go. I do not paint to make money; I paint because I am driven.'

'What drives you?' asked Mary, as he touched her elbow and led her forward.

'Something in here,' he said, putting his hand on his heart. 'But my heart is bold, far too bold for this life. Part of me exists elsewhere. That is why I must paint.'

She was deeply struck by his way of expressing himself. The mood that grasped him when he spoke of his work was filled with resolve. He was lost in the ecstasy of the human form seized by demonic sensuality and painted it into limbs on canvas, limbs that were copious with desire.

'And I must paint you too Miss Wollstonecraft, very soon.'

She was overwhelmed with disquiet at the thought of being painted by Fuseli. What did he want? What would he ask of her, and could she resist him? Such dreams as she had had of him filled her with foreboding. His mind was open to everything and any-thing. And the paintings spoke of an indomitable will to power. She had never felt such unease since the time she had spent at the asylum searching for her brother, she had feared then the dark pos-sibilities of life, and recognised the feeling now. He lifted his candle to the paintings, one then another.

'So will you join me with my paint?'

'I must go,' she said quickly, making to leave. The music had stopped. Everywhere was silent and the candle was burning low. 'Perhaps I will let you make a drawing,' she faltered. 'But you must tell me what you wish to draw. I cannot agree to sit in the postures of some of the images here.'

'Ah, they disturb you Miss Wollstonecraft. It is good to be disturbed. It aids the creative impulse.'

Mary stayed silent; she did not feel happy with his words. Fuseli disturbed her in the darkest of ways.

They went downstairs and met with a beautiful woman who leant leisurely against the wall, her fair hair falling down her shoulders. She looked pale and unearthly and had a wild ghostly smile.

'Henry,' the woman said languidly. 'Where have you been?'

'This is my wife, Sophia,' said Fuseli, looking at the woman lovingly. She appeared half asleep.

'I am just about to go,' said Mary.

'So soon?' said Fuseli's wife. 'I have only just met you.'

'I shall come again very soon,' said Mary. 'I will send you a note, Mr Fuseli, to let you know when.' Then she looked again at his wife. 'You play very well,' she told her.

'Do I?' said Sophia, surprised. 'Was I playing the piano? How nice.'

'Does your wife take laudanum?' murmured Mary, as Fuseli opened the door on to the street.

Fuseli ignored her. 'Do not make me wait too long,' he said. 'There is a nature in you I must capture. I do not know if you will like what I find, but I am urged to seize it.'

'What is it?' Mary asked urgently, gathering her cape closer around her shoulders. 'What do you see?'

'My dear Miss Wollstonecraft, I can no more speak of it in words than fly to the stars. But paint, paint, that is how we shall find it; paint will deliver your answer!'

# 24

## *Troubles in France*

Mary was soon translating important documents and writing reviews for the new magazine. She was pursuing her splendid work which was published by Johnson anonymously, for that was his preference in the main, reviews could be troublesome, he said, and you had to keep an eye on the politics. She wrote to Everina and Eliza about her successes, but she did not touch on anything personal about Johnson. He was "a father figure", she said, which was just how he'd put it, and he'd helped her financially. She was working hard, she told them, and his pay was generous. Her highly emotional nature however persisted and she confessed she could not bear it if he so much as wrinkled his forehead at something she'd written. But he dealt with her moods admirably which was quite an achievement and she believed they shared an unspoken understanding. A young Scottish fellow lived with him, she said, a lively and interesting character whose name was Thomas Christie. Christie had helped him start *The Analytical Review,* and was excellent company. She told them about her study at the top of the house, a quieter place to work, she said, than her lodgings in George Street, and she talked about the wonderful cook who provided excellent meals and fed Johnson's lively fraternity when they all came for dinner. The maid, Louise, who was French, had described the French situation tearfully. She had left her parents in France and as their only child, felt riddled with guilt, though they'd insisted matters would get worse in her country and she should try to make a life in England for there were violent outbursts everywhere and no-one could settle. King Louis, it seemed, had no idea how to rule, and Marie Antoinette was a doll of a creature who did not know her people, which was always dangerous. It seemed the French were on the verge of revolution. The nobles were jealous of the king, the bourgeoisie were jealous of the nobles and the peasants were starving.

And she told her sisters about Fuseli and his painting *The Nightmare,* the erotic picture of his wife sleeping on her bed. There were those who said she looked dead, she wrote, though Mary asserted she was well and truly alive for she had recently visited their home and talked with them both. She explained how she worked with Fuseli on translations for Johnson; he was a brilliant painter, she said, and spoke several languages. And she wrote of the lively crowd who gathered in Johnson's home and his bookshop, distinguished fellows like Joseph Priestley and others. Finishing her letter she felt the heartbeat of her new life quickening. She was becoming a new genus!

But she had not told them about Henry Fuseli's drawings of *her.* Nor did she write about her portrait. Fuseli's wife greeted her with warmth and seemed to enjoy her visits, sometimes resting her head on Mary's shoulder where she would fall asleep within minutes. Mary thought she was a woman who liked repose, she would fall asleep in her arms, breathing softly, her white skin milky and shiny, and though she was pale as a moonbeam she always ate well and didn't seem at all undernourished. But Sophia Fuseli was a creature of the night, and Fuseli said she would sometimes play her piano by candlelight into the early hours of the morning.

It was the year 1789. A great deal had happened in the last few years and the world had changed irrevocably. Weekdays, Mary visited Johnson's bookshop, always busy with people; this was one of the ways he recruited his writers. There she exchanged ideas and heard all the news. The first edition of *The Times* had been published to waves of excitement and wonder. Titania and Oberon, moons of Uranus, had been discovered by William Herschel, the astronomer, and people looked to the heavens for answers, for it seemed there were none on earth.

*Of the Importance of Religious Opinions,* a text by France's Finance Minister, Jacques Necker, lay on Johnson's desk awaiting publication. It filled Mary with unease, for she knew what it meant. Necker had considered it right and proper that the people should know the opinion of the nation on crucial issues, and religion was of great importance. Mary had worked assiduously on translating Necker's work and it was now ready for printing. In her heart she felt sympathy for Necker. His task in France was enormous. The national debt had taken on huge proportions. Constant funding of the American wars had depleted France's resources and poor harvests had left peasants starving. They'd also grown weary of constant conscription and taxation and were determined to end it.

With serious disruptions up and down the land no-one felt safe. Louis had invited his nobles to talk about taxation, but his suggestions had met with indifference and he'd had to convene The Estates General, the only national representative body of France's three estates. It hadn't been convened since the year 1614 and there was a lot of confusion over who held sway or if anyone still understood it. The estates had always been a bone of contention in France and many said it was time they were sorted out. The First Estate was the clergy, the Second was the nobles and the Third consisted of 97% of the nation, from beggars and struggling peasants to artisans, labourers, shopkeepers and commercial middle classes, some of whom were rich merchants. Peculiar things were happening in France and it seemed the right hand didn't know what the left was up to. Despite its size, the Third Estate was economically exploited by the others and their frustrations, grievances and sufferings fell on deaf ears. Mary heard this as a constant refrain in Johnson's bookshop. People argued that the three estates would discuss matters separately but had only one vote in unison, which meant the Third Estate was regularly outvoted by the others. The country was on the brink of revolution and there was need for urgent reform. After a bout of failed negotiations the Third Estate had formed into a National Assembly challenging the king's authority. It was calamitous.

Jacques Necker had been a favourite with the people but had now been dismissed. Might there be a royal coup, people murmured suspiciously? Must they take action? Demonstrators marched through the streets and threw stones at the cavalry in Paris. It was rumoured more troops were advancing towards the city.

Those who were gathered in Johnson's bookshop spread their newspapers wide. 'This is a revolution!' they cried. 'Paris is in turmoil!'

And in July, that year, the revolution swung into action. Rioters searching for weapons and gunpowder stormed the Bastille, the king's prison fortress. They murdered the garrison soldiers and freed its captives. Then they hacked off the governor's head with a knife and paraded it about the city on a pike, a brutal, vicious and barbaric action, and still more horror was to come. Tax officials and corrupt politicians were strung from lampposts and left hanging to die moaning and screaming, parts ripped from bodies, landowners were killed and châteaux were destroyed. The vile demon of hatred had been let loose.

In August that year, *The Declaration of the Rights of Man and the Citizen*, a radical document covering human and civil rights was passed through France's National Constituent Assembly. Feudalism was abolished, depriving the clergy and aristocracy of familiar riches. The king's troops were replaced by armed revolutionaries who called themselves the National Guard, France was changing overnight.

'It is sheer hell over there!' someone in Johnson's shop cried out. 'Men grow savage when they're starving!'

'And so do women!' another voice added. 'I heard from a coachman that the women of Paris are to march from Paris to Versailles with all manner of home made weapons. They are intent on demanding bread from the monarch.'

Johnson's shop went quiet at the thought. Would the heads of the king and queen be paraded about the city too? It was perfectly possible.

'The queen is slight and pretty,' someone shouted, 'while the king is short and fat. They are indeed a peculiar pair. She decks herself in precious gems and all while her people are starving.'

'It's expected of her,' someone else reasoned. 'The people are to blame for expecting grandeur and magnificence.'

'And look where it leads!' cried the first.

'People are calling her the Austrian bitch,' said another. 'There are vulgar cartoons circulating France and they can't do anything about it.'

'It was rumoured, you know,' the first speaker said, his voice almost a whisper, 'that the king hadn't known how to consummate his marriage at first. Her brother had to come and instruct him.'

'But he was scarcely into his teens,' another said sympathetically. 'He has sired four children, so enough said about that.'

Despite the amusement, Johnson's shop grew silent, and a baffled fear came upon them, as if a shudder beneath their feet were coming from across the channel.

Mary felt as if the arrival of hell in France had coincided with a hell in herself. That hell was Henry Fuseli who would not leave her mind. But she had grown into a competent writer now and could bury herself in her work. She'd worked that year on *The Female Reader*, the first educational anthology written by a woman for women. But she could not follow her own instruction and it troubled her. Emotion made her irrational. She thought on it long and hard. In *Maria,* her novel, she had explored the struggles of a woman searching for identity, and her latest work, *The Female Reader,* was meant to help women become learned rational adults, capable of thinking for themselves and examining their lives. But she needed to apply her reasoning to herself. This she found difficult to do. What right did she have to instruct other women if she could not instruct herself?

With Fuseli rooted in her emotions and dreams, she was losing hold of who she was. Her vision of Fuseli was of a powerful male who held her in bondage. Johnson had warned her of his power, but feelings had won. Whenever he made his drawings, or she sat before him for her portrait, she maintained a certain reserve. She did not look at him directly, and when she spoke it was quiet and formal. His wife often came and went, disappearing to play her piano, and Fuseli ignored her. Mary wondered sometimes if his feelings for his sitter might be stronger than those for his wife, and she allowed herself to drift into romantic fantasies, something she despised. But she continued to visit his house each week and Sophia would greet her with a kiss, then withdraw to play her piano. And Mary dreamed dreams of Fuseli, dreams that merged with reality until it was hard to tell one from the other. And she thought she loved him.

News of the French Revolution spread fast through England. Louis XVI had lost control of his country and had fallen from absolute power to nothing. He'd attempted to quell insurgencies but they'd swollen in force and the people had come to hate him. The greedy king and queen, along with the aristocracy had bled the poor of their very life's blood, they said, and were as rats only fitted for the gutter. The royal family had been taken from the Palace of Versailles to the Tuilieres Palace in Paris where a Paris Commune could observe their behaviour more closely. The Tuilieres Palace was a cold and miserable place compared to the grandeur of Versailles, but the country was hostile to the monarchy now. The people loathed them to the marrow of their bones and the cry for a republic sounded out loud and clear: "Liberté, equalité, fraternité ou la mort!" was heard from all corners of the city. The poor of France were mad as thunder and livid as lightning.

And the champion of their cause was a brilliant young lawyer by the name of Maximilien de Robespierre, an outspoken advocate of the poor. Robespierre campaigned for equality of rights, price controls, universal male suffrage and abolition of slavery in the colonies. People fell at his feet. Inflamed to the centre of their souls, they felt they were fighting for their lives.

In May that year Robespierre had been elected as deputy for the Third Estate in the Estates General and had witnessed the collapse of the monarchy. The overwrought state of the people had filled him with anger. He had heard the cries of mothers whose children had died from starvation, he had seen with disgust the excesses of the rich, and he knew from his personal life the cost of deprivation. He had lost his mother early in life and his father had as good as run away. Brought up by his aunts, he had not known the love of a

221

mother, though people said it had made him independent and bold, and now he was a lawyer of note. A forceful and impressive speaker, Robespierre would often address the radical and ruthless Jacobin Club in Paris. There were those who called him a genius; others were contemptuous and said he was all puffed up. But someone in Johnson's shop remarked that as the ancient philosopher Aristotle had said, nature abhorred a vacuum, and in such turbulent times it seemed that no-one was in charge and the people had turned to Robespierre.

Such matters were discussed over Johnson's dinners until the candles burned low and conversations of late were all about France. Mary listened intently to the different opinions. But one of the chairs was empty that night and the fact made her sombre.

'Fuseli cannot join us,' said Johnson, a little disappointed. 'He sends his apologies.'

'That's a pity,' said one of the group.

'Aye, his obscenities an' sarcasms will nae doubt be missed,' laughed Christie.

'He is probably painting a picture of his wife,' someone else laughed. 'One of those he sells privately.'

'He is a great artist,' Johnson asserted frowning. Then he looked at Mary, who was gazing ahead subdued. 'Do you not agree, Mary, that Fuseli's talent is immense? I believe he is painting your portrait, though I have not seen it. He does not allow me up the stairs. Though I daresay the rooms contain great works of art.'

There was a chuckle amongst the guests. The people in the gathering liked Fuseli in the main and admired his painting, though his manner could be arrogant and irksome.

'Yes, he is painting my portrait,' said Mary with a sigh. The men fell silent for a moment, then resumed their talk. She did not feel like joining their conversations that evening. She was thinking about the French Revolution and the women's march on Versailles. Women when united were a powerful force to be reckoned with. But in English law, a man and his wife were as one; the wife must bow to her husband's wishes, under whose protection she performed those things called *life*. Oh, for emancipation! Women must be better educated! Women must free themselves to feel and do as they wished! She had so much more to write. As well as her translation of Necker, Johnson had published her *Original Stories from Real Life*, a book she had written for children. She'd enjoyed writing it immensely. It featured a Mrs Mason, a governess, eager to direct the girls in her care into the ways of virtue, spurning vanity and appearance for sincerity, compassion and truth. Writing it though, Mary had felt the tug of her own inconsistencies. She had wanted to illustrate how girls might succeed in whatever role they desired and also live dignified lives. But she had come across many problems, for how could women possibly work for independence, when there was so little employment available that was not servile. But they must not marry just for wealth, she had warned, or for fear of becoming spinsters. She was troubled. How hard it was to show a satisfying way for a woman to earn money if she didn't find love and a compatible bond with a man. She hadn't succeeded herself; she was earning now with her writing, though not very much. And she wanted love. How she wanted love! She felt lonely as she sat by Fuseli's empty seat at the table. Perhaps it was time to go home.

# 25

## *Fuseli, Sophia and Love*

That morning as he continued with her portrait Mary saw Fuseli was anxious. His manner was normally calm and the tension surprised her. 'We missed you last night,' she said, a little pathetically.

'I am glad. It is good to be missed,' he said attempting a strained smile. 'Well, as you see, I did not disappear. I simply spent the night elsewhere.' He frowned and dabbed at the canvas irritably. 'Everyone needs to know Fuseli's whereabouts however. I have little privacy. My wife too wondered where I was. She has not forgiven me either. You do not know how she screams; it can continue for ages. Oh Sophia has a sort of madness in her I think.'

'But if she did not know where you were then hasn't she a right to be concerned? Mary reasoned. 'She is your wife.'

'Wife, ah yes. But my wife is not my keeper; I do not need to tell her my every move.'

Mary wondered how it was with him and Sophia, and where he had spent the night. The house was silent that morning.

Fuseli sighed and continued to paint. 'I spent the night at the house of William Blake, the poet and painter,' he said.

She looked at him surprised.

'I find his work intriguing,' he added abstractedly.

She straightened and breathed in deeply. There was a strong sense of disquiet in the air. He had said very little that morning and she could not hear the piano.

He mixed a couple of paints on his palette carefully, concentrating his attention on the colours. 'Blake is an interesting man, we talked until dawn.'

'There are those who say he is far too imaginative.'

Fuseli shrugged. 'He is an artist of the highest order. Blake's imagination is powerful. Who can tell where our imagination will lead us. The places we are taken to in dreams can be most entertaining.'

'Or else terrifying,' she added quietly. For several moments they were silent. 'Did you see much of his work?'

'Yes, yes, of course. It is quite extraordinary. His characters leap through the air as if they exist in a realm of their own. – Gods, demons, angels, they are all his familiars.'

'He professes to *see* them,' said Mary, in a serious voice. – 'Angels, that is, he believes they are with us.'

Fuseli smiled. 'And you?'

'I believe in them also,' she said profoundly. 'I saw a group of angels in a wood once when I was small, only a few but that was enough. I do not forget.'

'And were they magnificent?' he murmured, moving in closer to his canvas. Then he darted his eyes at her curiously, eager for more.

'Oh yes,' she said wistfully. 'More than magnificent.'

He drew a breath and went on. 'I have never seen angels, myself. Perhaps they prefer to stay away from the likes of me.' He laughed. 'I might corrupt them, you see.'

Again they were silent. Fuseli spoke again. 'Blake has published some poems. He has called them *Songs of Innocence*.' He stopped and gazed at space. 'And that is just what they are.' He dropped his voice, reciting softly as he painted:

> '"*Father! father! where are you going?*
> *Oh do not walk so fast.*
> *Speak, father, speak to your little boy,*
> *Or else I shall be lost.*
>
> *The night was dark, no father was there;*
> *The child was wet with dew;*
> *The mire was deep, and the child did weep,*
> *And away the vapour flew.*"'

'That one touched me best.' He sighed. 'What man does not feel that his father has deserted him, or indeed, is a sort of vapour. Yes, I feel it strongly. *"Do not walk so fast,"* says the boy, but it is just a vapour he follows. Such vapour has to disappear. There is something tender and innocent about Blake for all his ferocity. He is however, consistent and sees consistency as important.'

'And you do not?'

Fuseli frowned. 'I let my imagination wander; it is quite wayward, so I am not consistent. No, I am not consistent.'

For a moment or two they were silent.

'Me neither,' Mary said quietly. 'Though I believe I have a central strength that returns me to where I should be.'

'Do you?' he smiled, narrowing his eyes as he looked at her. He was by nature disdainful, and she saw in his face he would somehow hurt her that morning.

'Foolish or otherwise, consistency is an important preoccupation of Blake's, just as he is contemptuous of self-contradiction.' He became more personal, all the time, watching her face. 'You are often self-contradictory Miss Wollstonecraft, would you not agree?'

'I probably am,' she sighed. 'My thoughts move quickly and I am always assessing them. There are things I wish to discover. I reach conclusions, then see another idea and decide to go with that one instead. I think I am a sort of explorer.' Fuseli stopped for a moment and looked into her nervous eyes. 'Perhaps my writing is worthless,' she said finally, feeling unhappy.

'Not so,' he gasped, staring at her wildly. 'Your opinions are excellent. I am deeply impressed by your writings.'

She remained very still and silent.

'My dear Mary, you are my friend,' said Fuseli, laughing briefly with amusement.

'Like Johnson is your friend?' she whispered. Her skin tightened with feeling. She tilted her head towards him awaiting his answer.

'Ah, Johnson, yes, my very first and best, before the arrival of my gift'

'The gift of your painting?'

'Yes that. I was a writer first, then a painter. I had to draw in secret, however. My father would have had me a man of the church.

I was ordained at the age of twenty and preached for a while. But it never touched my soul. Well, not in the way that *he* did?'

She waited a moment in the silence, listening to the sound of his brush on the palette. 'Of whom do you speak?'

'I speak of a young male friend who I loved with a passion.' Fuseli stopped and lowered his voice, thoughtfully. 'It was a thoroughly erotic passion. I could not sleep for longing . . .' He sighed and shrugged. 'But he betrayed me, you see. They do. He got married. I hated him for that and wrote to tell him my spirit would be there on his lips whenever he kissed her. I told him I would scorn every pleasure a woman could ever have given me, just to feel his embrace. But he chose the woman over me. She was clever, you see. I hate clever women. I went to Italy for a while, then I started to paint.'

'You are a great painter,' Mary said painfully.

'I am,' he said, frowning seriously as he took his brush to her portrait again and again.

'Why do you want to hurt me?' she asked. 'Is it because I am a thinker – a *clever* woman, perhaps? You fear women who think. You hate them.'

'Ah,' he sighed. 'You are a sad creature, Mary.' His tone was piteous. 'Do move your hands; my dear, how can I paint your beautiful eyes if you cover them up? The portrait is almost finished. I want it to please you.' He pointed at her with his brush. – 'Your piece by the way, of Rousseau's confessions in the *Review* was quite amazing. I saw that you did not mention the fact, but when he reached the age of twenty, a clever woman took him as her lover along with the steward of her house. It was a ménage à trois, which I am told confused him, though he loved her dearly.'

'Yes,' Mary said quietly, wondering how she could save herself from her thoughts. 'And you – would you have been confused like Rousseau?'

Fuseli laughed at the ceiling. 'I do not think so. I would see it as adventurous and creative. But Rousseau was young. It made him feel uncomfortable. She had a splendid library though and introduced him to many ideas.' His voice fell to a whisper. 'I suspect she had certain inclinations also that stirred him.'

Mary listened in silence. Rousseau had been dead some time. How was it possible to know what had occurred in his lifetime, the real naked truth of it? She respected confessions however that came through diaries and writings. Though even then, did people really speak the truth, or did they dabble in fantasies of their own idealised self?

Fuseli continued emotionally. 'You excuse him his adulteries, the abandonment of his children.' He waved his heavy hand, and paint fell from his brush to the floor. 'Yet *me* you censure! I cannot be rescued and do not wish it.'

'Why do you say such things?' she asked shakily.

'Your look just now, suggested disapproval of my craving for another man. Be careful. You would not know how easily such things can happen.'

'Perhaps I would,' she murmured. 'I too have been obsessed with someone of my own sex.'

Her whispering tone made him frown. *'You?'*

'Oh yes,' she sighed. 'I know of the pain.'

Fuseli's dark eyes blazed with interest. 'And where is this woman now?'

Mary felt chilled. 'She is dead,' she said flatly. 'She has gone.'

'Be still,' he said. 'Or your left eye is going to look squinted.'

'I am trying hard not to move,' she said. 'But I think I am weary of sitting.' Just then she was exhausted with Fuseli. Finally, she said, 'I must go. I think you have played along with me enough today.'

'*I* played along with *you*,' he said, with a look of disbelief. 'Oh, my dear, it is you who play along with me. You pretend to care for me, but I know you do not, you are not consistent, you see. You play with my feelings. You would like to take ownership of me, take me from my wife, and then you would dig your claws in.'

*'My claws?'* There were tears in her eyes as she spoke.

'Oh yes, I know you have claws. I believe you despise us really – us men, I mean. You want to blot us all out.'

She clasped her hands in her lap, but could not stop them trembling. There was fury in his last sentence, the fury he had felt on having been rejected by his lover, she thought, back in his youth. She pitied him for it, but she loathed the words he had spoken.

They contained an element of truth that made her shiver, but there was more, far more to her than that. Did he not see it?

His wife entered the studio.

'Ah, Sophia,' he said, with a rare acknowledgment. 'I am happy you have come to see me. I did not hear the piano and wondered what you were doing.'

'I am sorry for interrupting,' she said, a little mournfully. 'But I am very lonely down there. My music ignores me today.'

'What nonsense,' Fuseli said laughing.

'No, no,' she retorted angrily. 'It will not let me play it. That is the way of my music, it does not come through the instrument today, however I try.'

Mary stared at Fuseli. He was uncomfortable and slightly vexed.

'Alright, my dear,' he sighed. 'But how often have I said you must not labour your playing too long or it will leave you?'

'You said it and it has happened,' she frowned. 'You should never have said it.' She threw back her hair and fell into a chair beside him. 'Why do you dictate my life? Do I not exist for myself? Am I just a dream for Fuseli?'

'Why not read from your library,' Mary suggested. 'You have so many interesting books, but you tell me you never read them.'

'Why would I want to read books?' snapped Sophia, looking at Mary confounded. 'Books are a bore.' She gazed at the colours on Fuseli's palette and dipped a finger in the red, bringing it close to her lips. 'See,' she murmured. 'Today I taste blood.'

Fuseli stopped his work, and Mary saw in an instant that Sophia was everything to him. 'Do not frighten me, my dear,' he cried, in a tone of despair.

'But you do not love me,' she whimpered, pointing to Mary. 'You love *her* more. How can I bear it?'

He went to her and gathered her towards him. 'I love you immeasurably,' he murmured, kissing her hair.

'But when are you going to do a painting of me?' she asked him tenderly. 'You do not paint me anymore.'

'The time will come,' he said gently. 'I shall know when it is right.' He frowned and sighed, then stroked his wife's long hair.

'This house is very large,' Mary said to Sophia. 'You need company. Why don't I come to live with you?' She spoke in a tone of passion. 'I believe we could be happy together, all three of us. Loneliness dampens the spirit. I beg of you, please let me come to live with you . . .'

'Never!' cried Sophia, looking horrified. 'How could you think such a thing? It is impossible. You are here too much already.'

To Mary's surprise Sophia began to weep.

'Oh, see what you did!' cried Fuseli, in the tone of a father. He held his wife even closer. 'You've upset her. She is not to be unsettled like this.' Again, he stroked her hair. 'There now my love, be calm.'

'No, I will not!' screamed Sophia. 'She wants to steal you away. I know it!' she continued unflinchingly, saying how she hated it when Fuseli made drawings of Mary. 'You must not make any more,' she begged him, sobbing. She glared at Mary and spoke like a petulant child. 'He used to make drawings of me, and now it is you!' She rose and went to a table, gathering up several sheets of paper. 'See, they are here! – Take them away!' She pushed them at Mary, and the drawings tumbled about her.

'Take them!' cried Fuseli. 'Take them all!'

Mary trembled. 'What am I to do with them?' she asked shakily.

'Anything!' cried Fuseli. 'Throw them on the fire if you wish! For my wife's sake throw them away. Now go! Johnson can bring your portrait around to George Street, for I do not think we will speak again in the way we have spoken before.'

Mary went down the stairs and Fuseli followed her to the door. She resented grievously the way they had mocked her needs and her proud feelings of love. But she felt there was something deep between Fuseli and Sophia that was theirs alone. As she left the house she heard them laughing.

# 26

# *Revolution*

When it came to independence, there was a need to think carefully about one's actions and deeds, Price had said. They were words spoken from his own particular vision of freedom, freedom through caring and beneficence. 'Methinks I see the desire for liberty spreading throughout the world,' he said to the crowd in Johnson's shop that morning, repeating words from a sermon he had given last year. 'The dominion of kings will give way to the dominion of laws and the power of the priest will be replaced by personal reason and conscience.' This he believed emphatically and had conveyed such thoughts in *Discourse on the Love of our Country*, an address he had given at the start of the French Revolution.

People gathered about him, in tune with his every word. It was now 1790 and the revolution was going fast. The air was filled with a sense of catastrophe and fear.

'Can change only happen through fighting?' sighed Mary, standing close by. Price had suffered considerable effort to deliver his Address, he'd been brave and bold, but she saw now how maintaining such strength had affected his health. He was pale and unwell and needed to take things slowly. It was a habit of Johnson's to remember passages from pamphlets, and there was obviously something on his mind, thought Mary seeing him biting at his lip. Then he began to quote from the Discourse. The others drew back to listen:

*"'I have adopted the words of the Scripture, Now lettest thou thy servant depart in peace, and expressed my gratitude to God for having spared my life to see a diffusion of knowledge that has undermined superstition and error, a vast kingdom spurning at slavery, and an arbitrary monarch led in triumph and surrendering himself to his subjects.'"*

Mary standing with Price saw a look of sad reflection in Johnson's eyes as he spoke. Price leant against the wall. He could scarcely keep himself upright and from time to time trembled as if with pain. Yet the world cared nothing for Price's health, and Mary's instincts told her there was trouble in store for this gentle, thoughtful man who she saw as a guide to humanity. He had been contrasted now with the anti-revolutionary Burke who had declared his position most forcefully in his political pamphlet *Reflections on the Revolution in France*, arguing the revolution was harmful to king and country. Burke's pamphlet had caused a lot of disturbance and whenever he was mentioned the name of Price was drawn in. Mary found his fearlessness inspiring. He had even sent a message of approval to the National Assembly in Paris and his words had been published, words that had been read and talked about throughout the world. He was a forceful fighter for liberty and justice, which made him a target for hostility. Then came the war of the pamphlets and Johnson's press was busy from dawn till dusk.

That day the bookshop was frantic with voices. Priestley too was a focus of government suspicion. Predicting the revolution would spread, he expected his house to be raided any minute, he said. Mary saw that Priestley had just walked in and was coming to talk with Price. Today though Price looked weary. In fits and starts however he still had his say, expressing the hope that the world might at last come of age and sound judgement would finally prevail. He firmly believed that a fair scheme of government would bring about natural equality.

There was a steady flow of banter, wit and crosstalk in the shop just now, spirited moments of freedom, moments of delight, and moments of intense concern as pamphlets were earnestly debated.

Mary standing with Price listened to his talk with Priestley. Price couldn't see why Burke had protested so strongly against his Discourse, he said. 'It seems like madness for a man who had once believed in the rebellion to turn so fiercely against it,' he said confusedly. Priestley agreed decidedly. He had written that many dissenters previously in support of Burke had now turned against him, and Burke had discharged a reply loud as thunder. Priestley though had been ready and had replied with equal vigour, denouncing him as sycophantic and a champion of religion and monarchy.

Mary watched Price as he listened to Priestley. He shook his head and frowned, his features tight and drawn as if some lingering fate had finally seized him. Were there really angels on earth, she wondered. How could she deny what she had seen that day in the woods, however long ago? Might they be there for Price in his hour of need? She prayed in the silence of her heart.

The noise in the shop quietened. People were thinking. It was difficult to know what to make of it all, for the news that came across the channel might be fact or fiction. To actually visit France though could be dangerous just now. Curiosity however would never be stilled and writers were eager to learn. She had heard several dissenters discussing passage that very morning.

'I wonder why Burke changed his mind,' she said, frowning at Price. She saw that Priestley had taken a couple of pamphlets and left.

Price answered quietly and seriously. 'It was the women.'

Mary looked at him curiously and waited.

'It was the women's march on Versailles, when the king and queen had been forced from the palace and taken to Paris; he thought it improper and savage. That was when he wrote his *Reflections*. What a curse it can be to think. There is pleasure in it, no doubt, but how perilous it is sometimes.'

'Burke can rave all he likes,' Mary said earnestly. 'But it is wrong to feed his friends such poison.' Words seethed inside her. A reply was forming in her mind.

Later at Johnson's dinner, talk of revolution swelled the sound in the room. There were many points of view and a lot of fiery contention. You must safeguard your beliefs, they argued, and it was important to have opinions, but Burke had been far too harsh. Mary sat silent and inflamed. She could not forgive the attack he had made on Price. France had changed fundamentally since the start of the revolution and its effects were encompassing the world. Letters and publications flew across great distances fast as comets. Everything was moving quickly, readers and writers could scarce keep up with the news which all too often was bloody. Yet somewhere in the mayhem of it all, dissenters held on to the hope that the beast would calm and grow sober, and France would experience the liberty and equality it yearned for.

The English government feared the dissenters more than ever, and hovered about their organisations like assassins. On this particular evening Mary saw that Priestley was anxious, turning towards the door, ready for anything. He was a man of immense talents, and most important was his talent for controversial writing for which he was constantly pursued.

'The majesty of the people is the only sacred majesty,' said Price, leaning towards him. 'All civic authority is a trust from them.'

'Yes, I believe you are right,' said Priestley gravely. 'On understanding his natural rights and feeling his own importance a man will consider himself totally equal to anyone.' He shook a finger in the air. 'The majesty of the people, my friend, yes, that is the thing!'

Mary seated by Priestley, said she had twice read Burke's *Reflections* and they'd incensed her. 'I sent something hastily,' she said. 'I cannot read half a dozen pages of his book without admiring his ingenuity or indignantly spurning his sophisms.' Her blood was up. Priestley folded his arms and gave her a serious look. Her eyes flashed with anger. Nothing less than a formal reply would do. Burke must know that what he had chosen to write had consequences.

She went to her room where she sat for a good ten minutes, thoughtful. Then the whole of her being fused like never before as she composed her heading: "*A Vindication of the Rights of Men.*" Her hand shook as the words took form on the page. First she wrote, "Security of Property". Oh, how it caused her to rage! She was deeply contemptuous of privilege and the complacency of those who lived rich and indulgent lives caring nothing for the poor. As she wrote she hoped Burke would feel the burning arrows of shame!

Her pen went fast across the page: *"Behold, in a few words, the definition of English liberty! And to this selfish principle every nobler one is sacrificed!"* Land that wasn't used, she asserted, should be divided into small farms so that people might work towards independence. She envisaged a society based on industry and talent where each person might attain rewards and where younger children in a family were no less than the eldest son, a society where women might aspire to be independent also and loved for themselves, not for what others dictated. She also believed the poor should be assisted, not in a charitable way, but more towards self-determination.

She wrote till well past midnight. Outside it was silent and dark. Just then there came a tap on her door. Then another. She opened it on to a very tired looking Johnson. 'It is 2 a.m.' he whispered. 'I was concerned.' He glanced at the fading candle on her desk. 'Your candle has almost burned down, my dear. You will damage your eyes.'

The sight of Johnson's worried face alarmed her. 'I'm just making notes,' she said tiredly. 'It's a reply to Burke. But I'll stop now, I am far too emotional. I shall address it again tomorrow.' She went for her cape and drew it closely about her.

'Now I shall take you to George Street,' he said. 'But I can see this room needs a bed.' Johnson went for his coat and they left.

He liked the streets after dark, he said, the bats intrigued him. A bat came on to his window ledge regularly, he told her, and he fed it meal worms. It was getting quite fat. 'Bats are mainly nocturnal,' he said, 'they emerge from their roosts while we're sleeping.' He laughed quietly into the stillness. His voice came soft through the night. 'Fuseli made a very good portrait, I thought. It arrived at my house the other day. I thought I should send it over. I presumed you'd received it, but you did not mention it, my dear.'

'I didn't want to,' she murmured. 'It faces the wall in the parlour.'

'But why don't you hang it?'

She answered with silence.

'Well, I think it a pity that you've turned it away rather than face it with pride. Fuseli is a great artist and I thought the portrait quite wonderful. – I believe he made some drawings as well, though I seem to have missed them.'

Mary was glad of the darkness so that Johnson couldn't see her expression as she remembered the way she'd left Fuseli's house so ashamed, the drawings in her arms, sometimes falling to the floor so that she must bend to retrieve them. 'They have gone. I have torn them to pieces and burned them.'

'You did what?' Johnson stopped for a moment shocked. 'Dear Mary, you are such a clever woman and have so many special qualities, yet you have all these foolish insecurities too. I see them in your eyes, even in your movements sometimes. You are quite extraordinary, and that, you know, can often make you afraid.' He sighed. 'Being ordinary is so much easier.' He gazed at the night sky, just a few stars shone through the mist. Shaking his head he murmured. 'You burned Fuseli's drawings, I cannot believe it.'

They walked more slowly. It seemed less complicated speaking her emotions to the darkness. 'I don't want to talk about Fuseli,' she said, her voice a little too loud so that a dog barked further down the street. 'I want to reply to Burke.'

'Oh yes,' said Johnson. 'By all means reply. And you won't be alone either; a lot of others feel the same. I'm expecting Paine to write next. I know he is fuming.'

'Paine is a man who always seeks fairness,' she said.

'He does,' Johnson continued. 'But it troubles me, Mary, when friends put themselves in danger. I could always refuse to publish them, of course, but I never do. You see, what they say is almost like a prayer. It is a force for enlightenment. I cannot ignore it, and neither can the world.'

But the next afternoon, as she wrote at Johnson's house, there came upon her a feeling of dread. Her words as they emerged on the page seemed far too weak and inadequate. An important energy had left her. She knew there were stages of loss that left you depleted, she had known them before, but in time the mind reclaimed itself. She prayed and waited for her stronger thoughts to return. But the feeling of loss plagued her. 'The loss of Fuseli is hurting,' she wept to Johnson later.

Johnson looked at her straight, his eyebrows raised as always when he grew emotional. 'You never actually *had* him,' he told her quietly. 'And anyway, I thought you wanted to forget him? You mustn't allow your mind to harass you, for it will, you know if you let it. You must write, Mary, write! You know I believe in you.'

'But do I believe in myself?' she said wretchedly. 'Have I the strength to reach the best that is in me?'

Johnson gazed at the floor, then spoke plaintively. 'What do you mean "*the best*?" We are only as strong or as thoughtful as the day allows. I have no desire to coerce you, but I think your work is valuable. And as for romance, well, there is nothing in this world I'd like better than to have you find love, my dear. – Oh love, ah love! How we are used by *love*.' He shook his head slowly. 'I warned you against Henry, but you would not listen. You must try not to think of him. It will get you nowhere. You have done no harm and need not worry about consequences. He did not love you, so there you are. He loves Sophia. But his love is fickle, you are better off without it.'

Johnson's words calmed her. 'You are right,' she murmured. 'Thank you.'

'However,' said Johnson, half serious, his features soft in the yellow afternoon sunlight shining through her window. 'I can discard what I have printed so far of this pamphlet if you wish. That is, if you fear Mr Burke.'

At that she started. 'Oh, I do not fear Mr Burke,' she cried, her eyes wide with resolve. 'Oh, no, do not destroy it. I intend to continue. I have a lot more to say.'

'That is true,' said Johnson, smiling wryly.

She covered her face, embarrassed for her weakness and knew he would berate her if she fell into hopeless melancholy. 'A very clever trick, sir, you know my mind too well.' She lifted her head and smiled.

'Godwin was here earlier,' he said, lowering himself into a chair and glad he had made her see sense. 'He says you don't talk to him. You ought to talk to him, you know. He is a fine writer and speaker, a man you might learn from.'

She pressed her hand to her breast. '*Me*, learn from *Godwin*?' She frowned.

'Oh yes, and he can learn from you. We all learn from each other. But you have something against him, you see, and I don't think it's fair. It bothers him.'

'He irritates me,' she sighed. 'He tries to interrupt when I'm talking. I was talking to Paine and he leant straight across. He is rude.'

'But Mary, I never knew rudeness bother you before? You are eager as a beaver to express yourself. Sometimes you make it hard for others to get a word in. I have seen you dismiss poor Godwin in the cruellest of ways. Why do you do it?'

'I'm not sure,' she murmured. But she felt an aversion towards Godwin, and did not like the way he so often fixed his eyes on her.

'Wasn't it something your brother said once in the street?' asked Johnson with a curious look. 'Oh, how high minded we can be, yet also how trivial sometimes.'

She was quite overcome for a moment as Johnson slowly got up and left. Yes, she could be cruel, but she hadn't liked the gorgon image. She touched her heavily curled hair. Might she turn people to stone if they looked at her? Perhaps she did in a way. Had she petrified Godwin? No, she decided, she had not! His self-possession, his fearless look was disturbing; she felt he saw into her soul. And it was all too true, she ignored him. But she would not connect with Godwin, not ever, for there was something about him that weakened her.

Her mind flashed over her youth with Ned, she had loved him dearly once. But Ned had changed, and her sisters too. What she remembered in the main was the history of their miserable childhood and the way it had shaped her feelings. She knew she must see them soon though before they were lost to her for ever.

Ned was difficult and must always play older brother, wiser, more astute and condescending, and he diminished her, assailing her with harrowing tales of the past and revisiting old concerns. But her writing, her writing! She had to get on with her writing! Her ideas came fast, but sometimes she wrote too quickly indulging personal thoughts and feelings while forgetting to scrutinize issues. But she had to publish rapidly, of that Johnson was adamant, speed was of the essence.

In her room at Johnson's house next day she read through what she had said in her reply to Burke:

> *"Mr Burke's Reflections on the French Revolution first engaged my attention as the transient topic of the day; and reading it more for amusement than information, my indignation was roused by the sophistical arguments, that every moment crossed me, in the questionable shape of natural feelings and common sense."* She had neither patience nor time, she wrote, to follow through what she had called his *"devious tracks"* and had confined the work *"to the grand principles at which he has levelled many ingenious arguments in a very specious garb."*

Yes, exactly! She wrote on intently, though she never felt the work was ready when Johnson ran off with it. It gave her immense satisfaction, however, to know she had written with passion about civic virtue and liberty in accord with her dissenting friends, and from the very depths of her heart.

There was a great noise in the dissenting community just now, and the rumble had spread to the cities. Her pamphlet sold far and wide and very soon Johnson was requesting a second edition, this time carrying her name. She edited this very carefully, honing her language so that it blazed like fire on the page. "Mary Wollstonecraft" was becoming known!

But Price grew ever more sick, and over the next few months increasingly frail. People whispered that the much loved man was dying. Mary fretted and spent a lot of her time alone in her room at

Johnson's reading and writing. Johnson spent most of his evenings with Price, sometimes sitting by his bedside, keeping him company, it was painful to see him declining, he said, but despite the love and respect of so many people, the man was mortal. Price requested few visitors, he had given all he could and now he could give no more.

It was hard to accept his death. Everyone in the dissenting community had a fierce sense of loss, and went about silent with grief. Mary wrote to Ned and her sisters and they sent their consolations, requesting she visit them soon.

One evening at Johnson's dinner, Mary saw that Paine was seated by William Blake who he had brought along as a guest. They were talking anxiously together. Close by, she heard what they said. Everyone feared for Paine who was constantly pursued by the government. 'I feel they are always in the shadows,' he said. 'I can scarce eat my dinner for thinking I shall feel a hand clamped on my neck. They know where I am every minute.'

'You'd be better off living in France,' Blake said gravely. 'I know what you want to write and so do they.' He glanced at the dark window. 'You are right, they are probably watching right now. You risk your life my friend if you stay in England. – Go, I say, soon! Do your writing in France and publish over there.'

'I have been thinking the same, myself,' said Paine pondering. 'But I don't know how France would receive me. There is always Robespierre, of course, constantly forming his damned committees, a committee for this, a committee for that. He is bound to see me as a threat. And where would I hide?' He sighed and straightened.

'You have work to do,' Blake said pointedly. 'You must write.'

Paine nodded slowly, then rose and put on his hat. He would proclaim revolution permissible, he said, if a government did not safeguard the rights of its people. Did it not make sense that all human beings were entitled to a decent life, with food, hopes and aspirations? – *The Rights of Man!*' he declared. 'That's what I intend to write about. What could be more important?'

'Go, my friend,' said Blake, 'for who can know why a man has been murdered on a dark winter's night?'

Paine paid little heed to such warnings normally, but matters were getting worse. 'You are right. I shall leave for France straight away, though my heart is heavy at the thought.' He spoke with resignation. 'Liberty and equality is all the people ask for, and soon they will get it. I shall answer Burke with gusto, and start on *The Rights of Man* this very evening just as soon as I am back in my house.' He smiled wryly. 'Provided my house is still there, and has not been razed to the ground.'

Rumour went round that week that Paine had arranged to cross the channel. Government officials had forced his door and ransacked his home. It was only what he'd expected, but he had gone, and he had taken his writing with him.

'The Girondin party are moderates and will see Thomas as an ally,' Johnson told the others that day in his shop. 'Wherever he is, nothing will stop him writing.'

'He will do well to steer clear of the Jacobins,' said William Godwin, standing close by. 'They are ruthlessly radical and follow Maximilien de Robespierre as if he were a god; but he is far too extreme in his thinking.' Godwin turned to Mary, standing by Johnson. 'Do you not think so, Miss Wollstonecraft?'

She sighed. 'I am not surprised Paine has left us, but I suspect he knows what he's doing.' She spoke in a tone of admiration, gazing ahead abstractedly. 'I pray they won't find him.' She recalled his words: *"These are the times that try men's souls . . ."* and wondered if he would be chased until exhaustion. What was happening in France, she wondered. Was it time for her to go and find out?

## 27

# *A Vindication of the Rights of Woman*

Mary felt she had a good rapport with Johnson as they strolled through the woodland together one mild Saturday morning. They talked over all sorts of subjects as they went along the lonely pathways. 'Your new edition of *Original Stories* is admirable,' he said as if with pride. 'And Blake's engravings look spectacular. I'm glad Fuseli recommended him, a most gracious gesture I thought.'

'I'm thrilled to have Blake's engravings enhance my work,' she murmured. 'It is a privilege. But I hate Fuseli.' His cruelty still had hold of her, she could not forget it.

'How soon we can move from love to hate,' sighed Johnson. 'I think you need to get away for a while. When are you seeing Ned?'

'Soon, I hope.' But she wasn't happy as she thought of it. 'And I shall see my sisters too. I have asked them to go to his house, that way I can see all three of them together. We have much to catch up on.'

'Good. I hope you will speak of your success as a writer. From the things you tell me, I wonder if they ever read your work.'

'They wouldn't tell me if they did,' she laughed. 'I intend to take something with me, though it will probably stay in my bag. Ned can be critical. He thinks I'm against him, you see.' She'd had a long struggle with her family of which Johnson knew very little. She wondered why her heart was heavy when she thought of them, but the young girl in her couldn't break free from her childhood concerns. She must still think about her sisters and help them financially, they were women, and therefore disadvantaged. Her other brothers

242

had lives far away and she rarely had news. She and Ned, though nearer in body, had drifted apart in mind. As a lawyer he must constantly argue his point, and did so heatedly. Her own convictions however about the rights of women were strong and she argued with an eloquence he couldn't compete with; then he would throw up his hands in defeat and walk off. Her father had always exasperated her. But she hadn't the least desire to talk with her father, so left him alone. 'I shan't talk about my work,' she told Johnson decidedly, 'but if anything is mentioned and I'm questioned, then yes, I shall speak of it. I want more than anything to be with my siblings a while and see they are well. They have changed I know. There are times I feel I hardly know them.' The world of her family existed so little for her now, she must confirm it was still there.

'Life changes constantly,' Johnson said pondering. 'We see our families as if at a distance for a while, then all of a sudden they move in close; in our minds that is.' He spoke pensively as if with personal knowledge.

'Then again just as suddenly, they are gone,' Mary said with a sigh, 'like images in a dream, and we cannot reach them. I daresay it's the same for them.'

'We cannot alter the way things finally will be,' Johnson said straightening. 'I believe we must search for the essential truths within us and allow them to guide us.'

'I know such truths in my soul,' Mary murmured. 'Women will become independent beings, I am determined. I shall persuade them through what I write.'

'And your determination is powerful. I am deeply impressed. You are always so passionate about it.'

She smiled wryly. 'Men generally laugh at a woman's determination, but let me tell you, I never resolved to do anything of consequence that I did not resolutely adhere to.'

Johnson stopped for a moment, filled with interest. 'I know it, Mary. And what is your resolve right now?'

She looked at him straight, her eyes intent and shining. 'Something very important; I think it is time.'

'You look triumphant,' he smiled, sharing with her a moment of vital aspiration. 'I'm curious.' They stood for a while in silence by a towering oak. She put her finger to her lips.

'Oh, come, my dear! You must let me in on your secret. What are you intending to write?'

'Dear Johnson, this will be my best work yet!' she said, smiling with rapturous purpose.

'I am sure,' said Johnson. 'But what will the work be about? And what will you call it?'

She turned her face to the sky and spoke as if uttering a prophecy. '*A Vindication of the Rights of Woman!* – Yes that is what I shall call it. I hope to persuade all women to seek greater strength and become independent beings.'

Johnson raised his eyebrows and held her gaze. 'And they are not?'

She flushed with emotion. 'They are slaves to their feelings and must set themselves free. Passions are their own masters and live in us constantly, but I try to take my own in hand and make them bend to my will.'

'Oh that we could.' Johnson smiled warmly. 'And you will forget Henry Fuseli, for to hate is to always remember.'

'When I return from my brother's and I have finished writing *Vindication*, I shall go away for a while.' She had read the newspapers and whatever else she could find about the French Revolution and was eager to follow Paine across the channel. 'Paine is a strong advocate for the rights of women. You will recall his words: *"Man with regard to them, in all climates, and in all ages has been either an insensible husband or an oppressor."*'

'Aye, we're bit of a rotten lot, aren't we?' Johnson smiled wryly. He had a way of not taking things too seriously. 'Shame on us, Mary. But it's all very complicated, you know. How hopeless it seems sometimes. Men, women, love . . .'

'Matters must improve,' she murmured. 'I shall disappear for a while and think.'

Where will you go?' Johnson asked quietly. They carried on walking and he gazed at the ground as they went.

'France,' she said decisively. 'I shall go to France.' The desire was urgent but the thought of visiting that bruised and battered country weighed heavy in her soul. That was the reason she needed to see her siblings, for what if she were killed in the chaos over there? She would see them once more. A wind was up and she fastened her cape more tightly. Johnson secured his hat and they quickened their pace. There was something strange in the air, like the beginning of a new life. She wondered if it might be hers.

'I have actually heard from Paine,' Johnson said through the wind. 'Discreetly, of course, this morning. I thought you'd like to know. He has completed his *Rights of Man*. I have a copy in my office and intend to publish very soon. Burke will be incensed with this piece, oh yes, and Paine's attack is bound to cause more controversy, but he is urging me to publish and everything he says is right.' They walked quickly, the wind moaned all around them. 'I believe he is in hiding at Versailles. No-one will stop him writing, not unless they kill him, that is.' The wind dropped for a while and they slowed down their pace. 'Paine used to be a corset maker once. He got married though and needed money.' Johnson laughed quietly. 'Reputation has him as a corset maker by trade, a journalist by profession, and a propagandist by inclination. You may have heard it said; the words trip off the tongue so easily.'

Mary gave Johnson a look of surprise. Paine was a complex man, a sort of subterranean creature, purely individual, he might do anything. So he was hiding away at Versailles was he, and about to shake England to the roots with his words. 'I dislike corsets as much as I dislike Fuseli,' she murmured.

'Yes, I imagine they are equally uncomfortable. Fuseli holds you in a vice.'

'Not much longer, I promise.' She was able to smile. 'What happened to Paine's wife?' she asked, frowning and concerned. He had never spoken of a wife. It was interesting to hear new things about people who intrigued her. She was a great admirer of Paine.

'His wife? Ah, one way and another Paine had it rough, his wife became pregnant, then his business collapsed and she went into premature labour . . .'

Mary waited, fearing she might hear an all too familiar story.

'Both she and the baby died. He fell into a sort of abyss after that but the man has great strength and found a way out.'

'Oh, for a revolution in female expectations,' sighed Mary. 'Poor Paine, he did not tell me.'

'And he wouldn't. It was far too terrible for him.' Johnson pursed his lips, his eyes suddenly dark as if searching the past.

'And you will publish *The Rights of Man*? Even though his life is in danger?'

'I must. I can do no other. Just as he must write, I too must publish. He cites his authority for the equality of man from the bible, while Burke cites his from the power of the monarchy, chivalry and other such ideas.'

As they walked on, she thought about Paine and his dead wife and child. Then her thoughts fled to Agnes, then Fanny. Anger rose in her that enough wasn't done to make childbirth less dangerous for women, and that female anatomy wasn't fully understood or considered. 'I think we might look to Nature for our lessons,' she said. A *natural* life is the way we should go, but how are we ever to achieve it?'

Johnson shook his head confounded.

'Fanny tried to achieve it,' she murmured with a sigh, remembering her drawings and the tender way she'd held flowers as if they were babies.

'You loved that woman didn't you?'

'Yes I did. But people die and leave us. I can imagine how Paine must have felt when he lost his wife and child in one fell swoop – the swoop of a demon! Oh, Blake would recognise its face!'

'Wordsworth has sent me some poetry,' Johnson said smiling. 'The man is as inspired as ever. He has such spiritual cognisance of Nature, I fancy he burst from some glorious flower, he is truly blessed!'

'I have never met him; though I have often heard others speak of him. Will you publish his poems?'

'But of course. Eventually, that is. I am taken up with the war of the pamphleteers at present, as you know only too well.'

'Is Wordsworth back home?' she asked, following his line of thought. 'I believe he was living in France?' Mary's thoughts constantly turned towards France. Who could know what was happening to its people in such tumultuous times?

'Yes, he returned. He was forced to flee. He says the revolution is chaotic and bound to get worse. The September massacres in Paris finally decided him, the killing of all the priests at the prison was barbaric. The revolutionaries had turned into an angry mob fearful of the queen's armies arriving in Paris. They got rid of their opposition in the cruellest of ways. Some 1200 prisoners died, half of the prison population that was in Paris. Wordsworth had to flee, him being English and all, there was no way of knowing what would happen.'

But Mary was undaunted. She was still intent on crossing the channel if it were possible. 'It is impossible to imagine the terror of the Princess de Lamballe,' she murmured. 'She endured such horror.' A loyal friend to Marie Antoinette, her loyalty had cost her her life. 'As much as I support the revolution, I cannot understand how its heart can darken to such atrocities.' She glanced at Johnson, whose features had turned hard and stern.

'Kingship is finished in France,' he said. 'And I fear the revolution will grow bloodier than ever before it is done.'

'And Paine will be in the thick of it,' said Mary, 'a price on his head most probably.'

'I believe he addressed the Revolution Society when the troubles first started,' Johnson added as if confirming the man's dedication. 'That maddened Burke as well. Paine asserted the right of the people to elect their leaders and dismiss them for any misconduct. The government was most perturbed.'

'I'm sure.' She frowned. 'It is men who betray progress for their own selfish ends, and women sacrifice themselves to whatever men desire. Women need better education so they might find a logical geography for their lives to help them think more sharply.' Fuseli entered her mind again and she thought of how he'd recommended Blake to Johnson. Yes, it was kind. Fuseli admired Blake, he was bold and brave and his work was magnificent, and after all, Blake saw angels. She was suddenly filled with emotion. For several minutes they were silent.

'I hope you will be with us for dinner, this evening,' said Johnson. 'Erasmus Darwin is to join us. He is a Naturalist and most inspiring. You'll enjoy his company I'm sure.'

She covered her face with her hands.

'What is it?' he asked, turning to her concerned. 'Have I upset you, my dear? You would tell me if I had, wouldn't you? Oh, my tongue is too loose!'

'I would be very happy to meet Mr Darwin,' she said, a little shakily. 'But I feel so . . . I feel so old.'

'"Old?" – But you are young!' he gasped. 'How can you say such a thing?'

She spoke in piteous tones, then she turned to him and pointed at her eyes. 'Look at the lines around my eyes. How did they happen?' She touched her hair. 'And I never take time to powder my hair or dress even half decent. I am a plain woman Joseph, and serious thought has devoured me.'

'My dear,' he laughed. 'You have eyes like a goddess. And you are never, never plain! I have seen men look at you. And as for powdering your hair and piling it high, I am glad you don't. Those piled and powdered hairdos are a breeding ground for fleas. It is better to have it natural.' He then made reference to women he knew who he said made their hair look ridiculous. 'We shall be looking as foolish as the French 'ere long,' he said. The French mocked the queen's high hairstyles, while aristocratic women frequently copied them at leisure, he said. He did not care for his wig, but as a publisher felt he should wear it; he must have his writers believe in him, he said, and had to look smart. But such matters, he asserted, were far too superficial to bother a mind like hers. 'I shall await your work with pleasure,' he said. Then he turned his eyes to the clouds. '"*A Vindication of the Rights of Woman!*" Yes, very good!'

She felt glad as she climbed into the chaise for her journey to Ned's. His reply had been favourable, and it seemed her sisters were eager to see her too and would be there at his home as requested. As the chaise moved on, she felt glad thinking of times they had all shared in the past. She had started her book that week and was making excellent progress. Her stay would only be brief, just a couple of days perhaps, time enough to hear their news and see how they were all faring, but not long enough to spark up disagreements.

The sun was shining as the driver cracked his whip and the chaise moved off. Thoughts of Henry Fuseli still assailed her, but she cast them aside, thinking of what she would say when she arrived at Ned's, what to reveal and what to hold back. She leant back her head, her heart beating to the sound of the wheels of the chaise: *How long must I wait for love? How long, how long, how long . . .*

# 28

## *Reflections*

What a strange family we are, thought Mary as she journeyed back to George Street. The time she had spent with Ned and her sisters had been a familiar tangle of memories, arguments, struggles and laughter, much as always. And however she tried to deny it, it did upset her. 'Well, what of it,' she murmured, staring through the window of the chaise at the cold, white, lonely day. 'We are what we are, and we have to put up with each other.' They were each a law unto themselves, passionate in their own spirits. Their mother had been pathetic when it came to their father's behaviour, suffering his abuse as if she could do no other. Ned had tried to govern his father's drunkenness with discreet behaviour and carefully considered words, while Everina and Eliza's eyes had glowed with a kind of impotent rage which it was Mary's lot to deal with.

But it had worn her down. She could not even deal with her own anxieties and felt umbrage in her heart for the burden of blood she'd been given. And it irritated her that her siblings thought her half silly, a woman of mad ideals who thought she could take on the cares of the world when she couldn't even cope with her own. Ned had laughed at her contemptuously when she'd talked about education for all. "Poor girls don't need education," he'd asserted, leant against the mantelpiece at his home. "They just want husbands and children." He was quite the lawyer now, no sleeves on his waistcoat in the manner of the upper classes and displaying his handsome legs in neat black breeches and shining silk stockings.

"They wouldn't know what education meant," he'd laughed. And her sisters had smiled. "We have to start somewhere," Mary had said indignantly. "Just because a thing seems impossible, doesn't mean it is. It might take years, but national education for all is the way we must go, and women, no matter what class, must experience the world for themselves." She had flushed with emotion; Ned could belittle her so easily. "The poor are too full of drink to care," Eliza had said with a sigh. "For just a few pennies they can escape into a bottle of gin." "Oh, no, not now," Ned had interjected quickly. "We have laws in force to curtail that gin business now. These people can't get their *Ladies Delight* and *Cuckold's Comfort* like they did, poor harvests have meant that the price of grain has increased; landowners are less dependent on income from gin production nowadays." "There will always be bootleggers, who can sell it to those who will pay," Eliza had replied curtly, determined not to lose ground. "Oh, not so many," Ned had said shrugging his shoulders.

And so it had continued. Even Ned's small son had looked at Mary sideways, as if she were a stranger in their midst. But she'd smiled and dismissed it. If the child didn't love her, then it wouldn't have to matter, she could not let it diminish her and must reserve her energies. Her work was like an instinct holding out its hand and beckoning her into the future, a future she perceived and felt in her soul but was blind to as yet.

Back in Johnson's house she got out her papers. Firstly she read up her notes on the French Revolution. The National Assembly's *Declaration of the Rights of Man and the Citizen* bothered her, for it only applied to men. Why? she asked herself irritably. Were women in a different world? Women didn't know who they were, whilst men usually did. It was just as if women knew nothing of their selves and others knew nothing of them, they might well have been locked in prison. Little wonder they often went mad. She knew that middle and upper class women living in opulence were no less abused than those who must live in damp and stinking cellars in the poor parts of London, with sometimes twelve to a room. It was a different form of abuse but nonetheless painful and a violent robbery of their souls. They did not know what was happening, and only felt the pain of loss, the terrible loss of self. She had to address it.

For a while she sat in silence, moved by passion as always. Instinctively she let passion rule her because through it came her best ideas. 'I need the words!' she moaned. 'Dear God, give me the words!' She sat quietly a little while longer. And then with triumphant power the words came into her mind and her thoughts moved swiftly. – Not only had women been omitted from *The Declaration of the Rights of Man and the Citizen,* they had also been excluded from government, and citizenship was only granted to men who were over twenty-five. Would this also apply to education? A French official named Talleyrand-Perigord had recommended a free education for children of all sexes. Though the education, Mary had noted, would follow Rousseau's ideal, in that a girl's education would be mainly to serve their husbands. But why, oh why? 'It is almost deathly,' she murmured. Prince de Talleyrand, a French bishop, was a politician and diplomat. She would send him a letter forthwith and see if she could influence his thinking, for hadn't the revolution in the first throes of its glory included the rights of women? He had to see sense.

She went through her papers and rooted out some of his words: "*. . . that to see one half of the human race excluded by the other from all participation of government was a political phenomenon that, according to abstract principles, it was impossible to explain.*" What had made him change his mind? She would dedicate her book to Talleyrand, she decided, and hope to tug him in the right direction by recommending an education for girls equal to that of boys. The thought soothed her. Did she not do Talleyrand a kindness by treating him with such respect? Her blood raced as she wrote. Might not the rights of women come to birth from a fair and universal education, and might patriarchal oppression disperse like the morning dew? She prayed it could happen.

She wrote all day until Johnson's maid tapped on her door and brought in refreshments. After that she continued writing till late in the evening, declining Johnson's invitation to dinner and eating on her own.

'Godwin asked where you were,' Johnson said the following week as they travelled to George Street in a chaise. The weather was too chilly for walking. 'I said you were writing. – He doesn't think you plain, not at all, he is quite enamoured of you, actually.'

'Never,' she laughed. 'I doubt he has cast me a glance.'

'Ah ah! Godwin is clever. He looks when you don't see him.' Johnson gave a little chortle. This was one of his night-time moods; he could forget his airs and make jokes in the dark, and often went without his wig when taking her home in a chaise. With a change of tone, he said, 'You have worked for days on your book, is it done?'

'It is,' she sighed. 'I have said all I can for now.'

'How soon can I publish?' he asked, a sudden spark in his voice. 'I shall publish you anonymously, of course. You need not fear, I shall protect you. We'll see how it goes, and if it does well, I shall want your name on the front of the second edition.'

She felt tender towards Johnson just then, and leant her head on his shoulder. He had been her father, her companion, the mainstay of her existence over the last few years. He had given her life and she had grown from his wisdom just as she had grown from Price's. And she loved her room in his mansion, her private abode where she could write and think as she wanted and come and go as it suited. Sometimes Thomas Christie came in for a chat and they'd enjoyed exchanging ideas, he was full of fun and made her laugh. But he too was intent on his writing and they didn't talk long. It seemed as if the whole world were abuzz with change. 'I'll give you the finished book tomorrow,' she told him.

'First thing in the morning,' he said.

He spoke with the excitement she liked. 'First thing,' she murmured.

As they reached her house he helped her out of the chaise and saw she was safe inside. Then he climbed back in and directed the driver to his home.

And the writing was delivered next day as promised. As the fingers of the clock moved to the noonday hour there came a knock on her door. It was Christie. 'Johnson tells me you've done it!' he said, glowing with enthusiasm.

'Yes,' she said laughing. 'He took it away like a greedy squirrel with a nut.' Christie, she thought, had a subtle, quick intelligence, always watchful and critical and he'd been waiting for her book almost as eagerly as Johnson. When he was critical he was usually right and she listened. He pulled up a chair and sat down. He was dressed in his smartest clothes that day as if he intended going out. If he didn't go out, he usually wandered the house in his dressing gown and cared little for niceties. But he was always warm and energetic and knew what everyone was writing. His normal manner was quiet and reserved until he got excited that was, then he would deliver a fast stream of words – the latest ideas, things he despised, other things he loved. He had a passionate heart and Johnson loved him like a son.

'Johnson tells me he likes it. So there you are, I am first to tell you.' Christie laughed in his usual jubilant manner.

'I shall leave for France very soon,' she told him, suddenly serious. So far, she had only told Johnson and her family.

'Oh?' he said, frowning surprised. 'When will you go?'

'In a couple of months. I need to arrange passage. I'm not quite sure how to do it.'

'I think I can help you with that,' he said, crossing his legs and folding his arms as if it were settled affirmatively. 'Though I hardly recommend it, Mary, you know how it is over there. Each day I am expecting someone to tell me Paine has been shot or even worse.'

'I know,' she said. 'I am hoping to seek him out. I think he's in Paris.'

Christie frowned. 'I know his address. But would you want to visit him there, would you even dare, and would Paine expect it?'

'I think it would please him,' she said flatly. 'There are things I must learn, things I must write, people I need to talk with.'

Christie gazed at her with thoughtful, concerned eyes. 'If I tell you his address you must commit it to memory. I can't write it down. All letters received are delivered discreetly just as ours are to him. It is a nerve-racking business.'

'We always hear the worst,' she frowned. 'People exaggerate.'

'Paine doesn't exaggerate,' shrugged Christie. 'He is a man of utmost integrity.'

They were both silent a while. She knew she must leave the country and quickly. She had to get away from Fuseli, to expel him from her heart and forget him. And she was starting to feel strangely old, as if she might be coming to the end of her life; she felt her features were falling and what beauty she might have possessed was starting to leave her. But perhaps she was wrong; perhaps it was true that Godwin looked at her. It pleased her now to think so. He was attractive certainly, and she was getting to like him better. She intended to be gone six months, she told Christie. If all went well, she would return to England with important things to write about. She would need to get herself organised and Johnson was busy publishing her latest work. There was a lot going on. She shivered slightly. The autumn was passing and she must buy warm clothing for winter.

# 29

## *To France*

It was a cold damp evening as she waited to board the vessel. A thin mist roamed across the harbour, drifting then returning, drifting then returning like a curious ghost. The coach lamps dimmed as they left. Christie had brought her but had quickly departed and dusk had fallen on the murmuring gathering at Dover. She saw that a woman waited close by, shifting about nervously when the men on patrol arrived with their lanterns. Her hood half covered her short loose curls and she held it close with her hand. The sea was relatively calm just then, calmer than the minds of the travellers who glanced at each other suspiciously. Spies! Spies! Everywhere spies! Mary wore a long woollen coat and a hat bearing one or two feathers, given her by Mrs Burgh. Though her clothes were unfashionable they were warm and of excellent quality.

As the patrol men moved about the harbour shining their lamps she saw that the woman standing near wore a blue silk Mantua gown, brocaded with designs of fruit and leaves. She wore a hooded coat, loose to show off her dress. Of a similar age to herself, Mary thought she might be an actress. Mary turned to her and smiled, surprised by the dazzling redness of her hair. She is Irish, she thought, feeling a sudden affinity. Had the weather been warmer they might have exchanged a few words, but the evening was cold and dreary and they expected any minute to be invited to board the ship. She thought on the last few months as she stood there. Johnson had published her book. She had become a successful author and the world spread itself before her. It was such an invigorating thought.

'I'm sure I heard seagulls singing,' the woman said suddenly, her light voice entering the dusk like a voice in a dream. 'Do seagulls sing?'

'I don't think they *sing*,' Mary replied pondering, as if the question were vital. She had never heard seagulls singing, not even in Wales by the beach. 'They scream though, and very loud too.'

'I hate the sound of screaming,' said the woman, her gloved hands covering her face. 'There is a lot of screaming in Paris just now.'

A man's voice came from the shadows. 'Is that you Miss Lamont?'

She turned to look. 'Yes, are you here to assist me?'

'I am,' he said, in a strong French accent. 'Où est votre baggage?'

'It has gone on the boat,' she replied. She turned to Mary. 'I think they took it with yours?'

'Did they?' said Mary, looking confused. 'I have only a couple of bags. A boy took them away.'

'It's muddy underfoot,' said the woman. 'Take care as you go up the gangplank.'

The gangplank jolted and rattled as the passengers climbed on board, while the shapes of the waves rose and fell with dark menacing intensity.

'Are you alone?' asked the woman.

'Yes,' Mary asserted. 'I always travel alone.'

'You need not travel alone today,' said the woman. She spoke in a pleading tone. 'That is unless you want to. I should be very glad of your company. I have done the journey before on several occasions but I am always nervous. There will be room enough for us both in my cabin. Do join me.'

They found her cabin and entered. 'I shall be just next door,' said the man, who introduced himself as Fabien, the woman's friend. The woman said her name was Laurette.

'And I am Mary,' Mary said, greeting them formally. The man's eyes were alert and watchful as he stood in the doorway.

'Do not fear me,' he said, seeing her look. 'I am here to see that

Laurette arrives safely in Paris. I can take care of you both, if you wish. It is good for Laurette to have company.'

'I do not fear you,' said Mary, smiling.

'Merci beaucoup!' Fabien laughed. 'We all wish to live, but fear is a common emotion in Paris just now.' They both took off their coats.

'A weary emotion,' sighed Laurette. 'Have you reserved accommodation?'

'Yes,' said Mary.

'And would it be difficult to cancel?'

'I doubt it. I took a cancellation myself; it is a popular hotel by the Seine.'

'Nothing is popular by the Seine anymore,' sighed Laurette. 'The rooms are empty around there. Paris is filled with beggars and the river stinks rotten, it is a place where people cast refuse and carcases. Better to live further away. The apartment I stay in has several spare rooms. You will be very much safer with us.'

Mary thought Laurette seemed unhappy, and she wasn't too pleased at the thought of living alone near the Seine, considering her words. 'Thank you,' she said. 'But . . .'

Laurette went on. 'You will have lots of time for yourself. The friend I am visiting needs support. It is disturbing work she is involved in. I thought I should visit.'

Mary had connected with this interesting woman straight away and wondered who she was. Would it not be better to stay with Laurette, she concluded than wander on her own around Paris. 'But wouldn't I have to pay you,' she said awkwardly. 'And the hotel would expect compensation. I have very little money.'

'Oh, you needn't pay us,' Laurette said laughing. 'And as for compensation, such a hotel would expect its guests to change their mind. The hotels do very little business the way things are. The room I have is in the house of a friend. She lives with her mother and her uncle Doctor Curtius, a medical man and wax modeller. They are very good people, you would like them.'

The cabin interior was neat and tidy, the atmosphere warmed by lamps. There were two small beds, a bookcase and a table. 'Provided the weather is good, the journey shouldn't take long,' said Laurette. 'The side of the cabin over there can be yours. I shall breathe much better with your company. – Ah, I see they have brought our luggage.' The boy from the harbour came with their bags and put them down on the floor. He stood awaiting a tip. Laurette gave him some coins and he hurried away.

'Till tomorrow,' said Fabien, closing the door. 'You know where I am if you need me.'

Mary and Laurette took off their coats and sat down on their beds.

'Why are you going to Paris?' asked Laurette, gazing at Mary curiously. 'Is it for love?'

'Oh, that it were!' laughed Mary.

'Then what?' Laurette's eyes held her with an intense and puzzled stare.

'I go because I must.'

'Then it is for love,' said Laurette, slowly shaking her head. 'Either to find it or lose it. But it is only for love.' She leant back and folded her arms. Mary saw that her fingers were filled in rings, and she imagined Laurette received lots of gifts for she was decked in jewellery.

'I go out of curiosity,' said Mary finally. 'I am hoping to write.'

'About what?' asked Laurette, waiting.

'The revolution,' Mary said, lowering her voice and thoughtful. 'Good experience means good writing, of that I am certain. I hope to talk with a friend from England. I must find him. We are both writers. I would like to write something for the people back home.'

Laurette's eyes shone with interest.

Mary's thoughts were of Paine, but she dared not mention his name. And in a way Laurette was right. She had mainly fled because of love, love for Henry Fuseli.

'Are you with child' Laurette asked, meeting her eyes. Her look lingered.

Mary leant away. 'Oh no, not at all. Why should you think so? I am not even married, nor do I have a lover.'

'You could still be with child,' Laurette murmured. 'Men can be selfish and careless.'

Mary began to wonder if she had made the right decision, in agreeing to share the cabin. But did she not advocate honesty and directness herself? Did she not scorn artificiality in words and manner? But directness was sometimes provocative.

'I am not with child,' she said, bending her head. She sighed. 'I am still a virgin.'

'Well, you needn't look ashamed,' said Laurette with sudden laughter. 'I am the one to be ashamed. I have had eight lovers since the age of sixteen. I fell out of love with them quickly. I had a child with two of them, and on both occasions I lost it just after birth. They were not meant to be, you see. Heaven wanted them back.'

Mary felt as if her heart would break as she listened. 'Poor medical assistance I suspect,' she murmured. 'I am appalled at the number of babies who die, even before their first breath.'

'How long will you stay in Paris,' asked Laurette, moving on.

'I don't know. I am eager to find things out and learn.'

For a moment or two they were silent. It was getting quite dark. 'And you?' asked Mary.

'I am going to visit my friend, nothing more. She is very nervous just now. In truth though, she is a great deal stronger than I am. We have been friends since childhood. I lived in Paris a while, then my family returned to England. I come and go. Marie's work in France consumes her and is often disturbing.'

'What does she do?' Mary asked softly, wanting to know more from this woman who had befriended her so easily.

'She is an artist. She makes marvellous wax models that look like their living subject.' She smiled with perfect teeth and bright red lips. Her manner and confidence were undoubtedly that of an actress.

'And where did she learn how to do it?' asked Mary.

'The doctor is an expert, he instructed her. She is his prodigy.'

'You say he is a *doctor*?'

'Yes, he is a doctor and an artist. It is possible to be both, you know. I would like to have been a painter myself, but I cannot do it. I think it is strange that our imagination will not bend to our will. My imagination would have me be a great painter, but I am an actress, I can make words matter more than when they are written.'

'I cannot imagine acting,' smiled Mary. And she did not want to think about painters just then. To be honest and sincere was what she searched for, acting was quite the opposite. She hated the way the upper classes in England acted a part and didn't really live. She took a breath, the thoughts made her emotional.

'The revolution is growing more violent,' said Laurette. 'Nothing is resolved, and we cannot tell who is in charge. There is need for good leadership, but it is sadly lacking.'

'I have heard about that,' said Mary. 'It is bad when people distrust each other, how do they ever make progress?'

For a few moments they sat thoughtful.

'Tell me,' said Mary. 'Who has your friend sculpted? – But perhaps you need rest. I am not so tired myself now I am talking.'

'She is very clever,' smiled Laurette. 'She has sculpted the heads of Rousseau and Voltaire. Magnificent work. You will have heard of those men, of course.'

'I have,' said Mary. 'I am familiar with much of their work.'

'I do think Voltaire was handsome,' said Laurette, clasping her hands and closing her eyes at the thought. 'He travelled the world, a lot, you know, escaping, I think. But he loathed corruption and hypocrisy.'

'I read he served as philosopher to Frederick the Great,' Mary added, fascinated by the thought that someone had sculpted his image. 'But he said the wrong things. I believe he went to Rousseau in Switzerland. They would not let him in France.'

'Ah no, they would not. He wrote bad words about King Louis. Marie is a royalist but she liked Voltaire a lot.'

For a moment or two they thought on their talk.

'Voltaire was good, you know,' Laurette said abstractedly. 'He set up businesses to give people work – watch making, that sort of thing. He was a great believer in equality.'

'His philosophy and political ideas are known,' said Mary, recalling some of her talks with Johnson.

'He read your Edmund Burke and thought it admirable that the

English were able to write as they wished and did not get thrown into the tower. He was imprisoned in the Bastille for a while, you know, for writing a satirical play. He suffered in there for a year before escaping to England.'

'And did Marie make images of others?' She had no desire to talk about Burke.

'Of course, one was of the Duke of Orleans when he came to be Regent in France. She is very much praised for her work.' She gazed into space for a moment. Her voice fell low. 'But Voltaire's was made for his funeral. I was fond of Voltaire. He would often come to the theatre to watch me perform. That's where we met.'

'Was he one of your lovers?' Mary ventured.

Laurette did not answer at first, then said a little wistfully, 'He was rather too old. But I did love him. He was a regular visitor to the theatre when he came to England.' She broke off with a sudden thought. 'And another man called Gilbert Imlay, not famous like Voltaire but certainly charming.'

Mary shook her head. 'I do not know him,' she murmured. She felt distant, listening about this life beyond her. She bowed her head, brooding. How little she had experienced of life's true perils.

'Imlay is an American living in France but he is often in London. He told me he served as a lieutenant in the Continental Army.' She laughed and tossed her hair. 'Oh he tells you such fascinating tales. But his creditors are always chasing him. He is an excellent escapist however.' Lines of irritation gathered on her brow and she brushed back her hair with her hand. 'He is sometimes at Marie's when I visit. He tells her his problems. They are legion! Only his dark good looks prevent her from sending him away.'

'Does she care for him?'

For a moment Laurette was thoughtful. 'No, not romantically. She is far too sensible for that.'

'And you?'

She smiled and poured them both a drink. They would soon be eating, she said, it was almost time. 'I do care for him,' she murmured. 'But I could never love him. I do not trust him, you see.'

'Is he in England?'

'Not now, he is in France, possibly visiting the Curtius household in Paris where Marie is living. You might meet him. But he does not stay, he only visits, he has a house of his own in Paris. He knows a lot of people who he likes to think are his friends, but he borrows money and does not always repay it. He is forever coming and going.'

Mary looked away. She had borrowed money herself. Sometimes she'd had to. But Johnson had paid her well for her writing and she'd paid back everything she owed. She breathed a sigh of relief. 'Perhaps he needs a little success. Success solves a lot. Without it you can fall into a hole you might never get out of.'

'You have experienced this *hole*?'

'Oh yes. It is dark and cold.'

'But you got out?'

'Yes, one way and another, I did. It was difficult. But I am always tottering on the edge.' She laughed quietly.

Laurette shivered. 'Are you hungry?'

'Indeed.' Mary confessed that so much talking and thinking had given her an appetite. They both found their shawls then walked together down the deck. Mary saw that Fabien walked slowly behind them.

30

*Paris*

It had been a beautiful crossing, the night busy with stars, the sea gentle and calm and excellent conversation with Laurette. It was good, all good! Mary felt a great mood of hope, as if she were stepping into an entire new world. Fabien had hired a carriage to take them to Paris and after they'd retrieved their luggage they all climbed in to travel to the home of Doctor Curtius.

The wheels of the carriage rattled along the poorly made roads while the coachman sang to his horses. It was mid afternoon. Laurette had spoken a lot about Voltaire, who had been a prolific writer and Mary felt he must have been a passionate man. She recalled what she'd learned about his life. As well as satirical plays Voltaire had written poems, novels and essays, historical and scientific works. He had also fought to eliminate the powers of the priesthood and aristocracy, hoping to see them replaced by a constitutional monarchy that gave rights to ordinary people. Laurette said he'd lived in Switzerland a while before his return to Paris in 1778 where he'd watched his tragedy *Irene*. The five day journey, however, had been wearisome for the 83-year-old Voltaire, who believed he was dying. Faint and sick, he had written: *"I die adoring God, loving my friends, not hating my enemies, and detesting superstition."* His body had been old and weak but his spirit had been strong and his debility had magically lifted. He'd had the pleasure of seeing his play, but died very soon after. Denied a Christian burial in Paris however, he'd been buried in an Abbey in Champagne, his heart and brain separately embalmed. But his passion lived on through his writing. Mary wondered what his hopes had been and whether he had felt fulfilled. Perhaps Marie had captured some of his feelings in her work. She was eager to see it. But in what way was her work "disturbing"?

They took refreshment on the road, then travelled on further. The carriage clattered up a thin cobbled street and stopped by a row of apartments. Paris was a huge city, boasting elegant shops and restaurants, but because of the revolution it was now dark and ghostly. The old celebratory Paris had gone and there was a strange chill in the air as they all climbed down from the coach. 'The poor are hiding in the alleyways,' said Fabien. 'They will appear if they hear us, either to beg or to steal. You have to be cautious.'

'The revolutionaries are suspicious of Marie,' said Laurette nervously. 'She has been teaching the king's sister to draw so is seen as supporting the monarchy.'

A woman looked down from the window of an upstairs apartment. There was the quick sound of footsteps on the stairs. 'Someone is coming,' said Laurette.

'I shall leave you now,' said Fabien. 'I have discharged my duty.' And with a quick light bow he returned to the carriage. After a shout from the coach driver, the horses were soon away.

The door downstairs opened hastily, and Marie, pale and breathless drew them inside. Her dark hair was untidy and her large beautiful eyes were nervous. She frowned at Mary suspiciously.

'Mary is a friend from England,' said Laurette, and she explained how they'd met on the journey.

Marie glanced up and down the road. 'Come inside quickly!' she whispered. 'And pull the door tightly behind you!' A few carriages travelled about, one or two people walked the streets. 'The September massacres have put an aura of gloom and fear over Paris now,' she said wearily. 'Hundreds of people were butchered. Anyone who does not think like the revolutionaries is seen as a threat.' She shook her head concernedly, 'So many people have been brutally murdered.'

'Mary is a writer,' said Laurette. 'She has come to see what is happening in France.'

'She is brave,' said Marie. 'That or else she is foolish.'

Laurette went on. 'She was to stay at a hotel near the Seine, but we can send a messenger to cancel. It is most unsafe to be there.'

'Do you wish her to stay with us?' asked Marie, glancing at the bags at her feet. 'That could be even worse.'

'Surely it is no trouble to let her live with us a while,' Laurette said assertively. 'Paris can be fearful at present, and there are two spare rooms in the apartment.'

'Of course,' said Marie in a changed tone of voice. 'Forgive me. Mary is very welcome.' She spoke sincerely though she was nervous. 'Life is a fragile business here, and I fear it is bound to grow worse. You are no doubt aware that Britain and France are about to make war. You are bold to cross the channel.' She frowned and bit her lip. 'We must always be on the lookout.' Her tone became serious. 'It is best you keep your writing a secret too. We are sometimes raided, and there are informers everywhere.' She narrowed her eyes as she spoke. 'Informers who like to bend the truth. Il est si troublant.'

There was the click of a door and Mary saw that the doctor stood in a doorway upstairs. He was a small but strongly built man, who looked at Mary warily. He was balding, and the top of his head shone in a beam of sunlight from the window. 'This is Mary from England,' called Marie. 'Do not be concerned. She is a friend of Laurette's.'

His tone was calm as they climbed the white stone staircase. 'How long will you stay?' he asked as they reached him.

'A month perhaps,' said Mary. She smiled awkwardly. Who were these people, she asked herself, who she'd trusted so easily, and who it seemed trusted her in return.

'I doubt it will be more,' Laurette told the doctor, greeting him with a warm embrace. 'We have no idea of the way things will go in Paris, have we. Mary might wish to return to England sooner rather than later.'

'Indeed,' murmured Marie, helping with their luggage.

'An *English* woman,' Doctor Curtius murmured, frowning worriedly. 'We shall have to hide you away. The king's sister sees my niece as her friend, she has been teaching her to draw, you see.

There is danger in talent. – Were you hoping to see the Palace of Versailles?'

'That would be interesting,' said Mary.

'Everything has changed,' said the doctor. 'The Palace is heavily guarded now and you cannot enter. The king and queen were moved to the Tulieres Palace here in Paris, it is dark and dreary compared with the Palace of Versailles, but there were reasons, you see. You will have read of them in England, no?'

'Yes,' said Mary. 'We read all we can.' It felt strange to be close to the heartbeat of the French Revolution, to be a neighbour of the king and queen.

Curtius went on. 'Much has happened in the last few years. Marie works at her art; she is a wonderful wax modeller, though life in France is very grim. The glittering corridors of Versailles have lost their wonder. No-one would look in its mirrors now for fear of encountering the devil!'

They entered a large furnished room. The smell of wholesome cooking came from the kitchen. 'I have a very good cook,' he smiled. 'I speak of Marie's mother, Anne Marie. She cooks for us and keeps the place tidy. The woman is a great treasure.'

Anne Marie emerged from the kitchen, an attractive well-made woman, whose large grey eyes moved from suspicion to acceptance as Laurette explained the situation. Marie came forward and took Mary to the room she would stay in while Laurette went off to her own.

It was a pleasant enough room, thought Mary glancing about, though it was small. But the windows were long and the room was light and airy with a desk and chair, a comfortable bed, a chaise longue and a dresser with a water jug and bowl on top. The window looked out on the boulevard. 'It hasn't been used for a while,' said Marie. 'But I hope you will find it agreeable. My mother is about to serve dinner so do come and join us soon.' With that she smiled and left.

Mary sat by her desk a while, oddly abstracted. Already she was aching for home. She was a woman in her thirties in a Paris apartment with strangers, an apartment with a strange secret; for she had seen how Marie turned the key in the lock of her studio before showing her to her room.

She went to the dresser and poured out water from the jug into the bowl. After that she washed her face then fastened up some falling strands of hair. She felt tired. But her determination was strong; nothing would sway her from her plans. She would write! And despite the September massacres and the other horrors she knew of, she was still behind the revolution, and would seek out Paine just as soon as she could and talk with him. Did the doctor know who he was? His writings were very well-known. But on second thoughts, Paine was a revolutionary and it might put his life in danger if she spoke of him to people seen as monarchists. She remembered the address given to her by Christie, who had told her to commit it to memory and not write it down. She had said it over and over in her mind so that she knew it like her own name. But when could she try to seek him out, and without being seen?

They all talked freely over dinner. Doctor Curtius talked with Laurette, catching up on her news, while Marie spoke of the new wax models she'd recently completed, talking to her mother in French, too fast for Mary's hearing. Marie told Mary that Doctor Curtius's work was celebrated in Paris and that he had done it at first to illustrate parts of the anatomy. But his skills had been noticed, and he had then moved on to much more interesting subjects. In July 1789, wax heads of the Finance Minister, Necker, and the Duke of Orleans, both made by Curtius, had been carried through Paris in a protest march just days before revolutionaries had stormed the Bastille and set the revolution in motion.

'Marie is a clever modeller,' said Curtius proudly. 'I have taught her everything I know.'

'And it has not been inherited either,' Anne Marie added, seated by Mary. 'It is pure labour and talent. Philippe isn't her father, her father is dead. He was a German soldier named Grosholtz. His face had been horribly disfigured in the wars; a part of his jaw was shot away. It was replaced with a silver plate.'

Mary looked at her sympathetically. 'It must have been painful,' she said.

'It was ma chère, especially in winter. The pain was always worse in winter. He died before I gave birth, so he did not see his daughter.'

She rubbed her arms and frowned. 'But Philippe has been wonderful. Marie calls him her uncle. It will do.' She glanced across at the doctor who talked on quietly with Laurette.

'. . . Oh yes, he was here yesterday,' the doctor was saying. 'Anne Marie prepared him some food. He tells me his business is in trouble again, but there is nothing new about that, Gilbert is always having problems. I believe he is in need of money.'

'And did you provide it?' Anne Marie called across.

'No. He does not return it.'

Laurette sighed. 'He came to the theatre in London just recently. He was in difficulty then as well. Oh, there is always something. I wonder what has happened now. Someone is after him in London.'

'He asked for you,' said Philippe, looking at her straight.

Her shoulders rose and fell. 'Does he intend to come back?'

'I think he might. He was troubled. He was here one minute, the next he was out of the door.'

'Probably to find someone else who might lend him some money,' said Anne Marie.

The doctor laughed quietly. 'He calls himself a speculator, and he certainly is. He is a charlatan and a gambler, a charming scoundrel is Gilbert. He needs a good woman.'

'He would break her heart,' said Laurette, as if with personal knowledge.

'I'm sorry Mary', said Marie. 'We are talking about a friend of ours − or he is more a friend of Laurette's. He likes to go to the theatre in London when she is acting, then afterwards he takes her to dinner.'

'It is *I* who take *him* to dinner, I'm afraid. Gilbert is usually penniless.' Laurette spoke wearily. 'But he lives beyond his means, what he cannot pay for he will acquire some way or other, consequences do not matter. I am easily taken in I'm afraid. Oh yes, he speculates, you see.' She reached for a dish of vegetables. Philippe poured them all red wine and passed around a plate of meats. 'So what is the matter with him now, I wonder,' she mused. 'He will probably have lost a ship's cargo, or possibly even a ship, knowing Gilbert.' She laughed lightly. 'I can remember him telling a terrible tale of woe to a man in a box at the theatre. He had reached some sort of crisis, and the man passed over a lot of silver that night when they'd been drinking.'

'And was the money ever repaid?' Anne Marie asked curious and confounded.

'Oh, I doubt it,' smiled Laurette. 'The man was just being generous I think. There are often people like him at the theatre, lonely people who always have plenty of money.' She nodded thoughtfully. 'I am sorry to say I have used such men myself at times.' She sighed. 'Needs must.'

# 31

# *Gilbert Imlay*

*"It would be an endless task to trace the variety of meannesses, cares, and sorrows, into which women are plunged by the prevailing opinion, that they were created rather to feel than reason, and that all the power they obtain, must be obtained by their charms and weakness . . ."*

Mary put down her pen and gazed at the page before her. She'd been writing for several hours and had risen early that day while everyone else lay sleeping. She felt comfortable in Curtius's home and had now been there three days. He had a candour and kindness about him and a natural way of relating, as if he had always known you. With his long studied looks and observations he might have been making a waxwork model in his mind. He lived an intense existence, carrying out operations, saving lives, and creating wax models, and he was deeply concerned about the politics of France, sometimes sitting on the chaise longue perfectly still for quite some time, as if trying to think it all through.

The previous evening, Mary had been given a tour around his studio, an extremely rare privilege Laurette had told her. She had thanked him, astounded by what she had seen, and thrilling with excitement as he'd gone around the sculptures with the candle. The waxen heads and figures were alarmingly lifelike and as the light of the candle found them she'd feared they might move. The head of Voltaire was so precise it might well have been the man himself. She had looked at it for several minutes, recalling his forced exile in

271

Britain and the way he'd been deeply impressed by its constitutional monarchy as opposed to the absolutist regimes of Continental Europe. Scrutinizing his image, tears had formed in her eyes and she'd felt the pull of his spirit like she did when reading his work. He had been a great thinker. There was something larger than life about Voltaire. It was important to mix humour with intellect, she thought, to be able to laugh at the world was special. Voltaire could laugh at tragedy; he could satirize it and make it more bearable at the same time extracting its important messages for progress. But she could not laugh at it herself, she must worry over it, lose sleep, allow it to enter her blood.

She rubbed her eyes. She was thinking too fast. She had talked with Marie at length, discussing her art, and she'd thought of her family in England, Johnson and her friends, and hoped she wasn't causing concern. She would send them news shortly.

Daylight had arrived and her room flooded with light. The others were up and talking. Hurriedly, she dressed and went to join them.

'Good morning,' said the doctor warmly. He was setting the table for breakfast; Anne Marie was busy in the kitchen.

'Good morning, Mary!' called Anne Marie. 'Did you sleep well?'

Mary said she did, though it wasn't exactly true, she'd spent most of the night in earnest, tossing, turning and thinking, until she'd climbed out of bed at 4 am to get on with her work. She must find Paine soon!

Marie was busy in the studio. 'She is perfecting something,' said the doctor. 'She cannot relax until what she is making is correct to the finest detail. She is always being asked to make heads of important dignitaries and she knows she must get them right. They are not always people she likes, of course, but the payment is good.'

'And what is she working on now?' asked Mary, seated on the chaise longue.

Curtius frowned thoughtful. 'I'm not sure. She is being a little bit secretive.'

'And she is nervous too,' said Anne Marie. 'I noticed something was covered last night.' She looked at Curtius, who continued to set the table without looking up.

Laurette came through, putting combs in her hair.

'There has been a note from Imlay,' said Anne Marie, pointing. 'It is there on the dresser. A coachman brought it this morning.' Laurette glanced over and went to look. 'What does he say?' Anne Marie called as she went to bring in toast and conserve. Mary saw that Laurette read the note quickly then put it in the pocket of her gown.

'He is here in Paris,' she said softly, in a tone of affection. 'He intends to call at the apartment.'

Philippe Curtius sighed, and furiously buttered his toast. 'And when will he arrive?'

'About three today. He says he hopes I'll be here.'

'He *knows* you'll be here,' said Philippe under his breath.

Laurette went with Mary to the table. 'What am I to do?' she murmured.

'Do you want to see him?' Anne Marie asked, pouring out tea.

'I always enjoy his company,' said Laurette, 'whatever his mood.' She straightened her hair and gazed about the room abstractedly. 'It would be good to see him, yes.'

'He probably wants money,' Anne Marie added, in a low and irritable voice.

Marie sat eating in silence. Her finger nails still held traces of wax from last night's work.

'She does not need to give it to him, though,' Philippe said, annoyed. 'She can always say no.'

'You cannot say no to Gilbert,' said Laurette. She sighed heavily. 'He tries so hard but he is very unlucky. He had got himself into a bit of trouble in England.'

'Ah yes, he has been *"unlucky",*' said Philippe. 'Unlucky, yes. It is a useful word.'

'Were you never unlucky, Philippe?' said Laurette, looking cross.

'I think not,' he answered quickly. He passed toast to Anne Marie. 'I have always been lucky in that I work very hard and do not lean upon others.'

'No, you do not,' sighed Anne Marie, giving him a warm smile. 'And you have always been generous to us.'

'But you will not give money to Gilbert?' said Laurette, fixing her eyes on him intently.

'No, I will not. I think he goes the wrong way.'

'But Gilbert says a man must speculate, and he thinks he is good at it too.'

'He is good at getting in a fix,' said Philippe. 'If he wishes to come to see you, then he is welcome here in my home, and that is all I can say. Now eat your breakfast, my dear, and we'll see what happens.'

Mary watched them, seeing how Philippe and Anne Marie were so attentive to each other. Anne Marie was a woman of constant activity. Mary had learned that as a single parent she had sought the best for her daughter and had encouraged her to practise wax modelling. And the doctor had delighted in her talent. Both mother and daughter had wanted the best for each other. Anne Marie had met Philippe in Switzerland and became his housekeeper there. Then she had accompanied him to Paris where he'd established a cabinet of portraits in wax which were put on display for the public. Laurette and her parents had lived close by and Laurette and Marie became friends.

Just now Laurette looked troubled. All that could be heard in the room was the scraping of knives on toast as they finished their food. Mary changed the subject. 'I would like to explore Paris tomorrow, if I may,' she said. All eyes were suddenly upon her. 'But I must leave at dawn.'

'And would you feel safe wandering Paris alone?' asked Philippe, surprised and concerned. 'Anything might happen.'

'There is someone I need to see,' Mary faltered. 'Can you get me a chaise first thing?'

'It can be done,' said Philippe, 'but where are you going?'

'I am not at liberty to say,' she said, looking downwards. 'I trust you will understand. I am not going plotting or anything. I have a friend here from England who I want to speak with. I shall only be away for the day.'

'And if you do not return?' said Laurette, raising her eyebrows worriedly. 'What then? People disappear all the time in Paris, we cannot search for you.'

'And I would not expect it. I shall return though, do not fear. I really must talk with my friend.'

'I see,' said the doctor. 'A friend from England . . . Yes, these matters are complicated, I know. And what about today?'

'I have much to write,' she said. Glancing outside, she saw that the weather was dry. She hoped it might rain tomorrow; it was easier to feel safe in the rain.

'Gilbert is to join us today,' said Laurette. 'He is arriving mid afternoon and usually stays for some time. Perhaps you would like to meet him. – Shall I knock on your door when he arrives?'

'Please do,' said Mary. 'Mr Imlay sounds intriguing.'

'Oh, he is certainly intriguing,' said the doctor, 'though in the wrong sort of way.'

Laurette looked ahead abstractedly but made no comment.

As soon as they had taken breakfast, Anne Marie cleared the table and went to the kitchen. The doctor and Marie went off to the studio where they locked the door behind them. The waxworks was a serious affair, there was always such tension attached to it. Only Laurette and Mary were left in the room.

'I must write,' said Mary, making to rise.

'When Imlay arrives I'll tell you,' said Laurette. 'Whether he will engage you in scholastic conversation I do not know. He is often strangely wanton.' She laughed quietly and looked Mary up and down as if with grudging admiration.

'If you would rather see him alone I can stay in my room,' said Mary. 'I know he is your friend.'

'*My friend?* Well, sometimes he is, sometimes he isn't,' Laurette said flatly. 'I think you should meet him though, I believe he would like you.'

'I have lots to write about,' said Mary. 'And I doubt I'd be very entertaining. I am far too dull and solemn.'

'Not at all, my dear!' gasped Laurette. 'I am sure he'll enjoy your company just as I do.'

Mary lifted her face and smiled. Just then she felt helpless and exposed. She did not know Laurette. She did not know Gilbert Imlay. And she did not know Anne Marie who bustled about the kitchen, or those who were locked in the studio. She didn't really know where to find Paine either. Life must unfold as it would, she had made herself hostage to fortune.

That day Mary wrote well. Anne Marie had brought her a sandwich at lunch time and she'd continued with her work. Then, just as the sun was growing low, a knock came on her door. It was Laurette. Imlay was in the apartment. Anne Marie had gone to her room; the doctor and Marie were still working in the studio. Mary went out into the parlour and sat down in a comfortable chair while Laurette and Imlay sat together on the chaise longue.

'Mary Wollstonecraft, I take it?' he said, standing and bowing lightly. He straightened the collar of his coat. 'I hope I am suitably dressed to meet with your illustrious self. I have heard of your work.' She thought him boyish and playful. Laurette giggled.

'I had not noticed your clothes Mr Imlay,' Mary said smiling. 'You are smart enough though I think.' Then she glanced at Laurette, who was now sitting in silence, occasionally sighing or giving a low little laugh.

Thoughts came to Imlay quickly. He joked. He cajoled. Mary thought he lived on the frothy effervescence of life, indulging himself, eager to surprise and shock, not the sort of man she would take to. He talked on easily about matters that might have embarrassed a less bold woman. Were English women demure, he asked her. Might they dare to be sexually uninhibited? All the while he glanced at Laurette, repressing his smiles.

'I believe women are every bit as sexual as men,' Mary said firmly, looking at him straight. 'And they might well be uninhibited too.' He would not embarrass her, she thought, she would evade nothing! His eyes searched her own flirtatiously. He was trying to make her uneasy, but it was something she'd often considered and she was ready. She spoke freely, for this was the kind of conversation she wanted, the kind she would have had at Johnson's dinners, something challenging and piercing. Wasn't she on a mission to inform the world that women were equal to men? Of course. Imlay was indeed an alluring man, she liked how he held his shoulders so straight, the way he crossed his legs, the way he clasped his hands, resting them in his lap with a sort of manly grace. Laurette fussed him and played with her pearl drop earrings, laughing like a girl in love. 'Yes, Mr Imlay,' Mary asserted, 'women and men are equal when it comes to sexuality. Why not?'

'And would they satisfy their sexual desires as men might, throw caution to the winds and take their pleasure?' He watched her and waited intently.

She braced herself; it was a battle. 'That would depend on the circumstances. It is important to consider repercussions.'

Imlay went on regardless. 'And must they *know* the man they desire?' he asked, his eyes asking for more. He smiled.

Mary knew that such matters were talked about openly in France in ways that weren't possible in England, and the changing times meant no stone was left unturned. But it surprised her he should speak so overtly in front of Laurette. She braced herself; she would not shrink from his gaze. 'Not necessarily,' she said, with the very same smile. 'But it might be advisable. Women, you see, become pregnant. Men do not.'

'Ah, yes. That can be something of a nuisance.' He pursed his lips and frowned. 'And what if the man . . .' he spoke now, in a curiously intimate tone, 'should *love* her.'

'Well, of course, that would be best,' she said, smiling a little self-consciously. 'But love can be fickle and women are often let down.'

'Indeed,' he said quietly, holding her gaze.

Laurette went for a glass of water in the kitchen. Mary could hear her talking with Anne Marie, who spoke in irritable tones. Imlay went on, speaking of what he had done with his life, his plans and hopes for the future. But in his dark blue eyes was a sense of failure, thought Mary, a deep rooted sadness. He was happy to laugh at it though and move on. It came to her then, that he resembled her father. And despite his reputation, she decided Imlay was a survivor. She thought he probably laughed a great deal about things better not laughed at and was a heavy drinker. He was an oddly separate being, quite independent, and just as Laurette had said, "Strangely wanton." He had a quick, carefree mind, an imagination that sometimes went beyond the boundaries of common decency, one minute speaking in the voice of a wealthy merchant, the next as a pauper or a rake. It was hard to believe he was as roguish as painted and she decided not to believe it.

# 32

## *Finding Paine*

Imlay had left the apartment just after dinner and Mary had retired to her room. In spite of her better judgement she had found him most beguiling, though much to Laurette's annoyance, for he had shown her more attention than was proper for a new acquaintance, leaning too close and passing her lingering looks. Yes, Imlay could be dangerous when it came to the heart, thought Mary, and it riled her that he had broken her reserve so easily. But her body felt warm and vibrant as she got into bed that night, and she hoped he would visit them again.

First though she must search out Paine. A chaise would arrive tomorrow at first light. She rehearsed his address again in her mind. As Christie had left her at the harbour, he had said he too would be visiting France very soon since the National Assembly had asked him to do some translating. Might he spend time with Paine, she wondered. She hoped so, then she could see them both. She was missing her English friends and her family more than ever.

The chaise set off in the cold white light, the roads frosty and slippery, which the driver said was often the way of Paris in December. He warned that his horse might be slow. She knew from Christie that Paine was living with Girondin leaders at rue des Petits Ecuries in an old farm mansion. He wasn't expecting her but she'd told him of her intentions when they'd talked together in England. It did not do to reveal too much and they had both been cautious.

278

As the chaise sped on through the city, it was as if her fate were in suspense and she prayed she would find him. She hoped also that the quiet light of dawn would be softer and less intrusive than the harsh light of day and that her journey might go unnoticed. She felt comforted at the thought of him living with Girondins; the Girondins were followers of Voltaire and Rousseau, mostly lawyers and writers and concerned about the rights of women, the plight of unmarried mothers and other significant issues. A sense of being part of a great new energy possessed her. Girondins were moderates, that was all to the good for they were rational men and to be rational was vital. But when she thought of the radical Jacobins she feared for Paine's life, for such men were extremists and had the National Guard supporting them and the Paris commune with its militant sans-culottes who called themselves that because they liked to wear working men's trousers in opposition to the upper classes who always wore breeches. All wore the badge of the tri-colour cockade on their hats, for it was now the emblem of revolution; you must side with the monarchy or side with the revolution and to wear the tri-colour cockade was crucial. Mary had been told that Paine befriended both Girondins and Jacobins alike, which would make the Jacobins ever more watchful and suspicious, and Paine argued compassion towards the king, which put him in a difficult position, for there were many who wanted King Louis dead and would have ended his life at a stroke.

Mary decided Paine might be living with Jacques Pierre Brissot, a Girondin leader who'd suggested the king should be sent to live in America, and argued that killing him could bring all the monarchs of Europe after their heads. Mary thought Brissot sounded interesting and hoped she would meet him. Paine had a habit of befriending interesting people. The thirteenth son of an innkeeper, Brissot had been born in Chartres. Much like her brother, Ned, he had shown an interest in law and had worked for a law firm in Paris. But Christie had told her that his need to write had come on him just like a passion and he'd gone on a tour of England examining its political systems and observing its social classes. There was a great deal of truth, thought Mary, in the fact that no matter what you learned, no matter what profession you pursued, your calling would register loud and clear in the end. She too had heard that calling and it had now brought her to Paris.

But it wasn't the Paris she'd read of. This was a devastated city, a place of desolation, broken statues littering the streets, châteaux razed to the ground, their windows burnt and buckled. She recalled how Brissot had criticised France whilst approving of Britain, and there were those who would do away with him for that alone. He had also insulted Marie Antoinette by publishing a pornographic pamphlet against her which was now in wide circulation. He was a man of immense energy but it seemed he'd been a little too daring. He'd been thrown into the Bastille prison for almost six months on returning to Paris. Once he was released, however, quite undaunted, he'd worked towards ending slavery in the colonies and publicized Girondist ideals far and wide. It had been his intention to take his family to live in America, but the revolution had thwarted his plans and he'd been dragged back into the fray.

According to Philippe, the Jacobins had now taken charge at the revolutionary club in Paris. Brissot's power had been supplanted by the power of Maximilien de Robespierre who had assumed authority when the club had split over a petition to remove King Louis after he'd tried to escape the country. Captured at Varennes with his family, the king had been returned to France as a traitor and was more distrusted than ever.

The chaise stopped by a garden of fruit and vegetables. Ducks, geese and hens wandered the grounds idly in the early morning stillness. It reminded her of her father's attempts at a farm and she stood for a moment watching the animals as the chaise drew away. The hens scattered and cackled loudly as she walked amongst them. Just then she saw that a boy stood in the doorway.

'Are you here to see Citizen Paine?' he asked, peering about nervously.

She attempted to look beyond the heavy oak door into the dark house behind him and nodded.

He glanced back over his shoulder. 'Mademoiselle, what is your name?' he asked, with a cautious look.

'Mary Wollstonecraft,' was the firm but quiet reply. 'I have come from England.'

'One moment,' he said. 'I have told Citizen Paine that someone has arrived. I am the lookout, you see. He said I should ask for your name. Your name is right, he has expected you.' He looked at her for a long moment, then turned and ran down the long dark corridor, leaving her alone by the door.

She felt unsafe standing on her own outside, not really knowing who lived there. The boy returned breathless. 'Mademoiselle Wollstonecraft, come this way. Je suis désole! I am supposed to address you as Citizen, but I forget. Everyone in France is addressed as Citizen now.'

She followed the youth as requested. 'Where are we going?' she asked him, dismayed by the length of the corridor and the dim lighting.

'There are many doors,' said the boy. 'But the rooms are empty, everyone has fled to England. Citizen Paine is talking with Citizen Brissot. There is no-one else here. The other Girdondins have gone.' The boy became thoughtful as they walked. Suddenly he plunged into talk: 'My mother is unwell. – She fears the Jacobins will kill King Louis. – She wept so long yesterday.' He spoke in a tone of hopelessness. 'The revolution is frightening. My father was killed for nothing. He was good and hard working. But my parents always loved the king. Do you think they will kill him?'

'I do not know,' Mary replied piteously. 'Only time will tell.' She glanced about; so many closed doors seemed somehow ominous. Not even a candle lit the corridor.

'Citizen Brissot wants the king to go to America. But you dare not have mercy on the king.' The boy spoke angrily.

Their footsteps sounded loudly as they walked along the cold tiled floors. She saw that the boy suffered, constantly pulling on the pocket of his trousers and murmuring fears for his mother, 'She is very unhappy . . .'

'What do you do here?' asked Mary.

The boy threw out his arms, as if to say *everything*. 'I run errands for Citizen Paine. I am a good rider. I am able to take messages at a gallop.' He stopped for a moment thoughtful, then continued. 'I sometimes screw the necks of the chickens as well. My mother showed me how to do it. She says you have to be strong and must not heed their squawks; they are only hens and have to be eaten. I am given money for my work. Everything I earn I pass to my mother; she is saving for when the revolution is over, then it will all be better.'

Mary was shown into a dimly lit room with a great glowing fire in the hearth. Two men sat beside it. They rose quickly as she entered.

'Here is the mademoiselle,' said the boy, glancing about nervously.

Paine gazed at her with gladness. 'My dear Mary, you are here!' he laughed. 'How good it is to see you. – Are you alone?'

'I am,' she said, with a deep sigh of relief. 'It is good to see you too, Thomas.' Swiftly, she dropped her hood, and she saw that the room was large and heavily furnished. The boy took her cape, murmuring to a woman who was removing plates from a cupboard. Paine bid Mary sit down, speaking words of concern and words for her safety. His companion stared at her curiously.

'This is Jacques Brissot,' said Paine. 'Jacques, my friend, this is Mary Wollstonecraft from England; she is one of our circle. I have told you about her before.'

Brissot bowed quickly. 'Miss Wollstonecraft, yes, I am delighted.'

'You will not forget her,' said Paine. 'She is a woman who has an important point of view.'

'On what?' she said smiling, taking a seat by the fire.

'On all things that matter,' laughed Paine.

She leant towards the fire; it warmed the cold of her face. 'It is *your* views I come for dear Thomas; my own are getting confused.' Paine and Brissot sat down.

'I can believe it,' sighed Paine piling more logs on the fire.

'We are all confused,' said Brissot, frowning deeply. 'We have talked for most of the night with our friends, but we are still no closer to knowing how matters will develop.'

'They are going to kill our king,' said the boy, standing close and listening.

The woman brought plates to the table. 'Hush,' she said. 'Do not go on, my son. You know how the thought makes me weep.'

The boy persisted. 'Citizen Brissot, is it true?'

'I do not know' said Brissot quietly. His voice fell low. 'But the queen's family will send their armies if we do.'

'We can hide him here. He can go down the stairs behind the cupboard,' urged the boy. 'Citizen Paine, what do you think?'

'Hush, I say!' cried the woman, clipping his ear. She stood still for a moment, bending her head. 'He hears all manner of rumours.'

The woman's long dark curls shone like silk as the fresh morning light came in through the window. Mary thought her quite beautiful, though she was obviously anxious, and constantly screwed up her face. Paine and Brissot gazed intently at the fire.

'Will you take breakfast?' asked Paine. 'Perhaps some cheese and bread? And Celine here makes very good apple juice. We have lots of apples in the orchard.'

The boy wandered off, all legs and awkward limbs, and his mother attended to the breakfast, slicing into a loaf of bread with a heavy sharp knife.

'We have wonderful cheese,' said Brissot, as if for something to say, all the time looking at Mary with a curious expression. 'I recommend it. I do like cheese. There is sufficient livestock here to sustain us.'

The powerful man seemed preoccupied, thought Mary, as she watched him wringing his hands. 'The National Convention has now declared France a Republic,' he said. 'But there is still more bloodshed to come, bloodshed itself is a disease of mankind; it takes hold of us just like a plague.'

'The cow in the orchard gives excellent milk for cheese,' said Paine, more cheerfully. 'That's good. And there are freshly boiled eggs if you like. Celine scratches her hands each day to reach through the thorn trees. The hens like to hide them, but she knows their ways, you see. It is good to have eggs, and it is good to have a cow. – Ah yes, I believe that a lump-sum grant should be given to each individual once they have grown into an adult. That way they can buy themselves a cow and implements to cultivate some land. The business of wage labour is criminal to me. Liberty needs economic independence and material security, not just for the rich but for all.'

'I abhor the idea of property as much as you do,' said Mary.

'Well,' said Paine, frowning thoughtfully, 'personal property is only acquired through society, isn't it? If a man is separated from society, how can he have personal property? Anything that is accumulated wealth – other than what a man's own hands can produce – comes from living in society and some of that wealth should be returned.' He passed a plate to Mary and a knife to cut her food with.

'And people are often paid too little for their labour,' said Mary, nodding for certainty.

'Exactly,' said Paine. 'The accumulation of personal property is, in many instances, the effect of paying too little for the labour that produced it; the consequence of which is that the working hand perishes in old age, and the employer abounds in affluence. It is exploitation by capital. Ah, society is produced by our wants and government by our wickedness.'

'I have read such ideas in your writing,' said Mary.

Brissot sat pulling on his long thin nose. 'There is a great deal to do and not enough time to do it,' he murmured.

'But we have food enough for now,' laughed Paine. 'And that is a blessing.' The sound of scuttling came from the floor.

'And food enough for animals that find their way in,' said Celine beneath her breath.

Brissot stretched out his long heavy legs and yawned. 'They are less trouble than men,' he said languidly

'I'm glad you have come,' Paine said to Mary, smiling at her warmly. 'I trust our friends are fit and well back in England.'

'They are certainly busy,' she said abstractedly. 'Johnson, of course, would have us write as fast as we think.'

'Ah yes,' said Paine, narrowing his eyes with remembrance, 'his press burns like the sun! He is a very brave man.'

Brissot took a boiled egg from a dish and tapped about it with a spoon until the silky white inside shone in his fingers, then he took a bite and the whole was devoured within seconds. 'Bravery is everywhere,' he said, 'and its opposite, of course – fear. I feel them both in my breast. But I am soothed if I know that my wife and children are safe.' For a moment all three were silent. Brissot spoke again. 'I cannot help feeling that American ideals can help improve the government here, and I must always declare what I believe in.' He smiled and waved a finger. 'I do not wish to spend any more time in prison, however. Oh, no.' He feigned a shiver, then fell into indignation. 'All experience is valuable, of course, but four months in that damned Bastille could have sent me crazy.' He tapped the sides of his head and turned to Paine. 'I believe I am sane, am I not? I hope you would tell me, my friend, if I wasn't. – Bah! A few saucy images of the queen, that was the extent of my pamphlet, but they could not take it.' He turned to Mary. 'And some have called me a spy . . .' He laughed loud at the ceiling.

'But Jacques . . .' said Paine. He sat back and folded his arms. 'The war on Austria went badly.' He spoke cautiously. It was a sore point for Brissot that as Head of the Legislative Assembly he had recommended war on Austria that spring.

'But they threatened to invade should we venture to harm King Louis.' Brissot spoke angrily. He stood then paced the floor with slow heavy strides. 'They knew not a thing of our plans, it was all surmise. Threats, threats, the soldiers hear of them, you see, and it stirs them to violence.'

'But the war had been a bad decision,' said Paine, 'for the French armies were crushed at the start, causing even more tensions.'

'It did not work as I hoped for,' said Brissot. 'And my heart is heavy for that.' For a moment he struggled with his thoughts. 'But it was just as my heart dictated. My heart goes one way and history goes another. But I am clever with foreign policy in the main.' He bit his lip thoughtfully. 'And it has to be remembered that I was not as hardened as the Jacobins. I said we should keep King Louis under arrest, not kill him! I had my reasons for that, as you know. Several reasons. But the Jacobins do not reason.'

'So what is Robespierre up to?' asked Mary, taking a bite of perfectly delicious cheese. Brissot was a man of immense power, but he too, made mistakes. What if the revolution became chaotic and France was ruined.

'Robespierre! Robespierre!' said Brissot, shaking his head angrily. 'He is a very persuasive speaker, but I know about armies and he doesn't. However, there are always obstacles.'

'I believe he is now taking over,' she said, recalling what Philippe had told her.

'He would like to think so,' Brissot declared, straightening. 'His followers increase by the day.'

'He could,' said Paine. 'We have all discussed it.'

Brissot glanced through the window. 'Only the clucking of hens,' he whispered. 'It is far less harrowing than gunfire.'

Mary could feel the tension and frustration of both the men she breakfasted with that morning. She recalled Paine's words, written that summer in answer to the charges laid against him, words that had brought about many stormy discussions around Johnson's table: *"If, to expose the fraud and imposition of monarchy ... to promote universal peace, civilization, and commerce, and to break the chains of political superstition, and raise degraded man to his proper rank; if these things be libellous ... let the name of libeller be engraved on my tomb."* And the beast of government had roared ever more loudly.

Suddenly the boy ran in. His mother, in the kitchen, looked round the door anxiously. 'Soldiers are coming!' he told them, breathless and fearful. 'I have seen them. It is a group from the National Guard. They are marching.'

'Good, good, Andres, that is what you are paid for,' said Paine, standing up quickly. He ruffled the boy's hair.

'Marching eh?' said Brissot, hardening his voice. He braced himself, his eyes flashing as if a fire were lit in his soul.

'The cupboard in the kitchen . . .' said Paine. 'Celine will draw it back. Come now!' He waved them onwards. 'Mary, you and Brissot, come with me – we must take to the steps!'

It was a full fifteen minutes before Celine gave the knocks that told them all was in order.

'Andre says they have passed,' she said as they emerged.

'Are you sure?' Paine asked the boy. 'You must be certain.'

'I am sure,' he said. A look of intense pride spread across his face. 'I have saved you Monsieur Paine.'

'You might be right,' Paine murmured. He went to the window. Outside all was well; the animals grazed tranquilly, the trees in the orchard waved softly in the light morning breeze.

'I must leave,' Brissot said urgently. He threw on his coat then bowed lightly to Mary. 'It is good to meet you,' he said. 'And I hope you will gain safe passage back to England, for I believe you would be wise to return as soon as you can, you cannot breathe the air in this country without breathing in death!' With that he went out of the door and left.

'It is true,' Paine said to Mary, thoughtfully. 'There is an aura of death everywhere.' They resumed their seats by the fire, but there was little ease to be had in the room that morning. 'Where are you staying?' he asked.

'I live in the apartment of a Doctor Curtius,' she said. 'You might have heard of his work.' And she told him the story.

'How lucky. You would otherwise have been in Paris alone.' His features creased with concern.

'Indeed,' said Mary a little worriedly. Paine looked at her, his large grey eyes troubled. She realised now that France was more dangerous than she'd thought. It was hard to know who was in control, if anyone was in control at all. The Jacobins and the Girondins fought for power, and the Jacobins appeared to be winning. She continued. 'It is comfortable there. I feel the apartment is safe. Marie's mother takes care of it. Marie is an artist.'

'"An artist?" What does she do?'

'Curtius creates wax images. He has taught Marie how to do it. She is highly accomplished.'

'Hmmm,' said Paine, pondering. 'Yes, I have heard of this Doctor Curtius. Did he not make an image of Voltaire for his funeral?'

Mary nodded. 'I have seen a copy in his studio. It might be his very flesh, the likeness is quite remarkable. Doctor Curtius has a salon in Paris as well; people like to visit, it is seen as a sort of entertainment. He makes heads and tableaux; his best, apparently, is of Marie Antoinette and her family taking dinner.'

Paine laughed quietly. 'Well, they can stare all they like at a tableau I suppose, but to stare at the queen like that while she eats her dinner might be seen as a treasonable offence.'

'Curtius's skill is fascinating,' Mary murmured.

Paine frowned curiously and stretched out his legs, his hands clasped behind his head. 'Ah, he knows what the people want. Nothing distasteful, of course. It is Brissot they chase for that!' He smiled wryly.

Mary's voice grew serious. 'I believe there is a part of the salon that is quite grotesque. It surprised me to learn of it. I should think they hated the work.'

Paine waited, curious.

She continued, sighing deeply. 'It is filled with obnoxious criminals, I'm told, suffering executions and such, all made from wax and quite fearful to look at.'

Paine held her gaze. 'And taken from real life?'

'The work is derived from life and death. If a subject is alive, oil is rubbed on the face and grease in the hair so that the plaster does not bind.'

Paine poked at the fire and grimaced. 'Art?'

'I know,' she sighed. 'But art takes us where it will.' She thought of days roving the woods with Fanny. Images of woodlands in England entered her mind, England flaming with colour, woodlands shimmering with dappled light and peace. For a moment or two they were thoughtful. The boy and his mother had left. The house was still. Mary spoke shakily. 'Marquis de Launay . . . You remember . . ?'

'I assure you, I do not forget.'

She saw that Paine contemplated the event with repugnance. The governor of the Bastille had had his head hacked off with a knife and the revolutionaries had marched it through Paris on a pike.

For a moment or two they were silent.

'What you do not know . . .' she continued slowly, 'is that Marie was required to make an image of his head . . . It was brought to their apartment.'

'What, his decapitated head?' Paine listened in disbelief.

Mary took a breath and continued. 'That is what Marie has told me. And there were others.'

'That's astonishing. Have you seen them?'

'No, but I know who they were.'

For a moment or two the room was silent.

'You understand what I'm saying?' Mary said quietly.

Paine stared at the fire, his eyes wide with thought. 'You are brave to speak of such things.' He lifted his face and looked at her long and hard.

'Not at all, it is good to tell you,' she assured him sighing. 'You are strong. It eases my mind.' She continued. 'Doctor Curtius entered a very dark place with his work and had no idea what was there. But history was waiting as always. Now he and Marie must partake of that history as artists.'

Paine moved uneasily in his chair, sighing and shaking his head. They were together now in the horror of the French Revolution, not knowing where it would lead. 'What are your hopes for the future?' she asked.

'"The future?"' he murmured. 'Is there a future? It seems a long way off. It is as if we must go through a million despairs to reach it.'

Again they were silent.

'I dedicated *Vindication* to Talleyrand,' she said softly. 'I thought it would help . . .'

'Yes, I heard from Christie.'

She nodded and smiled. 'But I did not like his educational ideas.'

'Are you writing anything else?'

There he sat, opposite her, looking at her with his large interested eyes. 'I am trying to write about the character of the French nation,' she said. She saw that he leant for a bag beneath the table. Thrusting his hand inside, he drew out a thin package.

'Money orders,' he said, waving them in the air, then handing them across. 'Christie brought them for you from Johnson. He knew you would visit me.'

'Thomas has been to see you?'

'Just briefly. He was only visiting. I suspect he'll be on his way back by now.'

'Johnson is good. And dear Thomas. Is he well?' She took the orders and put them in the pocket of her cape.

'He was deeply subdued by the state of France. Matters are worse than he imagined. He isn't too fond of the Paris streets either and misses the English pavements. He likes to look smart, of course, like Johnson, but chaises and carriages forever throw mud at you here.'

'Yes, it's a nuisance, especially for women. We must always organise our skirts, even before turning a corner. Though not only are our bodies corseted, our minds are bound too.'

He nodded thoughtfully. 'And you will keep on addressing it?'

'I must. But I fight a battle, I know. Women, however, are strong. The female peasants in France have shown that their veins can spark fire. Deprive them of food for their children and they will rise in vengeance against tyranny. And those who live in luxury live in a kind of madness, a dreamlike existence. They are as dolls in a dolls' house. Marie Antoinette is a doll. She is probably stunned by what has happened to the country. Her doll's house is shattered, and there is nowhere else for her to go.' She lowered her eyes. 'I wonder what they will do with her.'

'I fear the worst,' he murmured. 'What they did to the Princess de Lamballe, her lady in waiting, must torment her constantly.'

Mary shivered and rubbed her arms. 'I believe the woman was by nature placid and reserved. She was branded because she was close to Marie Antionette. What happened to her was vile. We talked about it a lot at Johnson's house. She was more than loyal, more than brave, but she was also naive. She might have stayed in Bath at the Royal Crescent where she was safe. She feared returning to Paris.'

'Many people in England and France were in favour of the revolution, but what they did to her was obscene,' said Paine, frowning. 'She went to the Tullieres Palace with Marie Antoinette out of loyalty, but she was murdered for that.' He shook his head and they went on talking till dusk. Presently the boy appeared in the doorway to ask if he was needed for work.

'Citizen Wollstonecraft needs to go home,' said Paine. 'Can you get her a chaise?'

'Cette minute!' replied the boy. With that he ran off through the fruit trees and down the long lane.

# 33

## *Laurette Returns to England*

A whole week went by after Mary returned to the apartment and other than the sound of Anne Marie in the kitchen, the place was uncannily silent. Marie spent most of her time in the studio with Curtius, though they did not speak of their work. Laurette had gone. Not a thing had she left behind, her room was neat and tidy, without a sign of her having been there. She had left France for England leaving a brief note of farewell but promising to write to them later. Mary had heard her crying that week in the night, but hadn't felt disposed to inquire, for it had seemed like a personal sadness.

'Is she sick?' Mary asked the others at breakfast. There was a strange tension amongst them, Mary felt awkward.

'Yes,' said Anne Marie sighing. 'It is *him*. I would not mind but we have warned her so many times. He will always play games.'

'And he wins,' said Marie. 'There will always be others; Imlay breaks hearts.'

'Oh, he always triumphs,' said Anne Marie, in a raw and irritable tone as if she had given too much counsel to Laurette that was lost on deaf ears.

'He does *not* triumph,' said Curtius stretching up in his seat. 'He is indifferent. He would no more understand his heartlessness than rain understands its wetness.'

'So Gilbert has upset her?' Mary said quietly. She took a sip from her tea. 'Have they been seeing each other?'

'Constantly,' said Ann Marie frustrated. 'She is a fool. They were lovers. But now she has left him, thank goodness. It is wise. He said he would come to the apartment to see her this morning. Ah, what a surprise he will get to find she has gone.' She laughed though tiredly.

'No doubt,' said Mary, trying to sound nonchalant, but the feelings she had for Imlay surged in her blood. She too, was a fool, but it was hard to be rational when he was always there in her mind. 'I wonder what has happened.'

'They argued badly – some woman I think.' Anne Marie sighed. 'Laurette will not learn.'

'I can read the man like a book,' said the doctor, 'but Laurette is a fantasist. She expected too much of him.'

'She loves him,' said Marie quietly. 'Love hides the truth and we are fair game for its antics.'

For a moment or two they were silent seeming to grapple with their thoughts.

'But he does not love her back,' said Anne Marie finally. 'He only loves himself. Women come and women go for Imlay, he is a type and will never settle down. He has a house on the outskirts of Paris, but he does not stay there, his work takes him everywhere.'

'Perhaps he needs the *right* woman,' Mary said softly. Her soul stirred as she spoke. She had taken him for herself already.

Her breakfast companions looked at her astonished. 'I'm surprised you should say such a thing,' said Marie. 'The man is impossible.'

Anne Marie ceased to listen and got up to remove the dishes from the table.

'So what will you do today then?' the doctor asked Mary.

'Write, I hope. I have much to record, and I must send some letters to England. People will wonder how I am.'

'So who will you write to?' asked Marie, glancing at Mary sharply.

'My friends and my sisters.'

'You must not write of my work in letters to England,' Marie said anxiously.

Mary glanced away. The warmth she had known in the apartment had cooled; everything seemed to have changed. She too was changing.

She went for her shawl, then sat on the chaise longue in the parlour with her reading, she would write later on, not yet. She was waiting for Imlay.

An hour went by. The morning was moving on. The doctor and Marie had gone to work in the studio. Anne Marie was busy with the ironing. Mary went to her room to do some writing. For some minutes she gazed through the window. She did not want to miss Imlay should he arrive, and tried to think of a plausible excuse to return to the parlour if he came. Just then she was alerted by the clatter of a carriage on the boulevard and the sound of horses snorting and clopping to the steady beat of a drum. Then out of the blue, a coach emerged accompanied by National Guards, it was a strange unreal image in the morning sunlight. Incredulously she stared. Then there came a persistent knock on her door.

'Oh, mon Dieu!' cried Anne Marie. She rushed in breathless, then stood peering outside. 'It is happening!' she gasped. 'Look! Look! The king is to be tried for treason! – See, he is there in the carriage!' They both gazed down on the boulevard. 'He cannot gain pardon for there are too many charges against him – a lot of them no doubt invented. – Oh, what will they do with him?' Anne Marie put her hands to her cheeks, which had reddened with emotion.

The boy's fears at the mansion came into Mary's mind. It was as if she had somehow expected it. She saw there were others watching from their windows, but no-one ventured outside.

Anne Marie's eyes blazed with irritation. 'It will not be fair,' she moaned. 'The king has no voice. He and the queen were but children when they got married. And all to bring Austria and France together. – Nothing but politics! He is not very good with politics, and eats to soothe away his fears. Marie says he is often bewildered. She has seen him like that at the palace when she's been teaching his sister to draw.' She threw up her hands in despair.

'It is such a theatrical existence,' murmured Mary, still looking on. 'The life of the court is all ritual, how can they know who they are when they are made to be so artificial?'

'The queen will be next,' said Anne Marie shakily. 'Those poor, poor children, what will become of them?'

When the carriage had passed and the street became silent Anne Marie went to the others. Mary could hear them talking noisily in the studio, the door closed against her. They had such a mysterious closeness, she thought, like people framed in a picture she could never be part of. Consumed with feeling, she wanted to write. But her hand shook as she did so and the pen fell out of her fingers.

It was the 26th December. What an awful Christmas letter it would be for Johnson, she thought, but it had to be sent. She sat for a while resting her head in her hands. So was this how the French Revolution would proceed, she asked herself. What would they do with King Louis? How might matters work out? Might the revolution, in spite of its horrors, have a central purity, an essential truth, a heart that might at last be victorious? Dear God, let it be so! She took up her pen and dabbed it in the ink, blotting the page as she went, she might have been blotting up blood:

*'About nine o'clock this morning, the king passed by my window, moving silently along (excepting now and then a few strokes on the drum, which rendered the stillness more awful) through empty streets, surrounded by the national guards, who, clustering round the carriage, seemed to deserve their name. The inhabitants flocked to their windows, but the casements were all shut, not a voice was heard, nor did I see any thing like an insulting gesture. For the first time since I entered France, I bowed to the majesty of the people, and respected the propriety of behaviour so perfectly in unison with my own feelings. I can scarcely tell you why, but an association of ideas made the tears flow insensibly from my eyes, when I saw Louis sitting, with more dignity than I expected from his character, in a hackney coach going to meet death, where so many of his race have triumphed . . ."*

She wrote for another fifteen minutes, detailing all she could. Then she lay on her bed and rested.

'They will cut off his head,' Anne Marie said later, in the parlour as Mary went to join them. 'It is inevitable.'

'I am finished with work for today,' said Marie. She rubbed her swollen eyes and sighed. 'I must try to breathe more easily.' She left the table and went to her bedroom, murmuring unhappily, 'I know what will come, and I know what they will ask me to do.'

Curtius turned to Mary. 'We are all weary, my dear,' he said gravely. 'It is a living hell.' Then he poured himself a glass of red wine.

Time passed much as before. Imlay hadn't been to the apartment at all, and Mary concluded he was working somewhere abroad. It was February, 1793. War had been declared between Britain and France and it was almost impossible for correspondence to flow between the countries. Now foreigners must have several witnesses to attest to their propriety before they could stay in France.

Mary felt anxious. She glanced around the apartment. It had been her home, but she did not feel welcome there now. Changes were happening quickly. Maximilien de Robespierre had taken control of the government, printing presses were destroyed and their owners were under close surveillance. More committees were established. Proceedings against the king had moved with cold alacrity and Louis XVI of France had finally gone to the guillotine on the 21$^{st}$ January at the Place de la Revolution watched by a jeering crowd. Now Paris was silent with shock. Curtius had bought a paper and they had huddled together to read it. The king, it said, after spending time with his family on the previous evening, had risen at five a.m. to a dull wet dawn, and at 8 o'clock a guard of 1200 horsemen had escorted him to the guillotine. It made for horrifying reading. Beside him, at his request, had been a Father Henry Edgeworth, who had described the event with both anguish and compassion:

*"The path leading to the scaffold was extremely rough and difficult to pass; the King was obliged to lean on my arm, and from the slowness with which he proceeded, I feared for a moment that his courage might fail; but what was my astonishment, when arrived at the last step, I felt that he suddenly let go my arm, and I saw him cross with a firm foot the breadth of the whole scaffold; silencing, by his look alone, fifteen or twenty drums that were placed opposite to me; and in a voice so loud, that it must have been heard at the Pont Tournant, I heard*

*him pronounce distinctly these memorable words: 'I die innocent of all the crimes laid to my charge; I Pardon those who have occasioned my death; and I pray to God that the blood you are going to shed may never be visited on France.'*

*He was proceeding, when a man on horseback, in the national uniform, and with a ferocious cry, ordered the drums to beat. Many voices were at the same time heard encouraging the executioners. They seemed reanimated themselves, in seizing with violence the most virtuous of Kings, they dragged him under the axe of the guillotine, which with one stroke severed his head from his body. All this passed in a moment. The youngest of the guards, who seemed about eighteen, immediately seized the head, and showed it to the people as he walked round the scaffold; he accompanied this monstrous ceremony with the most atrocious and indecent gestures. At first an awful silence prevailed; at length some cries of 'Vive la Republique!' were heard. By degrees the voices multiplied and in less than ten minutes this cry, a thousand times repeated became the universal shout of the multitude, and every hat was in the air."*

News had passed around the world fast as a comet. Correspondence with England was precarious and risky, for the English were viewed with more suspicion than ever as foes of the revolution. Mary's thoughts were of home. How good and holy seemed her past, the free open meadows, the woodlands, and Fanny her dearest friend, now dead; a part of Mary's soul had been taken on the death of Fanny, and she had lost part of it again here in France, for the ideals the revolution had set for the free individual appeared to be turning sour.

'You ought to have left with Laurette,' Anne Marie chided. 'What are we to do with you now? You cannot find a hotel, it is far too dangerous and anyway they all are closing their premises. But you dare not stay here, you are English.' She rubbed her face wearily. 'You cannot know how deeply involved we are here, deeper than you could ever imagine. We wish it were not so, but that is our fate.' They were distraught to the depths of their beings. For a few moments they were silent. They all sat tense and fearful. Anne Marie was shaking uncontrollably.

'I need to go out for a while,' said Mary, disturbed and confused. The apartment felt deeply oppressive. She spoke with difficulty, all words seemed lost just then. Should she try to get passage to England? Was there still time? She did not want to put the lives of her friends in danger and she was certainly in danger herself.

'Well,' said Anne Marie. 'Do walk out if you must, but it is snowing.' Mary saw that terror had entered Anne Marie and a sort of shame since the death of the king. They all gazed at space abstractedly. Mary reached for her cape and went to the door. As she made her way down the stairs, she felt a strange silence all about her. It was the silence of dread. The stairway felt colder than usual and the shadows seemed darker. She gazed downwards then froze suddenly. Thick splashes of blood made a steady line on the stairway from top to bottom. *It is the blood of the king!* she thought, with instant perception. The sight of it made her nauseas. Stepping aside, she went down carefully to the heavy front door and found her way outside where she took deep breaths and leant against the wall trembling. The snow fell heavily about her. At that moment Imlay came walking towards her.

'Well my dear,' he said, frowning. 'You appear to be getting quite wet.'

She looked at him surprised, then covered her face with her hands, embarrassed. 'You have no idea what is happening here,' she said miserably.

'I suspect it will be a fine wax image,' said Imlay dryly.

'You know?' she said shocked.

'But that is what they do, it is their work. It was inevitable that the head of the king would be sent to Curtius's apartment. Someone arrived in a carriage last night. I was on my way over and saw them. The man had a bulky package . . .' Imlay was silent a moment then lowered his voice. 'I knew what it was.'

Mary looked at him incredulous.

'It was bound to happen,' said Imlay with a sigh. 'Marie and the doctor are experts. It is their art. I cannot get used to it myself. Waxwork? Horrible stuff.'

'Why are you here?' she asked him shakily, brushing snow from her cape.

'Why do you think?' was his answer.

'If you have come for Laurette she has gone to England.'

'That's right, she has,' he smiled. 'She came to tell me.'

'But why did you come to the apartment so late when you knew she had gone? Was there something you wanted?' Bright morning light dazzled her eyes. She shaded them with her hand.

'There probably was,' he smiled. 'And she is right here in the snow.'

'I have nowhere to go,' she said feeling forlorn and ridiculous. Snow dripped down her face. She adjusted her hood. 'I can never return to that room. Not now.'

'I was concerned about you,' he said, quiet and serious. 'I know they are often up late, so I took the chance I might see you last night. But the blood on the stairs bothered me, so I have come now instead.'

Again she felt the strange fascination he had aroused in her before. 'My work is in the desk in my room . . .' she ventured. 'My writing . . . I need it.' Again she braced herself. She did not want to appear overwhelmed, though her state of mind was obvious. 'Where shall I live?'

'Listen,' he said, frowning and thoughtful. 'I'll go and get your things. – No, no, it is quite alright. I know how to deal with Anne Marie, and I suspect they'll be glad to get rid of you, matters as they are. I shall tell them I found you by the door of the apartment down here and you were almost frozen to death.'

'Oh, that I could freeze to death!' she moaned, tightening the strings of her cape. 'But I can't just leave them like that, I owe them so much.'

'If you are meaning money, let me pay them. I am quite flush just now.' He rubbed his chin and smiled. 'At least for a while.'

'No, not money,' she pleaded. 'I don't mean money; they would never ask me for money. I owe them far more than that. I owe them for giving me a home, for giving me food and care, and a beautiful room to work in.'

'And you will have the same with me,' he said, stamping snow from his boots.

'With you?' She looked at him puzzled.

'Yes, with me. I have plenty of room in my house. As a matter of fact I have all the room in the world. My last lodger has left and apart from a man who lives with me and takes care of the cooking and such I am all by myself. You will keep me company.'

For a moment or two they were silent.

'So what do you think?' he asked. He gave her an intense look. 'Am I to brave those stairs?'

Her voice fell to a whisper. *'Oh, the blood!'* she said shakily.

'Ah yes. I had better not step on the blood of the king had I, or I might have a bit of bad luck. Or more bad luck, I should say. For it does keep coming my way.' He frowned and gazed at the sky. 'I have somehow lost a ship. And let me tell you there is solid silver on it too. God knows where it has gone. These trading companies are useless!'

'The revolutionary principles are right,' Mary interjected. 'And I support them, but was it right to guillotine the king?'

He sighed and looked her up and down. 'Am I to take the cares of the world on my shoulders? I have enough of my own. This revolution does not know if it is on its head or its heels. It is totally without direction. There will be many more executions, and the worms in the earth neither know nor care, it is men who understand about death, living men! What matters is *us* and that we carry on breathing. Oh yes, there will be more executions. You can see how this business is going. It is obvious to anyone who thinks. I dare not imagine the worst.'

For a moment they were both thoughtful. Mary was struggling to convince herself that matters weren't as bad as they seemed that somehow the revolution would find a moral direction. 'Will you stay in Paris?' she asked him.

'Just for a while, I have work here. I am a diplomatic representative of the United States to France, and I am American, so there we are, they will have to be careful with me.'

'But not with me,' said Mary, shivering with cold.

'No, not so much. But you must keep out of harm's way.' He took off his coat and placed it about her shoulders. 'Wait here while I fetch your things.'

'Do speak of my appreciation!' she called as he opened the door. 'I am thankful for their kindness.'

'Have no fear, I won't be long. The man who brought me will come for us with his chaise; he is there in the boulevard. I shall soon have you safe and warm.'

# 34

## *Living with Imlay*

Mary loved travelling by Imlay in the chaise and he became in her mind a sort of protector. But she was troubled. She did not really want a protector, and it irked her that her emotions should make her think it. She suffered as they went for she knew theywould have to quarrel. She had lost her pride and dignity; she had shown her weakness and vulnerability. It was everything she loathed.

Imlay lived on the outskirts of Paris in a house surrounded by woodland. She loved the trees and shrubberies they went through as the chaise moved on, and December woodland had a sort of peaceful calm when covered in snow. As she climbed from the chaise, all about them was still.

It was a large stone house he lived in, two storeys high, and she saw through the trees that lamps were lit in a window downstairs. She grew less tense and anxious as she imagined an easier existence. The revolution had come so close to Curtius's apartment, as close as the king's blood, and she could not cast it from her mind.

Imlay had gathered her things from the apartment without any ado and her friends had sent best wishes. But they hadn't been down to see her. She knew however their opinion of the man she'd taken off with and they were probably jaded knowing the task before them. But Mary felt safer with Imlay. He was bold, confident and impervious it seemed to the trepidation around him and she let herself rest in his care.

As they went in he called to someone inside, 'Damien! Damien! – Find me a room for this lady, and light her a fire!' Damien, who came running, looked about 35, she thought. He had dark untamed curls swinging about his shoulders and a scar about three inches long down his left cheek. His features were hard and she saw that he peered at her suspiciously, bowing lightly before taking her cape across his arm.

'You need not fear him,' said Imlay, seeing her look. 'He has lived in this house a long time. In the old days, before the revolution, his wife was here also, but she left him and went to live in Switzerland.'

'Do you have bags?' asked Damien.

'Just these,' replied Imlay, pulling two bags from the shadows. 'Her writing is in the small one; ensure she has a desk in her room. She will want to continue her work.' Imlay smiled at her warmly.

'You have delivered me from misfortune,' she murmured.

'Something like that,' he said, so close that she felt the warmth of his breath on her cheek.

'You have many fine paintings,' she said, glancing about his hall. She saw they were scenes from the countryside.

'Yes,' he said wistfully, following the line of her gaze. 'I like paintings of woodlands. They are all from different countries, bought on my travels. They are not valuable, however, that is in terms of money. I mainly buy them from peasants and frame them myself.' He went to peruse them, staring at each with interest and straightening them up on the wall. Then he went to the parlour door. 'Come,' he beckoned.

She loved the melody of his confident American accent, and she followed him meek as a lamb, taking a seat by the fire, collecting herself as she enjoyed the warmth of his house.

'It is good you are here,' he said, gazing at her with pleasure. 'That chair you are sitting in came from America. Do you like it? You can sink right down and sleep in it if you wish. I have often done so myself.'

He came up close and stroked her hair, and the blood rose to her cheeks. 'My hair is tangled,' she said self-consciously, trying to tidy it with her fingers.

'I know,' he smiled. 'It is a nest of snakes.'

She frowned briefly. 'Please don't say that.'

He glanced outside unperturbed. 'And the damned snow still falls,' he murmured. 'A pity. I can't stand snow, but at least it's easy to see footprints should strangers creep up on the house.'

'Are you searched for?' she asked, frowning. Just then the relief of escaping the apartment had effaced her other concerns.

'For my debts, not my politics!' he laughed, striding the floor and stroking his chin as if troubled. 'But my mental vigour keeps me safe. Ah yes, I am glad of my wit, dear girl, it comes in useful.'

Damien appeared in the doorway. 'The fire is lit and the room is ready, Monsieur,' he said. 'It is all just as you hoped for, is it not? The mademoiselle is here. – Indeed, you are a magician!'

Imlay put out the flat his hand. 'Not so easy with your tongue Damien,' he said with a wink. 'I tell you too much when we drink.'

'The mademoiselle is lovely,' said Damien looking downwards, aware of his indiscretion.

'Well now Citizen Mary, go take a look at your room,' said Imlay. 'It is a very pretty room at the back there; I think you will like it. – And Damien, we are to address each other as "Citizen" now. Who knows what they'll do to us if we don't. Try to remember.'

She followed Damien upstairs and they entered a room at the back of the house. It was small and comfortable with a crackling newly made fire. Candlelight flooded a lovely chaise longue and dressing table, firelight danced on the walls and on the freshly made bed which was covered in a blue silk counterpane. It was obviously a room for a woman, she thought, and she couldn't help wondering who else might have slept there. The room looked neat and well kept, as if always available. How quickly she'd been conveyed from the sad apartment to this place of peace and charm. Just a small back room, but oh such a wonderful room! 'There is fresh water in the jug there, and a bowl also,' said Damien. 'Should you need anything else, I am always somewhere in the house.'

'Damien!' called Imlay. 'Come and heat the broth!'

'I am coming Captain Imlay!' the man called back, then he sped down the stairs.

So this was Imlay's home, she thought as she combed her hair by the fire. He lived in this large dark house hidden in the trees. Doves would no doubt awaken him at dawn in summer, and he might have squirrels in the garden. She liked the feel of the house, especially the large garden. His house was filled with curiosities bought on his travels, strangely shaped chairs, ornaments and sculpted dancers. He liked dancers, particularly naked girls in elegant positions as if frozen in time. A wall hanging with images of Egypt covered a third of a wall by her bed. She wondered how he had brought it and imagined him travelling on a ship with it rolled as if it held Cleopatra. She wondered if he had actually been to Egypt and seen the mysterious pyramids containing the coffins of Pharaohs. Her eyes turned to the bats flitting about the eaves by her window. Johnson would like the bats. Travellers told of bats as large as pigeons in the Great Pyramid of Khufu. In the sixteenth century, travel to Egypt had been made much safer. The Sultan Selim had provided protection for French traders and pilgrims and people had visited more freely.

She gazed about the room as she fixed her combs in her hair, then she poured some water in the bowl and splashed it about her face. Her skin was shining from the cold of the snow and her journey, and also from being with Imlay. 'Is this what love feels like?' she murmured. 'Has it at last found me?' The feeling suffused her being. How could it be that she had never felt it before? It had always been a great separate being only known as a stranger. Now it was with her it felt like hers and she owned it. Did he feel it too? There was a small desk in the corner. Yes, she could work from that. And she saw there was a bookshelf for her books. There came the call of an early owl near her window. Her bags lay on the floor, she would empty them later. Just now she would eat with Imlay.

Next morning she found him reading a book in his library, then saw with surprise that his name was printed on the cover.

'You write?' she said, taking a seat beside him.

'I try,' he smiled.

She looked at the title and spoke it out loud, '*A Topographical*

*Description of the Western Territory of North America,* I am most impressed.'

'I hope to encourage settlement in America with that.' He handed it over and she leafed through the pages.

His eyes sparked with pleasure as she held it. 'It is quite precise and thorough,' she said. 'You have done much research . . .'

He leant back and folded his arms. 'I'll be damned if there's anything missing.' He spoke grandly, theatrically. 'If you want to obtain a correct account of the soil, climate, natural history, population all that, then just read Imlay's book and there you have it.'

She cast her eyes around his book shelves. 'You have a good library,' she said. 'I see that a lot of your books are written in French.'

'I attempt to read them,' he said, 'though I'm slow.'

He watched her touring the shelves, removing odd volumes and searching their pages. They were quiet together and seemed at ease.

'I hear you are sympathetic to the rights of women,' she said softly. 'Laurette informed me.'

'Did she?' he laughed. 'It depends who the woman is.'

'And I heard from Christie that you never intend to marry. You dislike the institution, in fact you deplore it.'

'It seems I am talked about a lot,' he smiled. 'I have been in the clutches of women in the past, but never again. I do believe women should have rights though, and not before time. I can't imagine how I would live if I were female, if I could live at all.'

'Are you writing anything now?' she asked him curiously.

He stretched his arms above his head and yawned. 'Well, I've thrown down a few ideas, but they don't amount to a lot, other things get in my way.' He laughed quietly. 'It's a sort of novel. Very scrappy.'

'Where is it?' she asked intrigued.

He glanced about. 'Oh, it's knocking about somewhere. I'm not particularly proud of it.'

'I know the feeling,' she said abstractedly. She thought of *Vindication,* her recent publication. She had not written it as well as she'd wanted and intended to write it again. Next time she would give it the due respect it deserved.

She heard him sigh, then he rubbed his face tiredly. 'Books are one thing but life is another,' he said wearily. 'We need to live closer to nature I think. It is best for the human soul.'

'I agree absolutely,' she said, pleased by his comment. 'I see myself in a cottage in a wood with some dairy animals and a piece of land to take care of.'

'A bit confining perhaps,' he said soberly.

'Maybe,' she said, running her finger around the edge of his book as it lay on top of the table. 'But I would hope by then to have found myself someone to love . . .' She was playful with him and confident.

With a sudden change of heart he clapped his hands and laughed. 'Come, let's see what Damien has got us together for breakfast.'

'I expect you are awakened by doves in summer,' she said as they went.

'Turtle doves would certainly serenade you in that room in spring; they purr like kittens. But they're probably crossing the Sahara desert now. Courageous little beggars.'

She saw that the table held bread, cheeses and conserves and a large pot of tea. 'The snow has disappeared overnight,' he said, glancing outside. 'Just a brief change of temperature and it's gone.'

Together they gazed through the window, the branches of the trees hung damp and still, but the skies still threatened snow. As they sat down to eat, she felt gloriously happy. 'I had the strangest dream last night,' she told him, her voice suddenly fragile.

'Let me in on it will you,' he said, smiling and pouring the tea. He looked at her curiously.

'It was all very odd . . . The king was passing through the woods by this house in a carriage . . .'

'What, by here in a carriage? How the hell did the coachman do that, those tracks are so narrow and anyway the king is dead.' He shook his head at the thought.

'It was a dream,' she said quietly. 'Anything can happen in a dream.'

'So where was he going?'

'He was on his way to be tried. – Oh, I know it's too late, but dreams care nothing for time. You ran to the coachman and stopped it.'

'I did?' He looked at her incredulous.

'You told the coachman that the trial would be biased and ordered him to stop.'

Imlay frowned. 'You were confusing me with Doctor Curtius I think. He has sympathies with the monarchy. Marie has taught art to his sister, you see. But me? And besides, that carriage was probably accompanied by National Guard.' He laughed at the thought. 'So what did they do with me after? Lop off my head, I suppose.' He opened his eyes widely, waiting for her to deliver her imagination. 'It is only a ghost you see before you; Captain Imlay is no longer amongst us.'

She smiled at his easy humour. She wasn't very humorous herself; her soul was fettered by concerns. But it was good to see how easily the cares of the world passed over him; she loved his freedom of spirit. But she saw in his eyes there were other parts of him that struggled; perhaps she would learn of them in time.

'So, tell me, what happened next?' he asked, slicing off a portion of cheese and pressing it on to a piece of bread before taking it slowly to his mouth.

'Nothing more,' she lied, looking away. She would not tell him she had gone to visit him in prison, had made a case for his pardon and had brought him back to his house in a carriage, where she had then shared his bed. And how wonderful his love making was! She thrilled as she thought of it. Could it ever be so good in reality? He did not know how she'd loved the strength of his passion in her dream. And as she looked at him now she felt a greater intimacy with him, as if somehow it had really happened, not in a dream but in reality, for his eyes as they met her own were the eyes of a lover.

'I have to leave,' he said, drinking the last of his tea and standing. 'You will only have Damien for company today. You can rest assured though; he will take good care of you, I promise.'

She was silent for a moment, disappointed at losing him so soon. He went for his coat and returned buttoning it slowly. Then he donned his hat, and looked at her. 'How do you feel?' he enquired after a moment's silence. 'You are looking quite dismal.'

She moaned as if suffering. 'Why must you go?'

'I have work to attend to,' he said, looking perplexed. 'The house will be silent when I've gone, then you can do some writing and I won't be here to disturb you.'

'Please don't leave,' she fretted. 'I love being with you.'

'My dear Mary, I don't have a choice. I must try to discover what has happened to that damned ship's cargo. You can take repose in my house. There is a nice little balcony in your room and should the weather grow milder you might like to sit out there. Now that the snow has melted I shall take my horse and return early evening.'

She attempted a smile. Must she go the whole day without him? She drew a breath and straightened.

Within minutes he had galloped away.

For the rest of the morning she sat in her room attempting to write. The clock on the wall showed 11.30 a.m. She wrote, and wrote some more. Damien was down in the basement working, when all of a sudden there was a loud rap on the door. He came up the steps straight away, then walked through the hall at speed. Mary went to look and saw that he addressed a young female visitor. He spoke politely, but she strode right past him removing her gloves and in an obviously tetchy frame of mind.

'I am quite worn out,' she moaned. 'Here, take my coat. I have had such a terrible journey, the roads are so slippery.' She glanced towards the parlour. 'Where is he? Is he in there?' As she took off her hat a mass of auburn curls tumbled about her shoulders.

'He is out,' said Damien. 'He went off early this morning.'

'Where did he go?'

'He did not say. He just left.'

'How long will he be gone for?' The woman spoke despairingly.

Damien moved from foot to foot confused. 'He was good enough to help you when you needed him,' he faltered. 'He was kind. But he always has business to attend to. You cannot cling to him like this.'

'I do not *cling* to him,' said the woman even more vexed. 'I am not a leach. I am valued. You take too many liberties with your words Damien! If you upset me I shall tell him. Now at least make me a drink and let me get warm by the fire.'

Damien directed her to the parlour, but seeing Mary at the top of the stairs, she stopped on the way. 'Who is that woman?' she asked, looking annoyed. She went to call up. 'You there, who are you? – Come down!'

Mary made her way down, bracing herself as she approached. 'I am Mary Wollstonecraft from England,' she told her loudly. 'I am staying with Mr Imlay a while.' Curious how powerful her voice was, she thought, when she felt indignant. In a silk grey dress and pearls, the woman stood proud and superior. The buckles on her black brocade shoes shone in the sunlight from the window. Mary wondered how well this woman knew Imlay. Was she about to move in?

'I don't know anything about you,' said the woman, looking Mary up and down.

'Citizen Mary only came to join us last night,' said Damien. 'She has nowhere to live.' He sighed and looked bewildered. 'This is Citizen Colette.'

'"*Nowhere to live?*" That is bad.' Colette frowned and gazed at Mary with wonder.

'You are right,' said Mary. 'It is bad.' A chill passed through her as she thought of Curtius's apartment. What would she have done, she wondered if Imlay hadn't brought her to his house? She could never have stayed where she was.

Colette shook her head perplexed. 'Pourquoi? – Why have you come to France, it is nothing but revolution here. Are you mad?'

'I came to write,' Mary replied, trying not to look chagrined. But her blood was up in her cheeks. No-one would call her mad! 'I intend to write an account of the revolution for the people in England. I am a writer.'

'Ah,' said the woman, gazing at her with interest. 'A dangerous venture. I too am a writer. Or I was. The France I knew has changed. Who can write in these awful days without fear? Are you published?'

'Indeed,' said Mary. 'I am Mary Wollstonecraft. I am very well known in England.'

The woman straightened. 'Well, you had better not be known too much. It is unwise for a writer to be noticed in France, unless you are on the right side.' She ran her fingers through her curls and sighed. 'But you cannot tell one side from another at times; they blend then fracture and break. It is the breakage that causes confusion, for then our hearts are shattered and we are all in each other's way.' She stood very still in the hall, clasping her purse as if it were her very heart.

Mary glanced through the window; it was a clear December morning with a perfectly blue sky. All outside was still and silent as if sleeping. They both went into the parlour and Damien brought them drinks. The woman was beautiful and elegant; Mary thought she too might have been an actress like Laurette for such was her countenance. She had made an impressive entrance and had quite taken over the house as if it were a stage.

'I have never read your work,' said Colette. 'What do you write about?'

'Ideas,' Mary said abstractedly. 'First I make notes, then I put them together for a pamphlet or maybe a book. But life here changes very fast; I would like to talk with you about that, if I may. I had friends in England who I talked with a lot, I miss them.'

'Do you always write to be published?' Colette asked. With startling familiarity, she lowered herself into a chair and stared at Mary haughtily.

'In the main,' said Mary, taking a seat opposite. 'Though I do keep a diary. It is good to keep notes.' She wanted to find out more about this woman who was so acquainted with Imlay. Damien said Imlay had helped her. In what way had he assisted her? 'You and Monsieur Imlay are very good friends, are you not?' she said tentatively.

Colette smiled and changed her position in the chair. 'You might say that. I was involved in a wearisome love affair with a man from England. I stayed in this house for a while until I found an apartment in Paris.' Her face looked pained as she spoke. 'Gilbert can be kind, but he is very difficult to live with.'

'Do you visit here often?' Mary felt she had a battle on with this woman who seemed angry and frustrated.

'Whenever I can. Not very much though now, Paris is so unstable.' She talked on quickly. 'But Paris is where I was born. I live with other French women and a few expatriates in the city, some of us are female activists, we write and distribute pamphlets and meet for discussions; the revolution changes by the minute and the jaws of Paris can be vicious, there is violence everywhere. I have a friend who lives in Lyon; there has been terrible bloodshed there because of the revolts. There are Parisians who believe that the Convention must be cleansed of moderates; it is seen as counter-revolutionary and traitorous to be moderate, you see. Such people can be charged with treason and arrested. Since the Jacobins have taken control, the revolution has become more brutal. People are withdrawing their support for the Convention now. It is even possible to make convictions on nothing but hearsay.' She breathed in nervously and continued. 'I wanted to talk to Gilbert about that, but like the dark crow he is, he has flown!'

Mary was about to say he would return that evening, but decided on silence. It was interesting to hear of other expatriates in the city however, the idea aroused her. 'Might I visit you sometime?' she asked.

The woman put her hand in her purse and pulled out a pencil and paper, then she scribbled out an address and handed it across. 'Are you staying here long?' She gazed at Mary thoughtfully. 'It is best to return to England.'

'I shall stay for as long as I can,' said Mary firmly. She had got on well with Colette so far, despite the tumult in her mind. Colette drank from her tea as Mary continued. 'From all I hear, the experiences of the poor in France have been painful beyond expression. The people who stormed the Bastille were brave, but the violent mob is manipulated I think by those with self interest.'

For a moment or two they were silent. 'Perhaps we squander ourselves in caring,' sighed Colette. 'We put ourselves in danger because of it. You say you have ideas. But ideas can kill. See what is happening to France because of ideas. Ideas are flying round the world like locusts and we cannot breathe because of them.'

'This country is steeped in drama,' said Mary. 'Its people can be easily mesmerised by fanatics. It is all drama.'

'You mean Robespierre?' Colette looked at her sharply. 'He is quite a dramatist I know. Very theatrical.'

'He excites the people,' said Mary. 'His power is disturbing. Let us hope what he says is right, though I feel something bad about Robespierre.'

'And now they have killed the king,' Colette murmured, falling back into her chair. 'The Girondins didn't want him dead, but they could not stop it.'

'He had made some bad decisions,' said Mary. 'And now there are many who are bent on inflicting misery on others, misery for its own sake. The people seek a leader as a spider swings on its thread and seeks a hold. And the evil is that no leader comes forth, not one who can manage them altogether. I believe in the revolution but need it be so uncivilised?'

'Human nature can be barbaric,' Colette said wincing. 'I doubt it will ever change.'

Mary searched her mind, remembering Price's sermons; she would not let those beautiful perceptions wither, she would keep them alive through memory. Price's thoughts had fused with her own and had resolved into a strength in her blood. 'The revolution must work,' she whispered. 'It dare not be an accident like the fall of a comet that scorches the earth then dies. It has to be productive of good and we must try to see that it is. France needs able leaders, to show how things must be done with grace and humanity.'

'The people need someone who can guide the revolution to its proper conclusion without ferocity,' asserted Colette. 'Our so called leaders are all shouting at once. Who is to hear what they say in all the commotion?' She stood and straightened her skirts. 'Now where is my coat and hat? I shall have to be off.'

Mary called to Damien to bring them, suddenly feeling like mistress of the house. 'How did you get here?' she asked. Through the window she saw that a horse stood tethered to a tree. 'Did you ride?'

'I did, and my horse has been most patient. He is a very good steed, is he not? I have had him many years; he is used to this house.'

Damien brought her coat and she slipped her arms in the sleeves. Then she fixed on her hat and pushed her hands in her gloves. 'Remember to call on us,' she smiled. 'We will expect you.' She placed her hand on Mary's shoulder. 'And good luck with Gilbert.'

Within minutes she had gone.

# 35

## *Loving Gilbert*

If he loves her it will kill me, thought Mary as she sat at her desk that day trying to write. She seethed with jealousy and knew she would have to find out, or the thought would continue to torment her. If the snow fell heavily again he might not return that evening, he might even be away all week, she concluded miserably.

As the hours passed by, the weather broke fiercely and the wind moaned through the trees so that all her thoughts seemed sorrowful. She prayed for his return, constantly going to the window. Just then there came the sound of a horse! Quickly she went to the stairs. Damien was piling logs in the hearth in the parlour. 'Is it him?' she asked urgently.

'Yes,' he said irritably. 'Sit down and relax. – Did you write?'

'A little,' she said quietly. She did not like Damien's manner when he turned moody. She could hear the strain in her voice.

'So what did you write about?' he asked, his back still towards her. He threw logs on the flames.

She sat down slowly, waiting for Imlay. 'The revolution, of course, but I need to talk with other people. It is hard to believe that violence and suffering is the price to be paid for toppling such a selfish regime.'

'The longer such an order exists the more effort it takes to overthrow it,' said Damien, continuing his work. 'Only bloodshed can defeat it. But there is worse to come, which is why my wife went to Switzerland.'

'You must miss her.'

'Yes, but she is safe.'

'But why did you not accompany her?'

'I have an aged father in Paris. He is frail and ailing. That is why.' He brought more logs for the hearth. 'If you wish to see Citizen Colette, I will take you when I visit my father. We can go in the chaise. But you must speak to Captain Imlay first. He will probably advise against it.'

'I need to find friends,' she said, annoyed by his coldness. 'The time seems long when I'm alone.'

'That is all very true,' he said. Then he rose and went to the kitchen.

After a while, Imlay came through into the parlour. Tall and lean he fell into his favourite chair. It was now getting dark and Damien went through the house lighting candles. Imlay's eyes looked tired and ghostly in the firelight and Mary saw he was anxious.

'I don't know what her business was,' he murmured. 'Did she tell you?' He looked at Mary intently.

'You mean Colette?'

'Yes, Damien said she'd been to the house. What did she say?'

'We spoke of the revolution. She came to see you, but you'd left.'

'But she was here for some time?'

'Maybe an hour.'

Damien came in with a bottle of wine and a glass and handed them to Imlay, who opened the bottle quickly and poured himself a drink, then he rested his head on the back of the chair and rested as if sleeping. 'Colette gets on my nerves. I can't put up with her for long,' he said quietly.

'We exchanged ideas, it was a good conversation.'

He opened his eyes and sat up. 'You say nothing of where I go, of course – should you find out, that is.' He drank deeply. 'You can stay in my house as long as you like, but do not discuss my affairs. Do you understand?'

He spoke, she thought, like a tutor to a troublesome pupil. 'You treat me like a child,' she said coolly. 'Please don't do that, or I fear I must leave.'

'I doubt you will leave,' he laughed, taking a drink from his wine. 'By God it's bitter out there. Better in here by the fire.'

She was angry with him now, her heart beat fast with annoyance.

'I do not want to quarrel,' he said. 'But I need to know I can trust you.'

'Trust me about what?' Her tone was cold and measured.

He sighed. 'Matters are sometimes strange with me. You must accept I am not straightforward.'

'So it would seem,' she murmured.

'Something's the matter?' he said, lowering his voice and leaning forward. His eyes were gentle in the firelight. 'You're troubled.'

'Is she your lover?' she asked, too emotional just then for dignity.

'Who – Colette?' He laughed at the ceiling. 'She is rather alluring I admit, but no she is not. And you must not question me like this.'

'Yet you ask me what the matter is. *You* can question *me* it seems, but I am not to question you.'

'I am afraid you are right,' he said indifferently. 'The matter though is quite simple, you are jealous.' His voice was bold and flirtatious.

'I am nothing of the sort,' she whispered. 'And do not try to frighten me, for I will not be frightened by anyone.'

'I believe it,' he said, narrowing his eyes. He put down his drink and went to her. Then he wound his fingers through her curls. 'I think your hair is better off your face, like this.' He held her hair in both hands and drew it away from her forehead. Then he bent and kissed her cheek.

'You kissed me,' she said shakily.

'I know, I remember. – Ah, you tremble with feeling; I see there is blood in your veins. I feared they were filled with ice, your manner is sometimes so frosty.' He returned to sit in his chair.

'I am not frosty, I am a serious woman,' she said, taking deep breaths.

'I must eat,' he said, bracing himself. 'You will join me, I hope.'

'I would love to. Might I stay here a little while longer?'

'But I thought you wanted to leave?' He smiled wryly.

'I wasn't being serious.'

He bit his lip and frowned. 'But, my dear, I thought you were a serious woman?'

'You are very difficult,' she murmured.

'Am I? Well I apologise, but I can only be as I am. – Oh yes, do stay, but you will have to earn your keep. You will help Damien carry logs; make broth and sweep floors, and whatever else I can think of.'

She looked at him sharply. He laughed.

'Listen,' he said resolutely as they went through the hall to the dining room. 'I have found you a maid. She will be very happy to work for us. She lives in Paris and her name is Marguerite. You will like her. Her husband died last year and she's often lonely.' He gave her a long curious look as they took their seats at the table. 'She is poor. You are a zealous champion of the poor, are you not?'

'I am a champion of the destitute and distressed, those who suffer from lack of education and lack of money.' She spoke vehemently. 'They have no voice and must be heard.'

'Indeed,' he said abstractedly. 'So what can we be sure of then?'

'What do you mean?'

'We can be sure of the poor,' he said waving a finger. 'Oh yes, there will always be poverty.'

'It need not be so. Thomas Paine has some excellent ideas.'

'Oh, he does, but I doubt they will ever come to pass. His thoughts are good and I like what he writes, but I fear he is deluded.'

'You dare not say such things about Paine. He is a great thinker, a soothsayer and a philosopher.'

'And he will very soon be dead. The hounds are after him. But he has gone down a foxhole. Nobody knows where he is.' He glanced at her curiously. 'Do you?'

She shook her head. 'I know that he came to France . . .'

'Everyone knows he came to France, but where is he?' asked Imlay, passing food and looking at her straight.

'I do not know,' she said quietly.

'Is he your friend?'

She did not answer. She noted that Imlay was hungry and for a while he sat eating in silence. Then he opened more wine and poured them both a glass. His spirits grew vibrant as he drank. 'I asked what we might be sure of,' he said.

'Who can tell?' she answered. 'There are no certainties.'

'Not even one? Can I not be certain of your feelings?' he asked, staring into his wine and speaking in a sensual tone of voice. 'I mean *your* feelings for *me*?'

She looked at him vulnerably. He was firmly fixed in her heart; she was his for the taking. 'You can,' she said softly. For several moments they gazed at each other without speaking. 'And what about you, do *you* have feelings for *me*?'

He reached and touched her hand. 'Would I have brought you here if I didn't? I brought you because I cared. I was enamoured from the minute I met you. And I knew I would have you eventually.'

They were silent again, eating their food.

'And you think you *have* me?' she said smiling.

'Not quite, but I am getting close.' She was mad with desire for him now. Imlay would be her man. He was waiting, taunting and waiting. Oh, the agony of her passion, the fear of what it might bring, what it might contain once they were in that supreme of places, that sacred place of ecstasy she had denied her body so long.

He rose and took her hand, then led her upstairs to her room. As she lay on the bed, slowly he removed her clothes, kissing her naked flesh and moaning with pleasure at each discovery. Without doubt he was a practised lover, and he took her so easily. It was all so natural to him. But for her it was new, it was rapture. How she enjoyed being ravished. She wanted to keep him in her arms, to never release him. And she held him until the room grew chilled and the candles had almost burned away. In the shadowy light, she could not draw her eyes from his beautiful back as he sat on the edge of the bed putting on his clothes. 'I love you,' she whispered, running her finger down his spine. In the light of the dimming candles, he pulled on his trousers. He did not answer, but instead went to the door and she heard him descending the stairs with a slow determined tread.

She lay there confused for a while, wanting him to return and love her again. But she could hear him talking with Damien, speaking mere trivialities, then she heard them laughing. Was she forgotten so quickly, could it be possible? And she wondered about the mind of the man who was now rooted in her being.

But she was far too strong to be miserable for long. She prepared herself for bed and settled to sleep. Was this the way of a husband, she asked herself heavy hearted. But he wasn't a *husband*. If it was the way of a lover, it was cruel and selfish. She wondered how she should conduct herself tomorrow. He had reduced her to a sensuous heap of clay, something he could mould as he wished. And she knew in her soul she'd been wronged.

All through the night she was restless. At dawn, she heard Damien walking about in the parlour. Quickly, she descended the stairs and found Imlay seated at the table taking breakfast. She stood before him in her nightwear, though he was dressed and ready to leave. 'Good morning!' he called, beckoning her.

She took a seat, and he passed her bread and mutton but she pushed it away. 'You did not sleep in my bed,' she said, watching as he ate. He did not speak or stop eating, but looked at her surprised, and she hid her face in her hands, struggling to rationalise her thoughts. Now he was fully in charge. How weak she was to accept his dominion over her, she thought, but she could not help it, he had somehow made himself her master.

'Must I *sleep* with you?' he asked, raising his eyebrows and looking at her perplexed. He waved away the thought. 'You are free, Mary, free as a bird. You may do as you wish. Do I not have the same liberty?'

'But I wanted you by me in the night,' she said plaintively. 'I needed you.'

He sighed. 'Ah, you must not rely on me like that. It is most unwise. I am about to go away.'

She could not look into his face; the agony she felt was unbearable. And yet, he was right, she would hope to release women from the constrictions of romantic love, which she believed could drive them insane. And it did, it did! She could not think for wanting him. She rose and went to him and pressed her mouth on his hair. 'Come with me now,' she implored him. 'Come to my bed before you go.'

'But my dear, I must leave right now,' he said coolly.

'Not yet!' she said miserable and angry. 'Not yet!'

'Oh Mary,' he said. His brow creased with frustration. 'I thought you were strong.'

'And so did I,' she said wretchedly. 'But you see I am not.'

'Mary, my dear, 'he said softly. 'I know I can be thoughtless, but at least I am consistent.' His voice fell low. 'I do not betray myself like you do.' He took her hand and kissed her palm.

How soft his lips were, she thought, how she thrilled at his touch. She looked at him quickly, her eyes flashing fiercely. 'I do not think I betray myself. I speak from my heart.'

Imlay groaned, then stood. 'Listen, I really must depart, my horse is waiting. Try to compose yourself, my dear. If you're going to live in my house, you must accept me for who I am and not what you want me to be.'

'You dare not go!' she said frantically. 'How long will you be gone?'

'Two days,' he said, pulling on his coat.

'Oh, please make it only two days,' she pleaded earnestly.

'I shall try. But business takes as long as it takes.'

She saw he was emotional, biting his lip irritably.

'You can do some writing,' he said coolly. 'You have much to record. Damien tells me you would like to visit Colette. That isn't such a good idea. They are watching with the eyes of cats in Paris. Be careful. They constantly point at the English.' He stared at her, looking abstracted. 'But I understand your need to make friends. I cannot be a friend to you like that. As you see, I am often away.'

She stood there bewildered, moaning and unhappy. 'Might we not be together as a couple, just now and then?'

'That won't be possible,' he said, donning his hat.

'But what about our *feelings*? Did it mean nothing last night?'

'Feelings come and feelings go,' he replied. He shrugged. 'What the devil do you want from me, Mary?' He spoke angrily, but he went to her and held her, then kissed her hard on the lips.

'Only two days,' she murmured clinging to his arm. 'Let it be only two days.' She loved him yet she feared him. She was his prisoner now, both body and soul.

The next two days were dreary. She felt oddly like something old and ruined and no longer loved. It was as if there had been a sudden loss of her self. Where was Mary Wollstonecraft she asked herself? Where was her strength? The lassitude that seized her would not lift and she constantly went to the window and listened at the door for his return. Perhaps he would return early, she told herself hopefully, perhaps he longed for her as she longed for him. It was easier to think like that. She had written very little, and what she had managed was poor.

It was mid afternoon. How bright the sun was, she thought, yet how little of it entered her being, her soul felt dark and forlorn. Damien had brought her food and drink, but he had gone about quietly attending to his duties and had left her alone. She attempted to read, but that too was fruitless. There was something she needed, like a kind of food; she felt she might die of starvation. She rubbed her arms and paced the room. 'Imlay, Imlay!' she murmured over and over. 'Come to me now!' She glanced at the clock, ah! the day was so slow! Two days he had said, *two days!* That was if he kept to his word. She fell on her bed in despair. He was not known to keep to his word in anything much, he was a wild energy, a disruptive force like a storm, and she felt that storm in her blood.

She had changed her coiffure and had done her hair into plaits about her head with loose hair falling down her face, and she had taken it back from her forehead in the way that he liked. In doing so, she had discovered a few grey hairs on her temples; she feared them frantically and tried to pull them out with her fingers. Panic sped through her veins. Might she have a child? she asked herself hopefully. Might she yet have a child with Imlay? She would like to have a child and provide it with love and kindness. She did not feel she had had such love and kindness herself in her childhood, but she felt the spirit was within her to give it were she blessed. She glanced outside. All was quiet and still. In the silence of the night, she had thought she'd heard the rumbling of carts on the road. Strange to hear carts in the night, she thought, but in the light of dawn, she'd realised it was only a dream.

As the daylight waned and blackened and the night closed in, she knew that Imlay would not return that day. She did not want to reveal to Damien how it mattered however and as he brought food to her room she feigned to be absorbed in her work, whispering a quiet 'thank you' as he left. Then she put more logs on her fire. As they vigorously burst into flame, she felt the absence of Imlay more than ever.

He had been gone four days. When at last he arrived she fell into his arms with gladness. 'It has been too long,' she moaned. 'Far too long!'

'Mary, my dear,' he said frowning. 'Such need does not suit you.' He sighed at her torment and threw his hat on the table, then went to sit in his chair. He stroked his chin thoughtfully. 'You need to get out, though there might be a problem with that I admit. Damien can take you to Paris sometimes like you wanted. They are always watching but he knows how to dodge them.' His features lightened. 'The grounds at the back of this house are closed in; you can wander about through the trees, that is quite pleasant. The weather might be kinder tomorrow. It does not do to be always inside, the mind grows confused.'

It annoyed her to see him so liberated whilst she, herself, felt captured. She braced herself and sat down, then she urged him to talk about his business, asking him where he had been and what his hopes were. He had not found the ship he searched for, he said disgruntled, but he would keep on trying.

For a few moments they were silent as he took off his coat and returned to his chair. 'You are bound to feel lonely,' he ventured. 'I hear what you say. But I'm not going to argue about whether I should be here or there. I have no idea where I will be from one day to the next. In any case, Mary, it is plain from your writing that you hold the belief that women should be independent of men, it is an important mantra of yours.'

'Yes,' she murmured. 'That is what I believe.'

'But you do not practise what you preach,' he said, with a deep intake of breath and meeting her eyes.

She straightened. He was right. And it flooded her again, that burning sense of injustice she sought so fiercely to redress. 'Women can be harmed if they become dependent on men,' she said earnestly. 'Marriage can be a fatal contract for a woman; sometimes they might as well be dead, they behave so strange and ghostly.' She continued quickly, her strength returning as she talked. 'A woman loses all her rights and she will not be protected from her husband's caprices and cruelties either.' She stood and paced the floor. 'I do not forget my mother's sufferings, the way my father abused her. I shall never forget how it was!' Her anger was rising fast.

'But I am not such a man,' said Imlay, with a gentle smile. He gazed at her thoughtfully. 'I care for you a lot,' he said sighing. 'But you must not love me to distraction, Mary. What good will it do? You should heed your own teaching.'

'That's right,' she murmured. 'I should.' But she had lost herself already. Her desire for him now was such that she felt she could love him whatever he did, however her mind said otherwise. 'Your shipping ventures are bound to take you away,' she said, as if with sudden decision. 'But so long as you remember me on your travels, I think I could survive.' She saw that he looked at her pondering.

'You poor creature,' he said, rising. He went to her and held her against him. 'You feel and think so intensely, it quite wears you out.'

'Did you long for me?' she asked, turning her face to his.

'What do you think?' he said softly. He kissed her long and deeply. It was a kiss that left her wanting more.

'Come,' he said, taking her hand. And he led her upstairs.

## 36

## A Pregnant Mary

Mary went with Damien to Paris and made friends with Colette's circle, lively, excitable people who often gathered together to talk and share news. Other writers would join them, familiar with Johnson's crowd in London, and the English voices were reassuring. There was much to discuss and wonder at for each day was different in Paris, and it was impossible to predict which way the revolution would go. Everyone she encountered looked anxious, constantly glancing back for fear of what lay behind them.

Imlay was often away, mostly leaving at dawn and returning at dusk. She did not know where he went and he kept his counsel. She wrote to Johnson and her sisters, but correspondence between France and England was precarious. Marguerite took charge of her letters and had contacts, but there was always danger. Britain had declared war on France that spring and all British subjects living in France were threatened. Many were crossing the channel to return to their homes. But Mary's soul belonged to Imlay now; she must stay where she was. Their intimate moments held her.

While Imlay was away she sat in her room alone and made notes for her next publication, *An Historical and Moral View of the Origin and Progress of the French Revolution*. It meant so much and she wanted the work to be truthful. But how to record precisely what was happening was difficult, for there were many points of view and people were afraid to say anything in favour of monarchy. Much had happened since the king had been guillotined, and a great deal of emphasis was being placed on the notion of the "Citizen". The old rankings had ended and a new order had begun.

There were those in the Paris circle however, who argued the revolution was moving too fast, and as she gazed outside at the trees she felt distanced from England more than ever. Christie and Paine had speculated England might also go the way of revolution, for the poor were frustrated and angry. Now they were both marked men and the English government constantly tracked their writings and watched their activities. In the throes of her love she relished the hours spent with Imlay when he would give her his best attention; times when they talked together, laughed and made love, and she reported what she'd learned in Paris. Since the death of the king, Robespierre had grown in power at the Jacobin Club, and his faction in the National Convention was now known widely as 'the Jacobins'. It seemed that the Jacobins were against Church and atheism alike. Forever anxious to thwart anything injurious to their cause, they created rules of their own which had to be meticulously followed. Mary's Paris friends claimed it was impossible to know how ferocious the Jacobins might be, they were so determined.

'There is a need for sound judgement,' Imlay said to her one morning in the parlour. 'The Jacobins think they can force their way with brutality.'

Mary knew he was deeply aggrieved that day. Some of the Girondin leaders were his friends and the Jacobins were out to destroy them.

'It's looking bad for the Girondins,' he said. 'They must keep on their toes. It's damned poor business if they don't! Invasions and civil war have shaken the revolution to its roots, a lot needs addressing or the whole thing is going to run amok.'

Mary was often tired and sometimes sick in the mornings, but Marguerite was attentive. "You are *pregnant,*" she'd said flatly. "It is normal." The word *"pregnant"* itself held a reprimand, for Mary knew how Imlay would react once he was told. He did not want a family, he did not want to be tied to anything, freedom to him was paramount. But her soul was joyful. A child was growing inside her, the child of the man she loved. Might he not rejoice, just a little? Marguerite thought it most unlikely and went about the house sighing. She had never had children herself and her husband was dead, but she did not think she would want to have a child, she said, in such times.

Mary was strong with resignation. 'It is going to be difficult,' she said, 'for to bear a child out of wedlock is seen to many as sinful.'

'Not in France,' Marguerite said emphatically. 'Everything has changed. The sexual needs of women are now fully understood, regardless of marriage. It has always been so for men. Now it is the same for women. It is all about freedom and liberty. But to have a child out of wedlock just now is a sad mistake, for France is in the throes of revolution.'

'I will not blame Imlay for this,' said Mary. 'I am with child and I'm glad.' The glow of new life within her transported her into rapture. 'I do not believe, as you know, in the formality of marriage, but I believe that Gilbert and I have a bond that is deep and eternal. He must surely love me for he possesses so much of my spirit.'

'He does,' Marguerite said kindly, though her eyes were puzzled. 'You have been good to me Citizen Mary. You endure Captain Imlay's moods so well, it astounds me. I knew him through my husband years ago when he came to visit our home. We had very little to offer him, but he made a friend of my husband, and I liked him for that, but I knew he was fickle. My husband painted belles images, tender paintings of wild flowers and woodlands. Captain Imlay would buy them. There are some on the walls of this house. I had to sell most of what I had for I went through difficult times.'

Mary recalled her struggles with her school in London and the fear of having no money. And she thought of the support she'd received from Mrs Burgh, Price and Johnson and others. People could be good. She would never have survived without her friends.

'I also knew Damien and his wife,' Marguerite continued wistfully. 'They were happier days. Captain Imlay would sail to France from America and spend time with us. He was helpful when Antoine died. I was lost in grief.' She looked away abstracted. 'I thought I was going mad. But Captain Imlay brought food and drink or I fear I might well have perished.'

'Yes,' murmured Mary, Imlay was good like that. Here she was in France, carrying his child. But how long would she live there? Would her baby be born a little French citizen in the midst of revolution? What foolish thing had she done?

And life carried on. Mary went off to see her friends in Paris. Imlay went off on business. As support for the monarchy continued and émigré nobles created more provocative incidents, the Jacobins formed another committee. This they named: "The Committee of Public Safety". From April to July that year it was moderate in its dealings; officials talked in serious tones about serious matters and made notes. No more than that. But it could not deal with the formidable military situation. The monarchies of Europe observed what was happening in France with increasing dismay. The French had killed their king, might they not kill their queen also, and were not monarchies everywhere now imperilled?

Maximilien de Robespierre was bourgeoisie, though he sympathised with the sans-culottes and often spoke up in their favour, for their support had allowed the Jacobin faction gain power. He had said on the trial of the king:

*"You have not to pass sentence for or against a single man, but you have to take a resolution on a question of the public safety, and to decide a question of national foresight. It is with regret that I pronounce a fatal truth: Louis ought to perish rather than a hundred thousand virtuous citizens; Louis must die that the country may live."*

Some of the people winced, others applauded. But Robespierre's heart blazed with fervour and resolution. His eloquence was entrancing. Small and immaculately dressed, he was strong, arrogant and determined to have his way. His powerful and resonant voice captivated his listeners and his messages brimmed with an intimidating air of certainty. There were also other radicals, powerful in different ways. One of them was Jean-Paul Marat, a philosopher, physician and publisher, another Jacobin leader and supporter of the sans-culottes. Through his newspaper *"L'ami du peuple"* otherwise known as "*The Friend of the People*" he attacked his enemies and warned against counter-revolutionaries. Now he was eager for the names of citizens who had argued against the death of the king. He was out to execute Girondin leaders who were not of his own opinion and intent on making an example of any who defied him. Many Girondins fled, others were seized and imprisoned.

'Marat is a murderer!' Imlay exclaimed one evening in his garden with Mary. 'The country will react with violence if they execute any Girondins. – I tell you, they won't get away with it!'

'Surely, they would not dare,' she said, pondering. She watched him fixedly and saw he was seething with anger.

'I believe they would,' he said, narrowing his eyes and snapping off a twig from a hawthorn. A thorn pierced his finger and blood oozed from the wound as if it too were angry. He put his finger in his mouth and sucked at the blood. 'What is happening is unjust and devious,' he said, more calmly.

What would he do, she wondered, he was so incensed. He continued, 'Camille Desmoulins, will have something to say about this, I know. I must see him shortly. – Ah, Robespierre is damned ridiculous. He still wears a powdered wig yet likes to be in charge. And he claims he despises bloodshed, yet see how he lets it flow!' Camille Desmoulins, a noted journalist, ran a press. He was also a politician and made no secret of his sentiments, claiming the Jacobins were greedy for political dominion and wealth and would do anything to achieve their aims. He loathed the committees and his newspaper sought to dissolve them. His attitude was well publicised, but there was a heavy price for that and Robespierre opposed him bitterly.

Mary stood with Imlay, gazing at the evening sky. 'There's something I need to tell you,' she murmured. He turned to her curiously and she pressed her lips to his cheek. His skin was damp and fresh with the scent of evening. She wanted to reveal her pregnancy, but she feared his mood and knew the conversation would be difficult. But in a world of death and destruction the thought of new life seemed sacred. He waited and listened. 'I'm pregnant,' she told him quietly. She felt radiant and strong as she said it, to her it was wonderful, but the child was also his, would he too be joyful? She feared his reaction, her voice was small and tremulous in the evening air.

He took hold of her hands and his fingers tightened on hers. But he did not speak or look at her. Instead, he looked away perplexed, then turned to the quince tree beside him and plucked off a fruit. 'The quince has done well this year,' he said. 'The skin of the fruit is smooth and golden. Marguerite will harvest them and make us a delicious conserve . . .'

'Gilbert, did you hear me?' she asked softly. She took the quince from his fingers and cast it aside, then he frowned and looked downwards. This is what she had dreaded, the way he could distance himself and leave her feeling alone. But she told herself there could be nothing wrong with their love. 'Look at me,' she said, tenderly. 'Next spring you are going to be a father.' Again, she waited. How she longed for his words, even a look of warmth. But he gave her nothing.

He looked into her face, but he was silent and his features were still, then with a sigh he drew her towards him.

'Does it not please you?' she asked. His normally eager and enthusiast manner had deserted him. How unnerved she felt when his feelings fled from him like this, but he was bound to be confused she reasoned, even alarmed. His inner self remained separate, as always, in a world of its own. So far as she knew he had never fathered a child. Would it not give him joy to become a father? She gazed at the quince and the truth came to her clearly, next year she would bear a child, she too would bear fruit, and her life would be completely different. But would anything change for Gilbert? He would travel just as before, it was his work. Would she feel deserted and abandoned? The French were kind to pregnant women, there was always that, and Marguerite would take care of her confinement; she was practised in delivering babies. She gazed all about her. Oh, the harmony of the trees, the beauty of nature, she thought wistfully. Human beings let you down, but there was always nature. 'I don't want to make you unhappy,' she said, seeing his confusion. He was breaking twigs off the hawthorn again and again, breaking them into tiny pieces, letting them fall from his fingers like a shower of rain. 'And you mustn't feel captured.' She wanted so much to get it right.

'My dear,' he said quietly. 'When did I say I was unhappy?'

But he was still curiously distanced. 'You are pleased we are having a child then?' she said, daring to feel a little hopeful. 'You will enjoy being a father?' He touched her hand and frowned. Was this all she would get? Would he simply go away as always, and never feel the child in his heart? 'It isn't such a terrible thing,' she said sighing. 'Children are still being born even in the midst of revolution. Most people accept it, some even welcome it.'

'We are not "*most people*,"' he murmured, gazing down at the grass.

He was intense. How she feared his coldness, and she wondered if she could shoulder a future alone with her child should such a fate lie in store. Was she not Mary Wollstonecraft? Did Johnson not receive letters of admiration about her writing? She took comfort from the thought, and knew she must be loyal to her history and achievements, and she still had a great deal to do. But her spirits weakened as she felt Imlay's detachment. Might she have left it too late? she asked herself anxiously. Was she too old? The young might fall into raptures over a child, but she and Gilbert were in their thirties.

He spoke again into the evening. 'I need to spend time in Le Havre next year,' he said, pondering. 'I shall be away a lot come spring.'

He spoke as if she did not know him, as if she were unfamiliar with his comings and goings. 'I expect it,' she said quietly. 'But I hope I shall see you intermittently in the way I do now.'

'Of course,' he replied with a sigh. 'And Marguerite will take care of your confinement when the time is right; I trust you have discussed it. She is good with that sort of thing.'

'"*That sort of thing*,"' she murmured. She did not like his words. They did not fit with her feelings. And she hated the word *confinement*; it spoke of constraint and imprisonment, and were not women imprisoned by their husbands and children? The thought conflicted with the love she felt for the growing child inside her and the love she felt for him. She sighed. There were no such restrictions on a father, nothing needs change, men didn't have a confinement and could do as they wished. Those echoes that screamed in her soul came to her again in a flood of feeling – women were emotional while men were rational and strong! There were tears on her cheeks.

'How long are you going to be crying?' he asked, frowning. 'It really annoys me when you cry.'

She braced herself. 'I don't cry for long,' she said coolly. But still she loved him.

'Let's go inside,' he said finally. 'I think I need a drink.'

As they walked towards the house, he spoke quickly. 'You are in grave danger, my dear. You are English, and now you are pregnant. We shall have to declare ourselves married.' He turned to look at her, but her head was bent to the grass. 'It will only be pretence, of course,' he asserted. 'Neither you nor I believe in marriage. But to say we are married is expedient in these times, and it is safer for you and the child. We will need to sign a few papers . . .'

They entered the back of the house. Whatever he really thought in his secret heart of hearts, she was glad of his words. The evening had delivered her a husband and a father for her child. The child moved in her womb. She glanced back at the trees, they had ceased their songs. It had been like a sort of ceremony, a difficult ceremony, perhaps even a sacrifice.

Each time Imlay left the house, he instructed Damien to lock all the doors until his return. Paris was a city in turmoil, and she could not visit her friends, for soldiers had been to Colette's apartment and taken her with them. English expatriates had been visiting her, they said, and were trying to disrupt the revolution. Imlay had determined to intercede. He was proud and influential, claiming she would soon be returned when he'd prevailed on them to set her free. He had gone to them waving his fist, and Colette had been escorted back within the week. But the warning rang out clear. The Convention was more intent than ever on ridding the revolution of its enemies, and Imlay's Girondin friends were still in danger.

## 37

# Speculations and Contemplations

Throughout this unstable time, and ever more fearful as the days grew shorter and darker, Mary travelled to Paris with Damien to visit her new found friends. Damien's father was becoming increasingly weak, and tired of the revolution moaned that he wanted to die. Damien's mother had died from consumption four years ago and it would have pleased him to have his father in Imlay's house, but the old man refused all help.

The atmosphere at Colette's apartment had changed. Was it really true she could almost have gone to the guillotine? The thought was horrific. But the Jacobins were unpredictable, snapping and snarling like ferocious dogs on everyone's heels. The disconsolate queen, Marie Antoinette, had now been tried for treason against France and sentenced to death. In the clothes of a peasant, like those she had tried to escape in, she had gone to the guillotine, her hands tied behind her back. And she had gone to her death bravely, they said, not in a carriage like the king, but in a tumbrel like an ordinary citizen, a two-wheeled agricultural cart used for carrying manure. After her head had been severed, it was lifted for the people to see, and they had laughed and jeered at the dead head of the queen, while her body had been thrown into an unmarked grave with other unfortunate victims.

Mary's nerves were livid as her friends described what had happened. She could never have watched the death of the queen, particularly now she was pregnant and it seemed that the streets of Paris were uncannily silent after her decease. France no longer had a monarchy, the king and queen had been killed by their own people for treason against their own country. That or else politics, her friends said, for it was not the people themselves who did such acts, it was the words that came from the seemingly unshakeable beliefs of men like Robespierre. There were those who had used the gruesome spectacle for amusement, others for preferment.

Whatever Imlay had said to Desmoulins had obviously been ineffectual, for Colette said Brissot and twenty eight Girondins had been guillotined that very week for anti-revolutionary activities. But it was twisted and unjust, thought Mary, and she felt hurt and angry for Imlay's sake for it would certainly put him in a fury. She wondered what had happened to Paine, and decided he had probably fled. Colette said the Girondins had been taken by tumbrel to the guillotine, boisterously singing *La Marseilles* and acting like martyrs. Had Imlay heard the news? How she needed his stubborn strength just now. There was something untouchable about Imlay, whatever trouble he encountered he would find a way to surmount it, or cast it out of his life, and she never for a moment worried about his welfare, he was so independent.

One morning she went with Damien to the Place de la Revolution. The sight of the dark dried blood beneath the guillotine had made her vomit. Too many deaths. So many lies. So many misconceptions.

It was coming to the end of October. She had not visited Curtius's apartment since the day she had left with Imlay, but she trembled at the thought that Marie might be given more monstrous work to deal with. Was it already in progress? She shuddered.

After her day in Paris, she returned to the house with Damien and immediately went to her room to write to Imlay. She had not gone to see the death of the queen, she told him, but on her last visit to Paris, she had been to look at the guillotine, and wondered if the baby might have been mindful of her suffering, for she had felt it wince when she'd witnessed the blood on the floor. She begged him to return to her soon, even if only briefly. It would help give her strength, she said, for she could not even write her book, her ideas were afraid of her pen. As she cast her eyes about her room, she could not feel her beloved in the air and harboured the fear that he might not return at all and might even have left her. The hardness and coldness of loneliness entered her again, and as soon as she could smell the fire being lit in the parlour, she hurried downstairs to join Damien and Marguerite. She must hide her writing, Damien warned frowning, for in one fell swoop she might be seized and taken off. She always locked her door, she answered, and pushed what she wrote beneath her dressing table, hoping it was safe. She was determined to finish her book and send it to Johnson. But she could not write just now. She could not think. She sat with Damien and Marguerite, talking at a rapid pace and without waiting for answers. She feared for the baby, she said, and was constantly anxious. She needed to know why Imlay wasn't replying to any of her letters. Surely they knew, she said and she complained they were all in cahoots. But they knew her moods by now and took no notice.

'Write to him again,' said Damien nonchalantly. 'I will see he receives your letter, but I cannot guarantee he will answer it. He is searching after that ship he talks about, it is made of gold I think.' He sat in Imlay's chair by the fire, shaking his head and laughing to himself quietly.

Marguerite, in her steady and silent way, brewed tea and came back with it.

Mary talked on. 'The winter will soon be upon us. What if he does not return at all, I mean ever?' Her features were pale with dread. She glanced from Marguerite to Damien by turns, but they both looked downwards.

'He will,' Marguerite said quietly. 'But he will come at his own pace. He will not consider you though, however you plead. It is his way.'

'Then I must go and seek him out!' Mary exclaimed standing and biting her knuckles. 'I shall drag him out of his den!'

'It is not advisable,' said Marguerite quietly pouring the tea. 'And remember you might be noticed.'

'But he has made me angry. Do I not matter? I am carrying his child, but I doubt he gives us a thought. I know nothing of what he is doing. And what of the man who called here today for payment of a draft. What am I to say to such people?'

Marguerite and Damien fell silent.

During the next few days, Damien went about his work with a stoic detachment. He chopped wood and helped Marguerite with the cooking, the two of them sometimes sharing laughter, in the way that only those who had lived their entire life in Paris might dare. One evening in her silent room, Mary sat down to write to Imlay:

*"I am glad to find that other people can be unreasonable, as well as myself — for be it known to thee, that I answered thy first letter, the very night it reached me (Sunday), though thou couldst not receive it before Wednesday, because it was not sent off till the next day. — There is a full, true and particular account. —*

*Yet I am not angry with thee, my love, for I think that it is a proof of stupidity, and likewise of a milk-and-water affection, which comes to the same thing, when the temper is governed by a square and compass. — There is nothing picturesque in this straight-lined equality, and the passions always give grace to the actions.*

*Recollection now makes my heart bound to thee; but, it is not to the money-getting face, though I cannot be seriously displeased with the exertion which increases my esteem, or rather is what I should have expected from thy character. — No; I have thy honest countenance before me — Pop — relaxed by tenderness; a little — little wounded by my whims; and thy eyes glistening with sympathy. — Thy lips then feel softer than soft — and I rest my cheek on thine, forgetting all the world. — I have not left the hue of love out of the picture — the rosy glow; and fancy has spread it over my own cheeks, I believe, for I feel them burning, whilst a delicious tear trembles in my eyes, that would be all your own, if a grateful emotion directed to the Father of nature, who has made me thus alive to happiness, did not give more warmth to the sentiment it divides — I must pause a moment.*

*Need I tell you that I am tranquil after writing thus? — I do not know why, but I have more confidence in your affection, when absent, than present; nay, I think that you must love me, for, in the sincerity of my heart let me say it, I believe I deserve your tenderness, because I am true, and have a degree of sensibility that you can see and relish.*

*Sincerely, Mary."*

She read through what she had written and for a while sat troubled. Had she chosen the right words, or was she throwing herself at his feet and pushing him further away? Without doubt she loved him, each day she felt the stirrings of his child within her. But she felt pathetic and lonely. The letter was blotted and put in her drawer. Damien would post it next day.

Christmas came and she spent it alone with Marguerite. Damien stayed in Paris with his father and returned in the middle of January, bringing back loaves he had baked in his father's oven, a far better oven, he said, than the one in Imlay's kitchen. His father's oven was brick and clay, but somehow, he said, the taste of the clay entered the bread as it was rising and filled it with beguiling sweetness. It was indeed good bread, said Mary and they relished it with quince conserve.

Imlay had been absent all Christmas. Achingly, Mary had managed to write the final lines of her book, but there was little heart in the writing. She told herself she would need to look at it again when her mind felt better. Physically she felt healthy but there was still a darkness in her heart that would not be banished. Where was he? It was hardly possible he had been on his own all Christmas. Living in a world of conjecture her mind whirled with fears, the minutes and hours passed as if never having been. Every noise in the grounds brought her rushing to the window.

But she forced herself to take stock. Was their love but a dream, a dream only of hers and never of his? He was capable of staying away for as long as a year, Marguerite had told her. *A year!* And why was it always raining! The water ran fast down the walls of the house and windows. If she listened carefully she thought she could hear his voice coming through the rain, but it was only a romantic notion. The branches on the trees hung low and seemed to be weeping. The quince in the middle of the garden, which Marguerite loved so much, was naked and still as stone. Everywhere seemed black and stagnant. She would have left her food were it not for Marguerite urging her to eat; otherwise the child would be born mal-nourished, she said, which was true. And so she ate, but was often sick, for her whole body rebelled against Imlay's absence.

Where was the revolution going now in 1794, she wondered? She looked at Marguerite straight as they sat by the fire. 'He can do what he wants with his life, but why doesn't he long to see me,' she said bitterly. She felt annoyed and indignant that he had brought her to this state of having to seek counsel from the maid. 'If he doesn't want me, then once I have given birth I shall go to live somewhere else, that or return to England!'

She sat for some minutes brooding. Did the whole body of her work mean nothing? Had she learned nothing from any of it? If she could not learn from it herself, what use was her writing to others? She felt as if she could not exercise its lessons in her own affairs, to *know* was one thing, to *do* was another. She sighed deeply. 'I feel as if everything stops when he is absent,' she told Marguerite pathetically. 'Even my breathing. I can't really live without him, you see.' She went on anxiously, clasping her hands and frowning. 'If only he would write more often, just a few words of love in the midst of his business, that is all. I do like to hear of his work, of course, but can he not send me some warmth?' She looked at Marguerite desperately.

Damien poked at the fire. 'Citizen Mary, I cannot be involved,' he said. 'I dare not speak of Captain Imlay's affairs. I have promised.' He began to sharpen knives and lined them up in the hearth, carefully, precisely. The blades glowed in the firelight.

'Is there something you should tell me?' asked Mary, fixing her eyes on him steadily. 'Do I not deserve the truth?'

'I cannot say more,' Damien murmured, without looking up. 'Tu comprends?'

She shrugged angrily. 'Oh, very well; it is not as if I matter, is it?' Then she rose slowly, pondering. 'You can at least tell me how long he will be away. I'm sure you know.'

'I do not know,' Damien answered quietly, then he bent to the hearth and took up each blade in turn to test its keenness against his finger.

'We are about to leave January behind and move into February,' said Mary earnestly. She paced the room quickly. 'See how big I am with child. He has not been with me to share it.' There were tears in her eyes as she spoke. She felt imprisoned. The only place she could walk was in the grounds at the back of the house, for she didn't know if anyone watched. She saw that Damien and Marguerite looked at each concernedly.

'Perhaps I can go to find him for you,' said Marguerite. 'The heavy blasts of winter are done with I think, travelling ought to be easier. I have never minded the rain.'

'Soyez silencieux.' Damien murmured, touching Marguerite's hand.

Then he whispered something Mary couldn't hear. At that moment the sound of a rider came from the path by the house. Her heart beat fast. It was Imlay! She ran to the door and opened it. 'At last you are here!' she exclaimed, mad with relief as he entered. He was quite soaked through, though uncaring. 'I thought you had gone forever,' she cried. 'Oh, hold me my love, hold me!'

'I must remove my wet clothes' he laughed, looking her over. 'You are swollen as a ripe apple, and you look just as delicious!'

The day had come. He was here. In the bright glow of her happiness she could feel the blood rushing about her body. She felt as if the great celestial body of love was with her, encompassing her and holding her safe.

She was blissfully happy as Imlay strode about the house, calling instructions to Damien. – The window latch needed mending. He must chop more logs. He must see that the doors were securely locked at all times. She forgot about her weeks of loneliness and was soon smiling and caressing him again in her normal loving way. Did he not think her swollen fecundity handsome? Did he not think there was a special angelic glow about her skin?

He stayed home for a whole three weeks then returned to Le Havre. Mary talked with Marguerite about baby clothes and other things she needed for the child and she went out with Damien to buy them. From time to time people came to the door and made her feel anxious, but Damien managed the household with genius and strangers were soon dispatched. How skilled he was in the ways of the world she thought as she watched him pin the tricolour cockade to his hat, which he always donned before leaving. It was important to display the symbol of revolution, especially if you feared for your life.

She was now close to her time. Often tense, she prayed it would all go well, particularly when the child moved in her womb as if searching for a place to get out. Lying on her bed, she would feel for the tiny limbs, finding a knee or an elbow and wondering what the child looked like in the mystery of its lonely world. Did it sleep when she slept? Did it feel nervous when she did? Did it feel hunger at certain times of the day?

Today she felt bright and cheerful and the mirror said she looked beautiful. She must write to Imlay, she decided, about her hopes, her fears and the love she felt for him and his child. Did he receive her letters? No matter, he was probably busy. Marguerite said she knew of an excellent midwife in Paris who would come to deliver the baby, Imlay too had promised to be there for the birth. But would he remember? 'Please let him come,' she murmured. The evening star came and went time and again. And still she prayed.

But as the date of the birth loomed close and letters did not arrive she felt forsaken. Her friends in Paris did not visit the house knowing they were watched so closely, and she could hardly have gone to see them. The revolution was moving swiftly in its greedy diabolical way, swallowing every ounce of power it could grasp. Robespierre's ideas, it seemed, were a mass of bewildering contra- dictions. He despised power, yet he desired it. He hated violence, yet he promoted it. He was said to have whispered the revolution was going rotten, and many said he was fearful.

But Robespierre's friends now were few and far between and the deaths of the Girondins lay heavy in the hearts of their followers. Mary's circle in Paris claimed that Robespierre himself would be sent to the guillotine soon, for fingers pointed his way. The Committee of Public Safety, formed to protect France from its enemies, had now turned tyrannous against those it was meant to defend and thousands had been arrested without sense or reason. Countless numbers had been sent to the guillotine, others had died in prison. The picture was forever changing and today could no longer count on the loyalty of tomorrow, women wept in the streets for their husbands, husbands wept for their wives, children wept for their parents, it was as if the city were rampant with madness. The air seemed to palpitate with anguish. Even a look was dangerous; people went about with their heads bent low and were careful with whom they conversed, for 'informers' were everywhere and misinformation was all too readily delivered by those who thought only of themselves. Mary felt in a limbo waiting for her child. Resting on her bed that day, she wondered at the marvel of creation and fell into a reverie of speculating who the baby might look like and how it might be, then she awoke to the sound of his horse!

Imlay settled back quickly and was kind and considerate, playing the part of dutiful husband and prospective father.

'I do not think I have ever seen him so happy,' said Marguerite. 'But I doubt the feeling will last. The captain always grows restless.' There was a hollow sound to her voice, as if she spoke from the past.

'Leave him alone,' Damien chided. 'If he wishes to give us his best, then it is far better than his worst.'

'I shall be silent,' Marguerite murmured, brushing up ashes of fallen wood from the fire.

'I do not want a scrap of bitterness or sadness in the house just now,' said Mary straightening. 'Imlay is glad, and we must all be happy for the child.'

Damien stuck to his belief that Imlay was the best he could be, and Mary hoped he was right. But as Imlay went about the house, there was an air of guilt in his bearing. Occasionally, when he passed her, he did not look at her or speak, and he walked about the garden, his features strained and serious. He had not answered her letters and had made her anxious, but she did not question him about it, the post was often unreliable and perhaps his letters had been lost. Now though he was here back home and his presence sweetened her day.

Just then he entered the parlour and brushed his lips across her cheek. Then he gave a slight wince as if hating himself for something. 'I wish I could be better,' he said softly, 'but I can only be as I am.' Whatever sort of man he was, it was all she wanted for now.

The midwife's English was poor, but Mary saw she was attentive, advising and writing things down that she must not forget. Damien went about soft footed and Marguerite whispered as if the baby were born already and they must not wake it. Imlay said little, and spent a lot of his time deep in thought by the fire. He was always thinking. It was impossible to guess what his thoughts were, his world was so guarded, and to inquire might make him surly.

One afternoon as he sat in a chair in her room, he came up with the idea that after the birth she might like to return to England. 'You could live there in relative peace,' he said. 'It would be better for the child, I'm sure. I can arrange safe passage.'

'And you?' she asked, looking incredulous. *"Return to England,"* did he want to despatch her? The way his moods could change so fast always disturbed her. But he'd been drinking.

'I will join you later,' he said, stroking his chin thoughtfully. 'It would be good I think. I fear for you here, Paris gets worse by the day.'

She put aside her book and looked at him steadily. 'But when is *"later?"*' she asked. 'When would you come to me?' She flushed with emotion, wondering if he would sidestep his obligations, persuade her to go to England, then once he thought her safely ensconced with her family, simply disappear. It was perfectly possible. The desire for movement was strong in Imlay. Her feelings were so confused it was hard to make sense of her thoughts. She put her hands to her face and rubbed away the tiredness of the day. It would be good to see her family, that much was true, and to show them the baby would be heaven. But England too had changed. And would he ever *really* come to join her? She did not think so. But wherever she was living she wanted to see him, even if only periodically. She saw he was steeled with decision; he had thought about it a lot. Freedom burned fiercely within him, a flame in the darkness of his life, a darkness she could never enter. 'From all I hear, English society is going the way of France,' she said. 'They have been burning effigies of Paine. He is branded. They might burn effigies of me.' She spoke abstractedly, trembling slightly. 'I don't always please the powers that be with my writing, as you know.'

341

'Oh, Mary,' he murmured. He sighed heavily as if his life itself were a burden. 'It is nothing like the same situation. No–one is after you. You would be very much safer in England. It is dangerous and murderous here. – Oh, please, my dear, why are you crying? Do stop it.' He stood and paced the room. 'I simply want you to think about it, that's all. Consider it.' He shook his head as if bewildered. 'Sometimes you are so irrational.'

'How dare you!' she exclaimed. She braced herself and faced him. 'You rack my feelings with your words and then you call me irrational! This is what you do, you see. This is how men bring us down. I am emotional because I cannot trust you. I do not believe you would ever come to join me in England. No, you would simply forget me!'

'What nonsense,' he said, looking at her straight and shrugging his shoulders. He spoke slowly and quietly. 'I have no idea what you mean,' he said calmly, though his tone was self-conscious.

'Oh, yes you do!' she said harshly. 'You are a sort of chameleon Gilbert. Yes, a cold lizard-like thing that changes at will, that is what you are.'

He laughed loud at the ceiling. 'You are getting carried away. A lizard, indeed. Oh, lord! Now calm yourself down, will you. Is this not bad for the baby?'

'Ah!' she said angrily, her eyes flashing with anger. 'So I am damaging my baby am I, by getting upset? I probably am, and I must try to compose myself – yes, you are right.' She took deep breaths and sat down. 'Well, you provoke me, Gilbert. I do not think you care about this baby at all. You only care for yourself. You would ditch me in England and disappear like a puff of smoke. Oh, I know your game.'

'Do I have a game?' he said, amusedly.

'Of course you do, but perhaps you have no insight into that. You do not see how upsetting you are sometimes.'

'How do I upset you, my dear?' he asked, looking perplexed, and in a warmer tone of voice.

She did not answer. He waited.

'You can't say it, can you?' he said quietly. 'Because it is nothing but pure emotion, there isn't an ounce of truth in your accusations.'

*'"Accusations?"'*

'Yes, you accuse me of things that only exist in your fears. Why would I choose to abandon you? I am very busy, of course. – We have had this conversation before, so many times. What do you expect me to do? If I hang around here I won't earn a dime.'

'I hate it when you're away,' she said miserably. 'I feel so lonely.'

'But you are not alone. You have Marguerite and Damien with you.'

'They are not *with* me,' she whispered. 'I am neither here nor there to them.'

'As a matter of fact, that's my point. If you return to England you would have contact again with your family. They could be of comfort and support, and I'm sure they'd enjoy the child. Do you not agree?'

She breathed in deeply. 'No, I do not. Would you have me suffer the English middle class with their suffocating narrow mindedness and hideous affectations?' She threw up her hands. 'Oh, for heaven's sake no! I hate what is happening in France, but I do not wish to be forever striving after a way of life that will turn me into a doll. – Oh, to be a woman in England alone with a child!' She laughed wryly.

'But I would come to you, my dear. Have I not said so just now?'

'I do not believe you,' she said flatly. 'England is far away and the countries are at war. Also, I do not think your temperament would allow such a noble gesture.' She shrugged, then she went to sit on the edge of her bed, sighing. Why was life so difficult? She wondered if she would die in childbirth, it seemed a distinct possibility. Oh, the child, the child, who would take care of the child if she did; she could not leave it alone in such a cruel world. – But return to England? She could not do it. The position with her sisters and Ned was hardly agreeable. And they did not know the truth of her situation. The way she had described Gilbert was far from honest. Must she admit to Everina and Eliza that she had fallen into the very trap she had cautioned women to avoid? Oh, where was the tenderness of love. All her life she had dreaded this moment and knew it as her enemy. She stood and strode about the room holding the weight of her pregnancy in the palms of her hands. This baby was a part of Imlay; it would always be a part of Gilbert. Did he not care? 'Do you want to know what I think?' she murmured.

'Oh, I know what you think,' he sighed. 'You have made it quite plain.' He folded his arms and leant against the wall by the door as if ready to leave. 'Your withering rebukes are unsettling. But you think the wrong things. We are the sum of our hopes, our fears, our dreams. We dream of a life we want. We might even live in that dream, or at least try to. But you cannot live in dreams, my dear, none of us can.'

'You dare to philosophise *me*,' she laughed. 'Oh, you are full of conceit.' She shook her head trying to calm her emotions.

Imlay threw out his hands in a gesture of hopelessness. 'Listen. I have many problems. Ships do not return, the government is forever throwing obstructions in the way of my business. Our dreams rarely materialise. You hope for the dream, but it will not happen. It's impossible. And it isn't my fault. You dose your reality with ideals as if with laudanum. Ah, such ideals are only for those in heaven. Heaven is not on earth, it is only in dreams!'

'Well,' she continued quickly, closing her ears to his words. 'I think you are selfish, Gilbert. I think you do not want me. I think you do not love me – or why do you want to ship me to England like some worthless cargo you wish to be rid of. – Oh, not a cargo of silver like the one you constantly search for, but one you would like to forget.' She pressed her hands to her stomach. 'And I have this cargo here, this child you do not love. But how could you love it when you do not have a scrap of love for its mother? I have sent you loving letters. I have poured out my heart, while you, you . . .' She ran her fingers through her tangled hair and took deep breaths. 'Oh, Gilbert, you will kill me, I know it!'

He rested his hand on the door handle and stared at the floor.

'Go, go if you like!' she called. 'And do not think I shall miss you. I am quite used to your absences now, and the child will grow up without you. I shall teach the child not to think of its father, for thinking of you is indeed an unhealthy pastime. You are best forgotten Captain Imlay. Now leave this minute, I intend to forget you!'

But he did not leave. He wandered the house next day like a wounded animal, sighing and wringing his hands. But the uppermost thing in Mary's mind was the birth of the baby. She discussed with Marguerite how matters should proceed if she died in childbirth and Imlay had gone. It was sombre but necessary talk. Marguerite attempted to calm her, claiming the midwife had said the baby was perfectly positioned and eager to burst into the world.

'But the world is so cruel!' groaned Mary. 'Why should my child be born into so much sadness?'

'Not so,' insisted Marguerite. 'The spring is here. There is hope.'

'And Captain Imlay?' Mary said haltingly. 'Is he . . . Do you think he is well?'

Marguerite smiled warmly. 'You are very close to your time Citizen Mary; he vows not to leave until the baby is safely delivered.'

Mary took hold of her arm. 'But will it be "*safely delivered?*" Can you be certain?'

'Citizen Mary, you are strong,' said the midwife entering the room and hearing the strained conversation. 'All will be well, I promise. I have much experience. No mother or child has ever died in my care. Comprenez vous?'

Mary thought again of her family, and her friends in Johnson's circle. She hadn't been truthful when she'd written to her sisters about Gilbert and had described him in the gentle terms of her heart not the brutal terms of reality. In her heart she believed her beloved might be less self serving were he given enough reassurance and counselled on the error of his ways. And was her tongue not too fierce sometimes, too ready to criticise? It did not help. What terrible things she had said to him, how often she must have hurt him. She would force herself to take pains to stay silent in the future. Silent! Silent! Women must live through many humiliations and they must uphold their dignity as best they could. But as she thought of it she grew tense. She was not actually married to Imlay, but had hoped for a relationship where she might rely on his love. Could such a hope become reality?

Lost in thought, she suddenly became aware of a sharp stabbing pain in her abdomen. In an instant she knew was in labour! The pains came again, and again. She went to the top of the stairs and called for Marguerite to come quickly. Then she lay on her bed feeling strangely lost to herself, as if she were being used by some elemental force beyond her, a force that belonged to her body and the dark earth beneath her, a force that wasn't her own, making her bend to its will. Her mother had known this force so many times, it was a force that all women knew when bringing a child into the world. Sometimes they succumbed to it easily, sometimes they fought it, other times it took them with it and devoured them, their child also. Marguerite and the midwife raced upstairs and arrived breathless by her bedside.

Imlay followed and stood very still in the doorway, gazing intently on the scene.

'The waters have broken,' said the midwife. 'The baby is coming.'

'There is laudanum in the cupboard,' Marguerite said pointing. 'She may need it,'

The midwife nodded. 'Will you stay, Captain Imlay – or perhaps you will wait downstairs? I can call you.' She spoke over her shoulder while unfastening Mary's garments.

Imlay looked on perplexed then turned and left.

It was a grey dull day and the room was darkish. Marguerite lit candles and brought towels and hot water. The midwife said all would be well and as the birth pains strengthened asked Mary to push so the baby might be born. Even as she moaned, she felt victorious and knew she was winning. The baby was coming easily, and the warm bulk of it passed into the world alive and well. It was an easy and victorious labour, and the baby arrived at two o'clock that afternoon. Exactly, the midwife said proudly, as she had forecast.

Marguerite called down to Imlay who came to them quickly, delighted by the noisy infant and the rapturous Mary. 'And are you well, my dear?' he asked, lavishing her with kisses. The midwife swaddled the baby and passed her across and he gazed at his child in disbelief. Little Fanny Imlay was a very lovely baby indeed.

'How healthy she is,' Mary said blissful and thrilled. 'She hardly looks like a newborn baby at all; her features are so expressive.'

'I have given her a good head of hair!' laughed Imlay. 'And I see it is my very colour.'

'That can change,' said the midwife smiling. 'The colour is good though, no?'

'I wonder what it is like for her to find herself somewhere else all of a sudden,' said Mary. For a moment or two they both looked at the child in wonder as if she were an apparition.

'Why, she is quite perfect,' laughed Imlay.

'Oh, see, she wants to feed!' said Mary pressing the child to her breast. The baby snuggled in, and the sound of urgent sucking entered the room. 'She sucks so strongly and knows exactly how to do it,' Mary said delightedly. She suckled her baby proudly, baffled by the new found pleasure, while the midwife gathered her things and got ready to leave.

'Everything is done,' said the midwife. 'I never knew my work so easy. The birthing process was a pleasure. Une grande joie!'

Imlay sat silent on the bed, his aquiline features tight with confusion. Just as the child had entered an unfamiliar world, he too was unfamiliar with the new situation and it seemed fatherhood bewildered him. For a moment or two Mary felt sad. There was always a sense of evasion in his eyes; he could not resign himself to anything for long and was already drawing away. But she believed there was something he yearned for; something immensely important that no-one knew anything about, though she did not know what it was, and his look could change from joy to despair in minutes. She thought he wanted the sea, the great cold lunging waves. She had known that longing in others. He was fascinated by ships and the great open space of the ocean. The sea could be entrancing, like returning somehow to the womb. He had come into her life and she had borne him a daughter, but now she feared she would lose him. He was tense and afraid. 'There, there,' she said to the child, once she had fed her. 'You were such a wild creature in my womb, and now you settle to feed and sleep so calmly.' She asked Imlay to place the baby in her cot. And he did, tenderly and carefully, though abstractedly as if in a trance.

One day merged into another and the baby was the focus of Mary's attention now. She felt so well that she did not take to her bed as was usual after childbirth but walked about the garden instead, cradling the child in her arms so it might benefit from the warm spring sunshine and listen to the bird songs. Mary felt she was living in a time of grace. She could hardly believe the tone of her letters when she wrote to her friends and family, everything was bathed in sunlight. And she had never before felt so sensuous! Whenever she took the baby to her breast she wanted Imlay. Each day, each moment, brought them closer together as they celebrated their child. It was a time of love for love's own sake, a time of prodigious happiness. But she wished she could draw him into her soul, for he constantly drifted away.

He had been home six weeks. But at last his restlessness prevailed and she knew he was looking to leave. He was eager to find the ship he had lost and she could tell he was bored of his home, which meant he was bored of her, and also his child. But she would not reproach him for his faraway look and abstractions, the way he avoided her and went to his reading or walked about the garden and gazed at the sky. But he argued over trivia, and her heart ached with sadness. He needed to attend to his work, he said, and she agreed. She could not have him for herself, he was a separate independent being, and as much as she would clasp him to her breast, she must let him go free.

That morning he announced he was leaving for Le Havre and the brightness in her life darkened, for he might easily be gone some time. She sat in the parlour feeding the child at her breast while he sorted out his papers on the table. His life was all about going away, always going away. And her own life must inevitably be one of missing him. Her old fears were starting to surface again as she watched him packing his things. Might he leave her and start a new life? She wondered if she had lost her allure since the birth of the child and feared the dark depression that so easily found her. She was well grounded in the scriptures and perhaps prayer might help her, she thought, for she feared for their little daughter and being alone. But she knew that her feelings would win. She would be angry eventually. Not yet though. Not now. He finished his packing and embraced her. 'Don't be too long,' she said softly. She heard the echo of her words in her heart like a long despised refrain.

He laughed lightly. 'I've been idle for far too long, my dear, now I must work,' he said. He cupped her face in his large warm hands and kissed her.

'You are precious to me Captain Imlay,' she told him softly. 'Never forget it.' He made no answer. Soon he would be gone, even for months. This was what life had allotted her, this was her fate. Their child slept in her cot, and as Imlay cantered away, the house became hopelessly still. She turned to her bookcase and found *The Vindication of the Rights of Man*. How angry she'd been with Burke when she'd written it. The feelings flooded her again. She had gone through several quill pens while writing the pamphlet. Such passion! Such power! Where had it gone? She read through some of the passages:

> *". . . I perceive, from the whole tenor of your Reflections, that you have a mortal antipathy to reason; but, if there is any thing like argument, or are to reference the rust of antiquity, and turn the unnatural customs, which ignorance and mistaken self-interest have consolidated, the sage fruit of experience: nay, that, if we do discover some errors, our feelings should lead us to excuse, with blind love, or unprincipled filial affection, the venerable vestiges of ancient days. These are gothic notions of beauty – the ivy is beautiful, but, when it insidiously destroys the trunk from which it receives support, who would not grub it up? . . . I"*

How strong she had been, how spirited! She had not faltered in her desire to support Price and to put Burke right! And he had certainly needed checking. Her skin tightened as she thought of it. She was Mary Wollstonecraft, she had things to say, and people must listen! She read on further:

*"Man has been termed, with strict propriety, a microcosm, a little world in himself. – He is so, – yet must, however, be reckoned an ephemera, or, to adopt your figure of rhetoric, a summer's fly. The perpetuation of property in our families is one of the privileges you most warmly contend for; yet it would not be very difficult to prove that the mind must have a very limited range that thus confines its benevolence to such a narrow circle, which, with great propriety, may be included in the sordid calculations of blind self-love.*

*A brutal attachment to children has appeared most conspicuous in parents who have treated them like slaves, and demanded due homage for all the property they transferred to them, during their lives. It has led them to force their children to break the most sacred ties, to do violence to a natural impulse, and run into legal prostitution to increase wealth or shun poverty; and still worse, the dread of parental malediction has made many weak characters violate truth in the fact of Heaven; and, to avoid a father's angry curse, the most sacred promises have been broken. It appears to be a natural suggestion of reason, that a man should be freed from implicit obedience to parents and private punishments, when he is of an age to be subject to the jurisdiction of the laws of his country; and that the barbarous cruelty of allowing parents to imprison their children, to prevent their contaminating their noble blood by following the dictates of nature when they chose to marry, or for any misdemeanour that does not come under the cognizance of public justice, is one of the most arbitrary violations of liberty . . ."*

So much writing and she had written it all so quickly. Far too quickly in truth, but Burke's *Reflections* had incensed her and she'd needed to make a swift reply. Turning the pages she wished she had written more carefully. But Joseph Johnson was a man who understood the times and when he wanted a book a writer must jump to attention and write it quickly.

She returned her book to its allotted place on her shelf then rested on her bed. Oh, that she might be calmer and less emotional, more in the way of the person she wanted to be, the ideal she set for herself and what she wanted for all women. She looked down at the baby asleep in the cot beside her. How sweet she was, how lovely.

And she was healthy too. She gazed outside. What would she do with her time now Imlay had gone? The need to write still throbbed in her soul, more so when she thought of England and Johnson's gatherings. She gazed at her pen and ink and the wad of paper on her desk, she must finish writing *An Historical and Moral View of the French Revolution* and send it to Johnson soon. He would be waiting.

# 38

## *Desperation*

It was almost the end of July. Little Fanny Imlay had just opened her eyes to the world and started to smile. Never before had Mary seen such beautiful intelligent eyes on a baby and she felt certain her daughter had an exceptional share of brains! Imlay had declared he wouldn't be surprised if their child should write the second edition of *The Rights of Woman,* she was so alert and alive.

But there wasn't much else to be joyful about just now. Imlay had been gone several weeks, the days were long and a gloomy air of silence pervaded Paris. Damien had told her there was a great deal of whispering everywhere. On 27th July, called Thermidor now in the new revolutionary calendar, the National Assembly had arrested Robespierre and taken him to the Prison of Luxembourg. But the warden had refused to jail him and Robespierre had taken flight. It was rumoured he was hiding in Paris, his position that of a fugitive. He was now an outlaw. Down and out and miserable he had taken a pistol and shot himself in the head, but having misfired, he had only wounded his jaw. He was said to have tied a bandage around his chin to support it and was living in a secret location. The revolution had gone the wrong way indeed for Robespierre. But he could not escape the consequences of what had been done. The use of terror had taken on the form of official government policy and ruthless blind brutality had been sanctioned for what Robespierre had believed a more important objective. Now he was accused of having had grandiose delusions, and his stubborn belief that the means justified the ends – the ends being liberté, égalité, fraternité and a better way of life for the citizens – had not resulted in democracy, but had instead delivered an excess of bloodshed and horror. Some people said another way might have served him better, but he had set his foot on a certain road and his obsessive nature could take no other. He had appealed to the assembly in an attempt to justify his actions, arguing his own point of view. It was a sad and pitiful litany. There were aspects of the Terror he'd disagreed with, he'd said, and he was not totally to blame for all the excesses; there were difficult ambitious men on the Committee who had scorned his ideas for a virtuous republic, and what's more he had never been corrupt, and had indeed been called 'the incorruptible', and he had never used his position for private gain or self-advancement. But his words were to no avail and Robespierre's days were numbered. Many people still respected him, but to support him was dangerous and to voice such support could be lethal.

In Paris an atmosphere of fear and cynicism had frozen all sensible progress, brother had turned against brother, father against son and son against father, families had turned away from their loved ones, trust itself had passed away. Many recalled with fear and trembling Robespierre's unbending declaration: *"Terror is nothing other than justice, prompt, severe, inflexible."* But there were those who murmured in support of him, saying that during his time in government he had always been a man of virtue and had never amassed treasures or deferred to royalty, he was a true revolutionary and lived in simple accommodation on his deputy's salary, he did not even take a carriage when he went about Paris and generally made journeys on foot. But had he not been the mouthpiece for the Committee of Public Safety and actively involved in the Terror, said others. The troops of the National Convention finally sought him out and he was seized at the Hotel de Ville in Paris. On the 28th July without trial he was taken to the guillotine in the Place de la Revolution where they cut off his head and his body was flung into a common grave amongst other ill-starred fatalities. "La Terreur" was over.

Mary sat in the parlour with Marguerite and Damien contemplating the future. Was it true that the Terror had ended, could it be possible? They looked at each other incredulously; it was hard to believe. Each day she thought about Imlay, wondering if news about Robespierre's death had reached him. In the lonely afternoons after she had fed the baby, she settled down to write. But she did not know where she belonged or who she actually was anymore. She lived in a world of thought and was glad of the child who brought her back to earth and needed her.

Le Havre, where Imlay took lodgings when away, was in Normandy, north-west France. She longed to see him and decided she might pay him a visit. How long would it take to get there in a chaise, she asked Damien, but he never replied and simply continued with his work. Ignoring her though made her ever more determined. She intended to take the baby and would stay overnight at an inn; it was a long journey. The thought of getting away for a while was enlivening. Having suffered the pain and sweat of childbirth, she longed for a life with Imlay and their child. Was it really too much to ask? They'd known happiness together before, might they not know it again? There was little life to be had in the house with Damien and Marguerite who talked quietly in corners and laughed at their own private jokes, or would go to Damien's room, closing the door behind them. Her friends in Paris had all gone their separate ways, which made her feel somehow discarded. Gilbert had seemed so pleased about the baby, she reflected. Oh, that he could see her now! And what of their earth rending passion, was it not still in his mind? Did he not want her as she wanted him? Well, if all else failed, perhaps she could make herself useful to him. He was a sorry businessman indeed. His relationships with people were often uneasy, and he would argue aggressively with creditors who came to the door. But once they had gone he would assume his manner of repose and his strange air of nonchalance. It was a useful quality to have, she thought, how good to cast aside your cares! He and Damien had a kind of affinity and had known each other many years. Damien acted in the way of a brother, working for Imlay and always concerned for his welfare, and Mary knew they shared secrets. Imlay had helped take care of Damien's father, who at last on his death bed, had declared he was glad to see the end of the Terror for now he could go to his Maker in peace, and he soon passed away.

It was the middle of August, the height of summer in Paris, hot weather and lovely long days. 'I must go to Le Havre,' Mary asserted that morning. 'I have decided.' She was seated at the table, the baby on her arm, her finger tracing the journey on a map. 'Can you get me a chaise?' she asked Damien, who was preparing broccoli seed-lings for the garden.

He looked up quickly. 'What is your intention?' He waited, watching her anxiously.

'I intend to visit Captain Imlay, of course, and why not?'

'And will you go alone?' He shook his head in disbelief.

She answered briskly and straightened. 'No, I shall take our child.' She stroked the head of the baby tenderly. 'She is still being nursed at my breast and must stay with her mother.' She went to the window and looked out. 'The weather is good. There needn't be a problem, though we shall have to stop on the way. We must have a good driver and a strong sturdy horse. I have sufficient money to cover it. Can you arrange it?'

Damien's face grew sombre.

'I do not like it,' said Marguerite, who sat peeling apples. 'The August weather is sometimes unstable, and he does not expect you.'

'No he does not,' Mary said flatly. 'I wish to surprise him.'

'But will he be *pleased* with this surprise?' Marguerite spoke in a whisper.

Neither she nor Damien looked happy, but Mary was determined. A baby should make no difference to her plans. Little Fanny was perfectly well and if she took warm clothes and food, what could go wrong?

Her worries though were not about weather, there was something she needed to investigate, just for herself. For what life did Gilbert live beyond her and their child? Was his existence freer, more vigorous, more truly alive elsewhere? Again he hadn't answered her letters. Were they lost or had he ignored them. She could wait and forget her fears, but it did her no service to bury her head in the sand and pretend. It was obvious from their faces; Damien and Marguerite were not deceived.

'But the Captain might not be there,' Marguerite faltered. 'He is often away. What if you cannot find him? You are bound to be disappointed if the house is empty, no?'

Mary sighed. She needed the truth. A chill ran across her skin, for her mind half knew the answer. 'I shall take the chance,' she said quietly. 'If he is absent and the house is locked we can stay at an inn, people are kind when they see a woman on her own with a child, that is the way in France.' She drew the baby close and kissed her forehead. 'You know,' she said thoughtfully. 'If Gilbert loves us he is bound to be glad to see us.'

'I am concerned about the baby,' Damien added, bracing himself. He looked at her straight. 'I remember when I was tiny; my mother took me out in the rain. I was soaking and coughing and almost died. I have told Marguerite the story. It had better not rain. Ah, pauvre enfant!'

'No, it had better not,' said Mary, a little indignant. 'I would never allow Fanny to be soaked in the rain. But she is strong. And anyway, Damien, she is not your concern, leave my baby to me.'

'When do you wish to leave?' he asked agitated.

'Tomorrow, midday if possible,' she replied firmly. As he snapped twigs for the fire, she saw that his finger nails were dirty and broken. His hands were big and strong. He worked very hard for Imlay and had also cared for his ageing father in Paris. Damien was an excellent man. Marguerite sat on the edge of her chair, a thin though shapely woman with a tired looking face. 'The weather is warm and lovely,' said Mary. 'I need to feel the air on my face. How I love August!' She spoke with enthusiasm. 'I do not think it will rain.' Then she lapsed into reflection. People grew best she thought when they exchanged ideas with others. She did not think she had grown with Gilbert. There hadn't been enough conversation. And the more she considered it the more she thought that she didn't *really* know him. It occurred to her then that she might not have loved him with the same intensity had she known him a little better. Could the passion she felt for him only exist if there was mystery? Was what she felt only something imagined, perhaps even dreamed? Oh, but real or imagined, the thought of losing it was insufferable.

'The Terror is over but the revolution is not,' said Marguerite gravely. 'We must wait to see what transpires. My spirits do not rest as yours do. Not yet.'

'Do our spirits ever rest?' Mary said, suddenly pensive. 'My spirit does not rest like you think Marguerite, oh no.'

Damien was fixing the window. 'It rattles,' he murmured. 'You ask for a chaise for tomorrow. You will need a good one, better than the one we have here.'

'And can you get it?' As always she felt strong when making decisions. She looked at him and waited.

'I can,' he said.

'And I can pack clothes and food,' said Marguerite. She peeled her apples more quickly.

'Then I shall do it,' Mary said with certainty. Again, she gazed outside. The glitter of the sun on the leaves in the garden, the softness of the day kindled the life force within her. She wanted love, she wanted her future, if it did not come to her readily then she would seek it out and secure it. She saw in her mind the dark days of her past, and the long long days she had spent without Imlay waiting for the child, and she cast them out of her mind.

Next morning, she settled in the chaise, the baby cradled in her arms, its pale blue innocent eyes staring and awaiting its fate. As the carriage sped on, the midday air was warm and pleasant. The night had been rainy but the land yielded that sweet aroma that always came after rain. She breathed it in and looked around at the countryside. Nature was indeed healing. Everywhere smouldered with beauty. The sight of so many wild flowers and the magical sound of birdsong lifted her spirits as she went. It was good to be alone with the baby out in the open air, moving along the tree filled roads, and she felt a sense of freedom, as if she were somehow escaping. In the best of her dresses and with her hair tied up in a scarf, she felt healthy, strong and lovely. And she was about to descend on her lover boldly. Would he like such boldness? Well, what if he didn't, he would get it. Just then she heard a voice. – 'Bonjour, bonjour!' a man cried from the roadside.

The driver pulled up by a young uniformed officer with the tricolour cockade on his hat. Next there followed a brief conversation in French. It seemed the officer had no horse and had walked some 25 miles over hill and hollow. He hoped to purchase a horse, he said on reaching Le Havre, though horses were in short supply. He told them his name was Captain Pascal Berenger from the revolutionary army, and he must join his regiment soon. 'Forgive me,' he said. 'I am exhausted.' He looked at Mary and smiled. 'May I come up and ride with you?' he asked. His sword gleamed in its scabbard and the buttons on his tunic shone in the afternoon sunlight.

'I have a baby,' said Mary, glancing at the sleeping child beside her, but there was plenty of room in the chaise and the captain looked weary. 'I am going to see my husband, Captain Gilbert Imlay. Do you know him?'

'I have not heard of him,' said Berenger. He wiped sweat from his brow with his hand. 'Where are you going?'

'To Le Havre,' the coachman said brusquely. 'If I do not go to Le Havre on this road then I do not know where else! If the lady will allow it you can get in the chaise, but you will have to pay me for that. I am all but a poor man and I must stop at an inn in an hour. We will not make Le Havre today.'

'No,' said the captain. 'I need to stop at an inn myself to restore my vitality for I am weak as a leech on a rock.'

'Do come and sit beside me,' said Mary, leaning forward. The young officer's eyelids were closing with tiredness.

The captain put his hand in his pocket. 'There you are,' he said, handing the driver a generous amount of coins.

'If the two of us sit together,' said Mary, 'I suspect I shall be much more comfortable. These roads are very uneven and I am sliding from side to side. My baby cries very little, but I fear she might bruise.'

'Well now,' said the captain, climbing into the chaise and looking down at the child. 'I dare say the infant is a girl. She has the prettiest face I ever saw.' He lowered his voice to a whisper. 'I do thank you for your kindness. I will not disturb her. I see she is sleeping. And I think I shall do the same myself once the weight of my body is taken off my feet.' He settled himself beside her and leant on the side of the chaise. Within minutes he was sound asleep.

After an overnight stop at an inn they returned to the chaise and were soon back on the road. The captain appeared refreshed and spoke more in the manner of an authoritative officer, rather than the weary traveller of the previous day, and he now had a certain intensity about him like a watchful pursued animal. 'Thank you for sharing your chaise,' he said, glancing about. 'I fell weary in the fields and thought I might never recover. I had lost so much of my strength, but now I feel better. It is not usually the way with me; I am strong and enduring normally.'

'It has been good to have company,' Mary answered light heartedly. 'There are sometimes highwaymen on the roads. I have never experienced a highwayman, but I imagine it is something of a shock.' She glanced all about as she spoke.

'These rural roads in France are generally safer than your roads in England,' he said. He frowned at a sudden thought. 'I do recall that the first person to be executed by guillotine was a highwayman called Nicolas Jacques Pelletier. I do not know what his robberies entailed but I hope they were worth it.'

For a moment or two they were thoughtful.

'So many good people have been guillotined,' Mary murmured, frowning. 'Thankfully the Terror is over.'

'Ah, we humans are good at killing,' said the captain, shaking his head. 'If we do not do it one way, we will do it another. Evil is evil, and the last person we think it can come from is our self. But we are able to kill more easily when in uniform. It is somehow made to seem right, right for some cause or other. But I suspect it is all futile.'

'You have had enough of it?' she said glancing at him.

'It is unending,' he said with a sigh. 'Do you know that people kill themselves to avoid the horrors of war? Imagine?'

'Yes,' she said abstractedly. She shivered. It was as if strange energies were moving in on her, as if her life were about to change in some uncanny dramatic way. The chaise moved on towards Le Havre.

It was a still warm day, the trees hung over as if resting. The sky was a soft clear blue. The baby in her arms had her eyes wide open, watching the birds flying close and listening to their beautiful songs.

'Does this man know the time of your arrival?' asked the captain. His eyes lingered on her face.

She raised her head and watched the clouds racing over the sky, their broad, thick bellies soft on the air. 'Oh, the beauty of summer, she sheer joy of summer!' she cried. Then she shook her head and smiled. 'He does not know I am coming. I hope to surprise him with our child.'

They found themselves on a higher road with darkening fields below them. The captain took out his pocket watch. 'And how do you know he will be there?'

She laughed. 'I don't. He might be anywhere.' But her laughter turned to a frown and she shrugged. 'C'est la vie.' Meanwhile they were drawing close to Le Havre.

The captain braced himself soldierly. 'So what will you do if no-one is there and the house is locked up?'

'I shall wait,' she said.

He looked at her curiously. 'But where, and how long can you wait?'

'I do not know. I shall find accommodation.'

'You are very unhappy?' He drew himself up and folded his arms. He was intense and cautious glancing about guardedly.

Mary sat hugging her baby. 'I can't help it,' she said pitiably. 'I am always chasing after happiness. I grasp it for a while, then somehow it just slips away.'

'Ah, so sad,' sighed the captain. 'I have a wife and child, but I do not know how they are. The revolution has parted us so often.'

For some minutes they were silent, thoughtful.

'Would you like me to come to this house?' said the captain. 'If the man is at home then I will leave you. If not I can help you find an inn. But I shall have to be off very soon.'

'Thank you,' she said. It was all very well having found her way to Le Havre, but Imlay was hardly likely to do business from his lodgings. He would probably be coming and going. In her eagerness to see him she had not thought about that. She felt foolish. How often her needs superseded her common sense. She was making a reckless presumption and it unsettled her to know how precipitous she could be when her feelings were heightened. But it was summer, glorious summer! She was well, and her child was strong. Out here, moving through space, she could breathe. Come what may she felt wonderfully free. She sat back and talked to the baby. 'We are going to see your father, my pet. He will be quite surprised to see how much you have grown.' She smiled at the captain, but underneath she felt raw that Imlay had brought her to this, a near crazed creature who knew not who she was or where she was going. Was Imlay bad? No, he was not. No-one was truly bad; it was just that people kept a bad thing in their pocket sometimes and would not discard it. She remembered something he had said to her once; "Stop trying to shape your life, just live, and let your life shape you." But she was very different from Imlay, she was far more careful, while he was easygoing and apart. And his sexual passion was immense. She could not forget his loving. The child watched the trees as they passed. 'Trees are so beautiful,' Mary said to the captain. 'I love their innocent dignity. And they dance when we're not looking.' She laughed at her childish comment.

'They do,' laughed the captain. 'Sans aucun doute!'

As they entered Le Havre, the landscape changed rapidly. The air grew rich with the smell of the sea and the sound of seagulls. Situated on the right bank of the estuary of the river Seine, Le Havre was a major French city, some 31 miles west of Rouen on the shore of the English Channel. It consisted of two separate areas divided by a high cliff edge; one part included the harbour, the city centre and the suburbs where Imlay would be living. There were lots of green areas and hanging gardens and Mary saw that the streets were lined with a beautiful variety of trees. Imlay had had a lovely city to live in when he wasn't in Paris, and she thought enviously that she would like to live there herself and might even suggest it when they met. Between the start of the revolution in 1789 and the year 1793, Le Havre had been the second largest port in France after Nantes, sustained because of the grain trade and being close to the British enemy. The defence value of the city had been affirmed in the sixteenth century when Cardinal Richelieu, the then governor, had reinforced the port and built a fortress. From the middle of the eighteenth century affluent traders had built their homes there, and in 1759 it had been the staging area for a proposed French attack on Britain. Her brother James would have found it all most interesting, she thought, and she kept her eyes towards the city looking about in anticipation of seeing Imlay perhaps riding his horse. She was beginning to feel excited. She was a lot more nervous than expected, and wondered what he would think of her temerity. They went beneath tall old trees and passed by many grand houses. Then the horse reared and whinnied.

'She does not like all the seagulls!' called the driver. 'I must take her more slowly. She also needs water.'

Mary and the captain leaned back in the chaise and settled for a slower journey into the city. She drew Imlay's address out of her pocket.

'It is good you have a written address,' said the captain, looking pleased.

'Yes,' she sighed, as if with sudden sadness, for it seemed Le Havre was Imlay's actual home. For a moment or two they were silent. 'Does my child look like me?' she asked, smiling and gazing at the baby.

The captain laughed. 'She has the very same eyes. I swear it.'

She drew the child closer. 'I want her to look like me. That isn't bad, is it?'

'But why should it be bad?' said the captain, looking puzzled. 'I have a son who I think is my image.' He straightened and frowned. 'I hope my boy is well.' He frowned deeply. 'Must a man always fight instead of living? Ah, but I come from a military family, it is always the way.'

'I am a writer,' she told him. Somehow it felt like a lie.

He looked at her and raised his eyebrows. His large brown eyes shone in the strong light. He was a powerful man, she thought. And it seemed he was happy in his marriage. She did not believe in marriage, but it was comforting to think the soldier had a wife at home who waited for him and loved him.

'That is most interesting. What do you write about?' he asked, with genuine interest.

She was silent a moment, thoughtful. 'About things I believe we must change.' She nodded for certainty and straightened.

'"*We?*"' he said curiously.

'Yes, people in general,' she answered, 'even the whole world.'

He shook his head confounded. 'I fear you want too much.'

She cast him a serious glance. 'I do not think so.'

'Tell me about your work,' he said, bracing himself and ready.

She contemplated his words, then spoke. 'It is mainly about wanting a better education and social equality for women.' The captain remained silent. She went on quickly, impassioned. 'I abhor the way they are seen as adornments of a household, that is in the middle-classes, their existence is so confined in England they are often frustrated, locked into their minds, sometimes to the point of insanity. – Men are given education, so why not women? If women had an education they would understand the world much better and also their place within it.' She stopped on seeing she overwhelmed him.

'You set yourself a difficult task,' he murmured. 'But yes, women are often treated badly. It is wrong.'

'It is atrocious. I cannot bear it. And unless women fight it will continue.' They were now on the outskirts of Le Havre. 'I also write reviews of other people's work,' she added. The driver was moving quickly.

'Ah, you are also an authority?' he said curiously.

'A little. And I'm writing a novel,' she said self-consciously. Her novel revealed a lot about her person. She wasn't sure if she would ever allow Johnson to publish it, but she very much wanted to finish it.

'A novel? He looked at her amazed. 'But you must always be making things up. I cannot even tell a lie very well.' He laughed quietly. 'Je dis la vérité !'

She laughed with him, happily. 'I shall do it. I just need time.' She realised as she spoke that talking about her work had enlivened her. She felt stronger. She was Mary Wollstonecraft again. It annoyed her that she was forgetting the importance of her writing.

'I really must buy me a horse,' the captain said, biting his lip. 'I shall see you to this house though first.' He looked at her with dark concerned eyes. 'I can take care of the child if you wish, until you come out. You will be quick to see if he is there?'

'I will,' she murmured, though her voice was shaky as she spoke.

Imlay's house was the last in a terrace of high stone houses opposite the main road. She stood for a moment looking at the dwelling. There was nothing particularly distinctive about it. It was a high dreary house and all the shutters were closed. She saw it was possible to approach the property from the back and decided to make her way round.

Quietly, she trod through some overgrown shrubbery then found her way to a door facing a large garden with high trees heavy in leaf. The house looked more accommodating from behind, and through a wide unshuttered window she could see into a large kitchen. Her gaze fell on the three storeys before her. Did he live here with others? She had never inquired about that. For several moments she wondered what to do next. She took a breath and straightened, daring to think he might be grateful she had made the journey and overjoyed by the sight of his daughter. She prayed he was in as she placed her hand on the iron handle of the door. Amazed by the ease with which the door swung open as she pressed it, she felt as if an invisible person were somehow behind it.

She had entered a large kitchen, but glancing about she saw that the room was empty. The kitchen area she found herself in was spacious, with a fire burning in the grate. A strong smell of cooking came from the oven by the fire. It was a tranquil comfortable room consisting of padded easy chairs with large satin cushions. A brightly coloured Aubusson rug lay by the fire and several busy tapestries hung on the walls which looked very much like Imlay's taste. She wandered about and looked at things, always keeping in mind the captain waiting with the child, despite her immense curiosity, she knew she must hurry. Was Imlay somewhere upstairs? She stopped and sniffed the air. The scent of perfume pervaded the house, though she could not locate it. Then her eyes fell upon a large bowl of fruit on the table . . . and something lay beside it . . . something that caused her to freeze.

Her blood raced as her imagination took hold, a long string of pearls rested by the fruit bowl. And she almost stumbled over a pair of women's buckled shoes which it seemed had been briskly cast aside. Her skin chilled as her thoughts ran riot. But she stopped and breathed better. Perhaps there were others who lived there, other lodgers he did not speak of. How she hoped it were so. But she was jealous, outraged and angry. Her cheeks burned as she made her way up the stairs. Then she stopped again halfway. She could hear Imlay talking in tender tones and a woman responding likewise. 'My precious young goddess,' he was saying. 'I adore every inch of your body. I . . .' Mary put her hands to her ears and leant against the wall. Her heart raced madly. What ridiculous words! Anger made her dizzy and weak. She felt as if the world were revolving about her. They were obviously making love, and so engrossed they hadn't heard her. She wanted to burst into the room and confront him, or might it be wiser just to steal away and return to the chaise? She felt as if a world of demons was trying to destroy her, and she wanted to collapse and weep, but she knew she must return to her child. Carefully, quietly, she crept down the stairs. Passing the table in the kitchen she reached for the pearls and pushed them into her pocket. She would challenge him with those the minute he returned to Paris, she would fling them at him and demand to know the owner! They were very fine pearls, had he bought them?

She fled from the house, arriving breathless at the chaise. The captain was ready. His calm demeanour soothed her, but she wept before him like a child and poured out her sufferings. His face contracted with pain. 'I hope you will never set eyes on this man again!' he said, returning the baby. 'It is a monster who does such a thing to a wife like you.'

'I am not his wife,' she moaned shakily. 'We have pretended to be married for my safety. He is American. You know how it is in France.'

'He is the father of your child,' said the captain. 'He has duties.'

'I do not expect any duty. He is free.'

The captain shook his head, his eyes staring and thoughtful. 'My wife is also free, but I am her lover. She has no other. Though I could not answer for my actions should another man steal her away.' For a moment or two they were silent. 'Shall I help you find an inn?' he asked, seeing she was so disturbed.

'Thank you,' she said, drying her eyes. 'But you need not concern yourself. I know where to stay.' The coachman was preparing to depart.

The captain made to climb from the carriage. 'Now I must say adieu dear lady, and wish you a safe journey. Whatever has happened at that house today will pass. You will think on it better tomorrow. Your child is healthy and her temperament is good. And you, dear lady, are strong. Give thanks for such things.'

With that she watched him stride away down the road. Soon he was out of sight.

At eight o'clock in the evening next day, Mary arrived in Paris. It was a wet and miserable day. As she entered the house, she saw that Damien and Marguerite were having supper. She pressed her face against her baby's cheek, holding her close.

'You are wet,' said Marguerite, she stood and took hold of the baby.

'Yes, Marguerite, but Fanny is warm and dry.' She took off her coat and Damien laid it on a chair by the fire. Marguerite cradled the child. 'Put my daughter in her cot,' said Mary. 'She will probably sleep. I too am exhausted.'

'You will not eat with us then?' Marguerite asked, gazing at her with wide and wondering eyes. She laid the child in her cot by the fire.

Mary shook her head. 'And you need not worry about Fanny, she is clean and fed.' She stood fixed for a moment; the fitful memory of what had happened at Le Havre tormented her. The couple exchanged concerned glances but asked no questions. It was as well they didn't, she thought, for she had no answers, and had cried away all her tears. She pulled the string of pearls out of her pocket and ran them through her fingers, then she laid them down on the table. Damian and Marguerite looked on with anxious faces, watching her as she removed her gloves and hat.

'*Sleep, sleep,*' murmured Mary. 'I must sleep. I am going to bed. Please don't disturb me.' She turned to the stairs then looked back. – 'Take care of my child.'

'I have apple puree in the larder,' Marguerite told her, flushing at the strange situation. 'She likes it. And I can mash her some carrots. She is good with the solids now.'

Mary nodded and went towards the stairs. 'Let them be damned!' she whispered as she climbed to her room. 'Both of them let them be damned!'

A full half hour passed by. Damien went about the kitchen intensely, claiming something catastrophic must have happened at Le Havre, for Citizen Mary was not acting like herself.

'She will tell us in time,' said Marguerite.

'She looks very pale and she shakes as never before,' Damien replied abstractedly. 'Her mood concerns me.'

'She is tired,' Marguerite added.

Mary had closed the door to her room; next came the click of the lock.

'What do you think about these pearls?' Marguerite said to Damien, lifting them up from the table. They both gazed at them with wonder. 'They are very expensive.'

Damien frowned. 'She did not buy them for herself. She does not do such things.'

'And the captain did not buy them for her as a gift,' said Marguerite, scornful of him just then. She sat down by the fire and stared at the flames, the pearls glistening in her hands. 'She has found them somewhere. Where do you think she found them?'

Damien sighed. 'You know where she found them.'

'You should never have allowed her to go,' Marguerite said quietly, glancing at the baby. 'All manner of things might have happened. It was foolish.'

'Ah, now you are blaming me because she comes back here with expensive pearls she does not own. And in any case, you might have prevented her going yourself, but instead you packed her refreshments.'

'We are both to blame,' said Marguerite. 'We have been selfish. We stayed in our bed all day and did not care.' Damien placed his arm around her shoulder and drew her head towards his chest.

Just then they heard Imlay cantering up the lane to the house.

'He goes too fast!' Marguerite said running to the window. 'What is the matter, he is crazy.'

He burst into the house and threw off his coat and hat. 'Where is she?' he cried, glancing about madly. 'Dammit, she *did* take those pearls, I thought so!' he shouted. Lifting them up from the table. He looked at them for a long moment then threw them down on the floor. 'Who would have thought she would come to Le Havre and creep about like a thief?' He shook his head irritably. 'There's no telling what she'll do next.'

'How did you know she had been?' asked Damien, without looking up.

'Someone told me that a woman had been looking at the house and wandering around outside. I was given the precise description. I knew who it was.'

'And you fled back here,' Marguerite murmured.

'I had to. – Is she upstairs?'

Damien nodded.

Within minutes Imlay was trying the door of her room and calling her name, telling her not to take on so, that the woman was simply a friend, a companion in his lonely hours and that all men needed a female companion in long lonely hours or they would surely drink to excess. But shout as he would, knock as he would, not a sound came through the door.

After a couple of minutes, Marguerite came to join him. Imlay was pacing the landing.

Marguerite spoke quietly. 'The laudanum has gone from the cupboard, Captain. The last time I saw it was on the birth of the baby. Now it is missing.'

'What?' gasped Imlay. He banged loudly on the door. 'Mary, open this door!' he shouted pounding the wood with his fists. He turned to Marguerite. 'Do we have another key? – Dear God, I know nothing of this place!'

Damien brought a second key. 'Let me try this,' he said, pushing it into the lock. From the other side of the door, they heard the clink of the inside key as it fell to the floor. Very soon they were in.

They all three stopped, stunned by the sudden silence. 'She has taken an overdose of laudanum,' Marguerite said shakily seeing the empty bottle at her side. Slowly they edged towards the bed. Mary lay pale and ghostly. Her eyes were closed, her hands clasped tightly in prayer, her face looked ashen.

As Imlay drew near, tears came into his eyes. 'Mary,' he whispered. 'Please forgive me.'

Marguerite trembled. Damien held on to her hand. 'Marguerite,' Imlay said urgently. 'Make me a saline solution, quick! Perhaps we can save her. – And Damien, bring me that bowl!' Imlay lifted her head from the pillow, then gently opened her mouth. 'Ah good,' he said, as Marguerite arrived by the bed with salted water. 'We must try to get her to drink it. Come, Damien, help me, you hold her safe while I pour it into her mouth. No, no, keep her head held high, just a little at a time, or she'll choke!'

Slowly, by degrees the solution slipped down her throat and she started to cough and wretch. Damien held the bowl beneath her chin, and she vomited the laudanum, protesting as she did so. 'Oh no! Dear no! I wanted to die. Why can't I die? What use am I as a mother? I am no use to anyone.' She had failed, she moaned, she had failed in everything.

'Not so,' said Imlay, resting her head on his chest and stroking her hair. 'I am the one who has failed. You have not failed, my dear, not ever. I will not hear such things. Be calm.'

'But Gilbert,' she whispered, clutching his hand. 'That girl sounded so young.'

'She is twenty,' he said flatly, as if it were some justification. 'I do not love her. She sometimes comes to my lodgings. But I shall never see her again.'

'Did you . . . Did you buy her the pearl necklace?'

'No, I did not,' he said, taking a deep breath. 'I have no idea where she got them. Now be silent my dear. You have frightened us all with this.'

Mary closed her eyes. Behind her was a great silent past. Before her was a great silent future. Now though, just now, there was only the moment, her beautiful child and Gilbert.

Summer passed into autumn then winter. Icicles hung from the rooftops like strings of silver fishes and some days the snow fell heavily. Mary watched it as it chased itself over the sky. Fanny loved snowflakes and liked to stick out her tongue to catch them when Mary took her in the garden. She had started to crawl about the house and by the help of her arms could lift herself up, laughing at her small achievements. Mary would sometimes dance her on the table while Gilbert studied his papers. He did not go very far in winter and she was glad. But she feared the spring and knew he would be off wandering. But while he was with them he loved them. Or so it would seem. He was a man essentially of the moment, and each moment was its own master. She had forgiven him for what she'd discovered in Le Havre, but a certain bitterness remained. She could not shift it from her thoughts.

The spring of 1795 came quickly. Imlay had been coming and going as usual, though he was rarely away for long. He was seeing to unfinished business in Le Havre, he said. Mary made no inquiries, for she did not want him to think her weak and jealous. She remained sweet and trusting, there was no other way.

'Oh, my dear, if you only knew the funny little antics Fanny gets up to you would laugh,' she said one morning. 'She points to her eyes and says, 'eyes, eyes, eyes,' over and over. And she got her fingers into a jar of pickles yesterday in the kitchen and pulled one out . . .'

'And did she eat it?' asked Imlay, glancing up from his work, his eyes wide with surprise.

'No, she doesn't have enough teeth, but she sucked it and pulled the strangest of faces.'

Setting aside his papers he said, 'I must go to England this autumn. Will you come with me?'

She looked at him curiously. 'You mean for a visit?'

'Well yes. But I can't say how long the visit will be. Possibly even a year, business takes its own time.'

She crouched on the rug by the fire with the child. 'But of course,' she said, trying her best to sound pleased. 'I'm glad you have told me now, then I can prepare. And you will leave things here just the way they are, I take it?' She felt the old weariness of soul she had left in England. She shivered slightly. She wasn't fulfilled. She had not written as much as she'd wanted and had hardly been the woman she aspired to be in her writing, or the mother she would have wanted for Fanny. But it had been hard living in France and with Imlay who kept on confusing her. But fate took mastery in the end and she'd been forced to succumb to its power. What weariness she felt sometimes. But she did not want to return to England yet, not unmarried with a child. She rested in the fact that she had written some very good books and was highly respected in London; to spend some time there might be fruitful and she could investigate the lie of the land. She knew that Johnson's crowd would welcome her, and perhaps she would do some writing while she was there. The thought of her friends cheered her. And she would meet with her sisters again and Ned. It would be easy to find the love again she had shared with her sisters. With Ned though it was bound to be difficult, there was always the tension, and he took it personally if she complained how men treated women. He was happy with his wife and family, but whatever his circumstances, he still belonged to that army of men who crushed and suppressed women. And she still resented the privileges he'd enjoyed simply through being male. He knew all this and it made it hard for them to talk. Also, he thought she was married. The fact that she wasn't would prove awkward. But he did not know the way things were in France, and her experiences throughout the revolution had changed her fundamentally. But they would all love Fanny, of course, for how could they not?

The spring had been splendid in Paris, but summer proved rainy and dreary. Imlay had been coming and going as normal, tying up loose ends, he said, in Le Havre. Mary hated the long drizzly days of the last two weeks of August, and the child was constantly unsettled be-

371

cause she could not play in the garden and must always stay in. She threw her toys about and screamed at Marguerite's songs. There were days Mary felt tired and the thought of returning to England was too heavy even to imagine. But she prepared herself for it and felt happy with the thought that she would meet with Johnson's circle again and talk with interesting people. They would want to know what her life had been like in France, and she rested in the knowledge that her book about the French Revolution had been sent to Johnson and published; a lot of them were bound to have read it. It would be good to talk about that. And they would ask for news about Paine. That he'd been seen by Robespierre as an enemy was common knowledge and he'd been denounced as a traitor to the revolutionary ideal for consorting with the Girondins and the Jacobins had thrown him into prison. But by happy chance he had not suffered a Girondin fate and had completed his *Age of Reason* in captivity. It seemed to Mary that the whole of Paine's life had been one of constant tension. He must fight for the rights of men no matter what price, and she too would, in turn, fight for the rights of women. Apparently, his name had been listed for execution and the door of his cell had been marked, but the mark had somehow been missed and his life had been saved. He had then been released, largely on account of the American Minister of France arguing Paine's American citizenship. Absorbed in her pregnancy Mary had lost touch with his whereabouts, and her problems with Gilbert had drained her. But she was starting to wonder about her friends and family and there were days she longed to go home. She shuddered, confronted by the fact that she'd attempted to penetrate that space of ultimate darkness, and all of her own volition. Was it not wrong to try to end your life? And she wondered what it might have been like after death if she hadn't gone to heaven, but had instead gone to a kind of Hades where the ghosts of those who had died too soon, or tragically, wandered alone for ever. She had tried to die; she had actually tried to die. It was not possible to come back from such an experience and still be the same person, the ghost of it walked beside her.

But she clung to the glow of light that was her daughter and her love for Imlay. She opened the window and waved her hand in the rain, letting its wetness fall freshly through her fingers. Well, England was often rainy. It hadn't bothered her then; she had walked through the rain with her sisters so many times. She recalled the scent of the rain in England, that glorious woodland scent she had known when searching for wild flowers with Fanny. For a moment or two she allowed herself to think of those days. There had been love, real love, then. But it was all too soon snatched away. Sleep peacefully in the earth, dear Fanny, she thought, for there is little peace amongst the living. Gilbert tried to love, but his love was weak, and his eyes could be hard and cruel when determined, or like those of a beast at rest, vacant in a world of their own. And he didn't do *ordinary* things. Damien did those. Imlay was a man of books, papers and pens. That was when you loved people most, she decided, when you saw them doing ordinary things.

She came away from the window and placed more logs on the fire. Autumn was already in the air, time moved on so quickly she could scarce catch her breath. Imlay had organised passage to England now and they would soon leave Paris behind. September! September! She enjoyed September in England and would take Fanny to explore the woodlands where she would show her pine cones and point to the brightly coloured leaves.

Just then Marguerite rushed in, crying out frantically, her hands in the air. 'Oh, que devons-nous faire?' she cried. 'I cannot find her!'

'Have you looked properly?' Mary asked urgently. 'She is good at hiding.'

'But Citizen Mary I know where she hides,' Marguerite pleaded. 'I have searched all her places.' She trembled with fear.

Damien came running. 'What is it?' he cried. 'Ah, you have lost little Fanny!' He clapped his hands to his face. 'Captain Imlay is resting upstairs. We must tell him!'

They all three rushed upstairs and burst into Imlay's room. He was taking an afternoon nap but immediately sprang into action. They went through the upstairs rooms, looking beneath beds and wherever else she might have crept. They listened hard for her voice and called to her over and over. 'Just you wait,' shouted Imlay. 'Where have you gone little spider! Ah, wait until I catch you!'

'What if she has gone outside?' said Marguerite even more horrified. 'She can reach the latches now. I have seen her do it. What if she is lost in the woods?'

'Why weren't you watching her?' said Mary, guilty for leaving the child to Marguerite while she finished some reading. But Marguerite didn't seem to hear. The back door of the house was open and they all ran out into the rain calling and calling. Imlay and Damien ran frantically about between the trees while Mary and Marguerite searched through the dripping bushes.

'She is here!' called Damien breathlessly. 'I have found her beneath the quince!'

Mary gave a gasp of relief and joined him with Marguerite. The child lay silent and cold. She was pale and seemed lifeless. Mary lifted her while the others looked on anxiously. 'Oh my love, my darling little creature, dear God, why are you are so cold?' she cried. 'I am a bad mother. Please forgive me.' They all went quickly to the house. 'She needs dry clothes,' Mary said to Marguerite, 'And bring the bowl from the kitchen. She must have a warm bath. Why, she is scarcely breathing!'

'She will be fine,' said Imlay, striding about the room looking annoyed. He was annoyed with them all, and also with himself for resting. The child looked ill and in less than a week they would be sailing. Mary knew as she pulled off the child's wet clothing that Imlay would go to England alone if he must. Fanny gave a few little coughs, shivered and opened her eyes.

'Ah, she is with us once more!' cried Damien, filling the bowl by the fire with warm water. 'If she can sit in that for a while and get warm she will soon recover.'

'God, help her,' said Marguerite, bringing the child more clothing. We must get her a doctor. She shivers. I think she has a chill.'

There was silence. They all looked on as Mary lowered her child into the bowl and sponged her naked limbs. 'Here I am, my pet. Here is Maman,' she said gently. 'Soon you can have some milk, and sleep in your little cot. Oh, poor child.' Imlay sat staring from the chair beside them. Damien went out for a doctor.

Little Fanny lay sick and feverish all week, and the doctor attended her each day. There were times when it seemed as if all her vital energy had drained from her body and she was still as a winter pool. But her life force was strong and the doctor had assured them that with careful nursing she would recover and all would be well. But she could not travel. And neither could Mary. Never before had a child received such careful attention. Mary was constantly beside her and Damien and Marguerite gave her the best of their love. But Imlay left for England without them.

October dragged on and Fanny was erratic in recovery. 'I hope we don't see her fall back,' said Mary. The child's blue eyes shone brightly as Mary fed her strawberry puree from the garden's wild strawberries that year.

'You will cross the channel soon,' said Marguerite, as if it were inevitable.

'Yes,' said Mary flatly. 'I believe she is well enough now. It is a while since the captain left us. But our passage has been arranged and it excites me to think of taking my daughter to England.'

'The weather is good,' said Damien, sounding relieved. He was roasting chestnuts on the fire. 'October has been mild and the sea will be kind I think.' He was almost laughing, delighted the child had recovered, and also, thought Mary, pleased he would have the house to himself with Marguerite. Just then their thoughts were interrupted by the call of an early owl. 'We have one or two rabbits,' said Damien. 'Mild weather has brought them out.'

'And the owl is after them,' said Marguerite. 'There is little peace to be found for any living creature.'

The squeal of a rabbit came from the garden. After that there was silence.

# 39

## Mary Returns to England

Imlay had left. It was as if he intended staying in England for good, Mary concluded, for he had packed several trunks. She had known she must follow him quickly. Were she a bird, she would have flown to him that very minute, she told Marguerite. But she wasn't a bird; she was a woman and a mother, glad to have brought such a special child into the world. The responsibility, however, was sometimes overwhelming and she hoped as Fanny grew older she would never learn that her mother had once tried to die.

But the child would cry with the great joy of life, 'Maman! Maman!', whenever Mary appeared and would run to her with open arms, her little plump legs moving as fast as they could. Then Mary would clutch her to her breast. Her daughter loved her. It was good. And her heart beat fast with happiness when she thought of it. Her soul sought rest, but the happenings in France loomed in her mind like a nightmare. Her worst dreams were of soldiers coming to find her to take her off to the guillotine as they had done with Imlay's Girondin friends, and also the queen. She wondered what work Marie might be doing now. She shivered when she thought of the apartment; she had not visited it again after leaving, for it reflected the grim relentlessness of the Terror.

As she wandered her room that afternoon, she wondered what to take with her. There were paintings on her walls that Imlay had said she could have. But having seen such paintings in the house in Le Havre, she had no wish to own them. She would only take what she needed; Imlay would buy the important things when she joined him.

She'd had long discussions with Damien and Marguerite about the future and the French way of life compared to the life in England. England was the bedrock of her existence, the voice of her past, she had played in the woodland, and she had seen the angels, her youth had blossomed in England and her developing intellectual life. Such thoughts however, made her feel stupidly sensitive and sometimes brought tears to her eyes and she must summon her stronger self to recover her strength. It would not do to arrive there in such a frame of mind. She had travelled, she had experienced things others had never experienced, and she knew things others did not. Her family would not recognise her as the new person she had become, she would be the Mary of their childhood, it was inevitable. But her future had spoken. Her friends would know better and would accommodate her new found opinions, for they had no dream of the way she should be, and only wanted her to grow. Johnson and her friends saw each other as elemental forces, a sort of changing climate bringing sunshine or storm.

Soon she was sitting in the chaise with Damien and the child, the child quiet and thoughtful watching the sky. 'It's going to be alright, isn't it?' she said to him, suddenly nervous. 'I have no idea what I'll find when I arrive in England. I feel estranged from my brother and sisters, and they think I am married to Gilbert.' She glanced at her daughter. 'And I must take the child to her father.'

'You must follow him,' said Damien. But he spoke wistfully and did not look at her. As ever, he was kind and compassionate. He understood her and knew her fears. But she would not voice them for it made them far too real, and she could not bear the thought of Imlay being away from the address in her pocket, or worse. She was bending forward, enjoying the smell of her baby's young hair as she sat contented on her lap. Fanny was such a carefree creature and entered her days as easily as she'd entered the world. The child filled her heart with a singular marvellous pride.

Having boarded the ship, she watched the waves rising and falling, rising and falling and rolling onwards to home. It was a mild, clear day and the best all week, the sailors had told her. Oh, the joy of movement, and the freedom of the sea! It was easy to see why a life at sea was so attractive to her brother, she thought. Imlay too might have chosen it were he not consumed by business. The child on her lap gurgled with laughter at something in her own world while Mary glanced about at the passengers. The voices around her were from different nationalities and she did not always understand them, but their attitude was generally optimistic. She rested in the fact that she was now on her way to England and that the boat was excellent and safe. It was a Dover shipyard vessel and according to Imlay such ships were the best in Europe.

She went to her cabin and seated the child with her toys on the floor while she organised their things. There was a sleepy silence all about her and she allowed herself to feel happy. Soon she would be with Gilbert again and she would meet with her sisters and Ned. The strange empty feeling she had felt for some months had now been replaced by hope. – '*Hope, hope,*' she murmured, smiling at the thought. 'It is a wonderful feeling!' She looked at her daughter as she played with her toys, what a grand little thing she was. No words could describe the exalted feelings Mary had now as she watched the small busy fingers grasping the toys with delight, moving them about the floor with such pleasure. The child adored the little black horse Imlay had brought her from Le Havre. She could not imagine where it went in her daughter's mind, but she knew it would canter each inch of their cabin before nightfall. How lucky she had been with Fanny, for children could be difficult and tiresome, and she often felt sad that she could not give her the life she felt she deserved, and she held to the hope that perhaps life would be better in England.

'I could have walked it quicker!' someone grumbled as the passengers disembarked. 'Only if you can walk on water!' cried another. But Mary felt the time had gone quickly, for she had done some excellent writing whilst Fanny had played or slept. Now she sat at the harbour a while, looking about for Imlay and praying in her soul he would at last arrive to collect her. But as time passed by she accepted the fact that he had no intentions of coming to the harbour that day, and she wondered where to go first. She somehow managed to have constant heartache, and if there were heartache waiting, she could not suffer it yet, she would first find lodgings and settle her mind, then she would go to see Ned, after that she would seek out Imlay. She found a chaise and got in.

England excited a sort of religious fervour in her blood as the carriage passed through the streets. The sights and scents around her brought back important memories, and with them came their strengths and weaknesses. But she feared being hurt by Imlay, for in the darkness of his heart he was capable of casting her aside and his child too if it suited.

She found lodgings near Johnson's house. What a surprise he would have when he discovered she was back in London, she thought, smiling to herself. Her room was small, but no matter. And in any case, it was only until she gathered herself together and tried to make sense of her life. She would be gentler with Imlay here, she decided, she was hard on him it was true, she was persistent and difficult and first chance he got, he ran away. Yes, that was the answer. She flooded with warm feelings. It was such a pleasure to see English people peering into shop windows and to hear the traders on the streets calling and selling their wares. It was good too, not to feel the tensions of France.

It was a dull grey day as she made her way to Ned's in the chaise. The sky was a dappled grey and though it offered little sunlight, it did not threaten rain. She had sent Ned a message with someone who knew him and had asked him to arrange for her sisters to be there at the house when she arrived. The chaise turned into the street where he lived and she felt her heart race at the thought of meeting them all once again. He was at the door before she knocked, and greeted her warmly. She went inside and sat down on a familiar chair, smiling and saying how good it was to see them, holding her precious cargo to her breast, the child reaching and happy, her great eyes shining and busy. Her sisters sat on the chaise longue together. They took little Fanny in their arms, passing her from one to the other and giving her kisses. Neither of them spoke about Imlay or asked where he was. Ned's wife had come out of the kitchen and stood nearby, awkward and confused. The clock on the wall ticked on as they talked, careless of time or what it delivered. But both her sisters reserved their private thoughts, speaking only pleasantries. 'I dreamt about you just recently,' said Eliza. 'I thought you looked different, not at all like the Mary we knew. Your clothes and hair were changed. Though I see you are quite the same.'

'You too, Eliza,' said Mary. 'But considering what I've gone through in France, I suspect I have many wrinkles.'

'You are not wrinkly at all,' said Everina, immediately consulting the mirror as to the state of her own features. 'Not half so wrinkly as I am.'

Ned listened and shook his head. 'Well now, Mary, let us hear what else you are unhappy about, wrinkles aside.'

Mary gazed at him abstractedly. 'Life appears so easy here in England,' she sighed. 'It is hard to adjust.'

'What, to a bit of ease?' gasped Eliza. 'I can't say I've felt this ease myself. We haven't had death all about us like you but we still have our troubles.'

'Indeed, you do,' said Ned, nodding at Eliza. He smiled at his wife, who stood quietly beside them, then he talked about gloom and money. He liked to talk about money thought Mary, and she pretended Imlay was rich and that she and Fanny were well cared for, though it was far from true. Her sisters revealed very little about their lives as they talked, almost as if they were suspicious of her now, as if she had brought the demon of death along with her. Before long they were putting on their cloaks and saying goodbye. Next time would be better, thought Mary.

'I have tried not to think about France too much,' said Ned, Fanny seated on his lap. She had taken to Ned straight away and had an instant capacity for love. 'You will always do what takes your fancy, and if politics and guillotines interest you, then so be it. Strange for a woman, though.' She made no comment and he went on further. 'There is always a constant stream of information over here about matters in France, people talk, people write, but I rarely believe all I read. I do not want to demean you, my dear. If you can stomach all that and write about it as well, then congratulations! My other sisters are not cut out for it however, so

I'm not surprised they have gone.' He ran his fingers along the child's small arm in the way of a walking insect. 'But we all adore our little niece,' he said, pinching her cheek. 'But Mary, my dear, where is her father, and what is he up to?' He did not meet her eyes as he spoke.

Mary looked downwards confused. She had made her brother's her first port of call, and had not yet gone to find Imlay. She murmured he was living in London, and she intended to see him that day. She knew that everything she said sounded strange and didn't make sense. Ned looked suspicious.

'But where are you living right now?' he asked, frowning. 'Did he not come to meet you?'

'I am staying in a house I have stayed in before. The landlady knows me.'

'But will you not live with Gilbert?' He breathed in deeply and sighed.

'Of course,' she said quietly. 'Did I not tell you just now, I shall find him later today?'

'It's all rather odd,' he murmured. 'You are living in a lodging house with Fanny and you haven't yet sought out your husband? Worse still he was not at the harbour to greet you. Your sisters come over to see you, and you are so withdrawn, they go home. It is hardly fair. I'm sure you are holding things back. Your sisters aren't stupid you know, and neither am I. Had I known you would arrive in England with nowhere to go and no-one to meet you, I would have organised matters differently.'

'My sisters were far too silent; it was as if I'd done something wrong. I have not. I have just got on with my life.'

'Of course, and you might have got on with your death the way things were going in Paris. A letter would bring your sisters rushing to my home. They pored over every sentence.'

'The post was very poor.'

'I know,' said Ned, seating the child on the floor and straightening. 'Blasted nuisance.'

'I never asked for your help,' she whispered. 'I have always been very independent.'

'Oh, indeed,' he laughed. 'Least said soonest mended on that.' He looked at her straight.

'So I am still contemptible?' she said softly and slightly indignant. 'I am still *unloved*?'

He made a strange irritable sound. 'Oh, don't be ridiculous,' he said, throwing out his hands. 'For someone who professes rationality, you are quite the opposite, there is always such drama about you.'

She shrugged. 'Well, for a first visit, today has been quite a disappointment.' She bent to the child. 'Come my kitten, we must go.'

'I'm sorry, Mary. I do not mean to upset you. I too am a victim of emotion. I cannot be rational with you. You stir up my feelings, and I must say you worry me.'

'Well, do not worry,' she said, tying the strings of her cloak and making her way towards the door. 'I am just as I am. I know I can be difficult, even for myself.'

'I understand that as well,' he said, rising. 'I hope you will come again.' They stepped out on to the street. 'This first visit has been awkward. You have put our sisters through a lot of anguish, and not getting letters made it worse. It all lands on me, of course. It is I who must sort things out.'

She smiled wryly. 'You are highly esteemed and respected.'

His forehead wrinkled and he ran his fingers through his hair. 'No, I am not. Our sisters can be extremely awkward. Whatever I say is wrong. But I have to say something; the demand is there in their eyes.'

'Such is the way of families,' she said sighing. 'I shall come to see you again quite soon,' she said hopefully. 'I must also see Johnson and my friends. I hope they will prove less distant than my sisters.'

'Our sisters aren't really distant,' he said uncomfortably, as they walked to a chaise on the street. 'They are lost for words to tell the truth. Paris seemed like hell in the papers and there you were in the midst of it.'

'Yes,' she said, touching his arm. 'I thought about you all. I did not forget you.' She bent her head and lowered her voice. 'I do believe I have known the fires of hell. Perhaps I even died.' Then with renewed vigour, she looked at him straight and said, 'But see, I have risen like a phoenix!' She embraced him, then climbed into the chaise.

## 40

## *Strength and Sensibility*

Ned had been right to inquire about Imlay's whereabouts, but she dreaded finding him gone, and gone for good. He had not written since sending the address, and he had not met her at the harbour, she had wondered at first if he might have intended to surprise her, for he came and went like a shadow, but she could not chance the pain of discovery just yet, she was far too vulnerable. She had stared across the harbour lonely and miserable, begrudging those who were met by people who loved them. Ned would certainly have come for her had she written, just as he'd said, but he and her sisters believed she was married and she could not tell them the truth. Not yet.

Returning to her lodgings, she wondered how she might finally break the truth to them, for she would have to confess very soon. To be unmarried with a child in England made you an outcast whilst revolutionary France took a much broader view of relationships. The revolution had encouraged freedom and she had yielded to the new ideas. But she knew that in England people would either pity her or call her indecent. She hoped Imlay had kept his promise to be silent, for word got round in London very fast and her name was well known.

Having put Fanny down to sleep, she found Imlay's address and checked it over. She knew where the house was and her spirit reached out to it longingly, but her experience at Le Havre made her nervous. She bit at her knuckles. Ought she to go tomorrow? She feared the strength of her feelings and what it would do to her mind if he were living with another woman. Oh, she could not bear it! She feared that most. Her soul fell helpless at the altar of pain and she prayed. 'You have betrayed me, yet again, I know it,' she whispered to her fire as the flames flew fast up the chimney. 'Or why have you been so silent? You have left us. And whoever the siren is, I know she is with you!'

But again she summoned her strength and tried to cast aside her fears. Nothing was certain, it was the demon *fear* that tormented her, oh yes she had nurtured it in France, the revolution had been so terrible, and Imlay's infidelity had damaged her. Now fear was rooted in her soul and would not leave her. She knew she would have to banish it, if only for the sake of her child, but how?

Her landlady was kind and generous; she was fond of children and would come to the door with a sweetmeat or a toy for Fanny, who took it with delight saying, "Maman! Maman, oh, see!" And the woman would look at her happily, fancying the child was her very own granddaughter far away in America.

'And I do believe she has the very same stare – straight, innocent and honest,' she said that morning to Mary, who was putting on her cape to go out.

'Her look is very intense,' Mary said smiling. 'I think she is a dreamer like me.'

'Where are you going?' the woman asked, frowning. 'It is a cold, wet day.'

'"A cold, wet day,"' Mary repeated, as if the day itself were against her. She adjusted the child's hood. 'I am going on an errand to see a friend.'

'You are very sombre,' said the woman. She gazed at her curiously. 'Will you be late coming back?'

'I'm not sure,' Mary replied, confused. She couldn't say when she'd return. She wasn't even sure if Imlay would be there. But she could not deliver her fears and concerns to this good, though simple minded woman.

'Well,' the landlady murmured. 'Do not leave it too late, for the air grows damp in the late afternoon, and it might be hard to find a chaise.' She gazed warmly at Fanny. 'The child here mustn't fall ill.'

'No, not at all,' Mary said quietly. 'I am always in mind of her welfare.' She fastened a scarf around Fanny's little neck. 'The fog is heavy today,' she said, glancing outside.

'I don't want to meddle . . .' the landlady faltered. 'But she can stay with me if you like.'

'Ah, poor little mite,' said Mary pitifully. 'You are kind. I drag her hither and thither.'

'Well,' said the landlady diffidently. 'What I've been thinking is that you might need some time to yourself, and I am lonely, you see.'

Mary knelt down to the child. 'Do you want to stay here and play?' she asked her. She would much rather search for Imlay on her own, especially in the fog. Fanny was all but a baby yet, just learning to walk and talk. The child nodded and grasped the landlady's hand as if understanding the conversation. 'Only till Maman comes home,' said Mary. And the child kept nodding.

'I shall treat her as if she were my own,' said the landlady capably, removing the child's scarf and lifting her up on her arm as Mary opened the door. 'Let me have the little black horse,' she said, putting out her hand. 'I know how she loves it.'

'Ah yes, the little black horse,' Mary murmured, passing it across.

'Clippety clop, clippety clop,' said the woman, taking the horse across the sideboard. 'Now where shall we take it today?'

Mary struggled with her nerves as the chaise moved on. Closing on Imlay's lodgings she was ready for anything. She knew him well enough to think he would probably be aware of her arrival in England. One way or another, he'd find out, and she had sent him a letter from France which she earnestly hoped he'd received. But the fog lingered and it took the driver a while to identify the street.

All around her was the silence of spring, but the weather was cold and misty and people were probably staying in. She shivered, as much with the thought of her errand as she did from the cold. It was as if she knew what she'd find; Imlay wasn't happy on his own, had he not said so.

Climbing from the chaise by his lodgings, she took deep breaths, then stood by the door several minutes before daring to knock. She would not be timid, she would not be weak, she decided, she would be warm and tender, for as yet only the demon imagination had hold of her. She hoped Imlay would be loving. She prayed as she waited. Then she knocked loudly on the door. If it all went wrong, what would she do? Where would she go with her baby? Just then she heard footsteps in the hall and recognized Imlay's long stride! She was here at the door of the man she adored, the father of her child, he held her soul in his hands and she could not prize it away. She stood nervous and trembling.

'Ah, I expected you,' he said, opening the door quickly. He pursed his lips and looked into the street. 'Not today though in this mist.'

He was cool and aloof. It hurt her to the core of her being. 'It is nothing next to the fog in my mind,' she said. He invited her in but did not embrace her.

'Did you have a decent journey,' he asked. 'I mean coming across the channel.'

'I scarcely noticed it,' she said. 'I did some writing and Fanny slept most of the way.'

They walked down the hall and he led her into a large cosy room where she sat in a chair by the fire. He did not ask about the welfare of his daughter or why she was absent. 'Shall I take off my cape?' she asked, feeling uncomfortable. His eyes said he did not want her.

'So how is the child?' he asked finally, in a tone that made it sound like an effort.

'She is well, very well. You would be thrilled by her progress. I did not bring her today, of course, bad weather and all.'

'So who is she with?' he asked, poking at the fire. 'Did you leave her with Ned? I presume you have seen him.'

'Yes, I have seen them all, Eliza and Everina also. I have left Fanny with my landlady. She appears to love our little daughter.' He made a gesture with his hand and she took off her cape. She did not belong here, she thought, and neither did Fanny. He did not notice her dress, something feminine with a velvet collar she had bought for England. He did not offer her a single spark of warmth. Oh how his mood mocked her! She glanced about the room. 'Are you living on your own?' she ventured.

'Why do you ask?' he said, rubbing his hair as if annoyed. 'Is it good to think I am alone?' He turned away his face disdainfully.

'I thought I was coming to live with you,' she said quietly, looking downwards. 'And Fanny too, of course. Are we not your family? Or do you no longer know us?'

'Oh Mary, don't nag,' he chided. 'You English women do nag.'

She straightened, holding aloof, noticing again how white his hands were, how beautifully he kept his fingernails. Damien had done all the physical work in Paris. Imlay didn't dirty his hands. Yet his nature just now seemed coarse and callous in contrast with his clever mind. 'I'm glad you've seen Ned,' he offered. 'Has he sent you?'

'Not at all. He did not know where you were.'

'And did you not tell him?'

'Of course not. I am hardly proud of this arrangement.'

'Well, he won't be hearing from me,' he said smiling wryly. 'Beloved brother that he is, he will probably want pistols at dawn.'

It was obvious something was amiss. 'I manage my own affairs, Gilbert,' she said, bracing herself. 'I have never called on Ned for anything, apart from a little money. And that is all wrong. He was given a better start in life, he is male you see. For us women it is all quite different.'

He sighed deeply. 'Yes, yes, I am fully aware of your opinions.'

For a few moments there was silence. 'What am I to do?' she asked quietly.

'About what?'

'About me and Fanny, what are your intentions?' Her voice faltered as she struggled with her annoyance and his cold uncaring manner. 'Do you want me to bring her here?'

He rubbed his nose as he spoke. 'The landlord doesn't like children, and I shall often be away on business. You know how I live.'

'I do,' she murmured. She felt cut off from him and wretched. How she wanted to reproach him for his lack of communication, his cruel way of forgetting her.

'We have been through this before,' he murmured. He made an irritable sound. 'We have both had time to think, and our liaison has been a mistake.'

'"*Liaison!*"', she gasped. 'Is that what you call it?' Now she feared for her child and she feared for herself also. She felt so lost and could not envisage her future. She glanced through the window. The fog was beginning to lift. People were out on the street. She wondered where they were going and what their lives entailed. And she wondered what sort of life she could offer her child. 'Are you living alone?' she asked him again, scrutinizing his face as she tried to probe him.

'I suppose it matters, doesn't it?' he said, changing his position in the chair. 'I have to say I *do* have a friend. She is quite amusing and cheers me, whereas you, my dear, depress me.'

She chilled at his words and glanced at the door which was closed just then. 'Is she here?'

'I believe she is upstairs changing,' he said. 'I doubt she has heard you arrive.' He gave her a look of warning. 'Please don't cause me any trouble.'

She looked at him hatefully. 'You disgust me,' she gasped, her throat tightening with tears.

'Let's face it, my dear, you do have your tantrums,' he said, with a deep sigh of knowledge.

She knew he was thinking of how she had tried to kill herself. It had disturbed him. It had disturbed her too. What bothered her most was that she knew she could do it again; death was strong in her, stronger than the desire for life. Oh, the sense of disgrace, the gloom, the sorrow! She wanted to leave and weep. She had learned what she needed to know, though the knowledge tore at her heart. She rose slowly and reached for her cape. 'Do you not love me at all?' she enquired softly. He was silent. 'I believe you loved me once.'

'I can't imagine myself staying with a woman very long,' he said drowsily.

His shirt was open at the front. It was unlike him not to be neat and tidy, but today he appeared unkempt. She spoke again slowly, this time without emotion. 'But our daughter, Gilbert, surely you care for Fanny?'

He bit his lip irritably. 'It would be good to see her, of course. But I won't be tied to women and babies.'

Just now he seemed like a force of darkness dangerous to her existence. She stood lost in his power. 'I'm sorry,' she faltered. 'I had hoped for better.' Just then she heard footsteps on the stairs. The door opened quickly.

'Oh Mary!' gasped Laurette. 'I did not know you were here!' She stared at her shocked and surprised.

Mary smiled wryly. 'Ah, so it is you.' She laughed briefly. 'I ought to have known. I am just about to leave. You are two of a kind, I should think. Yes, quite a pair.'

Laurette looked past her and rested her eyes on Imlay. 'I didn't intend to . . .' she began.

'Of course not,' he sighed, uncrossing his legs. 'Well, now it is over and done with.'

Mary's heart beat fast. She felt it might shatter in her body, leave her all but a shell of herself, something dead and done with like an old fallen tree in the wood. In contrast to Laurette's loveliness, she saw herself now as old and ugly. She touched the crow's feet near her eyes, and felt again that eternal sense of wanting to get away from the world. She looked at them both by turns. 'How cruel you are,' she whispered. 'Both of you.'

'I'm sorry,' said Laurette. 'We never wanted to hurt you.'

'I doubt you have given me a single thought,' said Mary trembling. 'You simply do as you wish. But it doesn't matter does it? Little Fanny doesn't matter. I don't matter. – Laurette, I despise you!' They were all three silent a moment. Then Mary burst out pathetically, 'Don't you think you could care about others just the tiniest bit?' She looked at Laurette and Imlay by turns, her eyes pleading. And she fell into the state she hated, hearing herself and loathing herself as she spoke. 'I have nowhere to go. I can't be expected to stay with my landlady for good. I can't go to Ned's. And anyway, they think I'm married. Imagine?' She gave a mad little laugh. 'Could anyone be married to Gilbert? You know the answer to that Laurette, don't you? But you, oh you are quite perfect for him aren't you. You are an actress. You will play whatever part you must, for the time being that is, then you will leave the stage.' She felt dizzy and thought she might faint. She held to the back of a chair. Laurette stood still and silent, her hands clasped tightly before her. Mary continued. 'Well, if this is the way it is, then why don't I live with you both, and we can share dear Gilbert. An excellent idea, don't you think? That is what they do in France.' She trembled as she spoke, her eyes staring wildly.

Imlay sat watching the fire. He did not move or gesture.

Mary continued. 'I could bring little Fanny . . .'

Imlay gave a heavy sigh. 'I told you, didn't I, the landlord doesn't like children, and I am coming and going. It is best you stay where you are. I'll help with the rent.'

'You could move somewhere else,' Mary said hopefully. 'I intend to do some writing for Johnson. I'll take care of myself financially.' They were all three silent a moment. 'Don't imagine it pleases me to beg like this,' she said, collapsing in on herself. Laurette and Imlay had turned away their faces. She could hear the church bells ringing loudly, and something awakened inside her as she listened. She wanted to belong to the music of the bells, to have the kind of freedom the bells did, the freedom to peal and sing their beautiful song, a song that flew through the skies and then in an instant was over. It seemed so right, so splendid. 'Shall I go?' she murmured. Neither of them looked at her now. She felt contemptuous of herself that she had not suspected it. What an idiot she could be when it came to life and love. Did she have wisdom? No, she did not, she was a fool! But she stood with her head held high as she fastened her cape. Despair had followed her and had found her once again.

She did not get in a chaise, but instead went walking by the river. Oh, the water, the peaceful water, she thought as she watched it slowly meander, how calmly it went on its way. Imlay's lodgings were close by Putney Bridge. She saw that no-one traversed it just then and she stopped, suddenly imbued with purpose. Let the water take her where it would! She would let it return her to the elements, leaving her broken mind behind. But how cold and lonely it looked, how dark and perplexing. Her dress was soiled from the dirty bank of the river and she had torn her cape on a thorn bush. Was it difficult to drown, she wondered. She shivered. What if she could not die, and merely floated along, unable to find any peace, unable to sink into oblivion? It was raining hard. But never mind the rain. Would it not befriend her, make her clothes heavier, she thought, and help her sink in the water? A thin sun shone on the Thames. She shuddered and gasped. What was she doing? Was she not a mother? Did she not betray herself if she acted according to her feelings? Though all she could give to her child was anxiety and pain. The Thames was a venerable old river with ancient secrets; her death would just be another, it would not judge, instead it would clasp her to its breast and gather her in. She mustered her strength and climbed to a place she could fall from, then with one long moan leapt into its icy embrace.

But the Thames didn't want her either and she found herself lying in a bed at Johnson's house, Johnson seated beside her immersed in a book. 'Oh Joseph, I did not die!' she cried mournfully as she opened her eyes. 'Again, I did not die!'

'No, you did not,' said Johnson. 'You are very much alive, and I'm glad to see you're awake. You've been sleeping all day. '

'How did I come to be here?' she asked, trying to raise herself up.

'Somebody saw what you did last night and came to your rescue. There are a lot of good people about.'

She glanced about the room. 'Dear God, where is my daughter?'

'Fanny is safe with Godwin.'

'"*Godwin?*"' She could scarcely gather her thoughts and wondered if she were dreaming. Why was Fanny with Godwin? Then she became quiet and ashamed. What would he think of her, how would her friends judge her?

'Godwin has been very concerned. He wanted to take her, Ned was busy and . . .'

'Has Ned been here too?'

'Of course. He came as soon he could with your sisters but you were sleeping. He will come again soon. We are all upset by this, you know. You have a lot of writing to do, my dear, and you won't do much at the bottom of the Thames, will you.' He glanced at the fire. 'It needs more wood,' he murmured. 'I must go downstairs in a minute. Oh Mary, you do worry us. You did not die by guillotine;

you wanted to die in the Thames instead. My goodness, must we lock you up to keep you safe?'

'You have no idea what he's done,' she whispered. 'He did it before and he has done it again.'

'I think I know who you speak of, but it's beyond me why you let him matter. And what about that beautiful child? It is all quite sense-less to me. You would swat a wasp if it pestered you yet you let these thoughts plague your mind as if you had no power to stop them. I have to say, I have always considered you a sensible, intelligent woman and would like to think you still are.' He sat resting his head in his hands and sighing. 'You could have lived with me; you did not need to find lodgings. You know I would never abandon you.'

She stared at space confused. Johnson went on. 'And how many times have I told you of Godwin's goodness . . .'

'You say he has Fanny at his home?'

'Yes, I took the liberty. I spoke about it to Ned and he said he was happy with that. Once you are well, you can bring her here if you like. But Godwin has a few vacant rooms, and he is perfectly happy to have her. He'll take good care of her, I know. Can you imagine her face had she known her mother was down in the river with the fish? You are sometimes so foolish, my dear.' He was not wearing his wig and he scratched his head, frowning and concerned. 'And your choice of men disturbs me, first Fuseli and now this rogue. He certainly sounds a vexatious sort to me.'

She put out her hand and sighed. 'Don't Joseph, I love him. How can it be he cares nothing for my love?'

'Ah, yes. And I do believe Godwin loves *you*? But what do you care about that?'

'*Loves me?*' she exclaimed. 'You are mistaken. He doesn't even know me.'

'He has read your every word and is constantly concerned for your welfare.'

Her eyes shone with wonder. 'But he thinks I'm a gorgon.'

Johnson laughed loudly. 'Nonsense. Godwin is full of humour, as I have told you. You take him wrongly. He loves you for who you are.' He looked at her straight. 'Do you know who you are, Mary?'

She sat in the bed silent, hanging on his words. Did Godwin really love her? Could he love her as easily as that and she didn't even know?

Johnson continued. 'I don't think you do, you see. You think you are some silly little female who deserves nothing. Well, my dear, you are wrong, you are a very clever woman who doesn't even know it. We must teach you. This nonsense has put Godwin in a state. He is coming today with your daughter.'

For a few moments they were thoughtful.

'You know what I want to do, don't you,' she murmured painfully. She raised her voice a little louder. 'I want to help women out of their bondage, show them they need not be slaves. I want to make them see that their lives might be more fulfilling. Education would help them understand themselves and aspire to something more rewarding . . . But you see . . .' Joseph Johnson waited. Mary continued. 'I have done it all wrong. I cannot practise what I preach.'

'And who can?' said Johnson quietly. The maid came in and said she would bring some food. Johnson said to bring something light and a strong cup of tea. She went out and ran down the stairs.

Mary drew back the covers and sat on the edge of the bed. 'I should dress and sort out my hair, or I shall surely be a gorgon today, these locks have been washed by the Thames and I can still smell its breath. I must bathe and try to look winning.'

'But what are you trying to win?' said Johnson rising from his chair. He smiled. 'You have won already. You won Godwin's heart from the first.' He stuck his chin in his cravat and stared at her, clasping his hands before him. He turned as he went to the door. 'You scared the daylights out of that poor fellow on the bank. He dived in to save you, and thank goodness he did. Now you are here to tell your tale. If it is a tale worth telling, that is. I think it is best forgotten.'

'What happened?' she asked, as she gazed in the mirror.

'Someone on the bank knew who you were and he brought you here in a chaise. He left you with my maid. She put you in nightwear and saw you safely to bed. You were in a sort of stupor, she said. It seems the man disappeared. We do not know where he went.'

'He was the dark angel,' Mary murmured. 'But he does not want me yet.' She stared at the fire abstractedly. 'Fanny has his horse.'

'Angels don't come on horseback, my dear, they fly.' Johnson made a gesture with his arms.

'Ah, so you believe in them, do you?' she smiled.

'Well, of course not, but you do make me say the most ludicrous things at times. But I believe in Blake, the man, and he is quite at one with angels, so what can I say. He is extraordinary. They say he has second sight. Unfortunately however, I do not share his divination.'

Several hours later, after she had bathed and eaten and put on clean clothing, Godwin arrived with Fanny. The child ran to her laughing.

'She has asked for you constantly,' said Godwin, standing before her as the child danced around the room.

The clock ticked loudly on the wall and Mary took comfort in the fact that she was still living and hadn't left time behind. 'It was good of you to take Fanny,' she said. 'I feel so ashamed.'

'Well,' Godwin exclaimed, throwing out his hands in a gesture of nonchalance. 'We are all ashamed of something. Now, see how happy she is today. She has scarce found her legs yet she dances, there is so much joy in her soul. Be proud of it, Mary, be proud of it!'

'Yes,' said Mary, smiling with pleasure. He stooped to put wood on the fire. She felt at peace with him, as if at some fundamental level they knew each other well and had done so for years. 'Joseph wants me to write for him again,' she said, smiling.

'I know, he told me,' said Godwin. He breathed in deeply. 'But don't let him harass you. It is his way to get as much as he can out of all of us. Our writing is the air he breathes. You need to gather your thoughts together now, you are only just back from France and have much to consider. You have written about your experiences of course, and the work is extremely interesting. And moving too, oh yes.' For a moment or two they were silent. He continued. 'We have all been very busy. I have published my novel, *Caleb Williams*, Blake has published his *Songs of Experience* and Paine has published *The Age of Reason*, but his attack on organised religion has made him a lot of enemies. He writes some dangerous stuff.'

They went to sit on the chaise longue together, watching the child as she played.

'He is very courageous, like you,' she murmured, wondering what had happened to Paine and what he was doing.

'Did you write any more of your novel?' asked Godwin. He glanced at her curiously.

Fanny played quietly on the floor with her little black horse. Mary lit a candle on the dresser. The cloudy afternoon and the candlelight lent the little toy horse a shadow which insisted on following it about, making Fanny squeal with delight. Mary was stirred by the sight of her daughter at play, her eyes were quick and passionate and her imagination was immense, she wondered what she stored in her mind and who else took part in the games she played with the toy. Did she ever think of her father? Could Godwin take his place, she wondered if Imlay left them for ever. He was certainly taking his place with her. And ever so easily too. Her heart gave way to joy as she listened to his voice, the power of his tones and their confident strength.

It was a dark cloudy day, but summer was on its way and she wondered how she might spend it that year with Godwin. There were bound to be glorious days when they could walk out into the woods, sometimes alone, other times with Fanny. On summer evenings she could sit with him in Johnson's garden. Such thoughts brought solace. She watched him as he talked with the child, familiar and loving. He was a tall well made man with a firm and bold expression, almost menacing sometimes. He could make people laugh, and he could also make them afraid. Godwin was a leader and others took note of what he said. He had no hatred in his soul, but he was brave.

Fanny came to live in Johnson's mansion and time passed quickly. Mary and Godwin saw each other often, went to shows and strolled about London with the child or else walked the paths in the woodland and watched the ducks on the pond. And they made love. She felt triumphant and fulfilled. It was a shock at first to find love had found her so easily, bestowed like a gift from heaven, but she had seized it and knew it as her own. After a while, she took Fanny and went to live in Godwin's house. Her worries left her and her spirit became as frivolous as a skylark's in spring. Her past was forgotten. She lived with Godwin in affectionate peace and her heart beat fast with life.

Imlay had now left London. Laurette, too, had disappeared. There was immense activity in Johnson's house that season. His dinners were lively and most of the time the maid looked after the child while Mary talked with her friends. She had never felt better and her writing flourished. She had almost finished her novel, and sat in the evenings pondering how to write in fiction thoughts she had fostered all her life. It was the story of a woman who'd been committed to an asylum by her husband, not any particular individual, she asserted as she talked with Godwin one quiet afternoon in the parlour, it was rather a story about society and crossed all classes. It was the patriarchal institution of marriage that bothered her, she said, for it so often degraded women. Maria, her protagonist, could not renounce her romantic way of being and the way she'd been made to see womanhood. The novel explored her pain.

'What you say in your story speaks for a lot of women,' Godwin said as he turned the pages of her manuscript. 'You are getting to the heart of it, my love. This novel is bold and courageous. You speak of matters that are obvious, but need to be written.'

She sat back in her chair, watching Godwin's expression as he read out a chosen passage:

*"'Returning from the theatre, or any amusing party, I frequently began to relate what I had seen and highly relished: but with sullen taciturnity he soon silenced me. I seemed therefore gradually to lose, in his society, the soul, the energies of which had just been in action. To such a degree, in fact, did his cold, reserved manner affect me, that after spending some days with him alone, I have imagined myself the most stupid creature in the world, till the abilities of some casual visitor convinced me that I had some dormant animation, and sentiments above the dust in which I had been grovelling . . .'"*

He put down the page and shook his head. 'How sad and unfair,' he murmured. 'Is it true that men behave like this? It is quite despicable.' He looked at her and frowned.

'You are probably the fairest of all men' she said. She smiled good humouredly. 'The work isn't just about how badly some men treat women; it is also a tale to illustrate an opinion of mine, that a genius will educate itself. Circumstances can limit the opportunities women might have for self expression, but genius can work through that, whatever limitations society imposes. Women though, could achieve much more were those limits removed.'

'But you still fret about the way people insult you, my dear. — Oh, you do, you do. I see it in your eyes when things are reported.'

'I do not care in the least about reputation,' she said dismissively. 'Such words mean nothing. They are just like a bleak north wind.'

'A bleak north wind can kill,' he said, his eyebrows lifting with amusement.

'Then I put on my warmest clothing,' she murmured, and they laughed.


'But why on earth do you let people bother you?' a friend asked her one evening at Johnson's dinner. 'Anyone who matters will realise immediately why Imlay pretended you were married. It was to save your neck. And it did. Must you spell it out bold and have Johnson send out a pamphlet?'

'There are some who call her a whore,' a male guest murmured.

Godwin turned on him angrily. The child on his lap grew fearful of the fierce emotion. 'Mary,' Godwin said, frowning. 'Might the maid take Fanny for a while? It is getting quite heated in here.'

Johnson left the room with the child.

'I'm sorry,' the man said guiltily. 'I did not intend to be discourteous. I was being facetious. There are a lot of people who are whispering about you, Mary, as you know only too well. They are idle gossips, and now you are living with Godwin, you have given them more to talk about.'

'What a time they are having discussing me,' laughed Mary. 'Why do they get so excited? In France it means nothing to have a child out of wedlock. That's what upsets them, of course, that I was never married to Imlay and yet I bore him a child. People were bound to learn of it eventually. I always feared it would happen when I came back here. It is likely to be women who have set themselves up against me. A lot of them love to gossip. – Education, education, is the answer! Educate women and broaden their minds!' She brimmed with fervour as she spoke.

'Ah, I hate small mindedness,' said Godwin through his teeth. He touched her arm. 'I think we should get married, my dear, that would stop their tongues now, wouldn't it.'

The company laughed. '*You*, get married Godwin?' somebody shouted. 'After all you have said against it? Let us raise a glass to that!'

'Things change,' said Godwin quietly. 'And feelings change, too. I would marry Mary in an instant. What man could not love her?'

Mary turned up her eyes. She put down her knife and fork and brushed her lips with her napkin. 'And I would happily marry Godwin,' she said, smiling, remembering how they had talked about it in the still small hours of the night. She wondered now why she had ever gone to France. She had wasted what might have been precious, heavenly times. But she had learned a lot too. And she had Fanny. Imlay had given her a delightful child. She would though, she determined, have children with Godwin too. Oh, lots of children. He would make a perfect father; she had seen that for herself.

# 41

# *Godwin and Mary*

The months went busily along. It was now accepted that Mary and Godwin were living together with Mary's illegitimate daughter, and most people left them alone. When Mary took Fanny to the shops, shoppers occasionally whispered, but it did not bother her. She was happy, and the child was thrilled by the hustle and bustle of town. Godwin acted responsibly as if he were father and husband. He *did* want to marry Mary, and searched his mind as to why he should go against everything he'd formerly believed in. Or everything he thought he'd believed in, for his ideas about marriage were now in a flux. That they were in love was a serious truth for them both, and they wanted to be husband and wife. And when Mary discovered she was pregnant, marriage seemed sensible and right.

It was one of those slow weekends. Godwin sat writing while Mary sat sewing up a rag doll for Fanny. 'Eye, Maman, eye,' said the child, pointing to the button Mary was stitching on its face. The child was aroused by eyes.

'Yes, it is an eye, my pet,' said Mary. 'And soon I shall give her another. We are making a beautiful doll.'

'Mine, mine!' cried the child ecstatically.

'Yes,' said Mary, 'all yours.'

'And soon you will have a real-life sister or brother,' laughed Godwin turning from his work at the table.

'Well,' said Mary, laying her hands on her stomach and smiling gently. 'Who can know what secret develops in here. I love the mystery.'

Godwin laughed. 'It unnerves me all that,' he said, sighing. 'First there is nothing, then all of a sudden there is a new being in the world.'

'Or not,' Mary whispered. The colour drained from her cheeks as she spoke, but she took refuge in the ease with which she'd given birth to Fanny and the health and vivacity of the child. She pulled on the thread and fixed the second button in place. 'There now, two eyes,' she said smiling, handing the doll to Fanny. She looked at Godwin curiously. 'Have you seen her little black horse? It seems to have gone. The maid has searched everywhere.'

'Does it bother you that it is lost?' asked Godwin. 'You were speaking about it last night at Johnson's dinner. It is only a toy, my dear.'

She gazed about the room abstractedly. 'Things have a substance that is so very much more than their weight. I really believe it. We have substance ourselves that is more than what we stand up in, something that reaches beyond us I think, so why not toys. There were things I hated in my childhood because I thought they brought bad omens.'

'Oh, I do not know about *omens* . . .' smiled Godwin. 'But did you not like the little horse?'

'Yes, I did, but it left us.'

'Oh Mary, it is lost, that's all. Things get lost. It is a fact.'

'Not always,' she faltered, 'sometimes they are stolen, or they take themselves away . . .'

They were both silent a moment, watching the child as she played with her newly made doll. Mary spoke again. 'You will never leave me, will you?' she murmured.

He straightened and sighed. 'Of course not, why should I? And I hope you will never leave me.'

She gazed at him for a long moment. 'I might have to . . .'

He put down his pen and turned to her fully. 'What do you mean?'

She looked at him anxiously. 'I shall have to leave you if I die.'

He frowned annoyed. 'But my dear, why would you die?'

'Women die in childbirth constantly. – You must get me a good midwife, William. Promise.' Her voice was intense.

'It is arranged,' he said softly. 'Come and sit beside me,' he murmured, 'There, on that comfortable chair.'

She rubbed her arms and went to him. 'Let's light some candles,' she said, glancing about. 'The day is darkening; you are straining your eyes.'

Godwin stood and went to a drawer in the dresser. He lit four candles and the room flooded with light.

Fanny sat on the floor nursing her doll. There was an uncanny silence amongst them. Shadows spilled about the room. 'If only we could find the horse,' Mary said softly. 'Then I should feel much better.'

'Do stop it, my dear,' said Godwin. 'It is only a toy. It doesn't matter. She takes it out with her sometimes. Perhaps she left it at the shops.'

'She would never leave it at the shops,' said Mary, shaking her head. 'She always keeps hold of it.'

'Oh, Mary,' Godwin said, painfully. 'Fanny is happy with her new rag doll. It does no good to remind her of something she's lost.'

He put more logs on the fire, then fell to pacing the floor.

Mary would not be silenced. 'It's an omen,' she whispered. 'I know it. The horse has gone, what has it taken with it?'

'Hush, my dear,' said Godwin, angry how easily she became a servant of fear. 'Be strong.'

She braced herself and smiled. She was a woman who could fall into the darkest depths of her soul then rise again into the light. And she had learned how to do it quickly. 'Let us take a walk with the child,' she said. 'We'll walk down the little woodland path and stand by the pond. Leave your writing a while. It is getting dusky outside but I like the twilight. It is a warm June evening; the corn mint is heavy in the hedgerows. I like its soft pink flowers and their scent is lovely, that strong minty aroma heals the senses.' For a few moments they were silent. Then she whispered, 'Fanny always loved it too.'

'You haven't mentioned Fanny in ages,' Godwin said frowning and jealous. 'What makes you think of her now?'

She did not answer. They put on their outdoor clothes. It was a warm and beautiful evening. The woodland dark and mysterious opened before them. The wild beauty of the bluebells had finished, they hung now tired and withered; only the ghosts of their essence remained, a few bees hovered in the dusk over those that were left.

'See – a bluebell still going strong!' he laughed, bending to look.

'Don't pick it,' she urged. 'Let it live.' They stopped by the small pond. A couple of cows gazed sleepily over the fence. She talked on about the flora around them, using the Latin names of the flowers, names she had learned from Fanny. And she spoke again of her beloved's suffering in childbirth, her cruel death.

'Your mood is very strange, my dear,' he said worriedly. 'I do not like it. You have morbid memories of your friend and you shouldn't be thinking like that.'

'No,' said Mary, watching the ground as they walked. 'I shouldn't be morbid. I have much to be happy about. It is strange how pain will not leave us. It is sort of kept in a box and you open it now and then to see if it has gone, but it stays with its lonely self and you have to attend to it occasionally, fearing it might have escaped.'

'And mustn't it escape? he asked perplexed.

'No. We must heal it, you see. It can only escape when it's healed. Otherwise it just goes limply into the world and will suffer all over again.'

'A most unhealthy idea,' Godwin said frowning. 'You have a child here who loves you, and a devoted husband also. This talk vexes me, my dear.'

The evening was beginning to cool. Godwin turned to look back and put out his hand for the child. She gave a little laugh and looked at him, her eyes shining in the twilight.

'It's beautiful here,' said Mary. The child danced in the dewy grass, uncaring of the darkening woodland.

'The woodland always excites her,' smiled Mary. 'She loves to listen to the owls. She might stand for as long as five minutes enthralled by their calls. She did so in Paris when she was tiny. We lost her once in the garden . . .'

'Let's not talk about Paris,' he pleaded. 'It makes you think about *him*, and I want you to think about *me*.'

The days towards August passed slowly. They were struggling tiresome days in which Mary grew big with child and strangely big with fear. She went about pale and abstracted, often silent and thoughtful. Sometimes she would open the door on the night at the back of the house and enter the dark garden trembling and moaning while Godwin waited by the door until she returned. He considered sending for a doctor, but she chided him and would not allow it.

The first pains came at dawn on 13th August. She walked about her room excited, telling Godwin the child was on its way and he was bound to be a father by night time. All was in order the midwife said, and she was ready and waiting. Mary might take a dose of smelling salts should matters become too painful, she said, nothing more. Mary lay suffering on the bed. Godwin didn't keep laudanum and the birth must take place naturally. A hot piece of cloth would be laid across her parts if she tore. That would be the sum of her comfort.

'It is something women must endure,' Mary groaned as the pains grew stronger. 'But it is all so primitive. It need not be quite so horrendous.' The midwife did not listen, but instead attended to her task. How lonely and arduous it was, giving birth, thought Mary as she laboured. But it had all been so easy with Fanny and she wasn't expecting complications. The midwife though had spoken that very word as the pains progressed. Mary grew fearful.

'Please take Fanny downstairs,' Godwin told the maid.

'You too, my love,' said Mary, her voice straining with effort. 'You need not share my pain.'

'I want to be with you,' he insisted, gripping her hand.

'Your wife is right,' warned the midwife. 'My work will be difficult today. I must concentrate hard, you should go.'

Godwin's features were pale with worry. 'The fire mustn't go out,' he said, the words sticking in his throat. 'It needs more logs. Mary might like a hot cup of tea. Not now, I know, but perhaps . . .'

'Please leave us,' said the midwife in a hard tone of voice.

Godwin kissed Mary on the cheek, then he made his way to the door. This was beyond his strength.

To Mary the scene was familiar, and in the raging throes of her pain, she thought of Agnes, then she thought of Eliza, and she thought of her dearest Fanny Blood. There was much to be done, much to be written, when would she do it? Now she had to bear down. – 'Bear down! Bear down!' cried the midwife. Mary took deep breaths and forced the baby into the passage designed for its birth. But the pain was almost unbearable. She screamed in torment as she and the midwife battled. Then in the early hours of the morning came the cry of a second daughter.

But the midwife fell into a panic. Try as she would, she could not withdraw the placenta. She ran to the top of the stairs. 'Mr Godwin, please fetch the doctor!' she shouted from the top of the stairs. 'Your wife has lost too much blood. I fear she might die.'

'*Die?*' cried Godwin, coming quickly. 'She cannot die! The woman is my very life! If she dies then I die also! Where do I go for a doctor?'

It was still very dark outside. Godwin rushed through the streets horrified. Within fifteen minutes he was back. The doctor went to Mary quickly. He flung off his coat and rolled up his sleeves. He must try to extract the placenta by hand, he said, there was no other way. Mary lay on her back exhausted. The sheets were wet with blood. The doctor worked and sweated. The midwife stood by in attendance though there was nothing more she could do, the placenta had broken into pieces. 'I cannot grasp it,' said the doctor. 'I must get it all out or her womb will become infected.'

'Oh, my love,' pleaded Godwin, 'Don't die!'

The doctor struggled to pull out the dark clots of blood, throwing them carelessly into the midwife's bowl as she watched with horrified eyes. He worked exhaustively till daybreak, but could not be sure he had extracted it all, he said. 'I have removed what I can,' he told them. 'Now she must rest. Your daughter lies quietly in her cradle,' he said to Godwin. 'She is fit and well and unaffected. But I cannot say the same for her mother.'

'Is there anything else you can do?' Godwin pleaded. He had a daughter, but must he lose Mary?

'Nothing,' said the doctor exhausted. 'I can do no more. I shall return later today.'

'William, William,' murmured Mary, her voice shaking with pain. She put out her arms to embrace him. 'How we have loved each other. I will not leave you, rest assured. I shall fight the dark angel yet again.' Then she closed her eyes and fell into a deep sleep.

She slept for the whole of the day, occasionally moaning and delirious, but when the doctor came later that day he reported she was doing much better. Godwin stayed by her side, rejoicing as he saw the colour returning to her face and life returning to her body. He lifted her into a sitting position and she began to suckle her baby. It was a magical moment of recovery he told Johnson when he arrived later that day.

But Mary grew tired and was soon resting again. 'Do take a walk, my love,' she urged William. '*Please*. This house has closed in on you I think. I cannot walk with you today, but we shall walk together again in time.' He kissed her and went downstairs.

Godwin had been gone for an hour when the maid came running down the long woodland path, calling that Mary had a fever. 'She is shaking violently, I fear it is septicaemia!' she cried. 'Johnson has gone to bring the doctor.'

By the time Godwin got back, Mary was shivering violently. 'Why did you let me leave you?' he cried frantically. Milk was flooding from her breasts, soaking her nightdress, but she could not feed her baby. She was sick and delirious.

A whole week passed by in which Mary hovered between life and death, and it seemed the darkness of death was winning. 'This is how it must be for so many women,' she murmured to Godwin. 'This is our lot. There is much to be done and I will not be here to do it.' She grabbed his hand and clutched it to her mouth. 'Promise me,' she pleaded, 'that my work will not be forgotten.' She went on mumbling, though her words became incoherent and stayed in her throat. Then with one last gasp she gave up her spirit and died.

Godwin wept profusely and sat by her bedside moaning. 'She was not yet forty,' he said bitterly. He was angry at having her so cruelly snatched from him, and because she had suffered so badly.

She had hoped for many things, he said to their friends later. She had dipped her pen in the ink so many times, and had written so many words. Most of all she had wanted a better life for women. He glanced about at the least sound in the room, but she had gone. And he gazed at space, remembering her words that things had substance beyond themselves. How he longed for that substance. But he knew she could never return. He did not let others see the madness of his thoughts, believing that somehow madness might be a way of dealing with suffering for a while as a sort of relief from pain.

The grieving was to last some time, and he had also to comfort her siblings who were filled with misery. In time he found strength to publish her letters and reminiscences. His dead wife had been a brilliant woman, he said. She'd been a woman who had written with passion about her deepest thoughts and feelings and he knew that the bond he felt with her spirit would endure. She was buried in the graveyard of St Pancras, and at his instruction her gravestone held the inscription:

"MARY WOLLSTONECRAFT
GODWIN
Author of
A Vindication
of the rights of Woman

Born 27th April 1759
Died 10th September 1797"

He wrote to a friend:

*"I firmly believe that there does not exist her equal in the world. I know from experience we were formed to make each other happy. I have not the least expectation that I can now ever know happiness again. Do not – if you can help it – exhort me, or console me."*

No-one dared offer him comfort. He grieved until his grief was exhausted yet he spoke very little and tried to quell his suffering by striding into the woodland, treading the very same paths he had trod with Mary. On warm afternoons in the dappled light, he would stand and watch the sunlight on the pond where they had often stopped to embrace. In its glittering surface he might catch a glimpse of her face, smiling and at peace, while from behind him came the voices of two young women, laughing and talking. One of the voices was Mary's. He did not know the other.

# *Acknowledgements*

I am particularly grateful for the books listed below which illustrate the social, political and psychological mores of Mary Wollstonecraft's times and their role in shaping the intrinsic nature of her writing. I am also thankful for the knowledge and inspiration these books provided which helped bring her character to life and for the pleasure I experienced in reading them.

*A Vindication of the Rights of Woman*, Mary Wollstonecraft, Vintage, 2015; *Letters written in Sweden, Norway and Denmark*, Mary Wollstonecraft, Oxford World Classics, USA, 2009; *Rights of Man, Common Sense, and other Political Writings*, Thomas Paine, edited by Mark Phip, Oxford World Classics, 2008; *A Vindication of the Rights of Men*, Mary Wollstonecraft, edited by Janet Todd, OUP, Oxford, 2008; *Vindication, A Life of Mary Wollstonecraft*, Lyndall Gordon, Virago, 2005; *The Collected Letters of Mary Wollstonecraft*, edited by Janet Todd, Columbia University Press, 2003; *The Cambridge Companion to Mary Wollstonecraft*, edited by Claudia L. Johnson, Cambridge University Press, 2002; *Mary Wollstonecraft, A Revolutionary Life*, Janet Todd, Phoenix Press, 2000; *The Life and Death of Mary Wollstonecraft*, Claire Tomalin, Weidenfeld and Nicolson, 1974; *A Wollstonecraft Anthology*, edited by Janet Todd, Polity Press, 1989; *Reflections on the Revolution in France*, Edmund Burke, Penguin, 1968: *Maria, or The Wrongs of Woman*, Mary Wollstonecraft, General Books, Memphis USA, after the edition 1798.

I also thank John, my son, who despite his heavy work schedule and commitments to wife and children, found time to show interest and involvement. Also, I thank my writer friends who gave their support when energies were waning, and other sources who supplied information about Mary, including radio and TV programmes emphasising the continued relevance of her work.

Wendy Louise Bardsley 3rd July 2017

# Sources of Extracts

p31 – 'If I did not love you . . .' From letter to Jane Arden from Mary Wollstonecraft, *c* 1773

p35 – *Fare Thee Well.* The first published version of the song appeared in *Roxburghe Ballads* dated 1710

p51 – 'These are the times . . .' From a pamphlet by Thomas Paine, 1776

p232 – 'I have adopted the words of the Scripture . . .' From A Discourse on the Love of our Country, delivered, November 4th, 1789 by Reverend Richard Price

p239 – 'Mr Burke's Reflections on the French Revolution first engaged my attention . . .' From Mary Wollstonecraft, *A Vindication of the Rights of Man*, 1790

p241 – 'Man with regard to them, in all climates and in all ages has been either . . .' From An Occasional Letter on the Female Sex by Thomas Paine, August 1775

p252 – 'To see one half of the human race exchanged by the other from all participation of government . . .' From *Rapport sur l'instruction publique* by M. Talleyrand Perigord 1791

p264 – *Déclaration de Voltaire*, note to his secretary, Jean-Louis Wagnière (28 February 1778)

p271 – 'It would be an endless task to trace the variety of meanness's . . .' From *A Vindication of the Rights of Woman*, Mary Wollstonecraft, 1792

p349 – 'I perceive from the whole tenor of your Reflecting that you have a mortal antipathy to reason . . .' From *A Vindication of the Rights of Man*, Mary Wollstonecraft, 1790

p406 – 'I firmly believe that there does not exist her equal in the world . . .' Letter from William Godwin to Thomas Holcroft, c 1797/8